THE REBEL SON

ALSO BY ANDY MASLEN

Detective Kat Ballantyne:

The Seventh Girl

The Unseen Sister

The Silent Wife

The Lying Man

Detective Ford:

Shallow Ground

Land Rites

Plain Dead

DI Stella Cole:

Hit and Run

Hit Back Harder

Hit and Done

Let the Bones Be Charred

Weep, Willow, Weep

A Beautiful Breed of Evil

Death Wears a Golden Cloak

See the Dead Birds Fly

Playing the Devil's Music

Gabriel Wolfe Thrillers:

Trigger Point

Reversal of Fortune

Blind Impact

Condor

First Casualty

Fury

Rattlesnake

Minefield

No Further

Torpedo

Three Kingdoms

Ivory Nation

Crooked Shadow

Brass Vows

Seven Seconds

Peacemaker

Edged Weapon

Other Fiction:

Blood Loss – A Vampire Story

Purity Kills

You're Always With Me

Green-Eyed Mobster

THE REBEL SON

A DETECTIVE KAT BALLANTYNE THRILLER

ANDY MASLEN

THOMAS & MERCER

Published by Thomas & Mercer, Seattle

www.apub.com

EU Product Safety contact:
Amazon Media EU S. à r.l.
38, avenue John F. Kennedy, L-1855 Luxembourg
amazonpublishing-gpsr@amazon.com

ISBN-13: 9781662530654
eISBN: 9781662530647

Cover photography and design by Dominic Forbes

Printed in the United States of America

For Kat's midwives: Leodora Darlington and Victoria Pepe.

Be wary around your enemy once, and your friend a thousand times. A double-crossing friend knows more about what harms you.

Arabic proverb

Chapter One

Pulse racing, knuckles white on the steering wheel, Kat hurtled through the night, praying she'd be in time to save Riley and Van.

Ten minutes ago she'd been relaxing in a rose-and-geranium-scented bubble bath, ABBA singing 'Fernando' and a glass of Pinot Grigio within reach. Then Leah Hooper, one of her three DCs, had called.

'Kat, you need to turn on the TV or check Facebook or something. There's been a bomb. A threat, I mean. We're all getting called in. It's going to go off at 8.30 p.m.'

The bomb was at the Powerhouse, the venue Kat's husband and fourteen-year-old son had set off to that evening to see a band. And she had thirty minutes to save them.

Kat raced through Middlehampton, her body rigid with gut-churning, throat-closing terror. Her siren dopplered hysteria back at her off plate-glass windows, metal and concrete. Should have closed her window. Why hadn't she? No time to think about that now.

She swerved round a Honda Jazz dawdling along at twenty, yelling futilely at its driver to get out of her way. How could they not see the light on her dash, strobing its electric-blue semaphore into their rear window and lighting up the interior like a lightning strike? *Or a bomb blast.*

. . . pleasebeOKpleasebeOKpleasebeOK . . .

Her train of thought derailed, leaving this lone message repeating in her brain like a distress signal.

She was operating purely on instinct, spearing through the gaps in the traffic. Her foot alternated between being jammed down on the throttle until her calf muscle cramped and digging into the brakes to prevent a collision.

How could this be happening in her town? Terrorists didn't attack places like Middlehampton. That was for the big cities: London, Manchester, Birmingham.

Yes, they had their fair share of murders. But she could cope with that. Christ, it was her job! But bombs?

Images from news programmes crowded her mind. Other towns, other years. Other outrages. Kids in silver blankets after a concert turned into a bloodbath. Commuters with bloody faces clutching their briefcases, or each other. Faces riven with grief or blank with incomprehension. Cops, paramedics and firefighters moving through smoke and dust clouds with grim purpose.

The traffic lights ahead turned to red. Swearing, she hit the brakes, dropped two gears and swung her head left and right before blowing through the junction. A lorry came from the left, a motorbike overtaking a car from the right. She screamed, locked her elbows and shoved her foot down as hard as she could on the accelerator.

The Golf's engine shrieked. The truck's airhorns bellowed in protest and the biker swerved dangerously close to her rear wing. She felt the impact. The crunch of fragile plastic. Snatched a look in the rear-view mirror. The bike was wobbling, then skidding before the rider brought it under control, sending angry gestures her way with black-gauntleted hands.

She glanced at the dash clock. 8.05 p.m. She still had time.

Chapter Two

Kat swerved left, right, left, snaking through another junction, not even touching the brakes. Horns blasted at her from every direction as she threaded the Golf through a gap so narrow she flinched.

You could achieve miracles in twenty-five minutes. Reverse your fortunes in a netball match. Catch a killer out in a lie during an interview. Finish dinner with your husband and teenage son without anyone losing their rag or rolling their eyes. Oh, God, her beautiful, hormonal, stroppy, loving son. Who ought to be dancing and cheering to his favourite band, but instead some crazy terrorist had put a bomb right under the stage.

Riley had said he was going to get 'straight to the mosh pit'. He'd be shredded to pieces: far from the exit, hemmed in by other people.

Kat cried out involuntarily. Dashed tears from her eyes that were making her vision cloud with starbursts from the streetlamps and brake lights stippling the night.

Her phone rang. It was on speaker. She stabbed the accept call button. A male voice started to speak.

'Van?' she interrupted. 'Oh, thank God! Are you both all right?'

She scowled as Carve-up's voice filled the Golf's cabin. 'DS Ballantyne. Where are you?'

'Can't talk, I'm on my way to the Powerhouse.'

'What the f—? What for? I want you in here with everyone else. You're not equipped, qualified or permitted to attend the scene. Get back here now. That's an order.'

'My family are there!' she yelled as she swerved round a bend, earning herself another horn blast from an artic looming out of the dark like an ocean liner coming face to face with a sailboat.

'DS Ballantyne, get your arse back here. You can't help them.'

But she could. She had to. She couldn't lose her family.

Chapter Three

Kat slewed to a stop, stalling the Golf in front of a brace of fire engines.

Pumping Station Road was impassable from where Access Road Five met it at a right angle to the Powerhouse. She could see emergency vehicles and, held back beyond crime scene tape guarded by a ragged string of uniforms, a small crowd already capturing the event on their phones.

She jumped out, not even closing the door, already pulling her warrant card out of her jacket. Waving it at the firefighters who were gesturing frantically for her to move away from the venue, she jumped over the unfurling hoses and sprinted towards the cordon.

Someone shouted. She turned without slowing. A uniformed copper, not someone she recognised, was yelling at her to stop. She ignored her and ran on, stuffing her badge back into her jacket.

The air was thick with exhaust from the emergency vehicles. Something weird had happened to the air pressure and instead of floating away, the heavy diesel fumes were hanging at head height, a choking cloud that made her cough.

Spitting greasy saliva on to the pavement, she made for the right-hand edge of the knot of onlookers. Beyond the blue-and-white tape, there were armed response officers standing in small groups, the blue lights turning their black protective gear into eerie carapaces as if they were human-sized beetles bulging at the knees, shoulders and heads.

Her pulse racing, her chest tight, she skirted one group checking rifles and headed towards the police cordon. Two, both male, moved towards her, arms outstretched.

'Get back!' one shouted, his voice young, cracking. He sounded terrified.

'I'm job!' she screamed, pulling her badge free again and sticking it in his face. 'MCU. Let me through.'

The other cop, older, bearded, eyes narrowed, scrutinised her badge for a second.

'Sorry, Detective, but a major incident's been declared. Nobody but AFOs and crisis response officers allowed past this point.'

'My family are inside the venue,' she said, trying and failing to control her breathing. Aware of panic invading her mind and body and powerless to stop it. 'My husband and son, Ivan and Riley Ballantyne. Have you seen them?'

He sighed. 'No, but they're evacuating the venue now. I'm sure they'll be safe. The best thing you can do is wait back there.'

'I need to find them!' she shouted into his face.

She pushed forward but both men blocked her way. 'No,' the older one said again, forcefully. 'You'll only be in the way. Now step back, DS Ballantyne. Please. I'm asking nicely because you're job. But—' He gave her a light shove. 'We can do it different, if you won't comply.'

She backed away, hands held up in surrender. She didn't argue. What would be the point? He was right. What use were homicide detectives at a terrorist incident?

Then she turned and ran in a wide circle, well beyond his probing gaze until she found the edge of the crowd and of the cordon itself. Someone had tied the end of the tape to a chain-link fence. Another uniformed officer answered a call on her Airwave, then stared straight at Kat while nodding and speaking into the handset at her shoulder.

Kat turned away, ran back fifty yards and then stuck her clawed fingers through the chain-link. She toed her right boot into one of the gaps in the links and pushed herself upwards, snatching at the twisted top of the fence. Her foot came free of its precarious toehold and her leg dangled for a second. She bicycled her legs and found another gap.

She placed both hands on the top rail, and swung herself over the ragged edge of the fence before dropping down on the other side. Something ripped loudly on her front and pain arrowed across her ribs as a sharp end of wire sliced her. She looked down. Her white shirt was stained red. She swore. Messy, but not serious.

She sprinted away, down the wrong side of the fence. The cordon was coming up on her right. She swerved deeper into the shadows of the industrial estate's buildings and looped around a warehouse, coming out thirty yards beyond the cordon.

She grabbed the fencing and hauled herself up, taking just enough care to make sure she had secure footholds before swinging a leg over the top and vaulting down on to the tarmac on the road side of the wire. She checked her watch: 20:17. Thirteen minutes left to find Van and Riley and get them away and to safety.

Two hundred yards ahead of her now, the Powerhouse was lit up by the white spotlights the venue management had erected for the gig. Stark against the night sky, the structure seemed two-dimensional, a stage set. But the white of the spotlights was curdled with blue that slid across its concrete facade in drunken curves before reappearing on its far edge and beginning the sequence again.

Frantic to find her boys – oh, God, would she ever get to call them that again outside of tearful reminiscences with other bereaved families? – she raced towards the front of the building and the three sets of double doors.

Tear-streaked teenagers and white-faced adults were pouring out of the interior and stumbling, clattering and running down the steps before being steered away by uniformed officers and paramedics.

'You, there! What the hell do you think you're doing? Get away from there!'

Kat turned. A tall female cop in full dress uniform – silver flashing on her shoulder boards – was striding towards her. An unmistakeable figure: the Chief Constable herself – Ingrid Young. Her steel-grey hair, cut so short it sparked the usual misogynistic jokes on male-only WhatsApp groups, tinted blue by the emergency flashers like a party wig.

No time for Kat to show her badge. What good would it do anyway? Kat put her head down and ran around the outraged Chief Con, dodging a pair of cops as she raced up the stairs, threading herself between the crying children and their terrified parents.

She'd just reached the lobby when a man ran straight at her, his head twisted round to look back into the auditorium. His pumping elbow hit her in the cheekbone. Her vision whited out for a second and she staggered, then fell. On all fours, stars sparking round the edge of her vision, she went to straighten only for someone to crush her hand beneath a heavily cleated boot. She screamed in pain and yanked her hand free before dragging herself to her feet and running on.

She tried frantically to pick out Van and Riley among all the pale oncoming faces. Some were bloody. More collisions, she suspected.

A vision of Riley lying trampled in an aisle made her retch. No! This wasn't happening. She wouldn't let it. She swung her hips left then right as a group of six-foot-tall young men stormed towards her like a rugby pack, dodging their hurtling mass but taking a shoulder to the chest as one stumbled and rocketed forward as he struggled to keep on his feet.

Breathless, she wheezed in what little air she could manage and burst through a pair of doors and into the auditorium. It was half empty, and the remaining concert-goers were huddled against the emergency exits, their faces sickly green from the light of the fleeing-man signs overhead.

'Riley!' Kat screamed. 'Van!'

She ran down the central aisle, deserted as everyone piled out of the exits. But as she scanned left and right, bending to look under the nearest seats, she couldn't see either her husband or her son.

Instruments, amplifiers and the drum kit stood on the stage, abandoned like monuments to an old culture that believed in having fun without fear. Kat vaulted on to the black-painted boards and she spun round, straining to pick out Van and Riley in the stark yellow glow of the house lights. She couldn't see them.

She ran to the back edge of the last knot of people filing out of the emergency exit on the left of the stage. She grabbed a woman by the shoulder and spun her round.

'I'm looking for my husband and son. My son is—'

'Get off me, you crazy bitch!' the woman shouted.

A space opened up in front of her and she threw off Kat's hand and dived through the door and ran up the inclined carpeted walkway that led to the main doors.

Moaning with terror and almost paralysed by a strange foreshadowing of grief she was powerless to avoid, Kat checked her watch: 20:28.

Two minutes to find them.

Then her arms burned with pain and she floated upwards.

Two burly male firefighters had grabbed her by the biceps and lifted her feet clear of the carpet.

'Do you *want* to die?' one shouted, his face taut with stress behind his clear plastic visor. 'We have to go. Now!'

They wheeled her around and ran up the central aisle. The realisation hit her like a train. She'd endangered other lives trying to save Van and Riley.

'Put me down,' she said. 'I'll run, I promise.'

They dropped her to the carpet and together the trio sprinted through the central pair of doors to the auditorium and out into the lobby, from which the last few people were streaming.

Out on to the steps and down, into the floodlit plaza.

Kat stole a look over her shoulder and half-turned. The firefighter to her left grabbed her.

'No!' he screamed. 'No!'

He dragged her bodily away from the Powerhouse. Her breath was coming in short gasps that felt as if they contained no oxygen, only fear distilled into a breathable but still toxic gas.

'One minute, one minute! Clear the area! Clear the area!' someone bellowed through a megaphone.

Staggering, Kat ran away from danger, crying angry, terrified tears that she'd not been able to find Van or Riley. She checked her watch as she ran towards the milling crowd of shivering terrified concert-goers already being shepherded behind the protective convoy of emergency vehicles.

Thirty seconds.

Maybe they'd escaped already. She'd thrown herself into harm's way when they'd have done the sensible thing and headed out. Yes. Of course. She laughed disjointedly. What were the British good at if it wasn't keeping their heads in a crisis?

Van was a good dad, a great dad. And Riley, for all his teenage ranting and unpredictable temper, was a sensible boy. They'd have followed the instructions, formed an orderly queue and got out well before the deadline.

Fifteen seconds.

She ran towards the crowd, peering into the huddles of bewildered concert-goers, sure now she'd massively overreacted and that Van and Riley would be just feet from her, probably sipping hot chocolate and eating Mars Bars.

The bomb would be bad. Of course it would. But the emergency workers had got everyone out.

So, property damage. That's all, Kat. Property damage. That's what you have insurance for. Actually, have I renewed the house insurance?

Five seconds.

She jinked through the crowd, her anxiety a constant flittering buzz in her belly, her chest, the back of her neck, still not finding Van and Riley. Which was fine. They'd be here somewhere.

They'd be—

Chapter Four

She felt it before she heard it.

A subterranean rumble that vibrated in her chest.

Then the explosion, muffled by the thick concrete walls into a dull crump.

Around her people screamed, children began to cry and to her left a firefighter swore under his breath. As one, the crowd recoiled from the bang, a single-celled organism driven backwards by fear.

Then she saw it.

An obscenely swelling ball of orange fire that burst free from the side windows, rolled up and around itself, and blossomed against the night sky into a volcanic surge of flames, soot and whitish-grey smoke.

She heard the firefighter's radio crackle.

'Hold back. There might be a secondary explosion.'

They watched, paralysed, as flames licked up the sides of the building. Then, with an almighty crash, part of the roof caved in, and spears of vermillion flame shot into the sky, their rippling sides accompanied by swarms of yellow sparks.

Kat shook herself out of her immobility. Glass was tinkling down on to the concrete all around her as she walked, then ran towards the building. Someone yelled at her to stay back but she ignored them, placing one foot in front of the other as she picked up speed before breaking into a run and screaming the names that she was trying to avoid seeing written on gravestones.

'Riley! Van!'

A firefighter grabbed her by the left shoulder. She tore herself free, stumbling before regaining her balance and rushing towards the burning building.

Smoke poured out of the front doors, which had been blown off their hinges. Just as she reached them, a movement to her left stopped her. Two shadows emerged from the orange-tinted smoke, staggering away from the flames. One taller, with its arm around the other. Both stumbling, heads down.

Was it them? Had they made it out after all?

She ran for them, calling: 'Van! Riley! Is that you?'

Within touching distance, she wept with relief and horror. Their faces were blackened. Eyes white against the soot and grease. Lips parted to show teeth bared in a rictus of fear and the struggle to breathe.

'Oh, my God! You're safe,' she cried as she rushed to support Riley on his free side, helping Van, who was coughing convulsively, to haul him away from the carnage.

'Help!' she screamed. 'Help! Paramedic!'

Two green-garbed paramedics detached themselves from the crowd and ran towards the ungainly trio. With their help, all three Ballantynes made it to the sanctuary of the cordon.

Moaning softly, and coughing up black gunk, Riley was led to the back of an ambulance where he sat heavily. The female paramedic wrapped him in a silver blanket and fastened an oxygen mask over his nose and mouth.

'Stand back a little,' she said to Kat, calmly but firmly. 'Give him a little room.'

Van was sitting on the ground, also wrapped in silver foil, his eyes wide over his own oxygen mask, chest heaving, staring up at Kat with a look she'd seen on the faces of cops at bad crime scenes or traffic accidents. Blank, shell-shocked. Uncomprehending.

She was torn between trying to hug Riley, who was heaving the pure oxygen into his lungs, and squatting beside Van, her soulmate, who'd once rescued her from crushing depression on a Thai beach what seemed like a lifetime ago.

She settled for squeezing Riley and kissing his grimy forehead, whispering, 'I love you, Riley, I love you so much,' before kneeling next to Van and throwing a protective arm around him.

'Van, my darling man, I thought I'd lost you. I thought I'd lost you both.'

He doubled over as a racking cough seized him, then lifted the mask away from his mouth.

'There was a crush at the front. Everyone was trying to get out through the emergency exits.' He wheezed in a breath and lowered the mask to drag more oxygen down. Lifted it away again. 'We were getting trampled. It wasn't anybody's fault. So we went on to the stage. It was . . .' He stopped, coughed, moaned with pain and heaved in more oxygen. '. . . Riley's idea . . . and through the back. We got out through the kitchens.'

Kat couldn't hold the tears back any longer. As she wept with the sheer relief while the terror and the adrenaline left her, she gently replaced the mask over Van's face and returned to Riley.

'How's he doing?'

The paramedic was checking Riley's pupils with a pen torch while simultaneously inflating a blood pressure cuff around his right arm.

'He's fine. Nothing serious, but we'll take him to MGH for checks, just to be sure. Your husband, too.'

Kat cradled Riley's cheeks between her palms. She stared into his eyes. Once they'd been bright blue – in the first hours, days and weeks of life. Gradually they'd darkened. Now she thought she saw that tiny baby again.

'Go with the paramedics, OK? Dad'll be with you and I'll come in the car.'

Riley nodded mutely. She took his hand and squeezed. Was relieved when he squeezed back.

She stood and patted her pockets till she found the keys to her Golf. She tried to remember where she'd left it.

The crowd was thinning as people drifted away in twos and threes or small groups – back to their cars or public transport. Some accompanied by cops, others being ushered to ambulances. Out of the press, a familiar face appeared. Carve-up. His ginger goatee gone now – perhaps he'd realised it ran a poor second place to DC Faisal 'Fez' Mohammed's sharper black number.

She readied herself for the inevitable confrontation. Ever since he'd sent her and her former bagman Tom into a lethal confrontation with a murder suspect, her feelings for him had deepened from dislike through contempt to outright distrust.

He looked scared. Cheeks pale. Was that a fleck of vomit on the lapel of his suit?

'I need you back at the station, Kat,' he said. 'Please don't make this any harder than it already is. We've got work to do.'

The shock of the bomb was almost replaced by surprise that he'd used her name instead of his customary 'DS Ballantyne', a formality he used to put her down whenever he got the chance.

She was torn. Riley and Van were in ambulances, being taken to A&E, survivors of a terrorist bomb. But she was a homicide detective. A sergeant, moreover, charged with detecting major crimes and bringing the perpetrators to justice.

'Riley. And Van. They're hurt. I need to be with them.'

He glanced over her shoulder. Frowned. 'Go. Make sure they're OK. But then you get into work asap. I need everyone on this, Kat. Everyone.' He turned and walked off, pulling his phone out.

She hurried away, finally remembering where she'd left the car.

Fifteen minutes later she was parking at the hospital and slamming through the swing doors into A&E.

Chapter Five

Kat reeled at the sight of bloodied children and their terrified-looking parents.

'You can't be here!' a young nurse said, hurrying over, her hands out.

Kat flashed her badge.

'I'm a cop. My husband and son were there. Have you seen them? Riley and Van – I mean Ivan – Ballantyne.'

As the nurse checked a folded sheaf of notes, Kat scanned the room anxiously, her pulse skittering as if she'd mainlined coffee before a press conference. But she couldn't see them.

Horrific images flashed through her mind. The ambulance carrying them away from the bomb had crashed. They were maimed. Dead. She was certain of it. Images rose unbidden into her overstressed brain. A funeral. She'd have to buy a black dress. Or would one of her cop-suits be OK? Did people still have wakes these days? And then . . .

. . . and then the nurse interrupted her spiralling doom-thoughts.

'Your son's in the quiet room. He's fine. Barely a scratch. But your husband's condition is a bit more serious. He's suffering from smoke inhalation. We need to keep him on oxygen, for tonight at least. Maybe a day or two more, depending on how he's doing.'

Kat's mind reeled. She'd heard tales from mates in the fire service about the effects of smoke. The consensus was, short of being burned alive, smoke was far more dangerous than flames.

'Oh, my God, is that bad? He's going to be all right, isn't he?'

The nurse nodded. The muscles round her eyes tight.

'He's been taken up to Sheepton, it's a respiratory ward. Level four.' She glanced over Kat's shoulder, tightened her lips. 'I'm sorry, you'll have to excuse me. I have to go.'

'Of course, sorry,' Kat said. Her emotions swung wildly: relief that Riley was OK, but dread that something bad had happened to Van's lungs. She pictured blackened tissue, clogged tubes. Flashed on a post-mortem of a burns victim she'd had to observe as a rookie. 'Go. And thank you.'

She rushed away from the treatment space and pushed open a door labelled 'Quiet Room'.

Riley was there, looking lost in an oversized purple recliner. He cradled a brown plastic vending machine cup while he checked his phone.

Kat ran to him, falling to her knees before scooping him into a tight hug.

'Mum, I can't breathe!' Riley said, squirming out of her grip.

'Sorry, lovey. Are you OK? Let me look at you.'

'I'm fine. Get off me! Where's Dad? What's happened to him?'

'He . . . He inhaled some smoke,' Kat said, trying to keep her voice light. 'They're keeping him in overnight. He needs a bit of oxygen, that's all. Just to help him breathe.'

Even to her own ears, Kat's words sounded fake. The way you'd speak to a small child when you didn't want to alarm them.

Riley welled up. 'He's going to be OK, though? He's not going to die or anything?'

Kat held him close as he broke down in tears. Fought back her own. She needed to be strong for him.

'Hey, hey . . . Dad's going to be fine. I swear. The nurse didn't sound worried and she's a professional, yes? We'll go and see him if you like. Shall we do that?'

'Yeah.' Riley cleared his throat. 'Yes, please.'

'Come on, then,' Kat said, getting to her feet, swaying slightly as the blood temporarily left her brain.

Sheepton Ward was packed with staff. Every bed was full, and a few extras had been wheeled in, ranged in every available free space. Their occupants were hooked up to oxygen, administered via nasal tubes, green plastic nose-and-mouth masks, or in a couple of cases, full-face contraptions held in place with thick elastic straps.

Kat found Van in a bay at the far end, his bed hard up against a window overlooking the A&E department.

She rushed over, Riley following close on her heels.

Van was grey-faced, his nose and mouth covered by one of the green plastic masks. So, not the most serious it could have been, then. He had his phone in his hand. He let it fall on to the bedclothes and offered a small wave.

'Was just . . . texting you,' he husked as Kat bent her head to kiss his exposed forehead.

She sat on the bed and took his right hand in both of hers. Tried, and failed, to hold back the tears.

'My poor baby. Is it bad?'

He nodded. His thumbs danced over his phone screen. He held it up to her.

Really sore. Hard to breathe.

'Oh, darling, I thought I'd lost you.' She turned to Riley. 'I thought I'd lost you both.'

'Don't worry, Mum, we made it,' Riley said. He seemed calmer now he'd seen his dad, and that he was basically OK. 'Dad was a legend. I tripped and he, like, pulled me to my feet without even stopping.'

'You're *both* legends,' Kat said.

Her phone buzzed. It was Carve-up, demanding her presence at work. She had to go in. Wanted to. Whoever had planted that bomb was going to pay. But then a thought struck her. Where was Riley going to go? He'd never been on his own in the house overnight and now certainly wasn't the night to try that particular experiment. He'd claim he was fine, but no way was she going to leave him alone. Her heart sank as she realised her only option.

'Listen, you two. I have to go into work. I'm not sure when I'll be home.'

Van typed on his phone again:

go do your police thing get the bastards who did this

'I will. But, Riley . . . you need somewhere to stay tonight. I'm going to ring Granny.'

He groaned and rolled his eyes. She felt a surge of relief. If he was well enough to give her the full teenage treatment, there couldn't be too much wrong with him. If he'd agreed, *that* would have worried her.

'It'll only be for a night or two, I'm sure. And Granny loves you. Grandpa too. She'll probably say I'm not feeding you enough and buy you chocolate cake from Waitrose.'

Kat's mother probably would, as well. Never one to miss an opportunity to remind Kat of her deficiencies as a mother. *Pots and kettles, Mum, pots and kettles.*

Kat called her parents' landline. As it rang, Van began coughing, the spasms increasing in intensity until he was doubled up.

'Get a nurse,' Kat said to Riley, who was looking scared, like a small boy. He ran off.

Kat juggled her phone while comforting Van, rubbing his back between his shoulder blades. Thankfully, the coughing fit began to subside, although she was relieved when Riley appeared with a young Indian nurse on his heels.

'Morton residence,' her mother trilled in her special telephone voice.

'Mum, it's me. Can you have Riley tonight? Maybe tomorrow as well?' Kat gabbled, watching the nurse adjust Van's oxygen mask. 'You'll need to stop off at ours for his things – school stuff, clothes and whatever – and he'll need a lift to school. Home again, too. Oh, and Smokey, too.'

'And a very good evening to you, too, darling,' her mum said in a long-suffering tone.

Kat's temper flared instantly. She gripped her phone so tightly her knuckles cracked. 'He was at the Powerhouse, Mum! The bombing? Van, too. We're at the hospital. They're keeping Van in overnight, so forgive me if just this once I don't go through the social niceties, would you?'

Her mum's mood changed instantly, her drawing-room manners swept aside. 'Oh, my poor darling. I am so, so sorry. Daddy and I saw it on the news. Of course Riley can come. For as long as you need. Smokey, too. He can make friends with Sidney. Can you drop him off? No, wait. You'll be wanted at the station, won't you. To investigate.' Her mum's voice became muffled though still audible. Kat pictured her holding the receiver under her chin. 'It's Kat, darling. Van and Riley were caught up in that dreadful bombing.'

The line clicked. Her father spoke. 'It's me, darling. Which ward is Van on?'

'Sheepton.'

'I'll be there in fifteen minutes. Tell Riley to stay put with his dad till I get there.'

Kat swallowed against the lump that had formed in her throat. Even corrupt fathers were still fathers. 'Thanks, Dad. I mean it.'

'I know what you think of me, Kat. But I'm still your father. And I'm Riley's grandpa. Family matters, yes?'

'Yes.'

'I'm coming.'

The line went dead. The nurse turned to Kat. 'He is fine now. It is to be expected with smoke inhalation. We are keeping everyone under good observation. Try not to worry.'

Kat thanked the nurse. Then, once she had left, explained what was happening to Riley. Van nodded from the pillow.

'I'll come and see you tomorrow, darling,' she said to Van, then bent to kiss him again. 'Get some sleep. Do what the nurses tell you. Drink lots of liquids. I love you.'

She hugged Riley tight.

'I love you, too, my darling boy. Look after Dad till Grandpa gets here.'

Waving over her shoulder and turning at the double doors to the bay to blow them both a kiss, Kat made her way out, pausing to thank the nurse.

Outside the hospital, Kat fought to hold back tears as she replayed those terrifying few minutes at the Powerhouse. She yearned to stay with Van and Riley, but for once Stuart Carver was right. There was work to be done.

She wanted to find the bastards who'd attacked her town and almost killed her family.

Heaving huge breaths of clean night air, she walked the short distance to the car park and got in behind the wheel. She settled into the seat and closed her eyes, trying to ignore the cold damp sweat soaking her shirt.

Her phone rang. She glanced at the screen, ready to lash out at the telemarketer or scammer who'd picked that precise moment to try and talk her out of her hard-earned pay.

But it was Liv.

Kat's best friend lived in Wales now, although she'd grown up in Middlehampton. Until that fateful evening when she'd vanished, before a letter from a notorious serial killer had been sent to the police and the *Middlehampton Echo* claiming her as his seventh victim.

But Liv had faked her own death – including the letter – before disappearing from Middlehampton. When the killer became active again after fifteen years of silence, Liv had reappeared in Kat's life, turning it upside down. Kat had forgiven Liv – how could she not after learning that Liv had been terrified she was going to be the killer's next victim? Now they were friends again, bound by the shared secret that had almost broken them both.

'Thelma, oh my God, are you all right?'

'I'm fine, Louise,' Kat said quietly.

Thelma and Louise. Their favourite film. They'd quoted a favourite line, 'Always and forever', to each other as they'd sworn a blood-sister oath deep in the school field, far beyond the prying eyes of teachers or the sneaks who'd report them. Each had a fine silver scar at the base of their thumbs where they'd made that mutual bond flesh, carving their skin with Liv's penknife.

'But the bomb! And Van and Riley! They were there. Are they OK?'

'Riley's fine, Van's got some breathing problems from smoke inhalation. But he's OK, really. They're keeping him overnight.' Kat paused. Frowned. 'Wait. How did you know they were at the Powerhouse?'

'Been messaging with Riley.'

Of course she had. She and Riley had struck up quite the bond over the last year. To Kat's fourteen-year-old son, Liv was somewhere between a cool older sister and an even cooler auntie. Living on a commune in the South Wales countryside with people who owned shotguns and quad bikes. People who let Riley *shoot* their shotguns and *ride* their quads.

However deep into the teenage tunnel he went, he now had a human confidante as well as the canine one who'd pad around after him, claws clicking on the kitchen tiles, as he fixed himself a plate-defying 'snack'.

'How did you hear in the first place? Mutt-calf?'

'Of course. He was live-streaming. I have to say, Thel, that man must have been watching makeover reels on Instagram. Have you seen him lately?'

Kat had, but she really didn't want to devote even a second to discussing Middlehampton's very own true-crime podcaster – and her stalker. He'd backed off since Kat's friend, PC Abby Greene, had arrested him and issued words of advice, as the official phrase had it. That had worked: he'd made no further attempts to confront Kat in the street or the station car park.

Abby was a member of Hertfordshire Police's anti-stalking team. More than that, she was something of a fangirl when it came to Kat. 'Fiercely protective' might just about cover it. In the same way that 'a light tap' might describe how Kat had put down a murderer attacking her and Tom, her former bagman, with a blow from his own golf trophy. Kat didn't need protection, but Abby's devotion was harmless enough.

'Look, Liv, it's great to hear from you, but I'm heading into work. It's going to be an all-nighter. I'll call you soon as I can.'

'OK, sure, Thel. Message me, yes?'

'If I can. Love you.'

'Love you. Always and forever.'

The call over, Kat put the car into gear. She negotiated the hospital's perimeter road at a sedate 15 mph, and made the right turn on to the main road, her swinging headlights catching the moon-face of a barn owl cruising the fence-line for prey.

Riley and Van were safe, even if Van was hurt. So she could let her feelings of shock and terror fade away. But bad people had come to her town and committed the unimaginably evil sin of trying to murder children, her own included.

She felt it arriving without consciously summoning it. A dark, warlike emotion that had her jamming her foot all the way on the throttle, making the engine howl.

Kat wanted revenge.

Chapter Six

The assembled cops, Kat at the front, read the statement splashed over the home page of *the Middlehampton Echo*'s website and projected on to the wall:

> *The tyrannical regime with its boot-heel on the faces of the Al Jumairi people must face the consequences of its crimes. The Al Rashid family are guilty of imprisonment without trial, torture and summary execution, the widespread abuse of human rights and looting the country for their own enrichment.*
>
> *The cowardly, greedy West, in love with Al Jumairi wealth that buys weapons of war and instruments of oppression, has designated us as terrorists. The real terrorists are the Al Rashid family and their enablers in Al Jumairah and abroad.*
>
> *Now, these cockroaches are seeking to cleanse the blood from their hands. The deal to buy Middlehampton FC is a travesty and an affront to Allah. It must not go ahead.*
>
> *Desert Sun*

'Bloody nutters!' Craig Evers said. 'It's going to bring jobs and money to the town.'

The room filled with murmurs of assent and a few muttered threats about what would happen to anyone they arrested for 'murdering our kids'.

Chapter Seven

They worked all night.

And achieved nothing.

Kat had listened to the warning phone call so many times she knew it by heart.

Carve-up ran around for the first hour, issuing and then countermanding orders before retreating to his office and shutting himself in.

DCI Linda Ockenden, the Head of Crime, gathered everyone around her in the centre of the general CID office. Major Crimes simply didn't have the space to accommodate an entire station's worth of uniforms, plain-clothes detectives and civilian staff.

'Right, listen up. Sadly, I have to tell you that contrary to what we thought earlier, there have now been two confirmed fatalities.' She glanced guiltily towards Kat. 'I mean deaths. At 2.59 a.m., a girl – only fifteen – called Casey Hall died of her injuries at MGH after getting crushed in an incident on the Parker Street exit. Her father, Jonathan Hall, died trying to save her. He had a fatal heart attack at 3.05 a.m. Mrs Hall has been informed and is being supported by an FLO. I can hardly bear to use the word "fortunately", but anyway, tragic as Casey and Jonathan's deaths are, it looks like there are no further deaths. Most people got away with nothing worse than bumps and bruises or a panic attack.'

Kat's heart stuttered in her chest as she tried to imagine how Mrs Hall was going to cope with being told she'd lost not just her daughter but her husband in the same attack.

Van's grey face behind the oxygen mask swam in front of her eyes. She swallowed, hard. *There but for the grace of God . . .*

Beside her, Leah Hooper stretched out a hand and squeezed Kat's. Kat turned and mouthed, 'Thanks, mate. You all right?'

Leah could only nod. Her eyes were glistening.

Eyes front. The big boss was still speaking.

'Now, some deranged arsehole planted a bomb at a concert where kids were waiting to watch one of our local bands. I want them caught. Here's what we know. They phoned it in, giving us a whole thirty minutes to evacuate a venue holding two thousand. So hard as it may be to stomach, we have to assume maximum loss of life was not their aim.'

'Doesn't bloody sound like it,' an older cop protested from somewhere in the middle of the crush of officers.

'No, it bloody doesn't. But think about Manchester. That psychopath blew himself up in a crowded arena. Nails, nut and bolts, the works. He wanted to kill as many kids as possible. So what does that tell us about *our* perpetrator?'

Kat pointed to a transcript of the warning message taped to the incident board.

'He claimed he was representing a group called Desert Sun, ma'am,' Kat said. 'I checked online. They've got a website. They're against the Al Jumairi regime. So is this about getting publicity?'

'Or maybe they want to stop the deal going ahead,' Fez said.

Linda nodded. 'Without an explicit claim from them, we simply don't know. And, to be honest, I don't actually care. I want the bastards who plotted this outrage behind bars and questioned till they give it all up. That means evidence, evidence, evidence, people. I want you to sweat your assets: every snitch, snout and halfway reliable source. If anyone's heard so much as a mouse fart about bomb plots, strangers asking about the Powerhouse, whatever, I want it in detail. Names, descriptions, distinguishing marks, phone numbers, whatever. And I—'

Linda stopped. Scanned the room, frowning. The thin line of her mouth narrowed even further.

'Where's DI Carver?'

The room rustled as forty or fifty cops turned this way and that, looking for the missing DI.

'I think he's in his office, ma'am.'

Kat peered between a couple of taller officers. Standing near a water cooler was Abby Greene. She must have sensed Kat's eyes on her. She turned and shot her a nervous half-smile.

Linda rolled her eyes. 'Never mind. Everyone got jobs to do?'

A low chorus of affirmation.

'Right. Don't just stand there listening to me. Get on and do them!' She searched for Kat in the dispersing crowd. 'Quick word?'

Kat made her way through the press of departing officers until she was at Linda's side.

'Yes, Ma-Linda?'

They'd both grown used to the jokey nickname ever since Kat had tried and failed, on the first time of telling, to call Linda by her first name and not her title. But now it felt wrong.

If Linda felt the same way, she hid it well. 'What's your take on this?'

Kat didn't answer at once. She wasn't buying time. Not exactly. But her mentor, DI Molly Steadman, had once cautioned her about giving her opinion straight away.

'Everyone's expected to have an opinion on everything, Kat. But it's OK to say, "I don't know". In fact, it's good to say that. We're investigators, right? So we investigate, we don't pontificate.'

But Linda was looking at her. Expectant. She had to say something. She thought of Riley, uprooted to his grandparents' home. Of Van, lying in a hospital bed. She'd been terrified she was going to lose her boys. And now a girl and her father lay dead in that same hospital. She knew what it felt like to be Mrs Hall.

'I think they wanted to frighten people. To hurt them emotionally more than physically. Otherwise, why give a warning at all? Why not just send some guy with a rucksack full of plastic explosive and ball bearings to blow himself up?'

Linda nodded. 'That's what I think, too. Look, I'm going to be straight with you. I've never handled anything like this before. Terrorism?' She puffed out a breath. 'I've always been your basic crime detective. The closest I ever came was crowd control when a bunch of English Defence League idiots marched through the Bramalls. But with two dead, this is still a murder investigation. I'm going to be Gold Commander and that's not going to leave me time for anything else so I'm appointing you my deputy on this. You're on the SIO path, aren't you?'

'Yes, but it's early days. You remember what it's like. It's classroom stuff and case studies.'

'Well, this is going to be your biggest bloody practical so far, my girl.'

Kat hesitated. 'Does it matter that Van and Riley were involved?'

Linda shook her head. 'Maybe the College of Policing website has something on detectives not investigating terrorist outrages that almost killed their families. Me? I need every warm body I've got. Let's just say it'll give you a keener edge and leave it at that, eh?'

'What about Carve— I mean Stuart?' Kat blushed as she realised she'd been about to use the nickname for the senior officer.

Everyone called DI Carver 'Carve-up', although it usually wasn't in earshot of any of the bosses. A few origin stories regarding this name flew about the station, but the only one Kat believed was that he was a corrupt copper, who'd carved his way through any obstacles to further his career and pad out his bank balance.

Chief among the donors was her father, Colin Morton, a property developer with the moral code of a Mafia don. For him there were two priorities. His business, Morton Land. And the Morton family. Every*thing*, and every*one*, else he divided into two categories. Those who could help. And those who could hinder. The fact Riley was under his roof for a couple of days changed nothing.

'Stuart's too senior an officer to have an operational role on this one. There's going to be a ton of fallout from this so my senior team are all going to be locked down here helping manage this bloody shit-show. I've spent half the night on the phone to the mayor. The Home Secretary's apparently on her way down. Probably wants a selfie outside the Powerhouse talking to a bloody firefighter. The national media are already swarming down here. I mean, good luck getting a hotel room in Middlehampton by tomorrow morning.' She checked her watch. 'Great. Three forty-five. I mean *this* morning. And you might as well hear this from me now. We're going to be welcoming the Met at first light.'

Kat's eyes widened. Then she chided herself for her naivety. Of *course* the Met would be involved. They were the country's biggest and best-equipped force, and when it came to terrorist activity they were the people with all the resources.

'What do you want me to do?' Kat asked, having heard a note of rising anxiety in her boss's voice and not liking it.

'I want you to focus on the Powerhouse itself. Get CCTV, talk to every single member of staff. If the security staff are freelance or agency, find out from which outfit.'

'How about the band and their people? Entourage or whatever. They must have been there earlier, setting up and soundchecking.'

'Yes, good point. OK, you got enough to be getting on with?'

'Yes. And . . . Linda?'

'What?'

Kat extended her hand and gently laid it on the older woman's shoulder.

'It'll be all right. We'll get them.'

Linda sighed, the breath coming out in a shudder, and for a moment, Kat thought she was going to cry. But Linda Ockenden was made of sterner stuff. She squared her shoulders. Eyeballed Kat.

'Yes. We will. Now go do your job.'

Kat returned to MCU. Called out, 'Tom, Leah, Fez. Over here, please.'

Leah and Fez jumped up at once and headed over to her desk. Tom was facing away from her, tucked into a corner of the partitions between him and the walkway along the side of the room. His head was tipped back. Kat glimpsed something small and smooth. Rectangular. A flash of silver. Was that a hip flask? Was Tom drinking spirits on the job? She blinked. The flask was gone. Tom was on his feet and hurrying to catch up with the others. Had she really seen it? Or was the stress and the adrenaline getting to her?

'You OK, Tomski?' she asked as he arrived.

'Yeah, fine. I mean, apart from the obvious. Why?'

'Nothing.'

She inhaled deeply, hoping and not hoping to catch a whiff of alcohol on his breath. But he was too far away. 'Right,' she said. 'Jobs.'

Once tasks were allocated and the three DCs had dispersed to sort out the finer details, Kat messaged Van and Riley in their family WhatsApp group. She knew they'd both be asleep but it helped her anxiety.

How are u guys doing? xx

Shaking her head, she put her phone face down and logged in to her computer. It was time to start hunting a terrorist.

Chapter Eight

At 7.35 a.m., Kat finally admitted defeat.

She couldn't focus any longer. Promising the team she'd be back within the hour, she headed home. Before starting the car, she checked her phone. Still no reply from Van or Riley.

She kept her eyes focused on the road on the short drive home, resisting the temptation to check WhatsApp at every junction or red light.

Finally, when the front door closed behind her, Kat sagged against the wall. After a few moments, she was able to move again. She sniffed her armpit and recoiled.

Upstairs, she stripped off her smoke-infused trousers and shirt and chucked them in the laundry bin. Frowned. Didn't want to stink out Van's clothes too. She gathered it all up and hurried downstairs, hoping no neighbour would glimpse her in her undies as she nipped into the utility room and put a wash on.

She showered, taking a few extra minutes to wash her hair, changed into fresh clothes and started for the stairs. But the magnetic pull of her spare-room office drew her into its seven-by-eight-foot confines. As she did on the frequent nights when sleep eluded her, she stared at the details of the light-plane crash that had killed Connor and Tasha Starling, her half-sister Jo's parents. All she had was a sickening hunch that her dad, Tasha's business partner at the time, might have been involved. She shook her head. She didn't have time for a cold case, however much she was personally compelled to look into it. She had a red-hot case that needed her more.

The shower had made her feel halfway human. What she needed to complete the job was some strong black coffee. While she waited for the kettle to boil, she checked her phone again. Her heart jumped. WhatsApp notifications.

Riley had replied first.

> ok but still feel shaky granny made hot chocolate last night and

He must have hit return without meaning to.

> she put some brandy in it . . . bleurgh

That made her smile. Riley had broken his own 'punctuation is for old people' code and used three dots for some comic timing.

> Are *you* ok mum

Her heart clenched. He might be a hormone-tornado at times but Riley had a protective streak and she loved him fiercely for it.

She took a breath, swallowed the lump in her throat and tried her hardest to get her next message right.

> im fine if ur ill cu soon luv u lots xxx

Riley's reply almost had her sobbing with relief before it turned into a laugh.

u feeling ok

A pause.

x

No reply from Van, though. Anxiety juddered through her. Was he OK? Had he had a crisis? Been rushed into ITU? Visions of nurses wheeling crash carts and readying defibrillator pads flashed through her brain. Maybe he was asleep. No! Because they woke you up super-early in hospital, didn't they? She texted him instead.

Hey you. How are you feeling? Xx

Kat held her breath. Tried to banish the spectral medics and their worried frowns. Three grey dots started pulsing in the corner of her screen. Oh, thank God. He was fine.

mornin feeling better doc says i have to stay tonite too dont worry im fine xx

She laughed with relief at the message and Van's effortless use of teen-text. Then the laugh turned into a loud sob. She clapped a palm to her mouth, stifling the sound, over-loud in the kitchen. She turned to Smokey's bed, thinking a walk would do them both good, but it was empty. Of course. She'd asked her mum to take him as well as Riley.

Can you swap to WhatsApp? she texted, so they could talk with Riley, too.

Then, in the app:

Hey Riley, you OK about going into school today?

ye weve got a special assembly cos of trauma

Will you be all right?

i be fine gotta go granny serving up bacon and eggs and sausages

Van came in to the chat, then:

glad to see u got ur appetite

Kat's stomach rumbled. Riley wasn't the only one who needed to eat. She signed off with a quick Luv you both lots xxx and made herself a bacon sandwich with brown sauce. She tipped her coffee into a travel mug and headed back to Jubilee Place.

The traffic in the centre of Middlehampton was eerily quiet, as if the whole town had decided it needed to either stay at home or get to work early. It reminded Kat of the pandemic, and that weird sense she'd had of living through an apocalypse every time she went through town.

Lockdown. Such a strange word. And yet everyone had ended up dropping it into everyday speech. Now here they were, dealing with something even more reality altering. A bomb. Counter-terror cops taking over investigations. Linda, for once, looking subdued and out of her depth.

With thoughts of how she could best use her contacts and local knowledge whirling round in her brain, she drove the last half-mile to Jubilee Place and was soon at her desk, alternating between phone calls and database searches. The restorative effects of her shower, the coffee, and the bacon sandwich, which she'd eaten in the car, had worn off. Every few seconds, her eyes would close involuntarily. She shook herself, went to the kitchen, and returned with a black coffee. Back to the screen.

Kat caught movement out of the corner of her eye and turned.

Riley was standing over her, his face burned back to the skull. His charred lips parted with a dry whisper. 'u feeling ok' he asked, smoke trailing between his teeth.

She screamed. Jerked upright, spilling the coffee. The nightmare had seemed so real. She could still smell that filthy smell of smoke from the Powerhouse blaze.

Leah rushed over and squatted beside Kat's desk.

'It was just a bad dream, Kat. It's all right.'

Chest heaving, Kat struggled to her feet, shaken that she'd fallen asleep at work. She wiped the sweat off her forehead. Then mopped up the spilt coffee.

'It's not all right, though, is it, mate? Those nutters planted a bloody bomb. For what? Because they don't like some football takeover? I mean, Christ, what is *wrong* with these people?'

Leah shook her head. Dark bags hung beneath her eyes and her skin was pale.

Kat sighed. 'Sorry. We all had a crap night. Where are Tomski and Fez?'

'At the Powerhouse, interviewing staff.'

The double doors into MCU swung wide and as everyone looked round, a squad of ten or so people with guest passes on black lanyards swept into the room.

A woman in her early forties, black suit, dark hair, wearing the high ponytail all long-haired female detectives favoured, stood at the front.

'My name is DI Sharon Critchlow. I'm with SO15. That's the Met Counter Terrorism Command,' she announced in a voice that not only reached the back of the room but bounced straight off the poster-covered walls and ricocheted to all four corners like a flash-bang grenade. 'Or CTC, if TLAs are your thing. Me, I prefer ANB. That's the Anti-Nutcase Brigade. Sadly, it's your town's misfortune to be the target of the latest bunch of manifesto-waving lunatics. As of now, we are taking over the investigation into the Powerhouse bombing last night. This is my team. We need ten desks and a conference room. Who can help me?'

The room erupted with a cacophony of protest.

Kat got to her feet, anxious to prevent an inter-agency dispute gaining traction in the middle of the vital first few hours of the investigation.

Chapter Nine

Linda had appointed Kat acting SIO. So it fell to her to liaise with the abrasive CTC officer who stood with her arms folded in the centre of the room.

The humour-free quip about TLAs – three-letter acronyms – showed she was a woman who knew how cop bureaucracy worked, but didn't have much time for it. Although the Anti-Nutcase Brigade line sounded well-rehearsed to Kat's more cynical side.

She strode over to DI Critchlow, hand outstretched.

'I'm DS Kathryn Ballantyne. I'm acting—'

Sharon seized her hand and pumped it mechanically, twice.

'Sorry, DS Ballantyne, but you're not acting anything except under my orders now. About those desks? And we need a decent PC each, none of the rubbishy old clunkers you regional forces seem to love hammering away on.'

Kat's mouth dropped open. But before she could frame a reply, Linda Ockenden marched into MCU and clapped her hands loudly.

Linda's hair, usually neatly coiffed, was sticking up on one side. Kat knew the look. You got it from sleeping with your face squashed at one end of a sofa.

'Quiet, please, ladies and gentlemen. I want to see Inspectors Critchlow, Carver and Steadman, and Sergeants Ballantyne and Evers in my office.'

She spun and left. Kat had to give it to the big boss. She had the whole language of command, from tone of voice to the physicality of it, down to a fine art.

Wordlessly, she followed, glancing at DS Craig Evers as she passed the knot of Met CTC officers who were engaged in muttered conversations among themselves. Molly Steadman caught up with her in the corridor that led to the brass's offices.

'She's a charmer,' Molly said drily.

Kat rolled her eyes. 'For a moment back there, I thought I was going to like her.'

'Gossiping, ladies? I'd have thought things were a bit too dark for that.'

They both turned. Carve-up had caught up with them. Incredibly, he was smirking. Even as a Middlehampton family had been torn apart, and hundreds of others would be in shock, he was still intent on belittling female officers.

'Found the courage to leave your office, did you, Stuart?' Molly said, glaring into his face. 'What were you doing, hiding under your desk?'

Carve-up paled, two high spots of colour blooming on his cheekbones. 'Drawing up an operational spreadsheet, if you must know. And I resent your insinuation that—'

'You're a coward?' Molly shrugged. 'If the cap fits. Come on Kat, *we've* got work to do.'

Even ragged with fatigue and tension, Kat still found a moment to marvel at Molly's way with words and her unerring eye for the barb to take down Carve-up.

They reached Linda's office and entered. With seven people inside, the usually palatial office felt crowded.

'Thanks, my love,' Linda said as her PA Annie brought in coffee. Once everyone had a mug in hand, she cleared her throat. 'We've all had the chance to vent about the shits who perpetrated the attack on our people, so I want to keep this meeting strictly business. This is now a multi-agency operation with the codename Birdcage. I am Gold Commander. DI Critchlow—'

Critchlow leaned forward. 'Maybe we could put this on a first-name-terms basis? We're going to be putting in all the hours God or the Home Secretary sends on this and it'll save time.'

Kat sneaked a glance at the ramrod-straight Met DI. That was interesting. Using first names not out of solidarity, professional camaraderie or even politeness, but in the name of efficiency.

Very carefully – although Kat still noticed it – Linda let out a breath between lips she was forcing herself to keep relaxed.

'*Sharon* is taking full operational control of Operation Birdcage. Molly, Stuart, you still direct your teams but I want you to run any operational decisions past Sharon first.'

Carve-up held his tie so it didn't flop on to the tabletop. 'Linda, as ranking DI, I think it makes sense for me to act as liaison between MCU and CTC.' He turned to Sharon. 'I did a one-month rotation with some of your guys last year.'

Kat didn't bother disguising her own sigh. Even a terrorist incident was nothing more to Carve-up than an opportunity to curry favour with bigger dogs.

Sharon regarded him with a raised eyebrow.

'SO15? I didn't hear of us having a regional detective with us.'

She made 'regional' sound like 'pretend'. Normally Kat would have bridled, but as Sharon was aiming the insult at Carve-up she felt she could live with it.

Carve-up either took it in his stride or was too thick-skinned to notice.

'Not SO15, no.'

'Oh, right. Which unit was it? Drugs? Firearms? Gangs? Specialist crime?'

‘Er, no.’ Carve-up fiddled with his tie then sipped hurriedly at his coffee. ‘RPOCU.’ He pronounced the acronym in full, so it came out as ‘Ar-pockoo.’

Sharon frowned. Then a smile ghosted across her lips. Just for a moment.

‘The Royal Parks Operational Command Unit. Oh, well, you know, that’s good, too. I mean, we can’t have people riding their e-bikes where deer might be mating, after all. Well done you.’

Kat thought the woman must be wearing asbestos undies to withstand the heat from Carve-up’s cheeks as he retreated behind his coffee mug. Clearly she didn’t mind making enemies. Kat wondered what she knew about Carve-up. And whether it might be helpful to her own mission to take him down.

Ever since she’d met him, she’d felt he was off. But certain events had deepened and solidified her hatred of the man. His part in a conspiracy to get her indicted on corruption charges was bad. But worse, and at the top of the charge sheet, was him sending her and Tom unprotected into the violent confrontation with the murderous cop Tim Paxton. The confrontation that had ended with Tom in a coma.

Linda ended the awkward silence, although Kat thought the wait might have been just a few seconds longer than it needed to be.

‘Yes, well, if we could park’ – tiny push on that word – ‘any incipient inter-force friction, it’s been a long night for all of us. Stuart, you’ll be Silver Commander.’

‘What about us, boss?’ Craig asked.

‘Keep working the streets. That’s what we can bring that Sharon and her team can’t,’ she said, looking at Sharon, who nodded. ‘Someone in this town knows something. I want them in here, in an interview room, spilling their guts.’

Kat put her mug down on the table, which it hit with a *clonk*. ‘Aren’t we forgetting something? A young girl and her father are lying dead in the mortuary at MGH. Casey Hall died in the crush and her dad had a heart attack trying to protect her. That makes this a murder investigation. Maybe they didn't die in the explosion, but they'd still be alive if this bastard hadn't set the bomb off.' Her heart was pounding, but she didn't care. All the talk about Gold and Silver didn't obscure the one terrible fact about the night. Two Middlehamptonians were dead. 'You put me in charge of this last night, Ma-Linda' – Kat caught Sharon's quizzical glance and cursed herself for the slip – 'I mean Linda, and that's what I should be focusing on. This is still murder.'

Sharon turned to Kat. 'Look . . . Kathryn, wasn't it? Obviously, any loss of life is tragic. But you have to see the bigger picture. Twenty-two people were killed at the Manchester Arena bombing. On 7/7, it was fifty-two. Not to mention all the ones with life-changing injuries. It could have been a lot worse here. We already know the culprits for this one. It was the Desert Sun group and whichever member planted the bomb. If you want justice for the girl and her father, work with me and my team to find them.'

It was a good point. Kat opened her mouth to argue but found she had no words that made sense. She tried to connect with Sharon on an emotional level.

'I get all that, and of course I'll work alongside you. But my own family were almost killed last night. I need to be front and centre on this.'

As soon as the words left Kat's lips, she knew she'd made a mistake. She wished she could withdraw them, like deleting an unread text. But they were loose, flying round the room.

Sharon eyed her coolly. 'Well, that's a problem, isn't it? You've got a conflict of interest. I can't have you investigating a terrorist incident your own family were involved in,' she said. 'The CPS would have kittens. And *those* kittens would have kittens. No. You're off the case.'

'What?' Kat said, lunging forward, her heart thumping. 'You can't! This is my town.'

'And it's *my* investigation. I assume Middlehampton has other crimes that need investigating? Investigate those.'

Kat turned to Linda, wordlessly appealing for support. But Linda just shook her head. 'DI Critchlow's in charge on this one, Kat. And she has a point. I'm sorry.'

Fighting back tears of frustration and anger, Kat rose from her chair. 'Well, in that case, if you'll all excuse me, I'd better get back to my desk.'

Sparks flying around her peripheral vision, she left Linda's office, almost blind with rage at the casual way Sharon Critchlow had sidelined her. And how Linda hadn't backed her up. Not even tried.

She couldn't face MCU with its pack of strutting Met officers. Critchlow thought she should be investigating other crimes. Fine. Then that's exactly what she'd do. The old-school way. She took the stairs down to the shift room. Maybe there'd be something down there for her.

She knocked and entered the shift office. Behind the desk sat Harry Nightingale, the C-shift supervisor. Harry was a twenty-year veteran with the sort of sound instincts only a really top-quality uniformed sergeant could develop.

Grey bags hung from his eyes. He looked up and smiled wearily at her.

'Hi, Kat. All right?' He sounded as exhausted as she felt.

'Hi, Harry. Not really. The alpha bitch from the Met sent me to sit on the naughty step.'

He grinned ruefully. 'What did you do, turn up for a meeting with straw in your hair?'

She told him about Van and Riley, and how Critchlow had used that as an excuse to bounce her.

'Anything come in overnight that needs looking at by a problem child?' she asked.

Harry wrinkled his nose. 'Maybe, maybe not. Paramedics got an odd 999 call last night at 21.32 p.m. A mate referred it to me. Do you want to have a quick listen?'

She nodded and waited while he loaded a sound file. Kat leaned closer as the recording started with the call handler's trained, well-modulated tones.

'Emergency. Which service do you require?' A man's voice. Wheezy. Agonised. 'Help me! It hurts so bad.'

'Sir? Sir! You called 999. Which service do you require, please?'

'The amber . . .' a three-second pause . . . 'the medical one. The amber— Come quick. Please it . . . it hurts so much. My chest. I'm . . . dying. I can't breathe.'

'OK, sir. I'm going to need your address. Can you do that for me? Can you tell me where you live?'

'It's 31 Viking Way.'

'What's your name, sir? Can you tell me your name, please?'

'Pete. Vau . . . Vaughan. Please, help me.'

There was a click on the line. And a long pause. Kat straightened.

'Why are you playing me this, Harry? It's some guy having a heart attack by the sound of it.'

He held up a finger.

The call hadn't ended. Out of a hiss of static the man spoke a final time.

'They killed me.'

Then, the click that signalled he'd hung up.

Kat rubbed a hand over her mouth. She looked at Harry. '"They killed me"?'

'It came in an hour after the bomb went off. I followed it up. He's in intensive care. Alive.' A brief pause. 'Just.'

Kat nodded. Pete Vaughan had sounded not only in excruciating pain but confused mentally. He'd struggled with saying 'ambulance'. It had *sounded* like he was having a heart attack. He'd said his chest hurt and he was struggling to breathe. But men suffering heart attacks didn't usually tell the call handler they'd been killed, did they? She shrugged mentally. She didn't have much experience of dealing with heart attack victims. Maybe he was talking about cigarettes. Or doughnuts. Or double whiskies.

She left Harry and called the hospital as she took the stairs back to MCU. Finally, she got through to a doctor in ITU – the Intensive Therapy Unit. Pete Vaughan was still unconscious. OK, well, so much for that, then. Now she had time on her hands, she could pay him a visit later when he woke up. *If* he woke up.

As soon as Kat reached her desk, Tom came over. His face was dark with rage.

'Those shits from the Met have taken our PCs. And our desks. We've been working in the canteen. Can't you do something, boss?'

Kat caught it full in the face this time. The unmistakeable smell of stale alcohol. She glanced at his trouser pockets looking for a telltale bulge that might be a hip flask.

Tom stared at her incredulously. 'What are you looking at? I just told you – me and Leah and Fez have got nowhere to work.'

She could see how upset her fast-track graduate DC was. If his indignant tone of voice hadn't done it, the grammatical slip – 'me and' – would have.

'I don't know, Tomski. This is all new to me, too. Let me talk to Linda.'

Kat went back to Linda's office, nodding at Annie.

'Kat, don't go in . . .'

But Kat was in too much of a hurry to wait for Annie to finish. She knocked on the door and went in. Her jaw dropped.

'Ma'am!'

Chapter Ten

Kat stared open-mouthed at the Chief Constable for Hertfordshire.

Behind her, she caught the second half of Annie's warning.

'. . . Linda's not there.'

Too late. Ingrid Young was staring at her from behind Linda's desk.

'Can I help you?' she said. Then she frowned. 'Have we met, Detective . . . ?'

Kat flashed uneasily on their sudden confrontation the previous night. Her keeping her head down as she swerved round the Chief Con on her way into the Powerhouse.

'DS Ballantyne, ma'am. Not formally. I've heard you speak at events and you congratulated me at my passing-out parade at Hendon.'

'Well, I'm extremely busy, DS Ballantyne, so make it quick.'

'I was actually looking for DCI Ockenden, ma'am,' Kat stuttered, feeling like she'd blundered not into the headmistress's office but somewhere altogether scarier.

'You'll find her in CID. They had a spare office. Things are going to be a bit hectic around here until this bloody business is put to bed. Now, if there's nothing else?'

Being looked at by Ingrid Young over the top of her trademark black-rimmed spectacles was enough to turn the stoutest-hearted cop's knees to water. Kat's felt like water would be a step up in rigidity. She mumbled a 'nothing else, ma'am' and fled for the safety of the outer office. Where Annie greeted her with a rueful smile and a cup of 'the boss's' special coffee. Kat took it gratefully and sipped it.

'Sorry, Kat, I tried to warn you.'

Kat shook her head. 'No need, mate. That was a hundred per cent on me. Jesus, I think I might've wet myself.'

Annie snorted. 'Better than Linda then. I thought she was going to have a heart attack. The colour of her! God, I was one nine away from calling an ambulance.'

Kat frowned, thinking of Pete Vaughan's 999 call. After asking a couple of people, she found Linda in an office with all the space and comfort of a broom cupboard.

'Ma-Linda, I just went to your office. What's going on?'

'Well, Ingrid "how-does-she-look-so" Young has taken overall control of everything that the Critchlow woman hasn't. I'm still Gold Commander, but Ingrid wants hourly briefings to keep her updated on my progress. Anyway, enough of my troubles. What did you want?'

'My team have lost their desks and PCs and they're in the canteen. We can't work like that. I know DI Critchlow needs resources but she's just throwing her weight around. We all get that she's CTC without the power plays.'

'You're just going to have to be creative,' Linda said with a tight smile. She waved her arm around to indicate the parameters of her new office. 'As you can see, we're all having to adjust to reduced circumstances.'

Kat nodded. 'Sorry, Ma-Linda. It's just I know I could do more. And Van and Riley being involved won't affect my professionalism.'

'I know that, Kat, but Sharon's got a point. If and when we have someone in a cell, their defence lawyers will have a field day if there's even a whiff of impropriety—'

'But it's not impropriety—'

Linda's eyes flashed dangerously.

'Please let me finish, Kat. A cop with family members hurt in the blast. They'd argue you weren't seeing straight. Maybe planting evidence, which' – she held up a hand – 'obviously I know you wouldn't do, but it's not my opinion that counts. It's best you stay off it, OK? For now.'

Recognising she'd already gone too far, Kat backed down. Almost all the way. 'For now?'

Linda shot her a death-stare. 'Don't push it, Kat. I haven't got the bandwidth.'

Kat went down to the canteen to find Leah and Fez sitting side by side at two pushed-together tables, their force-issued laptops open before them. They'd found some blue cloth-covered office partitions from somewhere and had erected a makeshift cubicle. Their heads were bent in towards each other and they were so deep in conversation they didn't see Kat arrive.

Fez noticed her first. 'Oh, hey, Kat, what do you think of the new MCU?'

'It's bostin', our kid,' she said in what she hoped was a reasonable impression of Fez's accent.

He regarded her coolly. 'That, boss, might be possibly the worst Brummie impression ever attempted. I should probably arrest you.'

Leah grinned. 'Yeah, that was definitely a hate crime, Kat. Are you Brummie-phobic?'

Kat smiled. Despite the seriousness of the situation, cops would always find a shaft of humour. You had to. It was either that or go under. And she was pleased to see how hard Leah was working to repair the damage she'd caused to her relationship with Fez in the first few days after he'd arrived. Leah had made an ill-judged and unwarranted assumption about Fez's views on gay people. He'd shot back that he didn't care whether she was a lesbian or not, but racism was racism however you cloaked it.

'I spoke to Linda, and she told me we had to do what you already have, which was to get creative. So, well done on that. Have you guys got anywhere with the Powerhouse? I mean, I'm too *compromised* to help directly, but if you need to bounce ideas around, I'm always available.'

Before either DC could respond, Tom rounded the dogleg and entered their new quarters.

'Hey, Tomski,' Kat said. 'Any joy?'

He shook his head. 'I talked to seven people. Bartenders, front of house, the assistant manager. Nobody saw anything. All too busy focusing on their own tasks to keep an eye out for terrorists. It wouldn't be so bad, Kat, but every time we turn around there's one of those Met arseholes looking over our shoulders, asking what we're up to.'

Kat reached for something professional to say. 'They're just doing their job, mate. And unlike the Powerhouse staff, they are looking for terrorists.'

He sighed and slumped into a chair. 'I suppose so. Still think they could do with some ART, though?'

Kat grinned. 'Go on, I'll bite.'

'Arrogance Reduction Training.'

'Very good. If coppering doesn't work out you could always get a job doing stand-up.'

He tilted his head in acknowledgement of the routine quip, then frowned. 'I've been thinking about the bombing, Kat. I spoke to a friend in the fire service. He was out there last night. I mean, they all were, but anyway, he said the bomb was some sort of almost amateur device. No shrapnel and no high-explosive either. Their investigator is on it but early word is it was like some sort of homemade thing,' he said. 'Bleach, sugar and fertiliser. You can make pretty devastating bombs if you use enough and in the right proportions, but what he told me was that this was almost like it was designed to make a lot of noise and start a fire but not to actually kill or maim. They've not found any shrapnel for example.'

'What are you saying?'

'I'm not sure. It's just, despite everything that happened, I've just got this nagging feeling there's something we're not seeing,' he said. 'I mean, what if it's not some Gulf state resistance outfit at all? What if it's a far-right group from here in town? A false flag operation, trying to stir things up against foreigners buying a British club.'

Before Kat could answer, even though Tom's feelings about things not adding up exactly mirrored her own, a familiar, if new, voice silenced them both. 'I'll thank you to leave the theorising to those qualified to do it, DC Gray.'

Seconds later, Sharon Critchlow rounded the corner and came to stand with her back to the partitions, facing Kat and Tom.

Tom bridled. 'I was only speculating.'

Critchlow eyed him the way Kat imagined a bird of prey would eye a rabbit. '"I was only speculating, *ma'am*".'

Kat got to her feet. No way was she going to let another DI, let alone one from London, bully her team. Even if Tom's newly spiky behaviour was causing her the odd moment of concern.

'Look, Sharon. Let's not get into a dick-swinging contest, especially since neither of us has one. Tom's right, there is something off about this whole thing. We've got two locals dead. We are still MCU detectives, and if we want to speculate, hypothesise or bloody well daydream then we're going to.' A beat. 'Ma'am.'

The silence thickened to the consistency of window putty. Or canteen custard, widely held to be the tougher substance of the two. Kat held the DI's gaze, wondering if she'd just earned herself an official reprimand.

Sharon laughed. A brassy trumpet that carried far beyond the cubicle and had the servers looking over. 'You've got balls. Or given our lack of dicks, maybe front would be better. Look, I know you've had your collective noses put out of joint and I'm sorry,' she said, not looking sorry at all. 'But this is grown-up stuff now, and CTC are the best at this kind of thing so leave it with us, OK? You in particular, Kathryn.'

Leaving Kat open-mouthed and Tom fuming at his desk, Critchlow swept out.

Kat leaped up and ran out of the canteen after Critchlow. But as she rounded a corner she slowed and then stopped. What would be the point? Picking a fight with a Met counter-terror DI investigating a bombing? Yeah, because that would work. She returned to her desk. Biting her lip, she called the hospital. Maybe Pete Vaughan had woken up. At least a drive over to Middlehampton General would get her out of Jubilee Place, and she could visit Van.

She reached the ITU doctor she'd spoken to before. 'It's DS Ballantyne here. We spoke earlier. How's Pete Vaughan doing?'

'Better, actually. He's still very poorly, but he regained consciousness about half an hour ago. Sorry I didn't call you. It's been a bit hectic here since last night and it didn't sound like it was that urgent.'

'It's fine. Jodie, wasn't it?'

'Yes,' the doctor – Jodie – replied.

'Thanks, Jodie. I'll pop up now, if that's OK?'

'Of course. You know where to find us.'

Kat headed out into the car park. She found herself checking all round in case Ethan Metcalfe was waiting to ambush her as he had done so many times before, but obviously Abby Greene's anti-stalking caution had got through to him.

Breathing easier, she climbed behind the wheel of the Golf. She could get to MGH, clear up what Pete had meant by 'They killed me', spend a few minutes with Van and then find a way to work on the bombing without causing problems.

Chapter Eleven

A young woman in green scrubs came over as Kat showed an ITU nurse her warrant card.

'Are you here about Pete Vaughan?'

'Yes. I'm DS Kat Ballantyne.'

'We spoke on the phone. I'm Jodie.'

They shook hands.

'How's he doing?' Kat asked.

'He's stable, but beyond that, there's not much I can say at this point. We're running tests and he's already been down for a thoracic CT scan. His lungs are full of fluid,' she said with a sigh. 'We've put a chest drain in, but it's proving hard to control. So why the interest in our patient? Looks like a straightforward medical emergency to me.'

'It might be nothing, but he said "They killed me" when he called the ambulance.'

'Really? That's weird. Although he was in a lot of pain.'

'Do you know what caused it?'

'I wish I could say, but it's early days. We'll know more when he's strong enough for us to do more tests.'

'Can I see him?'

'He's in bay three just opposite the nurses' station. The bed in the far-right corner. His wife's with him.'

Kat entered the softly lit, four-bed bay, its silence broken by the bleeps of the different life-support machines gathered around each bed. At the far end, a bed poked out from a partially drawn blue curtain. Kat walked on the balls of her feet, anxious not to wake anyone, even though the bay's other three occupants also lay in silent slumber.

Kat peered round the curtain. An olive-complexioned woman who Kat thought might be Middle Eastern sat on a hard chair beside the bed. She looked to be in her early forties. Beneath the sheet, an overweight white man whose face, puffy and pale, was marked by thin red lines where Kat supposed the blood vessels might run. Even without the effects of his heart attack, he looked to be at least ten years older than his wife.

The monitor on the other side of the bed lit the right side of his face with its yellow and green traces. The beep of a drug driver sounded every few seconds.

The woman looked up at Kat and her dark, sad eyes widened. 'Are you a doctor?'

'I'm a detective. My name is Kat Ballantyne. Can I ask your name?'

'Dalma. Dalma Vaughan. I'm Pete's wife.'

'Dalma, I listened to your husband's 999 call and I wanted to speak to him about something he said.'

Dalma frowned. 'My husband is sleeping. Your questions will have to wait.'

It wasn't outright hostility, not quite. But the woman's obvious stress had revealed a distrust Kat was becoming depressingly used to encountering when she interviewed members of the public. A case the previous year had amplified that, when she'd tracked down the killer of a celebrity author whose public persona had concealed a far more toxic personal one.

'I know, and I'm sorry to intrude. If you don't mind, while your husband is asleep, could I ask you a few questions?'

Kat saw a second chair and sat, applying subtle pressure on the other woman to agree.

'Fine. And I suppose I should apologise for my rudeness. It's just what with all this, well, I'm not being the best version of myself.'

'Don't worry about it,' Kat said with a smile. She showed her warrant card and took her phone out. 'Would you mind if I recorded this conversation?'

The woman looked down at Kat's phone. 'Actually I would. And we shouldn't talk here. I don't want to disturb Pete, or anyone else. There's a coffee shop downstairs.'

After asking a nurse to call them if Pete woke up, Kat accompanied Dalma down to the hospital's coffee shop, a branch of Costa.

She bought them both a coffee and offered Dalma a pastry or a sandwich, which she politely rejected.

'How did you and your husband meet?' Kat began.

It was usually best to offer up easy, non-threatening questions with members of the public. Especially those who didn't initially appear pleased to see a police officer.

'In Al Jumairah. He was doing voluntary work there in the 2010s and fell in love with the country, and its people. I was one of those he fell in love with.'

'What does Pete do for a living?'

'He's a journalist. Freelance. He specialises in investigative work.'

Kat's cop antennae twitched. People who investigated things – cops, journalists – often made enemies. Chiefly among the people they were investigating. Had Pete Vaughan got too close to something? Like the takeover of Middlehampton FC?

She nodded, smiled. Pleased that Dalma appeared to be warming up. 'I think I've seen his byline in the *Echo*.'

Dalma nodded and sipped her coffee. 'He does a few stories for them. That big one three years ago about the unsafe factories? That was his.'

'I remember it. And if I can ask, what is he working on at the moment?' Kat asked.

Depending on Dalma's answer, she might be back on the terrorism investigation, whether or not Sharon wanted her there.

'The so-called Eel Deal. How much do you know about it?'

'Not much, I'm afraid,' Kat said, feeling the ground firming beneath her feet. 'Though if my husband was here, he could probably tell you exactly who owns how many shares.'

Or my father, a quiet but insistent voice whispered between Kat's ears.

'Much of this is in the public domain and some of it I know from Pete. The deal isn't just about football. The amount of money that will flood into Middlehampton will be enormous,' Dalma said. 'New housing developments. Retailing. Public amenities. Nightlife. It's all bundled in, and it all takes planning permission, licensing, agreement from the council. It will bring jobs, prosperity, all kinds of good things.'

Kat frowned. 'Sorry, Dalma, where's the angle?'

'There are two angles, not one. The first is the lesser of two evils. Where there is business and local government and pots of money sloshing around, there is corruption. Pete hates that with a passion. He saw enough of it in Al Jumairah.'

She paused, looked around. It was almost a theatrical move, as if a bad amateur actor had been given the direction 'Check you're not being spied on'. But somehow, from Dalma Vaughan, such a gesture felt totally believable.

Apparently satisfied, Dalma leaned closer to Kat and murmured softly, 'The second, and greater, evil is why the Al Jumairah regime is so keen on British football. Have you heard of "sportswashing"?'

'Sorry, it's a new one on me.'

'You run a regime with a bad human rights record. Secret police. Political prisoners. Internal exile. Torture. Rape as a weapon of war or political suppression. Summary executions. All the usual filthy tactics.' Dalma swallowed. Kat wondered whether she had experienced any of those tactics first-hand. 'And you decide you need to get a rebrand. So you hold a tennis tournament. Or you set up a golf tour. Or you buy a football club. You don't just acquire the asset, you acquire the fans and their goodwill, too. If a club is struggling, and let's be honest that describes the Eels, your money means it can buy new players, improve its facilities, even build a new stadium. Now everybody loves you and will defend you against your critics.'

Kat nodded. Dalma's summary, which echoed the statement from Desert Sun, was as clear as it was succinct. She wished HQ policy papers were as good. And Dalma had, wittingly or otherwise, supplied a possible motive for someone to wish her husband dead.

What did Kat know? *Really* know, as opposed to just suspect. Facts, in other words.

One, she had an investigative journalist who'd apparently suffered a heart attack, claiming in his 999 call 'They killed me'.

Two, he was married to a woman from Al Jumairah.

Three, the Al Jumairah sovereign wealth fund was on the brink of acquiring his hometown club.

Four, he was investigating the so-called Eel Deal.

Five, on the same night Pete suffered his heart attack, a terrorist group called Desert Sun had planted a bomb, apparently to draw attention to the deal and stop it going ahead.

It didn't take a genius to make the connection.

Did that put Desert Sun in the frame? Surely not if he was poking his nose into the deal they wanted to stop. The participants, then? The Al Jumairis and their British counterparts. It was, she felt, a reasonable suspicion.

She filed her suspicions away. As Linda had said, '*for now*'. Jodie had told her they were running tests. If the results came back and said an overweight, middle-aged smoker who drank too much had suffered a heart attack caused by his lifestyle then she'd take it and return to investigating other crimes. Maybe try again to get back onto the bombing investigation.

'I'm wondering if Pete's illness is linked to the takeover,' she said.

'But how? The doctors told me they think he might have had a heart attack.'

Kat frowned. 'Well, because of what Pete said in his 999 call – "They killed me".'

Dalma's deep-brown eyes popped wide. 'What? Why wasn't I told this?'

Realising her error, Kat backtracked frantically. 'I am so sorry, Dalma, I thought maybe they'd have told you in A&E.'

'They only told me he was very poorly.'

She drew a tissue from her sleeve and dabbed at her eyes.

'If I can ask, where were you when the hospital called?' Kat asked.

She tried to see if there were genuine tears in Dalma's eyes. Because despite her suspicions, if someone *had* attempted to murder Pete Vaughan, the most likely suspect wasn't a terrorist group from halfway around the world, or their political enemies. It was his wife.

'I was out with colleagues. When I got home, I found our front door smashed down. Luckily a neighbour was there boarding it up for us. The doctor called me just after I went inside.'

'What time was that?'

'I don't know. Ten? Half past?'

'You said colleagues. What do *you* do for a living, Dalma?'

'I'm a freelance translator. Arabic to English.'

'Did Pete ever mention anything that made you worried for his safety?'

'No. Never. He didn't scare easily.'

Kat sensed a dead end looming. Was she reaching? Looking for something substantive to investigate because Sharon had booted her off the taskforce? Maybe Pete had been hallucinating when he'd cried out 'They killed me'. Maybe he'd been drunk. Or maybe he'd just spluttered out some random curse against the forces in the universe that had sent such pain to him.

Her phone rang. It was Jodie. Pete was awake and asking for his wife. Now Kat could get an answer. One that would confirm her hunch or send her back to MCU with her tail between her legs, begging scraps from Sharon's table.

Together Kat and Dalma hurried back to the ITU, and Pete Vaughan's bedside.

Dalma sat close and clutched his hand. 'Hey, darling, it's me,' she said, before bending to kiss his forehead.

'Can I speak to him?' Kat asked.

When Dalma nodded, she leaned closer to Pete. His face was pale and blotchy. The transparent green oxygen mask added to the graveyard pallor.

'Pete, my name is Kat Ballantyne. I'm with the police. I'm a detective. You said "They killed me" when you called 999. What did you mean?'

His eyes swivelled in their sockets to lock on to hers. The angle revealed yellowish sclera streaked with inflamed capillaries. His lips parted with a click. They were crusty and flaked with ragged wisps of dry skin like rice paper.

Kat bent closer, but all she could pick up was a hoarse whisper. He raised his right hand off the sheet and crooked the index finger. His eyes slid sideways to look at the bent digit.

She lowered her head still further until it was almost touching his chest, straining to catch even a syllable that might reveal the mystery.

Another rasping whisper escaped the oxygen mask.

Kat shook her head. 'I'm sorry, Pete. I can't make it out. What are you trying to tell me?'

She heard the rattle as, with enormous effort, he inhaled and spoke on the out breath: 'Buh—'

'I got that, Pete,' Kat said, pulling back a little to smile at him. 'Buh— what? What are you trying to say?'

'—buh . . . buh . . .'

Kat's pulse picked up. She was aware she shouldn't jump to conclusions in advance of the evidence, but she was certain that she knew what he was going to say. 'Are you trying to say "bomb", Pete? Is it connected to the bombing at the Powerhouse?'

He groaned. Dalma elbowed Kat aside and began stroking her husband's forehead. Suddenly, the trace on the monitor started jumping. The trace hiccupped and then flatlined before dancing around on the screen in spasmodic jerks. Pete's left hand flapped up and down. Then his eyes squinted shut and he clamped his teeth together around a long, ragged hiss.

The monitor emitted a continuous scream. Dalma leaped to her feet.

'He's dying! Oh, Pete. Don't die! Stay with me, my honey.'

Kat jumped up and rounded the bed. She yanked the red crash button on the wall panel, starting a loud alarm. Within seconds, the sister, a couple of nurses, a carer and a doctor rushed into the room. *Just like when one of us hits the emergency button on our Airwave*, Kat thought, as the room filled with even more staff.

Kat stood well back, watching, horrified, as they started CPR while another nurse wheeled in a bulky red-and-white crash cart festooned with curly leads. Jodie arrived, issuing commands as she hit the power switch on the defibrillator. The machine whined on its charging cycle. Kat could only stare as the medics worked on Pete's body.

'Everybody clear!' Jodie shouted.

Pete's whole torso arced off the bed as she hit the switch that activated the pad pushed against his chest. The thump as he fell back on to the mattress was unsettlingly loud.

'Nothing!' a second nurse called.

The first nurse went back to her compressions as Jodie powered the machine up for a second hit.

Whine.

'Clear!'

Thump.

'Nothing.'

Whine.

'Clear!'

Thump.

'Nothing.'

Kat caught Dalma's eye. She was staring at Kat blankly, uncomprehending. Kat had seen the look before. Too many times. The next of kin of a murder victim confronting the grievous reality that the person they loved was gone and in the most violent circumstances.

Jodie tried once more before a newly arrived doctor, older, more wrinkles around the eyes, more grey hairs on her head, laid a hand on her forearm.

'That's enough, now.' She sighed. 'He's gone. Would you take this lady outside, please?'

Dalma allowed herself to be led out of the bay by one of the carers.

The older doctor checked her watch. 'Death occurred at 11.39 a.m.'

As the medics began the professional, clinical and administrative processes that would always happen when one of the living entered the realm of the dead, Kat's mind ran on ahead.

At the precise moment that the doctor had called time of death, Kat had begun, if only in her mind, a murder investigation. And she already had her first question.

What had Pete been trying to tell her? *Was* it 'bomb'? Was his death connected to the Powerhouse explosion? Sharon had booted her off that case, but if Kat was right, here was a link she couldn't ignore.

Chapter Twelve

A third doctor arrived. This one was a fortyish male consultant, dressed in smart trousers and a white shirt with the collar unbuttoned, no tie.

'Am I too late?'

'I'm afraid so, Dr Evans,' Jodie said. 'Patient died a couple of minutes ago.'

'Oh, dear, that's the third this week. Have we pronounced recognition of life extinct?'

She nodded. 'Dr Williams did. Patient died at 11.39 a.m.'

'Cause?'

'Looks like a massive myocardial infarction.' She turned to Kat, her face drawn, and said, 'Heart attack.'

On Jodie's face, and in her voice, Kat detected sadness mixed with a professional reflex to explain the medical term. Kat had hung around the hospital enough times – as a mum as well as a police officer – to have picked up more than a smattering of doctors' jargon, but she said nothing beyond a murmured 'Thanks'. Jodie was just trying to keep her looped in, after all.

'Do we have any medical history?' Dr Evans asked.

'Mr Vaughan had a history of alcohol and smoking-related illness,' Jodie said. 'He's been a patient on the respiratory ward a couple of times for short stays.'

'Looking at the state of him, I'm not surprised. I'm going to go out on a limb and say he was a stranger to both exercise and a healthy diet. So, to summarise, we have an overweight, middle-aged man with poor cardiac and pulmonary health. A drinker and a smoker, admitted with suspected heart attack in the first place. What did the thoracic CT show up?'

'Acute pulmonary oedema,' Jodie said, 'which isn't an obvious symptom of a cardiac event.'

'No, but based on what I can clearly see and you yourself have confirmed, I think it's obvious what happened here. So, cause of death, cardiac infarction with' – a nod to Jodie – 'complications resulting from pulmonary oedema and his own lifestyle choices. I'll authorise a basic post-mortem.'

'Excuse me, Doctor,' Kat said, stepping out of the shadows.

The doctor frowned as he finally noticed her. 'And you are?'

'DS Kathryn Ballantyne,' she said, producing her badge. 'I'm not sure this was natural causes at all. I think we need a full forensic post-mortem to determine cause of death.'

He smiled indulgently and folded his arms across his chest. 'I see. Let me ask you something, Sergeant. Do you have any medical training?'

'No. I don't.'

'Interesting. I do, you see. A lot. It enabled me to reach the rank of consultant before my fortieth birthday. So forgive me if I question your clinical judgement, but why, exactly, do you think your opinion counts for anything here? This is an ITU, not a police station.'

The nurses and carers and the two other doctors had fallen silent. Kat glanced at Jodie, who was standing behind the consultant and shaking her head. Her meaning was transparent. *Don't go there.*

Kat went there. 'Before he died, Mr Vaughan used the phrase "They killed me" in his 999 call. That leads me to suspect his death was not just sudden and unexpected, but also suspicious.' She glanced at Jodie again before continuing. 'Now, I don't have your medical training, but I do have a lot of *legal* training. And that, coupled with my professional standing as a homicide detective, gives me the authority to call for a forensic post-mortem. I'd be grateful if you could note that in your paperwork.'

He glared at Kat, but she smiled back patiently. He'd have to yield, and the only question in her mind was how gracious he'd be about it.

'Fine,' he said. 'It's not as if the pathologist doesn't have enough on his plate without fanciful requests from detectives. But you're the boss.'

He scribbled a signature then stalked out of the bay. The sister dispersed her staff with a quiet, 'Back to work everyone'. Then, slightly louder: 'Can somebody order a cottage, please?'

Cottage. Another bit of hospital jargon Kat had picked up. A bland euphemism for the black vinyl-covered trolley the porters used to transport bodies from wards to the mortuary.

Back in the main area of ITU, Kat buttonholed the nurse who had been looking after Pete. 'Hi. Can I ask you a couple of questions about Pete?'

'Of course. What do you want to know?'

'Can you tell me if there was anything unusual you noticed about Pete when he was admitted. You changed him into hospital pyjamas I assume?'

'Yes. But there wasn't anything in particular. An old appendix scar.'

'And I know this is going to sound a bit OTT, but any puncture wounds, ligature marks, bruises? Anything that might indicate he'd been attacked?'

The nurse shook his head. 'Not really, no. He smelled a bit of alcohol. But quite a few patients arrive smelling like a pub.'

Kat thanked him. Alcohol. Maybe Pete had been trying to say 'booze' not 'bomb'. Although it was still a strange coincidence, his murder, if that's what it was, being on the same night as a terrorist bombing.

Could someone have slipped a poison into his drink? He was a journalist after all, so perhaps he'd been in the pub earlier in the evening. But which pub? If she could find it she might get lucky and catch him on CCTV with his killer. Maybe Dalma would know if he had a favourite watering hole. Kat looked around. But Dalma had gone.

She saw the carer who'd taken her out of the bay. 'Where's Dalma?' Kat asked. 'Mrs Vaughan, I mean.'

'She said she was going for a coffee.'

Kat ran down to the coffee shop, but Dalma was nowhere in sight. Kat took a table and waited in case Dalma was in the ladies. After five minutes, and no sign, Kat checked the toilets. Dalma wasn't there.

She went down to the mortuary to speak to Jack Beale, the forensic pathologist based at MGH. They hadn't spoken for months. With no new murders, and her time consumed with twice-weekly trips to London to consult with the Met over a dead author's many rape victims, she'd had no reason to. No time, either, to do much about investigating the deaths of her dead half-sister's parents.

Jack was in his office, slumped over his keyboard.

Kat hurried over to him and touched him lightly on the back. 'Jack? Are you all right?'

He lifted himself upright. The imprint of the keys marked his cheek. His eyes were red-rimmed.

'Hi, Kat. Yeah, I'm fine.'

Jack sounded tired. Low, even. None of his usual flirtatiousness that surfaced whenever they met.

'You don't look fine. What's wrong?'

'Nothing. It's all good. What can I do for you?'

Clearly something *was* wrong. But if Jack didn't want to talk about it, Kat could wait.

'A man just died in ITU,' she said. 'Pete Vaughan. The consultant thinks it was a heart attack, but I'm not so sure. Can you book him in for a forensic post-mortem?'

'Sure. How about first thing tomorrow morning, 9.00 a.m.?'

She'd never heard him sound so down. 'Perfect. Thanks, Jack.'

She wanted to say something more. To ask what was bothering him. When the answer came to her, her heart went out to Jack as he sat in front of her, shoulders rounded, head hanging.

'You did the post-mortems on the two bomb victims, didn't you?'

He sighed. It sounded like it came from the deepest pit of despair.

'Back-to-back. The dad first. Then the girl . . . Oh, God, Kat, that poor child. All she wanted was to see a band with her dad and she ended up crushed to death in a stairwell.'

He sniffed. Then his lips seemed to twist as if he'd been given an electric shock. Before she could react, he sobbed. Tears rolled down his cheeks and he scraped them away with the heels of his hands.

She crouched down and without thinking put her arms around him and hugged him close.

As if he were a puppet and someone had just cut his strings, Jack fell against her as the sobs ran through him in great, shuddering waves.

'She was a kid, Kat. A kid! I went into medicine to save lives and now look at me. All I could do for her was cut her open and describe what had happened to her organs and her bones and then weigh her— her . . .'

'Hey, hey,' she murmured, speaking into the top of his head. 'It's OK. You treated her respectfully, I know that. And you *are* helping people. You're helping me catch murderers and hopefully the bastards who planted that bomb.'

From below her chin she felt him nod, or she chose to believe that was what she felt.

He cleared his throat and uttered a drawn-out sigh. 'You can let me up now, I feel stupid. Sorry for embarrassing you. That was really unprofessional of me.'

She released him, and he sat back in his swivel chair, wiping his eyes with a tissue from a box on his desk.

'No,' she said sharply, but kindly. 'Don't be sorry. And don't feel stupid, either. I'm not embarrassed, and you shouldn't be either. One of the best things about you, Jack Beale, is you still have empathy. Not like the arrogant twat I just met in ITU. He more or less implied Pete had chosen to kill himself for eating too many curries and drinking too many wines.'

Jack cleared his throat again and blew his nose. 'Early forties, sandy hair, white shirt, no tie?'

'That's him.'

'Dr Greg Evans. Youngest emergency medicine consultant in the trust's history – and isn't he proud of the fact?'

'Wanker,' Kat said, feelingly.

Jack smiled. 'Glad to see *your* empathy's still in full working order.'

She rubbed his shoulder briefly. 'Look after yourself, Jack. Try and get home on time today. Maybe call Gina and see if she wants to go out.'

Jack frowned. 'Gina?'

'Yes! Get a meal or see a film. Have a few cocktails. Whatever you two like to do together.'

'Gina lives in Leeds.'

Well, that was a puzzle. Since learning Jack and Gina had gone to a jazz festival in Bruges the previous summer, Kat had found her troubling feelings towards Jack – ones she was sure she shouldn't have as a married woman – cooling right down.

But Leeds? She couldn't see him as the kind of man to enjoy a long-distance relationship.

'That's a long way to go for a booty call,' she said, aiming for a jokey tone and wondering whether anyone even said that anymore.

He looked at her oddly. Was that a hint of a smile? 'Gina's my sister, so I think a booty call would be . . . problematic?'

The heat rising from the front of her shirt could have charred a steak. Her cheeks flamed and it was all she could do to not turn and run, so acute was the embarrassment she was feeling. Oh, God, not only had she jumped to a conclusion, she had taken a bloody great run-up and scored a new personal best.

'Oh. Of course. I mean, I didn't . . . I wasn't suggesting you and she were . . .'

He tilted his head to one side. The smile was fully there now. Indulgent, amused, enjoying her discomfort. She didn't blame him. She was too busy cursing herself.

'. . . were, what? Involved in an incestuous relationship with my sister? That's a pretty serious charge, DS Ballantyne.'

She finally broke free from the grip of her mortification and grinned at him. 'OK, stop it. Stop it now! I'm sorry.'

He shook his head, and his expression softened. 'No, *I'm* sorry, Kat. I mean, you were comforting me and I let you dig yourself into a hole.'

'Yes, exactly! You could have saved me but instead you handed me a bigger spade.'

He wrinkled his nose. 'Not that you needed one. The progress you were making, ten more minutes and you'd have reached Australia.'

'You're impossible, *Dr* Beale. I'm leaving. But I'll see you at 9.00 a.m. tomorrow.'

Still smiling she made her way back through the endless hospital corridors, heading for Sheepton Ward and a brief visit to see Van. Why was she suddenly feeling so happy, despite all the trauma of the past twenty-four hours? Surely it couldn't be because Jack Beale didn't have a girlfriend. Although he hadn't said that, had he? Just that it wasn't Gina. A pang of guilt skewered her. *Your husband's being treated for smoke inhalation and you're thinking about whether Jack Beale's single? Shame on you!*

After checking on Van, who was sitting up in bed and looking perkier, she left him there. Whatever else was happening in her life – and it was a lot – what took precedence was that she had a murderer to catch.

Maybe more than one.

Chapter Thirteen

Kat reached the Jubilee Place canteen at 12.25 p.m. The makeshift office composed of the chest-high screens was deserted.

She called her mum on her mobile.

'Kat. Is everything all right, darling? Have you got any leads yet?'

'Everything's fine, Mum. I can't talk about the case, but Van's looking a lot better. He might be coming home tomorrow. Can Riley stay another night?'

'Of course he can. Didn't I say? As long as you need.'

'How did he seem this morning?'

'We let him sleep in, so he was a little late for school. I'm sure they understood. But he ate a walloping great breakfast, so I'm not too worried.'

'But in himself? Was he OK? Was he tearful? Angry?'

'Just quiet. But boys that age are, aren't they? I mean, it's hard to tell.'

'It is. Look, thanks, Mum. I mean it. I know we haven't always seen eye to eye but you're being brilliant. You and Dad both.'

Her mum cleared her throat. She sounded as embarrassed by Kat's display of emotion as Kat felt. 'Yes, well. As Daddy said to you last night. Family is important.'

After ending the call, Kat headed up to MCU. She needed to let Linda know Pete Vaughan was dead and that Kat had a potential murder investigation on her hands. The office was abuzz with phones ringing, outbound calls being made and the hum and chatter of the full complement of Hertfordshire cops added to by the Met contingent. She could swear more had arrived since she'd left for MGH to interview Pete Vaughan.

Sharon Critchlow was addressing the room. She glanced up as Kat arrived. 'Ah, Kat. Good to see you. I was just briefing the team on what progress we've made.'

'Which is?' Kat asked, pleased that Sharon had found out and was using her nickname.

Sharon puffed out her cheeks. 'Honestly? Sketchy. Reliable intelligence is proving hard to get. I've been over to the scene this morning and spoken to the fire investigators and our explosives bods. The consensus is we got off lightly. No shrapnel. Just a load of improvised explosive. Literally a lot of bang for the buck.'

Kat bit back her rejoinder that two lives lost in the event itself, as well as a third, which looked increasingly likely to be related, didn't feel much like getting off lightly. She knew what Sharon meant. Compared to what could have happened – she swallowed as she remembered the terror she'd felt the previous night – it really was a miracle.

'If I can ask,' Sharon said, 'where have you been?'

Kat nodded. Sought out Fez, Leah and Tom and nodded to them.

'I've just come back from Middlehampton General Hospital. That's MGH if you fancy adding another TLA to your collection.'

This earned her a brief smile. Kat raised her voice a touch and addressed her next remarks to the office as a whole.

'This morning, at 11.39 a.m., a local investigative journalist named Pete Vaughan died from a probable cardiac arrest. But' – she held up a hand for silence as a few of the Met detectives started muttering to each other – 'before you ask me what I was doing rushing around after an overweight smoker with a drink problem who died of a heart attack, I think he was murdered. He said, "They killed me".'

'Who's they?' This was DS Michael Olusoga, Sharon's bagman.

'I don't know. But Pete was investigating the Al Jumairah takeover of Middlehampton FC, so I'm thinking there could be a connection to last night's bombing.'

Michael nodded. 'I agree. That makes perfect sense.' He turned to Sharon. 'We should roll it into our investigation, boss, don't you think?'

Sharon nodded. 'Yes. Put a team together. Use locals as you see fit.'

Kat had held her tongue before. But this was going too far. Pulse racing, she glared at Michael and then Sharon. 'Right. First off, we're not "locals". This is MCU. We're specialist homicide investigators. You lot are counter terror. I admit I don't know one end of an IED from the other, but I know a hell of a lot about hunting down murderers.' Her pulse was thumping in her throat as she spoke. 'Second, absolutely not! This is a Middlehampton resident we're talking about and he died in this town. That makes it our jurisdiction. I was up at MGH this morning, twice. I interviewed Pete Vaughan before he died and I've already sorted the post-mortem with the pathologist.'

'Which is brilliant,' Michael said. 'Saves me the trouble. But you said yourself, it's linked to the bombing, which is *our* department. And you're specifically excluded on account of your family connection. It's cleaner if we fold it into our investigation. Saves duplication of effort. And you're right about us being counter terror experts not homicide, which is why you're my first pick to handle the day-to-day side of the case.'

'Whoa, whoa, whoa! You need to back off,' Leah said indignantly.

Beside her, Fez and Tom were nodding and eyeballing a couple of nearby Met officers.

'The only ones backing off are you, love, and your boyfriend there,' a male Met cop said, lifting his chin at Tom, who'd clenched his fists. 'You want some then, mate?'

A new voice silenced the squabbling. 'That's *enough*! This is my house and I will not have you, sonny, or anybody else, insult, belittle or patronise my officers.' It was Linda, eyes flashing, as she strode into the centre of MCU and came face to face with Sharon. 'Bombs are your department, murders are mine. *We* will investigate and if' – she paused for breath – '*if* DS Ballantyne finds anything that points to the terrorists, she'll let you know, won't you, Kat?'

Kat nodded, at that moment so in love with Ma-Linda she'd gladly have taken a bullet for her. 'Absolutely.'

'Right, unless you want to take this up the chain, DI Critchlow, which is going to piss off at least two lots of brass, that's how this stands. Are we in agreement?'

Perhaps Sharon wasn't used to not getting her own way when she rolled her tanks on to another force's lawn. But she seemed to have lost the will for a fight.

'Yes, we are.'

Linda folded her arms. 'Yes, we are . . . ?'

'Ma'am,' she murmured.

Resisting the urge to punch the air, or, possibly, DS Olusoga, Kat gathered Tom, Leah and Fez up like a lioness with her cubs and ushered them out of MCU and back to their temporary accommodation in the canteen.

'I think I'm in love,' Leah said.

Tom and Fez burst out laughing.

'I can tell Emily if you like,' Fez said, referring to Leah's girlfriend.

Leah put her hands on her heart. 'Would you? It'll be better coming from you.'

Tom rolled his eyes at Kat.

'Right,' Kat said. 'Comedy break over. If my instincts are right, we have a murder to solve. Tomski, get started on Pete's background. Fez, I want you looking at his finances. Leah, can you get in touch with Dawn Jacobson at the *Echo*? I want to know if Pete had a favourite pub, maybe for meeting contacts. If he submitted expenses, she might know from them.'

All three DCs settled at their desks to start the laborious but vital process of victimology.

Kat grabbed her car keys. She was going to visit the woman she now had to think of as Pete's widow. Because, unpleasant as it was, she was a person of interest. Possibly, *the* person of interest.

Chapter Fourteen

Formulating different approaches to questioning Dalma Vaughan, Kat drove towards Northbridge, a once prosperous neighbourhood south of Bowmans Common.

Questioning a murder victim's next of kin was one aspect of the job she'd never felt really comfortable with. It wasn't their grief. That she could cope with. And there was a certain amount of training, formal and on the job. Experience helped, too. Plus, Kat was blessed, or perhaps cursed would be a better word, with a healthy dollop of empathy for those whose lives had been upturned by murder.

So, no, it wasn't their grief that made Kat uncomfortable. It was navigating that crushing, disorientating emotion while also teasing out of them possible motives, alibis and any signs, however slight, that things had been less than rosy between them and the deceased.

Euphemisms and delicate little dances around the truth were worse than useless. People became suspicious, hostile or just more distressed. Molly Steadman, in Kat's early days as her bagwoman, had once advised her, 'Just get to the point, Kat. Quickly, and directly. Don't dress it up, but be respectful. And take what comes.'

Once, 'what comes' had been a full willow pattern teapot flying across a sitting room towards her head. She'd got lucky that time, although a bill for new wallpaper had duly arrived at Jubilee Place.

At the Vaughans' house, she walked up to the front door, its glass panels obscured by screwed-on panels of plywood, and rang the bell.

The door opened. Wearing a dark-brown tunic and trousers, Dalma had 'the look'. Fatigue was leaking from her as if she'd been clinging to a lifebelt in a storm-tossed sea. Her eyes were half-closed, red from crying. The wings of her nose red from too much blowing. Slack muscle tone in the cheeks and lips.

'Hi, Dalma, can I come in, please?'

Wordlessly, Dalma stood back and beckoned Kat inside.

There were socially prescribed routines for this sort of meeting. Dalma followed them. Were they the same the world over, Kat wondered as she accepted a cup of tea and declined a biscuit.

They took their tea into a living room pleasantly cluttered with mismatched armchairs, a sofa draped in a patterned woven throw, and several low tables with tops of coloured glass.

'Dalma, I am so sorry for your loss,' Kat began. 'I really thought Pete was going to be OK.'

Dalma nodded, then sipped her tea. 'Me, too. Do you really think someone did that to him?'

'On its own, his remark on the 999 call was suspicious, but given what he was working on, and other factors, I have to assume he was murdered.'

Dalma frowned. 'But according to Occam's razor the solution requiring the fewest assumptions is the most likely. That would be a heart attack, like the consultant said.'

Kat had come across the odd phrase a couple of times before. She'd looked it up. William of Occam was a thirteenth-century monk. His idea was useful for cops as well as philosophers. But you still had to use your judgement. And, occasionally, trust your gut.

'You studied philosophy?' she asked Dalma.

Dalma nodded. 'I took an Open University degree when I first came to Britain. I was amazed such an institution should exist. In Al Jumairah, women are not permitted to go to university.' She sniffed. 'But if you really think Pete was murdered then it was them. The royal family. OBH ordered it. He must have done.'

Kat frowned at the acronym. 'Sorry, Dalma, OBH?'

Dalma laughed bitterly. 'Sheikh Omar bin Hamad Al Rashid. The Crown Prince of Al Jumairah. For some reason the media love to give these men cute little nicknames. They should call them devils or vampires, for all the blood on their hands.'

Kat wrote the name down in her notebook. After Dalma's refusal to allow Kat to record their previous conversation, she thought an old-school approach to note-taking might be less of a problem. 'We'll be looking at the delegation from Al Jumairah, obviously, but I wonder if we could talk about Pete a little, too?'

Salma sniffed, nodded her consent. 'Whatever you like.'

'You met Pete in Al Jumairah, you said?'

'Yes. He first came to do voluntary work but he kept returning. He fell in love with my country. The people there, when they got to know him, they loved him back. When I met him, he was covering a project to educate women and girls. It was his first brush with the authorities. They arrested him and he needed a translator. I was appointed. Things went from there, you know? It should never have worked, but we fell in love and were married six months later.'

Kat smiled. 'I met my husband while I was grieving for my best friend. You never know how life will play out.'

'Oh, I'm sorry. Not about your husband. Your friend. That must have been hard.'

Kat's breath hitched. Yet another person she had to lie to. 'It was. Very hard. But in some ways I feel she's still with me. That she always will be.' OK, so not a total untruth, then. 'When did you and Pete get married?'

'June 2016. Last week we were talking about what to do for our tenth wedding anniversary. Now I have to organise his funeral.'

A single tear crept down Dalma's cheek. She brushed it away.

'And yours was a happy marriage?'

Dalma shrugged. 'As happy as any other. I nagged Pete about his smoking. His drinking.' She smiled crookedly. 'Well, basically his whole lifestyle. He told me I was a shrew. I didn't know what that was the first time he used the word. I looked it up. It said a small rodent. So I said if I was anything I should be a jerboa. It was our joke. Pete said our marriage was *The Taming of the Jerboa*.'

'How about his work? I know he did pieces for the *Echo*. Did he have friends there?'

'Well, the editor, Dawn Jacobson – obviously. Though perhaps she was more of a client. But they went out for drinks and curries together.'

'On that subject, did you know if Pete had a particular pub he liked to drink in?'

Dalma shook her head. 'Pete used to say, "If it's got a decent bottle of red, a low ceiling and even lower clientele, I'm in".'

Kat nodded, returning Dalma's smile. There was one pub in Middlehampton that definitely met Pete's quotable description. She made a note to pay the Hope and Anchor a call.

Now to circle back and risk an interview-ending question.

'You said your marriage was "as happy as any other". I'm married, too, so I know the compromises we have to make to keep the damn things rolling along in one piece.' This was true. She'd once, mistakenly, thought Van was involved with one of his clients. Marnie Pryce possessed a husky voice, a lovely bottom, and a website catering to married people looking for affairs. She flashed guiltily on her conversation with Jack earlier. Squashed it down. 'Did Pete ever stray, do you know? I don't mean an affair or anything. Maybe just, you know, an ill-advised drunken kiss at a Christmas party? Anything that set your wife radar pinging?'

Dalma had started shaking her head halfway through Kat's story, but she hadn't leaped to her feet, eyes blazing and asked her to leave, so that was something.

'I know why you are asking these questions, but the answer is no. If Pete had a passion outside our marriage, it was for his work.'

'Of course. I'm sorry that I have to ask these questions.'

'You're just doing your job. As I do mine. As Pete did his. But I still think his work is where you will find his murderer.'

'Let's talk about that, then. Did Pete have any enemies? People he'd rubbed up the wrong way?'

Dalma pulled her mouth to one side and regarded Kat quizzically. 'You do *know* what kind of stories Pete wrote? Rubbing powerful people up the wrong way was what he did. He *lived* for it. In fact, that's one of the things we argued about. Never mind his drinking, or his cigarettes or his burgers. Pete got a kick out of receiving death threats. He said they meant he was turning over the right rocks.'

Never mind wife radar, that phrase – 'death threats' – set off Kat's *cop* radar like an incoming missile.

'Death threats from who? Do you have examples?'

'I have more than examples. Follow me.'

Dalma led Kat upstairs and into a small room kitted out as a home office. It reminded her of the back bedroom in her own house.

With practised fingers, Dalma riffled through the suspension files in the second drawer down and pulled out a green cardboard folder at least an inch thick.

'Help yourself,' she said.

Kat took the chair Dalma pulled out for her and opened the folder, while Dalma stood at her left shoulder.

Here were dozens, maybe hundreds, of poison-pen letters, printed-out emails, printed screen grabs of social media posts and direct messages. Even an old-school assemblage of letters cut out from newspapers and magazines.

YOU NEED TO STOP

BEFORE SOMEHTING

BAD HAPPENS TO YOU

There was something about those transposed letters in 'something' that gave the garish collage a flavour of the desperate. Yet the handwritten date at the top in green biro was seven years earlier. Surely the kind of person who composed death threats using letters clipped from the sensationalist 'pink top' women's weeklies wouldn't take their grievances from the kitchen table to the real world?

'How many are there?' Kat said, flipping through the sheets of A4.

'Last time we counted, 197. If you're going to waste time on them and not looking at the Al Jumairis, then there are two people you should start with.'

'Go on.'

'Gerald Hynde and Nick Chater.'

'Who are they? Did they send threats?'

Dalma nodded. 'Gerald Hynde's wife died from an industrial disease. Pete was investigating the factory where she worked. Toxic chemicals, you know? Anyway, after her funeral, Hynde basically went mad with grief. He started sending abusive messages to Pete and also to the *Echo*. It's been going on for years. He accused Pete of being in the company's pocket. Of taking bribes.'

'How about the other man? Nick Chater?'

'He's the founder of Middlehampton Supporters' Trust. He doesn't have shares in the club, or not enough to make any money out of the takeover, but he's been cheerleading the deal since it was first proposed. He's publicly slagged off Pete on social media.'

'Why is he such a fan? Of the deal, I mean?'

'He says it will secure the club's future. Give it the resources it needs to compete properly again. He accused Pete of trying to sabotage the deal to gratify his own ego.'

Kat nodded. This was good. Two solid leads she could pursue without getting tangled up in Sharon's investigation. A disgruntled local football fan and a grief-maddened widower sounded far more likely as murder suspects than some shady foreign . . . what?

Kat realised she had no idea who would actually carry out the murder of a journalist. A spy? A hitman? Was that even a thing? But then, there'd been the nerve gas poisonings in Salisbury a few years back, hadn't there?

The two men who'd smirked their way through an interview on Russian TV had turned out to be Russian military intelligence agents. Some hotshot DS from an unnamed covert branch of the Met had even come down from Scotland Yard to deliver a series of presentations on it to the whole station.

And hadn't there been that horrific case of the Saudi journalist Jamal Khashoggi? Strangled and dismembered by a gang of Saudi 'operatives'. That was the word they'd used at the time. Made it sound neutral. Like the sign on the dustbin lorry. 'Operatives working at rear'. A grisly image of body parts in black bin liners floated briefly into view.

Three lines of enquiry, then. Chater. Hynde. And one or more Al Jumairi 'operatives'.

She could picture Sharon and her tame DS licking their lips wolfishly at the mere mention of a covert assassination squad holed up in the Al Jumairis' hotel.

But she needed to pivot her thoughts back to the victim.

While Dalma was willing to talk, Kat needed to get as many questions answered as possible. And the next was extra-sensitive. She decided to take the scenic route.

'If Pete was freelance, and you are, too, I'm wondering if he felt the need to buy insurance. For if he couldn't work?'

'He had a couple of policies. Critical illness. Permanent disability.'

'Life?'

Dalma laughed brokenly. 'Life insurance? Who'd take him on? The other two premiums were more than we could really afford. Anyway, no.'

'A will?'

'You think I might have killed Pete for his fortune, Detective? Well, let me tell you. I *do* get everything. I get his credit card debts. I get his half of the mortgage. I get his overdraft. I think he even had a couple of Klarna things going on, so I get those too. Lucky me!'

She crumpled physically as her tirade ended. Sobs filled the room like wet, grey clouds, drowning Kat in the other woman's grief. She proffered tissues and waited out the storm. You didn't get immune to others' suffering. To do that you'd have to be some sort of psychopath. But you found a way to box it off in your brain so you could carry on doing your job.

'I'm sorry to put you through this, Dalma. I hope you know I simply want to catch Pete's killer.'

Dalma raised her head, reddened eyes glaring. 'Yes? Well, then, instead of looking at me for some sort of tawdry domestic murder scenario, why aren't you interrogating the rich and powerful people who stand to gain hundreds of millions of pounds? If Pete's investigation had reversed the deal or brought the police in, they would have had all that money taken away. That's quite a big motive, wouldn't you say?'

Privately, Kat agreed with Dalma. She imagined a room full of cigar smoke and bad intentions as gangster-like figures in pinstriped suits worked out how to remove an irritant like Pete Vaughan. One of the figures turned to her and blew a narrow stream of smoke, arrow straight, in her face.

'*You're not thinking of* me, *are you, Kitty-Kat?' her father asked.*

But she was. Men like her father had been dumping concrete over the bodies of their enemies since the damned stuff had been invented.

And the sums were eye-wateringly high. She'd worked cases where people had been murdered for less than the price of a packet of cigarettes, so when the sum ran into seven figures it would certainly provide an incentive.

Except people lost out on business investments and deals all the time. Yet the papers weren't full of corporate executives or journalists getting topped. Not in Britain anyway. Most murder victims were guilty of nothing more than burning their husband's toast, or looking at the wrong person's girlfriend.

But then the phrase Kat had started thinking of as Pete's dying declaration flashed back into her mind.

They killed me.

If it was Chater or Hynde, surely he'd have said "He"?

Or Dalma, "She"?

Kat pointed to the folder. 'Can I take this?'

Dalma nodded. 'For all the good it will do.'

'I'd like to take Pete's phone and laptop, too, if that's all right?'

She held her breath, but this time Dalma agreed. 'Yes. But the phone's on facial recognition and the laptop's password-protected and I don't know what Pete used. He was paranoid about it being stolen and changed the password every month. He had some system.'

Kat avoided sighing, despite her frustration. Now Pete was dead, they'd probably have to wait months before whichever firm made the phone would give her a code to unlock it. But maybe Digital Forensics would have better luck with the laptop.

She thanked Dalma for her time, and the tea, and expressed her condolences once more before leaving.

Kat had a folder full of death threats. A dead man's phone and laptop. And a strong connection between the victim, the Eel Deal and its apparently murderous Al Jumairi participants.

But thanks to William of Occam, she also had a few lingering suspicions about Dalma Vaughan. After all, given that she now thought Pete had been murdered, the line of enquiry requiring the fewest assumptions was that his wife had done it.

Dalma had told Kat at Pete's bedside that she'd been out with friends when Pete had collapsed and called 999. That alibi would need checking thoroughly. And she'd assured Kat that their marriage was fine.

Which was exactly what a murderous spouse *would* say.

Chapter Fifteen

Before pulling away from her spot outside Dalma's house, Kat called Darcy. Time was of the essence if she was going to get Pete's phone unlocked. She knew she was reaching, but she had to try.

'Hey, Kat, what's up?'

'I've got Pete Vaughan's phone and laptop. The phone's locked with facial recognition. Do you know if it's possible to unlock a phone from a dead person's face?'

Darcy 'hmmed' down the line. 'Not sure. I don't think so. I know the latest ones have all kinds of extra security built in. I think the face has to be moving, even fractionally. Eyes open, too.'

'What about the older ones?' Kat asked, feeling even the slender straw she was grasping slipping away.

'I don't know. I guess all you can do is try.'

'OK, thanks, Darce, got to run.'

Kat flicked on the blue lights on her dash and behind the grille and activated her siren. With a shriek of rubber from her tyres, she peeled away from the pavement, heading for MGH.

Traffic was heavy. She swore at each new hold-up, picturing Pete Vaughan's deteriorating skin colour and muscle tone as the inevitable process of decay progressed. But maybe Jack's body fridge would slow it down enough that she'd get lucky.

She burst through the double doors of Jack's office at 3.37 p.m. Pete had been dead for three hours and fifty-eight minutes. Was that too long?

'Jack,' she said. 'Sorry to interrupt.' He looked up from where he had been deep in conversation with his assistant, Ashleigh. 'I need to see if we can unlock Pete Vaughan's phone.'

Jack got to his feet, Ashleigh following suit.

'Do you know how many cops have presented mobiles to me asking me for a miracle?' he asked with a half-smile as he rounded his desk.

'Have you ever performed one?'

He passed her and led the way to the bank of refrigerated drawers ranged along one wall.

'There's always a first time.'

'Which one is Mr Vaughan, Ash?' he asked.

'Four, Dr Jack,' she replied.

She caught Kat's eye and grinned.

So it had happened. The mash-up of Jack's title and given name caused by Ashleigh's initial overly respectful attitude had solidified into a nickname.

Jack unhooked the heavy handle, pulled the rectangular door wide, and slid out the body beneath its white sheet. Without ceremony, he pulled the sheet back. Gasping wasn't in Kat's repertoire, or not when in the presence of a relatively unmarked corpse such as Pete's. But still, the grim reality of a dead human being still stirred a strange brew of feelings. Pity. Compassion. Sorrow. And, given the unwelcome greenish tinge to his skin, doubt and frustration. Not so much grasping at straws as clutching at thin air. Still, she was here now, and as Darcy had said, she had to try.

She swiped the phone's screen and held it over Pete's face.

Checked the screen.

Nothing.

'Shall I try opening the eyes?' Ashleigh asked.

'Please.'

Ashleigh gently lifted the eyelids, revealing only the lower edges of the irises. The remainder of the sunken white was a soft cream and looked dry. She let go and before the lids could close again, Kat replaced the phone over the dead man's face.

She turned the phone round.

Nothing.

'Shit.'

'If it's any consolation,' Jack said, 'that line of miracle-seeking cops I mentioned? It would stretch from here to the front desk.'

Kat sighed as she pocketed the phone. 'Thanks, anyway. I'll let you two get back to your meeting.'

'Hold on a sec, Kat. I'll walk you up. I was going up to the canteen anyway,' Jack said.

As they climbed the stairs, Jack cleared his throat. Kat turned to him.

'You thought Gina was my girlfriend, then?' he said, smiling softly.

She shrugged and kept climbing. 'Silly of me. I assumed, which we all know makes an ass out of you and me.'

'So why do I get the sense it mattered?'

She resisted turning to look at him. Rounded the half-landing, focusing on the strange way their out-of-kilter footsteps echoed off the hard surfaces. But she could sense it. The quizzical, teasing smile on his face.

'It didn't. Doesn't.'

'My bad. Anyway, that probably means my next question is redundant.'

'Oh? What was that?' she asked, knowing she was falling into a call-and-response pattern she'd frequently practised on interviewees.

'Do you want to grab a drink? After work one day? I know a nice place out in the country. In Sheepton,' he added. 'Like the ward. Nice little pub with a restaurant and a decent wine list. You like Pinot Grigio, don't you? I was hoping to tempt you with a lovely little white Burgundy.'

Kat was powerless to stop the blush that crept over her neck and up to her jawline. Or the not altogether unpleasant squirm of excitement that flickered into life low in her belly. In recent years she'd felt some of her true self getting lost to her roles as wife, mother, detective and doggy-mum. She'd met and married Van, and had Riley, before her twenty-second birthday. But there had been a time before that, before Liv screwed it all up, when Kat had been carefree. Going to bands or clubs. Drinking, dancing. Going out with boys who'd unashamedly ogle her body. Sometimes she felt nobody saw her as a woman anymore.

'Are you asking me out, Dr Beale?' she asked, then immediately regretted both her words and the tone in which she'd delivered them.

'For a collegial drink,' he said with a smile. 'Is that a yes, then?'

She inhaled. Then reality kicked in, hard. What the hell was she doing, even flirting with this man?

'Sorry, Jack. I'm in the middle of a murder investigation. And I'm married,' she added, hurriedly.

'It's just a drink, not an invitation to stay the night.' A beat. 'Although they do have a couple of rooms.'

Cheeks heating up, she pointed to the door. 'Canteen's that way. I have to go. Bye, Jack.'

She made it to the car park before she exhaled loudly.

Oh, God, what had just happened?

'Nothing,' she said loudly, causing a passing staff nurse to look round.

And that quiet, mischievous voice in her head that often asked her uncomfortable questions piped up once more. *Nothing? Really? Could have fooled me.*

Ignoring it, she reached her car and climbed in. The phone would have to go off to Apple. Maybe Darcy would have better luck with the laptop.

Chapter Sixteen

It was nearing 4.00 p.m. when Kat entered Forensics, carrying Pete Vaughan's bagged laptop under her arm, with his phone in her pocket.

Darcy took one look at the iPhone and sighed. 'That's the latest one. We'll start our usual process with Apple but I wouldn't hold your breath. The last one we had took five months.'

'What about the laptop?'

Darcy took it from Kat. 'Great, a MacBook. I'll send it to Digital, but to be honest, you might get the phone back first. I'll raise another ticket with Apple just to be on the safe side.'

Kat thanked Darcy and joined Leah, Fez and Tom in their makeshift office in the corner of the canteen.

'Hey, boss. What news?' Tom asked. 'Any leads?'

'Well, if your maths is good enough to solve the square root of sod-all, have at it. Otherwise, nothing. How about you guys?'

'Lots of digging. Result: a big empty hole.'

'I asked Dawn Jacobson about Pete's expenses,' Leah said. 'She said he drank so much they had an agreement he wouldn't submit every receipt. But as far as she knew, he didn't have a favourite boozer.'

As they bent over their screens again, Kat leaned back and rolled her head. The crack of her vertebrae betrayed how tense she'd been feeling since the Met had arrived. It was a weird one, all right. Pete Vaughan had called 999 and effectively reported his own murder. If only he'd given them something useful. Ideally, a description of whoever "they" were.

A familiar if unwelcome voice pierced her reverie, singing softly under his breath.

Carve-up emerged from the dogleg among the screens. Finished his song. '. . . piece of meat.' He smirked. 'Like it, DS Ballantyne? It's a rock classic.'

'What is it, Stu?'

'I've been reviewing the case with Sharon. The main one, I mean. The bombing. We were just wondering whether you'd closed your little offshoot yet. Or have you, I don't know, found something that links them. Was Vaughan making bombs in his home office?'

'He was murdered, I'm sure of it. And that means there must have been a link. No way could the two events be unconnected. Surely even you can see that.'

He leaned over her desk. Behind him, she saw Fez and Leah looking over, their faces hostile.

'Watch yourself, Kitty-Kat,' he murmured, using the hated nickname she knew beyond a doubt her father had shared with him. 'I'm still a DI *and* your line manager, so I'd advise you to keep that mouth of yours in check.'

The overpowering stink of his Aramis aftershave – the same brand as her father wore – made her recoil. But only physically. He ought to have learned by now that she didn't respond well to threats.

She stared into his eyes. 'He was murdered. I'm investigating, with Linda's full support. And in case *you'd* forgotten, she's a DCI and *your* line manager. Was there anything else or has Sharon not given you anything to do?'

He straightened, stroked his tie, fuchsia silk, fastened with an ugly gold pin. 'Fine. If Linda wants you to look at some hack who carked it after eating too many lamb vindaloos, smoking too many fags and drinking too many bottles of cheap *plonk*,' he said, leaning on the final word – a favourite term of misogynistic male cops everywhere used to describe their female colleagues – 'be my guest. Meanwhile DI Critchlow and I are trying to figure out who tried to massacre half this town.'

'Someone taking my name in vain?'

It was Sharon herself. Rounding the dogleg and increasing the number of cops in the tiny space to six, at least three more than it could comfortably accommodate.

'I've been looking for you, DI Carver.' She turned to Kat. 'Kat. What's going on with the journalist case?'

Before she could answer, Carve-up rode over her. 'It's nothing, Sharon. This Vaughan bloke gave himself a heart attack by basically living like a slob. DS Ballantyne here is, I'm afraid, guilty of typical small-town homicide cop frustration. Some random bloke drops dead and she's there with her magnifying glass and her deerstalker talking it up to murder.'

Sharon's lips had tightened as Carve-up delivered his latest piece of wisdom. When he'd finished, she turned her back on him. 'Kat?'

Barely able to control her temper, Kat shot a look at Carve-up so deadly, by rights it should have killed him. 'DI Carver is wrong, ma'am. As, to be honest, is the A&E consultant I spoke to earlier.'

'Go on. I'm listening,' Sharon said, raising an admonitory finger as Carver opened his mouth to speak. 'Hold your horses, DI Carver. Let Kat finish, please.'

He clamped his jaws shut again.

Kat suppressed an urge to smile. 'Two things happen within a couple of hours of each other in a – and it pains me to say this, ma'am – but a provincial town,' she said, earning a brief smile from Sharon. 'One: a terrorist bomb explodes, killing two. A group opposed to the Al Jumairi regime and its takeover of Middlehampton FC claims responsibility. Two: an investigative journalist who has the same deal in his sights – and who's married to an Al Jumairi woman – dies suddenly, unexpectedly and suspiciously, saying with virtually his dying breath, "They killed me". Now, if you agree with DI Carver that I'm indulging in, what did you call it, Stu, "small-town homicide cop frustration"? Well, just tell me and I'll go back to reviewing cold cases. I have a particularly interesting one I'm looking into at the moment, in fact.'

Sharon shook her head. 'Quite the speech, Kat. But also, exactly the same conclusion I've come to. If these two cases aren't linked I'll apply for a post in Traffic.' She glanced in Carve-up's direction. 'They always need people. What I really need from you, though, is something concrete. When's the post-mortem?'

'It's 9 a.m. tomorrow, ma'am.'

'Good. Let me know the moment you have a cause of death.'

Kat nodded and watched with satisfaction as Sharon beckoned Carve-up to follow her out of their space. She hadn't clicked her fingers. Not quite. But Kat caught Carve-up's disgusted expression all the same.

Once Kat was sure they were alone, she addressed her three DCs. 'Sharon's right,' she began. 'We do need a cause of death. I spoke to one of the nurses and she said she hadn't seen any marks or wounds on Pete's body when they changed him out of his own clothes. So, obviously they would have spotted blood if he'd been stabbed or shot, but I'm also ruling out blunt-force trauma and strangling.'

'What's left, Kat?' Fez asked. 'Poisoning?'

'Maybe. He was trying to say something to me just before he died. I think he was trying to say "bomb". But he could only manage the “b”. When I asked him he shook his head. He was quite distressed.’

‘Maybe he was confused when he denied it,’ Tom said. ‘Especially if he was pumped full of drugs. You said I wasn’t making much sense when I came out of my coma.’

‘Maybe it wasn’t “bomb”?’ Leah said. ‘You said he was a drinker. Maybe it was “booze” he was going for. Like somebody poisoned his wine.’

Tom rolled his eyes. ‘Agatha Christie, much?’ he sneered. ‘You’ll have us looking for a vicar with a lead pipe next.’

‘That would be Cluedo, not Christie,’ Leah shot back, eyes flashing. ‘Anyway, I don’t hear you coming up with anything.’

Kat caught Fez’s worried glance at Tom. Anxious to quell the incipient squabble between the two DCs, and bothered once again by Tom’s mood swings, she intervened.

‘Good point, Leah. And poisoning really does look like a possible MO. The nurse said she hadn’t seen any puncture marks but it could have been given orally, in his wine, for example. We know he liked a drink.’

‘Or injected somewhere it would be hard to spot the puncture mark,’ Leah said. ‘Under the tongue or in his ear.’

Tom wrinkled his nose. ‘Now you’re reaching for James Bond.’

‘Well, that’s because the whole thing is a bit James Bond, Tomski, isn’t it? I mean, look at it? It’s like Kat just said to Critchlow. A terrorist bomb plot and a dead investigative journalist. It’s hardly the average Tuesday night, is it?’

‘Jack will find out what happened, and how,’ Kat said. ‘But if Pete Vaughan *was* poisoned, what does that suggest to you guys? Because I know what *I* think.’

‘Somebody wanted Pete Vaughan dead before he could ruin the Eel Deal,’ Fez said.

'Yeah, but do businesspeople really go around administering poison through someone's soft palate or whatever?' Tom countered.

'No. But they're only half of the deal, aren't they, bab?' Fez said. 'You've got the Al Jumairis on the other side and from what I've been reading, they're not exactly shy of using brute force to get their own way.'

'Go on, Fez,' Kat said, once again delighted with her newest DC's breadth of knowledge.

'Two years ago, these women's rights activists were protesting outside the Al Jumairi embassy in Paris, right? Three weeks later, their leader, Hélène Dubois, dies in a car crash. Her Renault goes off a bridge into the Seine,' he said, growing more animated as the story progressed. 'It floated for five minutes, right? Plenty of time for her to get out but she couldn't. The car sank with her inside. By the time police divers reached it, she'd drowned. They tore the car to pieces. Guess what they found?'

Leah took the bait. 'What?'

'The driver's seat belt had been tampered with.'

'Bloody hell,' Kat said with feeling. 'Right, so if the Al Jumairis were a single nominal, we'd say they had form.'

'You said you knew what you thought, boss,' Leah said. 'Which is . . . ?'

'Pete was murdered in a way undetectable to regular doctors and nurses. We think it might have been poison, but maybe there's another way we don't know about. Either way, this MO says three things.' She counted the points off on her fingers. 'One, premeditation. Two, resources. Three, organisation. And, building on what Fez just told us, that points strongly to the Al Jumairis. Either one of theirs or possibly local talent hired in for the job.'

'Should we be closing off the other lines of enquiry so quickly, boss?' Fez asked. 'What about the death threats?'

'No, and you're absolutely right, Fez. As of right now, the Al Jumairis are one of our "persons" of interest in Pete's death – which might link it to the Eel Deal and the bombing. But so are Nick Chater, Gerald Hynde and, to be honest, anyone who sent Pete a death threat. And as we know, there were plenty of those.'

The three DCs were all nodding. Even Tom, who had been a little more pugnacious since his coma than before, wasn't offering any more counter arguments.

'Tomski, I want you to check out Pete's financials. Leah, can you start profiling Chater and Hynde. Fez, I think it's time you met one of Middlehampton's finest.'

Chapter Seventeen

Fez followed Kat into the Hope and Anchor, noting the battle-scarred front door, its lower half kick-proofed with a rectangle of steel plate.

Inside he surveyed the dimly lit room and formed a conclusion. In the pulp fiction detective novels he loved, places like this were inevitably referred to as 'low dives'.

And how about the patrons? They favoured him with stares in which curiosity, hostility and grudging respect were mixed. He was with Kat. And Kat clearly had standing in this community.

He clocked the heavyset guy at the bar. The one Kat had said would be Frank Strutt. Five-ten, broad shoulders and a deep chest that strained but did not part the buttons of his white shirt. A decent make, then, and chosen deliberately to accentuate but not be ruined by the bulk beneath.

Kat had told Fez to follow her lead before they entered. Fine by him. He'd known pubs like this back in Brum where he'd meet snitches. On the surface, they might all look the same, but every dodgy boozer had its own codes, customs and characters. He was here to learn.

A fat middle-aged man in a corner decked out in wannabe biker attire eyeballed him with undisguised hatred. He caught the tops of two rounded characters tattooed on his neck, peeping shyly from the neck of his Black Sabbath T-shirt. Great band. Birmingham's finest. Not so much the sneering fifty-something inside its XXXL folds. Those rounds were all-too-easy to decipher. 88. Alphanumeric code for HH – neo-Nazi code for 'Heil Hitler'.

Fez stared the guy out, committing his features to memory. He and Naz had brought Leila to this town and here was the first inkling that they would always have to devote a percentage of their energies to making sure their daughter was safe from men like this.

They reached the bar.

'Afternoon, Frank,' Kat said. She turned to Fez. 'This is DC Faisal Mohammed.'

Frank gave Fez an appraising stare. Then stuck out a hard hand. Fez gripped it, expecting the usual power play. A bone-crushing grip, knuckles of the unsuspecting rookie ground to powder. But the handshake was firm, warm and dry.

'Pleased to meet you,' Frank said. 'Fez.'

Fez smiled easily. No prizes for guessing how a man like this knew his nickname. Someone at Jubilee Place had leaked information about the new DC. Probably for a few quid or a free drink. Or just a small favour owed. He wondered about Carve-up again.

'Likewise,' he said, withdrawing his hand. 'Frank.'

'How are you finding Middlehampton?'

'I like it. Good place to raise a family.' He leaned forward. A little power play of his own. Fixed Frank with a stare at once confiding and firm. 'The guy in the corner with the evils for people like me – name?'

It was bold. They'd never met before. But Fez believed in establishing ground rules early.

Frank's eyes never left Fez. He was calculating, Fez could see it. The trade-offs being assessed. The equations being run. The flow of intel, both ways, being weighed in the balance.

'Tyler Fisk.'

Fez nodded. Committed it to memory.

Frank straightened and turned back to Kat. 'Drink?'

'Not today, Frank. I need to talk to you. In private.'

'This about the Powerhouse?'

'It's where we're going to start.'

He nodded. Turned to his left. 'Max! Bar, please.'

A young woman in tight black jeans and a salmon-pink mohair top came out through a door. 'All right?' she asked Fez.

'Hi.'

'We'll be in the back room,' Frank said. 'If anyone needs me, tell them to take a number.'

'Yes, Uncle Frank.'

He led Kat and Fez through a door into a snug, furnished simply with a battered table with a cast-iron base, and a few hard chairs. Fez looked around. Prints of foxes in hunting gear and dogs playing cards punctuated the nicotine-yellow walls.

Once they were all seated, Kat put her hands flat on the table. But Frank beat her to the punch.

His face darkening, he leaned towards them.

'It's not right, Kat. Foreigners – bloody terrorists, for God's sake – coming to our town and murdering innocent people. There's business, and that's understood by both sides. I mean, we go back, we understand how the world works.' He slammed a meaty fist down on the table. 'But this? This is an outrage!'

Fez had heard this moral philosophy before. Hardened criminals like Frank Strutt operated to a strict code. The details varied but for the most part there were certain lines they never crossed. Paedophiles, rapists, perverts who did what they did for pleasure, not power or financial gain? They were beyond the pale for men like Frank. Fez had scored some notable successes in Birmingham against proscribed groups with help from men who would cheerfully point a shotgun at another man's head and pull both triggers.

But the boss didn't have time for moral philosophy. Probably on account of her husband and son nearly being blown to pieces.

'Have you heard anything about it?' Kat asked.

'No, and I tell you, it's not for want of trying. I've got my people sniffing around. Places Critchlow's bunch of dimwits'll never reach.'

Fez chalked up another mark next to Frank's name on the mental list he'd been compiling since arriving in Middlehampton the previous year. Knowing a lowly DC's nickname was one thing. But the identity of a Met counter-terror DI? That was impressive. Even if it was another transparent little power play.

'You'll let me know if you learn anything,' Kat said.

A sentence, not a question. Fez loved how she worked this gangster. He could see how she'd built the relationship based on mutual respect and trust. Even though they both had to know she'd slap the cuffs over Frank's thick wrists if she had enough evidence.

'Yes. But if we find out who planted that bomb, I can't guarantee their safety. Lot of very vengeful people in this town, Kat.'

'Vigilante justice doesn't belong here, Frank.'

'I agree. But if some rag-head fell down a flight of steps and cracked his head open, that'd be what some might call *poetic* justice.'

Fez tried to remain impassive as the racist slur slipped from Frank's lips. Leah's early aggression in the workplace was something he'd been able to forgive after she'd explained her treatment at the hands of an older Muslim officer in her previous station. Her racist language had stung – no, it had hurt – at the time, but there were battles you fought and battles you avoided. He'd made that choice and he could live with it. But this was different. This was the kind of hatred men like Fisk exhibited. Frank turned to him nonetheless.

'Don't worry, Fez. I'm no friend of Tyler out there,' he said with a dead-eyed smile. 'But you have to admit, whenever there's a bombing or a beheading or whatever? Well, let's just say, they're not shouting "I love the Baby Jesus!", are they?'

Fez smiled back. 'You mean because they're Muslim?'

'If the *kufi* fits.'

'Funny. Did you look that up on Wikipedia when your friend at Jubilee Place told you we were coming in?'

Beside him, he caught a motion as Kat flicked her head round to look at him. Too late. He wondered whether Kat had been lulled by the usefulness of her relationship with this gangster into complacency. But Fez had seen what men like Frank Strutt were capable of given a bigger city to play in. And he didn't like it. Trafficked girls from poor countries forced into drug addiction and prostitution. Kids bought and sold like dolls at a car boot sale. He had his contacts, of course he did. But he was always careful to maintain a boundary between him and them. He just hoped the boss was doing the same.

Frank Strutt had blinked at his jibe. Not much. Too early in Fez's own relationship with Strutt to know if it was a tell or not. But he was aware now that, degree or not, here was no fast-track DC with his My First Detective suit and his eye on his next promotion.

'Maybe I mis-spoke, as the politicians like to say these days,' Frank said. 'You're a Muslim yourself?'

'Yes.'

'So tell me, what does the Qur'an say about murdering women and children?'

'It's forbidden. *All* of it,' he added.

'So we're in agreement. This bomber has to go down for what he did, yes?'

Fez was young. But he wasn't so green he'd fall into the trap of letting Strutt run the conversation.

'Al Capone,' he said.

Frank's heavy brow furrowed. 'What?'

'He was a noted Chicago gangster of the Prohibition era.'

'Yeah, I know who he was. I mean, what's he got to do with all this?'

'He organised the St Valentine's Day Massacre. Murdered seven men. But the Feds couldn't lay a finger on him. Know what they put him down for in the end?'

'No.'

'Tax evasion. He got eleven years.'

'What's your point?'

'My point, Frank, is that big men can be brought down for small things like tax fraud or hate crimes as much as by grand larceny or murder,' Fez said, ignoring the thrumming pulse battering his eardrums. 'Something to bear in mind next time you use that kind of language in my presence.'

Fez returned the bigger man's stare, wondering if this was what a bank vault door would feel like when confronted by a thermic lance.

'What do you know about Pete Vaughan, Frank,' Kat said, breaking the silence.

Fez felt gratitude wash over him. He should never have let his feelings get in the way when Kat had expressly told him to listen only. Too late now. He went back to his role as a silent observer, and hoped he hadn't ruined the usefulness of the meeting.

With what looked to Fez like physical effort, Frank turned to refocus on Kat. 'Who?' he asked.

'Pete Vaughan. Freelance journalist. I think he was murdered last night.'

Frank shrugged. 'Never heard of him.'

'So no whispers of a contract being put out on someone by that name?'

Frank glanced at Fez for a moment, then back at Kat. 'I run a pub. I don't know why you'd think I'd know about contracts.'

Fez cursed himself. Frank was pulling back. Retreating behind the old 'legitimate businessman' facade they all used. The smart ones, anyway.

'If I find out there was one, and one of your guys took it, I'll come back, Frank. You know that.'

Frank got to his feet. 'Like I said, I have no idea what you're talking about. Now, you'll have to excuse me but I think a barrel needs changing and Max is too skinny to do it.'

He looked at Fez. 'I'll be seeing you, DC Mohammed.'

Fez climbed into the car beside Kat. He twisted round in his seat. Needing to apologise. The encounters with Fisk and Strutt had unsettled him, and he was still angry. But he'd also leaped in when he'd said he'd listen.

'Kat, I'm sorry. I shot my mouth off and he clammed up.'

Her eyes blazed. 'Hey! No! You don't apologise to me for that. Frank never does, or says, anything by accident. Him calling the bomber a "rag-head"? The "Baby Jesus" bit? That was him seeing how you'd react. It *was* a racist thing to say, and I'm sorry you had to hear it, but my best guess? He did it to test you. You pushed back. Hard. Did you notice he wasn't expecting it? That's not bad, rookie. Not bad at all.'

Fez sighed with relief, felt his stomach unclenching. Though the sting of Frank Strutt's words, and Fisk's tattoo, still burned.

'Thanks, boss. I thought I was in for a right bollocking.'

Kat grinned. 'Oh, if you've ruined my carefully nurtured relationship with Middlehampton's premier organised crime figure,

I'll give you a bollocking you'll remember when you've clocked out with your thirty.'

Fez laughed. 'Do you think he meant it? That he'd not heard anything about a contract on Pete?'

'It's hard to say. When he said that thing about business being understood by both sides, I'm wondering whether contract-killing falls under that heading.'

Fez nodded. It was a good point. Whatever they thought about kiddie-fiddlers or serial killers, old-school moralists like Frank Strutt wouldn't have any qualms about murder-for-hire.

He looked forward as Kat started the engine. A skinny guy in a bright red Adidas tracksuit was sitting on a wall outside the Hope, a roll-up dangling from his fingers. He waved at them.

'Looks like we've got a friend,' he said to Kat.

'He's a snitch. Won't be a minute,' Kat said.

Chapter Eighteen

Kat climbed out of the car and joined Isaac Handy on the low wall.

The small-time drug dealer was one of her sources. He hung around on the fringes of Frank Strutt's world and usually came up with the goods. Whenever they talked, she sensed a vulnerability in him. A lost little boy who'd made what his teachers would have called 'poor choices'. With a son of her own, she felt an almost motherly concern for him.

'Hi, Kat,' Isaac said.

'Hi. You all right?'

He wrinkled his nose. Looked away. 'Yeah, yeah, all good.'

'Listen, I'm investigating the death of a journalist. A man named Pete Vaughan. Have you heard anything?'

'Nope. All anyone's talking about's the bomb. Whoever did that, I hope they all die. If Frank gets to them before you do, it'll happen for sure.'

'Never mind, Frank. If you hear of anything, Isaac, I want you to call me, yes? Usual rates apply.'

He nodded. He looked about as uninterested in the idea of a payday as it was possible to get. Completely out of character for a man always looking for cash to fund his low-level drugs business. Or his next fix.

Kat turned to him. 'Hey, Isaac. *Is* everything all right? Really? Is it your mum? Is she back in chemo?'

He sniffed again and turned back to face her. His eyes were wet. His sharp Adam's apple bobbed in his scrawny neck.

'She died, Kat. Mum died. What am I going to do without her?'

Kat's heart went out to him. Nominal or not, he'd never done anyone any harm and she knew how much his mum meant to him. Kat had even given him the odd lift up to MGH to see her.

'Oh, Isaac, I am so sorry. Really. My condolences.'

Her words sounded insubstantial to her ears. Like the rote phrase they uttered to the relatives of murder victims, '*I'm sorry for your loss*'. Kat always meant it, and tried to show them, but here was another grieving person and she knew nothing she could say would touch his pain.

She put her arm around his bony shoulders and drew him close. Maybe it was unprofessional, but right now she didn't care. He needed a hug. And she doubted there was a single soul in Middlehampton who'd offer one.

'She didn't suffer,' he said, sobbing into the crook of her neck. 'She was in the hospice. I was with her.'

'Well, that would have been a comfort to her. To have you there at the end.'

'Yeah, but now what, Kat? She's all I had.'

To her surprise, she felt tears welling up behind her eyes. This had never happened before. And then she realised. When she'd thought Van and Riley were inside the Powerhouse, she thought she'd lost them. Riley was safe but Van was still in hospital. Anger fired deep in her soul. Maybe Frank wasn't so far off the mark after all. She'd love to get the bomber alone somewhere dark, out of sight of CCTV cameras.

'I don't know, Isaac,' she said. 'When I lost my best friend, I just cried and cried. I thought it would never stop. But little by little I found a way to get past it. You'll probably always carry your grief for your mum. But it'll get to be a lighter burden. Something you can forget about most of the time. And when you think of her, it will be the good times. Birthdays. Christmas. Holidays.'

He sniffed loudly, and slowly righted himself, lifting her arm gently from his shoulders. He turned a tear-streaked face towards her. 'Thanks, Kat. I know you're a copper, but you're a good person.'

'I'll take that,' she said with a smile.

He looked down. Picked a loose tag of skin at the side of a nail. 'The funeral's at 2.45 p.m. on Friday,' he murmured. 'Northbridge Crematorium. If you can come . . .'

The lump in her throat returned. 'That's very kind of you. I've got a lot on but if I can be there, I will.'

He sniffed. 'Nice one.'

She left him there, on the wall, rolling another cigarette. Without a solid lead, somehow she doubted there'd be much time to see her own family, let alone grieve for Isaac's.

Chapter Nineteen

Kat left Fez in their improvised canteen office and went to update Linda. It was 7.00 p.m.

Normally the big boss would have gone home long since, but she'd made it clear there was no room for anyone to be working to the clock as long as the bomber was out there.

Linda puffed out her cheeks when Kat popped her head around her door.

'Oh, God, Kat, please tell me you've got something.'

Kat sat down, trying to formulate an update that would give her boss at least a shred of comfort. 'I spoke to Frank Strutt. It wasn't the most cordial of meetings but he said he hadn't heard of Pete Vaughan, or any contract to have him killed,' she said. 'Which he would have, if one existed. Nothing like that gets past Frank.'

Linda snorted. 'No, because he's either the one putting it out or the one collecting.'

'Which is true, but I think I believe him.'

'And this means, what?'

'It means that, if Pete *was* murdered – and I'm sure he was – it was either by a personal enemy, and I have two strong leads there, or it *was* the Al Jumairis, and they did it in-house. Which points the finger at someone in the Crown Prince's security team.'

'Tell me about the personal enemies first. Because if this is linked to the Al Jumairis then it's linked to the bombing, and that's a can of worms I really do not want to open.'

Kat nodded. 'Nick Chater runs the Eels' Supporters' Trust. Very anti-Pete Vaughan because he didn't want his investigation to scupper the deal. Gerald Hynde blamed Pete for his wife's death from an industrial disease. He's been sending hate mail care of the *Echo*. I'm going to drop in on Dawn on my way home tonight.'

'Maybe focus on those two for now. Getting in the faces of an international delegation might require a bit more finessing.'

'Will do. But I'm good to keep investigating them for the murder?'

Linda sighed. 'Quietly. And you run anything beyond background research by me first. Clear?'

'Yes, Ma-Linda. How's the other investigation going?'

Linda groaned, running her fingers through her hair. 'I swear, Kat, if that bloody woman gives me one more lecture about her "front-line experience in the war on terror" I'm going to scream.'

'Inter-force relations as peachy as ever?' Kat said with a sly smile.

Linda favoured her with one of her trademark frosty stares. Kat felt her core temperature descend by a few degrees.

'Let's just say we won't be inviting each other to our birthday parties.'

'Have they got anything concrete?' Kat asked.

'Concrete, yes. Useful, no. The bomb was some kind of basic DIY unit. Not even C4. Just a hacked-up mixture of household chemicals like the world's biggest bloody banger. Takes us precisely nowhere.'

'What about the fact there was no shrapnel round it? That has to be significant.'

'If you want to discuss the intricacies of terrorist bomb-making with DI Critchlow, be my guest.'

'I'll pass. How about CCTV?'

'Nope. Bomber was clever. Must have known where all the cameras were.'

◆ ◆ ◆

After her meeting with Linda, Kat returned to the canteen. Leah and Fez were nowhere to be seen. Tom was at his desk, staring at a screen.

'Hi, Tomski, you all right?'

'Tired.'

'Maybe call it a day, then. Go home and get something to eat. Or see if Eleanor wants to come round. That is, if you two are still good?'

'Yeah, we're good. You're sure, Kat? I don't mind staying.'

'It's fine, Tomski. Go, go. You can't solve a murder if you're not sharp. I'll see you tomorrow.'

Kat stared after him. She really hoped things were good between Tom and his girlfriend. The coma had done something to his personality, and spending some uncomplicated time with Eleanor could only be a good thing for his mental health.

With the space to herself, she called Dawn Jacobson. She was still working so Kat arranged to meet for a quick drink in a pub near the *Echo*'s offices.

◆ ◆ ◆

The pub was quiet. Kat wondered whether the bomb had frightened people into staying at home. Dawn sat at a corner table, nursing a gin and tonic. She smiled when Kat arrived with her own drink, a lime and soda.

'Hey, Kat, how've you been?'

'Off the record, those bloody Met counter-terror lot are doing my and everybody else's head in. They've commandeered MCU and even Linda's working out of a broom cupboard.'

'Any leads on that – that you can share?'

'Just this. And it has to be an unattributable source.'

Dawn nodded. 'A senior police source revealed . . .'

'Thanks for making it "senior",' Kat said, smiling. 'So, there's something that doesn't add up about the bomb itself. Normally, right, these people, they pack their devices with nails, or nuts and bolts.'

Dawn nodded. 'To cause maximum casualties. Like Manchester.'

'Or 7/7. Exactly. But this guy, or these guys, they didn't. It was just a medium-sized load of a basic home-made substance. Not even a high-explosive mixture. Plus they called it in.'

'I know. It reminds me of how the IRA used to operate, back in the day.'

'They still murdered two people, though, but I don't think that was the intention. Doesn't make it right, by the way, and I absolutely want you to make that point in anything you write. But to my mind, what we have here, if it is terrorism, is a very strange kind. Nothing like the MO of previous atrocities in the UK claimed by IS or other Islamist groups.'

Dawn narrowed her eyes. 'What are you saying, Kat?'

Remembering that she was now acting as an anonymous police source, albeit a senior one, Kat thought hard before she spoke. What was she trying to achieve here? Compromising an anti-terror investigation was a very serious step. But the more she thought about it, the more convinced she became that this was not a terrorist attack at all. She had to choose her words very carefully.

'I'm saying, despite the tragic deaths of two wholly innocent people, something about this terrible crime doesn't add up. The perpetrators caused great fear and anxiety, and grief, for Middlehampton, but if they were trying to stir up opposition to the Al Jumairi regime, they achieved the complete opposite.'

Dawn leaned forward. 'You just shared a lot, Kat. In fact, I'm going to be kind and say you shared far too much. I've lived in this town my whole life, like you, and I want whoever planted the bomb to rot in prison,' she said, her mouth tight, her eyes sparking with fire. 'So, and I can't believe I'm saying this, but I'm only going to use a couple of words from you. Just general stuff. But let me share something we found out ourselves this afternoon.'

'What?'

'Desert Sun are denying responsibility for the bomb.'

'You believe them?'

'Why would they lie if they'd really done it? That's the whole point with groups like that. They want the publicity. They revel in it. If they're denying it, and I can't reveal my source but it's one hundred per cent reliable, then yes, I believe them.'

Kat couldn't believe it. And then, because she'd always enjoyed a mutually trusting relationship with Dawn, she found she could. Something had been bugging her about the bombing since she'd recovered from her shock at almost losing Van and Riley.

Her homicide cop's brain kicked up into a higher gear. And where it took her brought her back to the reason she'd wanted to meet Dawn in the first place. What the bomb had done, with devastating effectiveness, was to divert police resources away from the other crime that had been committed on the exact same night. The murder of Pete Vaughan.

'Dawn, tell me about Gerald Hynde,' she said.

Dawn blinked, clearly surprised at the sudden switch in direction.

'Gerald is a very sad – in the literal sense – old man,' she said. 'He blamed Pete for his wife's death.'

'Did you report the death threats?'

'I wanted to but Pete insisted they weren't really serious. Just the product of a man deranged by grief.'

'But deranged people can do all sorts of bad things, Dawn, you know that.'

'I do, sadly. But Pete was adamant. He said, and I remember this as if it were yesterday, "The trouble is, Dawn, Gerald has a point. My work wasn't good enough. If I'd done more, Esther Hynde would still have died, but not in vain."'

'He blamed himself.'

'Always. That man had a moral compass forged out of iron, Kat.'

And there, in that heartfelt character portrait, Dawn unwittingly set Kat's thinking down a different line. Because in her career as a police officer, one thing she'd learned was the more someone was painted as a saint, the more likely they were to be a sinner.

And, as unwelcome as the cold wind that entered the pub with a group of laughing twenty-somethings, came another thought.

Just like my half-sister.

After leaving Dawn, Kat paid a quick visit to MGH to see Van. The medical staff were keeping him for another night, although the promise was he'd be home the following day. She called Riley. He cried down the phone. She did her best to comfort him and made him promise not to spend too much time on his phone before bed.

With no husband, no son and not even Smokey for company, she ate a quick microwaved supper of leftover spaghetti Bolognese and went upstairs to her makeshift incident room. If she had time on her hands, she could put it to use on her personal investigation.

Kat stood before a large whiteboard, staring at a photo of Jo downloaded from her personal trainer website. A vicious bully at school, Jo had been murdered for her crimes. Here, Kat's half-sister was smiling. Her skin was golden, her hair shiny. Beneath the straps of her fitness top, her shoulders were rounded, muscular.

Kat's heart felt heavy. Where was the woman behind the artfully composed studio shot? Kat had reached out to Ian Morris, Jo's husband. But he'd refused point-blank to talk to her, claiming he'd been unfairly accused of murdering his wife.

Beside Jo was a 2014 article from the *Echo*. 'Local Property Developer and Husband Killed in Fatal Air Crash'. She re-read the article about Jo's parents, Tasha and Connor Starling, even though, as she'd done with the media coverage of Liv's disappearance all those years ago, she knew it off by heart. And here she was again, consumed by a mystery she might never solve. After all, if Liv hadn't staged her own resurrection, Kat would have gone on believing her best friend was dead.

According to the Air Accidents Investigation Branch inspector who'd looked into the crash, the cause was a mechanical failure in the engine fuel pump. No foul play was suspected and the police closed their own investigation. The coroner recorded a verdict of accidental death.

She closed her eyes and tugged on her earlobes, a habit she'd developed at school when her problems, academic or otherwise, threatened to overwhelm her. Just like now. *Was* it an accident? Was she trying to invent a murder so she could investigate? It sounded like the sort of accusation Carve-up would make and she shook her head. 'No!' she said into the silence of the little room.

One thing she knew that the AAIB inspector didn't was that Tasha had had an affair with her dad. Also, that her dad – if not Tasha herself – was corrupt.

Call it by its correct name, Kat, she admonished herself. *Criminal!*

Yes, flying light planes was inherently risky. You didn't need to be a murder detective to know that. People died in them without being criminals. But when she added in the relationship with her dad, it looked at least possible that Tasha's and Connor's deaths hadn't been accidental.

But when was she ever going to find time to investigate the potential murders of Jo's parents when there was always a live case? The hot had to take precedence over the cold.

Or did it? Were the hot and cold cases more intertwined than she'd thought?

Pete Vaughan had told the 999 call handler he'd been killed on the same night as a terrorist group opposed to the Eel Deal planted a bomb at the Powerhouse. Hot.

Jo Morris's parents had died ten years earlier in a light-plane crash. Cold.

Jo's mother-in-law was Daniela Morris, an investor in Middlehampton FC. Warm.

Whose payoff from the Eel Deal would be jeopardised if Pete Vaughan's article came out. Hot.

Kat pulled out her phone.

Chapter Twenty

Daniela Morris answered just as Kat was readying a brief voicemail message, staring at her half-sister's photo on the whiteboard and feeling an emotional tug like she was a fish on a hook, being reeled in by a woman she'd only known in death.

'Hi, Daniela, it's Kat Ballantyne.'

'Hi, Kat. Long time.'

'I was hoping to ask you some questions about Jo.'

'Oh?' Daniela sounded surprised. Maybe she'd thought Kat would be calling about the bombing. She was one of the shareholders in Middlehampton FC, after all. 'Well, come round any time. I mostly work from home these days.'

'I'd love to. The problem is, I'm really up against it at the moment. The next few days, probably weeks, are going to be difficult. Could we speak now?'

'On the phone, you mean?'

'Yes. If that's OK with you?'

Daniela sniffed. As she spoke Kat caught a telltale thickening in her voice. She'd been Jo's mother-in-law, not her birth mother. But ever since the case had reignited, Kat had formed the impression Daniela regarded Jo as her own flesh and blood.

'Bit personal for the phone, Kat,' Daniela said. 'If you're busy during the days, come round now. I'll open something cold.'

Kat checked her watch, 9.30 p.m. 'Yes, I'd like that. Where do you live?'

Kat knew the address Daniela gave her. A fifteen-minute drive at this time of night. She promised she'd be there soon and ended the call.

◆ ◆ ◆

As Kat drove down Priory Walk West, looking for the Morrises' place, she marvelled at the idea that anyone should actually live in one of these immense period houses.

When Riley had been a baby, they'd often pushed the pram around Middlehampton Cathedral and its grounds. Until 1971, when the Diocese of Middlehampton had been carved off from the Diocese of St Albans, it had been Middlehampton Priory. The large churchyard and accompanying green space – the Glebe – was a favourite hangout of older students at Middlehampton College, Riley's school. Now, lit by a half-moon, the expanse of land, punctuated by graves, benches and electronic donation points, had a tranquil air.

The wrought-iron gates guarding the privacy of the occupants of The Charter House parted as she drove up to them and nosed the Golf on to the curving gravel drive.

Unlike her parents' mock-Tudor house on Gadelands, with its gold-painted replica of Eros at Piccadilly, this house was an altogether more stately affair. Four storeys of Georgian stone-faced brick, panelled windows decreasing in size with each floor according to some architectural formula she didn't understand but could appreciate for its harmony.

She rang the doorbell. Suddenly nervous, she looked down, checked her shirt, ran the back of a nail down her fly just to check it was zipped.

The door opened wide, spilling warm yellow light on to the stone-flagged doorstep.

Daniela Morris smiled. 'Kat, come in. I was having a glass of wine in the library. Care to join me?'

Kat, who would have cheerfully necked a bottle of Pinot Grigio just to settle her jangling nerves, said, 'Better not. I'm driving.'

'Diet Coke, then? Fizzy water? Tea, coffee?'

'Tea would be lovely.'

Daniela led her out of the vast hallway – which was hung with paintings of dogs with dead birds in their mouths, military men and sailing ships – into a book-lined room painted a dark, comforting green from floor to ceiling.

She motioned for Kat to take a chair facing hers in front of a fireplace in which a couple of logs burned, snapping and popping occasionally, and releasing a sappy, smoky aroma that made Kat think of school camping trips.

Daniela pressed a button set into the wall. *Some sort of intercom*, Kat thought, looking for a mic, or a grille to speak into. But Daniela merely smiled at her.

'I wondered how long it would take you to come here asking about your sister.'

Kat frowned. 'You know?'

The older woman nodded. 'I've known for a long time. After she lost her own mum, Jo and I got really close. We spent a lot of time in here, talking about the past. And now you're here, wanting to do the same.'

The door opened and Kat looked round. A clean-cut man of maybe thirty-five entered the room. He wore a beautifully made suit. Similar to the Italian designer numbers Carve-up liked to sport. Lower key, though. Kat pictured a discreet tailors' shop in a cobbled mews in a pricey part of London.

He came to stand a few feet from Daniela's armchair and bent slightly from the waist. 'Yes, Mrs Morris?'

'Would you bring some tea for my guest, Robert?' She turned to Kat. 'Any preference?'

Still stunned by the appearance of what she realised was a butler, Kat stammered out, 'Builders' would be fine. Thank you.'

The butler smiled. 'English Breakfast it is, then.'

Kat watched him go then turned to find Daniela smiling at her.

'Easy on the eye, our Robert,' Daniela said.

'Oh, no. I wasn't . . .'

'Checking him out? I wouldn't blame you – I do,' Daniela said. 'He's been with us for three years. The last one was OK but a bit old school. Kept calling me "Madam".'

Floundering, Kat tried hard to reassert herself. 'You don't come across many butlers in this neck of the woods, was what I meant.'

Daniela dipped her head. 'Wealth has its privileges. John's not so keen, but I told him, "If we're moving into a place the size of an office block, I'm having staff." I think he expected me to handle the place myself.' She rolled her eyes. 'Men.'

They made small talk until the butler returned with a tray laden with tea things. Perhaps sensing Kat's discomfort he made no attempt to pour for her, instead indicating by a subtle hand gesture that she was welcome to fend for herself among the sugar tongs, milk jug and strainer.

'Will your husband be joining us?' Kat asked, as she poured her tea, added milk.

Daniela shook her head. 'John's got a work thing. Dinner.'

Kat sipped her tea, which was perfect. She resolved to start buying loose leaf. 'With the Crown Prince?' she hazarded.

'Yep.'

OK, so there was a topic to be handled sensitively. Much like the reason she was sitting in a Georgian library having tea with one of Middlehampton's most successful businesspeople. After all, Kat had lost a half-sister whose existence she'd only discovered after her murder. Daniela Morris had lost a woman she regarded as her own flesh and blood.

'I want to know about Jo.'

Daniela sighed. Picked up her wine glass and took a healthy swallow. 'So ask me.'

'I just want to understand her. How she could have been, I'm sorry, Daniela, but how she could have been so evil at school, the way she and her little gang of bullies tortured Goneril Pickering?' Kat said, masking her embarrassment about her clumsy phrasing by sipping her tea.

'That's a very good question. I asked her myself, when I found out. You know she did loads of charity fundraising?'

'Yes. I assumed it was her trying to atone for what she'd done.'

'You're right. That's exactly what it was. It's not an excuse, but she was trying to make amends. To atone, as you put it. Jo found out the truth about her biological father when she was thirteen. She overheard her mum talking on the phone. The conversation got heated and Tasha shouted, "I don't want your money, Colin. I want you to acknowledge your daughter. *Our* daughter."

'Jo wasn't the brightest girl, academically, but she wasn't stupid. She could work out what that meant. Connor wasn't her real dad. Some other man – your father, Kat – was. Jo said everything changed for her in that moment.'

'Is that why she started bullying?'

'No. She told me that at first she was just withdrawn, angry. She hated Tasha for what she'd done and Connor for not, I don't know, being enough for Tasha.'

Kat saw it, then. The pivotal event in Jo's life that had marked the fork in the road when she'd chosen viciousness and violence.

'It was when the plane crashed, wasn't it.'

'She said her feelings about her parents felt like a betrayal. Like she'd caused their deaths. That was when she teamed up with Elise Burrluck and Hayley Edwards to form the Three Sisters.' Daniela pulled a tissue from her sleeve and dabbed at her eyes. 'What Jo did was unforgivable. I can't even begin to imagine the agony she put that family through, but she was hurting inside. She was in such pain, she was so *angry*, she tried to get rid of those feelings by inflicting pain on other people. But in the end, she realised the harm she'd done. How viciously she'd behaved. She was distraught. It was too late for Goneril, but she did try to put good into the world. If she hadn't been murdered, I think that would have been her life's work.'

When she finished talking, Daniela subsided physically, sinking back against the armchair. She was crying openly. Kat felt close to tears herself. But she forced them back. Ever since learning about her half-sister's crimes – because what else could you call the actions of a girl who branded her gang's symbol into the living flesh of another child? – Kat had struggled to reconcile her disgust and horror with her sense of loss over a sibling she'd never known.

She cleared her throat. 'Do you know what happened to Jo's parents?'

Daniela straightened in her chair. Her eyes widened. 'They died in a plane crash. You must know that, surely?'

'But *why* did it crash?'

'It was an accident, wasn't it? That's what the report said.'

'I'm not so sure.'

Daniela narrowed her eyes. She grabbed her wine glass and emptied it, then leaned forward, fixing Kat with a frank stare. 'You're saying they were murdered?'

'I'm saying I want to know more.'

Daniela refilled her glass. The bottle now only held a couple of inches. 'You know, I'm a very rich woman, Kat. In my own right, never mind John's holdings. If you need anything, anything at all, you call me or come to see me. Because my daughter-in-law changed that day. She's beyond harm now. But if you tell me that her parents' deaths weren't an accident, I will take a little bit of comfort from that. And then I'll help you find their murderer. That's a promise.'

Kat nodded her thanks. Daniela Morris seemed determined to help her. But would her resolve weaken if it turned out her business partner in the Eel Deal, and Kat's father, was mixed up in it? That thought spawned another. Dangerous, given Sharon Critchlow had warned her off investigating – 'poking your nose into' – the Powerhouse bombing.

'Will your husband be discussing the bomb at the Powerhouse with the Crown Prince, do you think? Or the—' she almost said 'murder' but decided to hold something back, 'death of Pete Vaughan?'

If she was surprised at the swerve from matters familial to criminal, Daniela didn't show it.

'I expect they'll come up. Why?'

Kat shrugged. 'A group opposed to the Al Jumairi regime detonate a bomb, drawing attention to human-rights abuses. Pete Vaughan tries to do the same thing with an article.'

'I don't know about the Desert Sun lot, but I knew all about Pete Vaughan. The man had some sort of white saviour thing going on as regards Al Jumairah. He wasn't going to change anything with an article. He was just boosting his own ego,' Daniela said.

'Although if he created a stink about them sportswashing their reputation by buying a Premier League club, it could lead to enough negative publicity to torpedo the deal.'

Daniela shook her head firmly. 'Sorry, Kat, but you're being naive. People like Pete Vaughan love to think they're changing the world with their' – air quotes – 'exposés, but they're like jackals hanging around a pride of lions. They get enough to live on, but do the lions change the way they hunt because a few scrappy little wild dogs bother them at kills? No. They do not,' Daniela said with finality. 'The only thing that could stop the deal would be if the Competition and Markets Authority ruled against it or the council denied planning permission for all the additional development. Neither of which are going to happen. In fact, you know what? I wouldn't be at all surprised to learn Vaughan had been in league with Desert Sun all along, seeing as how he seemed to hate the Al Jumairi royal family as much as they did.'

Kat wrinkled her nose. This was an angle she hadn't considered. Would a journalist be in league with terrorists? She thought the word was the right one. Whatever the rights and wrongs of their cause, or the Al Jumairi royal family, planting bombs in concert venues was terrorism in her book, pure and simple.

But why? What would he have to gain?

Maybe it was time to share the piece of information she'd held back moments before.

'Do you think that's why Pete was murdered?'

Daniela's immaculately shaped eyebrows shot up. 'Murdered? I thought it was a heart attack.'

So despite her connections, it appeared she didn't know everything.

'We believe it was deliberate,' Kat said. 'I'm heading the investigation.'

As soon as the words left Kat's lips, she had the disconcerting sensation that she was drinking tea with a woman who, because she stood to make millions from the Eel Deal, had to be considered a person of interest in her murder investigation.

Daniela had apparently reached the same conclusion. A guarded look entered her eyes. 'You're not really here about Jo at all, are you? You came to see if me or John looked like we had something to hide.'

'No, no! Not at all. I swear it wasn't that.' Kat held back from the easy question that presented itself. Begging to be asked. *'Do you have something to hide?'*

She had zero evidence connecting the Morrises to Pete's death. If she discovered some, fine, she'd return with a different set of questions. But for now, she wanted to make a graceful exit.

Kat thanked Daniela for the tea, and her time, and left her alone in the vast house.

As soon as she was home, she added what Daniela had told her to the murder wall, as she'd started thinking of it, in her private incident room. She fell asleep in her office chair staring at the interlocking scrawls.

She awoke at 5.01 a.m. and decided to call Liv as soon as the hour was halfway reasonable. She thought she could wait until 6.00 a.m. Farming folk made early starts, didn't they?

After all, who better to discuss a cold case with than a woman who didn't exist?

Chapter Twenty-One

Nobody in Middlehampton could know Liv Arnold was alive.

Every one of the original Origami Killer cases would have to be reopened and Stefan Pulford's conviction would be thrown into jeopardy. But soon that danger would be over. Liv was staying off the grid on her farm commune in Wales and getting married. She'd become Olivia Jones, one of thousands in Wales. A legally acquired new identity for a woman everyone already thought was dead.

Which made her the perfect confidante.

'Hi, Louise,' Kat said when Liv picked up. 'All right?'

'Lush,' Liv answered, pushing her South Wales accent – '*lash*'. 'You, Thelma?'

'I wouldn't say lush, but I'm OK. How are the wedding plans going?'

Liv spoke for ten minutes. Kat had to smile. Her best friend's obvious joy and excitement was like sitting beneath the noonday sun. Some of the tension and anxiety that had plagued her since hearing about the bomb at the Powerhouse left her.

Finally, Liv paused right around when Kat had begun to wonder if she'd acquired the trick of breathing through her ears.

'Enough about my wedding, Thelma. I want to hear about you.' A beat. 'What do *you* think about my wedding?'

That cracked Kat up. It wasn't a new joke, but Liv had that magic ability to make her laugh even with the tiredest lines.

'I really *did* want to hear about your wedding plans, but there was another reason I called. It's about Jo.'

Liv didn't miss a thing. 'What do you want me to do?'

At that moment Kat felt that old pull towards Liv. The unwavering loyalty, a readiness to look out for Liv or follow her anywhere.

'When Jo's parents died in the plane crash, the Air Accidents Investigation Branch sent a field investigator to look into it. His name is Ben Warwick. Riley told me you're great at online research. Could you try and track him down?'

'I'm on it. Listen, I have to go. It's my turn to cook breakfast for everyone. But I'll start today, OK?'

'Thanks, Louise. I love you, mate.'

'Always and forever, right?'

'Always and forever.'

Smiling at the way they'd never dropped their declaration of true friendship, Kat hung up. She went for a shower. Cleaned her teeth. Took a little plastic tube from the medicine cabinet. Oil of camphor.

Jack had scheduled Pete Vaughan's post-mortem for 9.00 a.m. One way or another, she'd learn whether she was investigating a murder.

Chapter Twenty-Two

Kat reached MCU at 6.51 a.m.

The Met crew and their supreme overlord, Sharon Critchlow, were also in early, and in apparent overdrive.

A large whiteboard had been set up and scrawled across the top in flaring red letters were the words: 'Local terrorist/OCG links???'

Organised Crime Groups? That was a stretch, surely? Gangs committed all manner of heinous crimes but always with the profit motive at their heart. Even murders were over turf or unpaid debts or disrespect. OK, so maybe that last one wasn't money-related, not directly.

But one thing they didn't do, in Kat's experience, was plant bombs in public buildings. It brought precisely the kind of heat Middlehampton was now experiencing. And that was bad for business.

She looked around for Sharon. If she was serious about researching local OCGs, Kat could be helpful. And maybe regain her territory on the fourth floor. She was tired of working out of the refugee camp in the corner of the canteen.

Loud male voices boomed along the corridor outside. One voice was instantly recognisable. She rushed over and pushed through the doors into the corridor.

Frank Strutt, hands cuffed behind his back, was being frogmarched by three Met officers into the smallest, smelliest and dirtiest interview room in the station. They usually reserved it for nonces, rapists, and people who committed the very worst kinds of murder.

Frank caught her eye. It felt like being trapped in a laser sight. Her chest tightened instinctively as if she could ward off the incoming fire with muscle tone.

'You are making a very big mistake,' he growled.

Kat was helpless. She wanted to protest that it was nothing to do with her. But that was out of the question. And anyway, what if he *had* had something to do with it? He'd been voluble in his anger the previous evening when she'd taken Fez to the Hope and Anchor. But what else would she expect him to say?

'Get in there and shut up,' a burly Met DC shouted at Frank, as a second detective opened the door.

'I'm going to hit you with a suit for wrongful arrest,' Frank yelled back into the detective's face. 'And anything else we can think of. Only it won't be half as fanciful as the bollocks you and your mates have cooked up.'

'Nobody's hitting anyone with anything. Unless you misbehave and then you'll find out what a Met-issue baton feels like,' the detective snapped. 'Get in there, sit down, and be quiet.'

'I want a lawyer.'

'Yeah? Well, I want a Ferrari. I guess we're both going to be disappointed.'

'You can't do this. I have rights.'

The young detective laughed in Frank's face. Kat though it was a bold move. In other places, Frank's, for example, that sort of move would end up with you seeking the help of a cosmetic dentist. A plastic surgeon. Or both.

'You've been arrested under Section 41 of the Terrorism Act 2000,' the cop sneered. 'And guess what? That means you do *not* have the right to legal advice. Not till my guv'nor says so, anyway. So be a good boy, sit tight, and keep your trap shut. If you behave, we might even bring you a cup of tea.'

Frank's response – an expletive delivered with so much force it made Kat flinch – bounced off the interview room door as it closed. She half-expected to see a hole punched through the plywood.

The Met cops were all high-fiving and bantering with each other as they sauntered off. Feeling it wouldn't do her profile any good if she went in to talk to Frank, Kat headed for the stairs.

She found her team assembled in the canteen office and assigned tasks for the day. Basically that meant everyone combing over Pete's last days, looking for anything, a second of CCTV, a witness who'd seen him in a pub talking with someone, a mysterious credit card payment, anything that might take them closer to the point where he'd been targeted for murder.

Kat sat at her own desk and cradled her head in her hands. She took a gulp of strong black coffee and pulled a face. Eyes closed, she tugged on her earlobes.

Someone tapped her on the shoulder. She spun round.

It was Abby Greene, her friend in response and patrol. R&P, everyone called it. Abby was dressed in a black suit and a pale blue shirt. Low, black heels. She wore her hair in a high ponytail.

Kat frowned. 'Hi, Abby. You started coming in on your day off? That's a dangerous habit.'

Abby smiled. Her eyes flittered left and right. Was she nervous? Why? She and Kat had known each other for years.

'You haven't forgotten, have you, Kat? My rotation in MCU? I got the authorisation through last week. It starts today,' she said. 'It would have been Monday but I was in court. Then, what with the bomb and everything, you know, it's been a bit hectic.'

Kat sighed inwardly. The last thing she needed right now was to be handholding an eager-beaver uniform with CID ambitions on her first plain-clothes rotation. But then she chided herself. That was exactly what she herself had been like. And at least now she had another warm body to help investigate Pete Vaughan's murder.

She smiled at Abby as she got to her feet. 'I'm going to be honest, Abs, I *had* forgotten. Like you said, it's been mental round here the last forty-eight hours. But you're here now so we'll get you set up with a desk,' Kat said. 'In fact, you know what? I'm going to talk to Sharon Critchlow. She's the DI leading the terrorism investigation. I'm going to insist we get our old desks back.'

Abby nodded. Then she looked down and brushed her fingers over her jacket front.

'Is this OK? I wasn't sure what to wear so I copied you. Yours is M&S, too, isn't it? I went out on Saturday, specially.'

'Good old Marks & Sparks. The detective's friend. Smart, professional and, most importantly of all, washable.'

Abby grinned. 'I did my hair, too. I usually have it pinned up when I'm on shift. But this looks more appropriate for plain clothes, don't you think?'

Kat nodded. Hoped Abby wasn't going to go *Single White Female* on her. Having one stalker was bad enough, even if Ethan seemed to have found a new hobby these days – promoting himself on national TV as a 'crime investigator'. Two would drive her crazy.

Leaving Abby with Leah, who started filling her in on how the case was going, Kat went to find Sharon. It was time to re-establish some boundaries.

Chapter Twenty-Three

Sharon surprised Kat, readily agreeing it was unfair her team had evicted Kat's from their own quarters.

'Half my lot are out and about now so grab your old desks back,' she said. 'They'll have to hot-desk, which is fine. Might teach them a bit of flexibility.'

Kat thought that was an interesting word for the DI to use. Surely counter-terror work was all *about* thinking laterally.

An hour later, she and her team were back where they rightfully belonged. Tom, Fez and Leah were shooting her appreciative glances as they lugged their boxes of files up from the canteen.

Kat was hunched over her keyboard when Leah called out. 'Kat! You have to see this. Quick!'

Leah aimed a remote at the wall-mounted flatscreen TV and boosted the volume.

Ethan Metcalfe was being interviewed by a BBC news reporter. But it wasn't the fact he'd attained the heights of a spot in conversation with the national broadcaster that shocked her. That emotion was reserved for his appearance.

Ethan wore a black polo neck beneath a dark-brown moleskin jacket. Leah and Kat called the look FTM – Fast-Track Modesty. It had definitely applied to Tom when he'd joined MCU a couple of years back, and now it seemed Ethan had taken it on, too. But it wasn't just Ethan's clothes that had caught her eye and caused her mouth to drop open. His hair was neatly cut, and he appeared to have lost a couple of stone at least.

'Looks like Ethan's been hitting the gym,' Leah said. 'Next thing you know he'll have a girlfriend. Although maybe that'll be good news for you, Kat.'

Kat shushed her. A chyron scrolling along the bottom of the screen described Ethan as a podcast host and crime investigator. So she hadn't been speculating. He really was trying to rebrand himself. A horrifying thought occurred to her, further souring her mood. What if he started approaching Linda, trying to get hired as a consultant? Linda wouldn't. Would she?

On screen, Ethan was pontificating about the bombing. 'Well, Meghan, anyone with an ounce of insight into how these things go down can draw a straight line between the Novichok poisoning attacks in Salisbury in 2018 and the recent poisoning of Pete Vaughan. No other explanation fits the known facts.'

'What known facts?' Kat shouted at the screen. 'There aren't any!'

'Are you saying there was Russian involvement, Ethan?'

He pursed his lips and glanced upwards for a second. 'There are very few state actors with the resources to perpetrate something like this. Given their track record, you'd be mad not to have the GRU or a similar outfit at the top of your suspect list.'

As he referenced the Russian military intelligence agency, he stared straight into the lens, just for a second. Kat had the disconcerting feeling Ethan was speaking directly to her.

Worse, by far, was the fact that Ethan, with the connivance of the BBC, was actively spreading panic in Middlehampton. Even though there was zero evidence for a nerve agent, he'd set that particular dog running.

'Usual Metcalfe bollocks,' Tom said, throwing a balled-up piece of paper at the TV.

'The guy's a loser, bab,' Fez added. 'I listened to a couple of his shows. It's fifty per cent fantasy, fifty per cent boasting and fifty per cent cut-and-paste off Wikipedia.'

'That makes a hundred and fifty per cent, our kid,' Leah laughed.

'Yeah, well, the man's fifty per cent crazier than the average loser we get ringing up confessing to every murder that gets committed.'

Kat wanted to take comfort from her team's jibes. But the trouble was, Ethan had a point. Not as far as the identity of Pete's attacker. As usual, Ethan was more interested in headlines than actual investigative work. But the general thrust of his argument was valid. The state actor she had her eye on was already in town on legitimate business. No need for cock-and-bull stories about visiting Middlehampton for its Gothic town church or medieval butter cross.

Leah snapped off the TV. 'Wanker,' she said.

'But what if he's right?' Kat said, addressing all four members of her team. 'He said what I've been thinking. That this could well be the work of the Al Jumairis.'

The three DCs all wore identical expressions – scepticism mixed with a reluctance to challenge her.

'Not being argumentative, boss,' Fez said, 'but all we have so far is a journalist lying on the pathologist's slab with no obvious cause of death beyond his own poor health.'

Kat opened her mouth to disagree when Abby jumped in. 'If the boss says it's the Al Jumairis, we should go with that. She's the one with the experience.'

'I don't *say* it's them,' Kat said, irritated that Abby had interrupted her with an unnecessary defence of her thinking. 'I just think it *might* be. And yes, I *know* we have no evidence, which is why I want you guys to find me some.'

'But aren't we putting the conclusion cart before the evidential horse?' Tom asked.

'Wow,' Leah deadpanned. 'Even by your standards that's a tortured metaphor, Tomski.'

He frowned. 'Fine. We should be drawing conclusions from the evidence, not the other way around.' He looked at Leah. 'Better?'

'Much,' Leah said, crossing her arms.

There it was again. Ever since coming out of his coma the previous year, Tom had struggled to keep his temper under control. Kat had even been to visit his neurologist at MGH to find out if it was normal for coma patients to behave differently after recovering. The consultant's answer was anything but reassuring. It amounted to, 'Yes, no and maybe. Depends on the patient.'

Kat spoke up, trying to head off yet another flare-up between the two young DCs.

'Never mind carts and horses, or – while we're at it – stable doors. My gut is telling me that not only was Pete Vaughan murdered, but his murder is linked to the Eel Deal. Now, before anyone says, well, why are we still looking into his background, let me explain,' she said, feeling her way into her argument. 'It *could* be the Al Jumairis. They, as a whole, have a motive. Keeping the deal on track and acquiring Middlehampton FC. But I'm not going to put all my eggs in one basket—'

'Especially with all these horses galloping around,' Fez said, to laughter.

Kat let him have that one. Anything to break the tension. 'Thank you, Fez. So that means we follow up on all leads of any quality. Right, jobs.'

She assigned victimology to Tom. Building their knowledge of Pete's life. Everything from his favourite restaurants to previous girlfriends.

'Maybe it was his investigative work that got him killed. But for all we know, he did something else to piss someone off badly enough for them to kill him. If nothing else, we have to close down that line of enquiry completely. I don't want Linda coming back on me saying I didn't dot my i's and cross my t's.'

She assigned Leah and Fez to work through the full list of people who'd sent hate mail.

'What about me, boss?' Abby asked.

She was standing right in front of Kat, well inside her personal space.

'You can choose. Pete Vaughan's post-mortem or helping Tom on victimology.'

Abby squared her shoulders. 'Post-mortem, please, boss.'

That impressed Kat. Maybe the new girl was going to work out after all.

Chapter Twenty-Four

With Abby beside her, Kat drove up to MGH. Abby fidgeted the whole way there. Her anxiety about attending the post-mortem felt like a third presence in the car alongside them.

'I thought you were right, boss,' Abby was saying, having barely drawn breath since closing her door. 'What you said in MCU about how it could be the Al Jumairis. I've been researching them. Did you know they have the death penalty still? The Crown Prince said he wanted to scale it back, but actually his father still controls the kingdom and he's like this super-hardline figure. My point is they're like these terrible people. I can easily imagine them ordering a foreign journalist to be taken out.'

Kat forgave Abby her burble of assertions, questions and thriller-movie terminology – 'taken out'! A detective's first post-mortem was a rite of passage. Everyone feared it. And those who claimed they didn't were lying.

At the hospital, walking from car park 9 to the mortuary, she gave Abby the same little pep talk she'd given Tom in his first week. Now that *had* been a baptism of fire.

'Try not to worry, Abs. We all have to go through our first post-mortem,' she said. 'Remember, focus on the details, take notes if it helps, and, if you *are* going to throw up, find somewhere away from the body.'

'I'll be fine,' Abby said with a determined jut of her chin. 'This isn't my first DB.'

Flinching inwardly, and reflecting that most uniformed cops saw many more dead bodies than the average detective, Kat still felt the need for a gentle correction.

'I don't have a lot of rules for my team, Abs, but there is one I'd like you to follow, please,' she said, keeping her tone friendly. 'We don't refer to murder victims as DBs, vics or any other trivial term. They were people when they were alive, and I like to keep it that way when they're dead, too. You know, so we don't lose sight of the person they were. So we'll stick to calling him Pete, OK?'

Abby blushed furiously, her whole neck and throat turning cherry red.

'Oh, God, boss, I am so sorry. It just slipped out. It's what the older guys call them. I just thought that's what we did. But it won't happen again, I promise.'

Kat turned to the young PC, worried by the hitch in her voice. 'Hey, it's fine, really. That wasn't me telling you off or anything,' she said, smiling. 'And I can totally imagine some of those twenty-year geezers in R&P giving it all the usual. But we're MCU and we do things differently. Oh, and one other thing.'

'Yes, boss?'

'That. The "boss" thing. You *can* call me that. Sometimes the others do. Especially if I'm in their faces about something. But you can call me Kat. It's fine. Just not "guv" OK? Never "guv".'

Abby smiled nervously. 'OK. Kat.'

'Right, we're here,' Kat said as they approached the doors to the mortuary, formally known as the James Frobisher Forensic Medicine Suite.

Abby stopped dead, causing Kat to bump into her.

'What is it, Abs?'

'How were you at your first post-mortem?'

Kat remembered the day. The dead woman on the dissection table, skin mottled green and purple. The smell of menthol in Kat's nostrils and how it had failed utterly to mask the stench of decay. How she'd swallowed down her gorge and concentrated on what was happening. Until her curiosity blotted out all other feelings and her nausea vanished.

Back when she was still a teenager, she'd seen what she'd believed at the time to be the 'death photo' of Liv. When she'd reappeared in Kat's life, Liv had admitted that she'd faked it. But it had inoculated Kat against the fear of dead bodies.

She lifted her chin and took a sharp breath.

'I lost my lunch into a bucket Dr Feldman always used to put in the far corner.'

Abby sighed. 'Thanks, Kat.'

Kat pushed open the doors.

Chapter Twenty-Five

Inside the mortuary dissection room, other police staff were already present. Two CSIs: one 'wet' for body fluids and tissue samples, the other 'dry', for everything else, from pocket lint to jewellery.

Standing beside Kat, Abby glanced at the green-draped body on the table. Snatched a quick breath.

The previous pathologist, Dr Feldman, now retired and on to more fragrant pastures, had told the young DC Ballantyne that it wasn't the sights that had greenhorns retching, but the smell. That disgusting mixture of bodily decay, from a mild, cheesy ripeness to full-on putrescence, disinfectant and formalin.

Abby groaned quietly, but the small sound was packed with dismay, horror and fear. Maybe she had seen more than her fair share of corpses, but there was something about the dissection of something that had once been a living, breathing human being that was unique.

Kat knew what caused fear in detectives in this situation. It was the threat of disgracing themselves. Of having to turn away to be sick in a strategically placed bucket. Enduring the knowing looks – and jibes – of more experienced officers.

She took the tube of oil of camphor from her pocket and offered it to Abby. 'Here. It helps a bit with the smell. Do it like on the telly,' she said, demonstrating with a little under her own nose.

'A little smear on your top lip. Don't get it anywhere you wouldn't want shampoo – it really stings.'

At his first PM, Tom had attempted to show some bravado with an off-colour joke about certain activities he wouldn't be attempting with the stuff on his hand. Kat smiled at the memory. But the smile slid off her face as she reflected on his now regular bad-tempered dismissals of his colleagues' suggestions and theories. Was it a permanent change, or would she one day get her old bagman back again?

'Morning, Kat, something you want to share with the rest of us?' Jack asked, smiling at her, his visor up and mask under his chin.

'Probably one for the pub, Dr B,' she replied, happy for once to be engaging in non-sexually charged banter with the pathologist.

'And who is this?' he asked, smiling at Abby.

'PC Abby Greene, Dr Beale. I'm on rotation with MCU.'

'Well, you couldn't have a better mentor than DS Ballantyne.'

'Oh, I know. She's the reason I asked for MCU.'

'Please, guys, it's already hot in all this PPE. You're making me blush,' Kat said.

On Jack's side of the table his assistant, Ashleigh Collinson, stood beside a photographer. Both were fully garbed in PPE. Kat made eye contact with both, nodding a friendly greeting.

'If we're all ready, let's begin,' Jack said.

He switched on the overhead mic and began talking in a steady, clear voice. He asked Ashleigh to cut away the hospital pyjamas with a pair of trauma shears. Each item was bagged and labelled, then put aside.

'Time of death we know practically to the second,' Jack said. 'Mr Vaughan breathed his last, actually probably an unfortunate term given cause of death, but anyway, it was at 11.39 a.m. yesterday.'

'What was cause of death, Dr Beale?' Abby asked.

'Jack, please,' he said, glancing to his left at Ashleigh who dipped her head. 'It's been given as a heart attack plus acute pulmonary oedema, or APO . . . Which means, please, Ash?'

'In layperson's terms, fluid in the lungs. It collects in the air sacs and makes breathing difficult. Or, as here, impossible.'

'Thank you. So, we have an official cause of death, which I have no reason to doubt, given the battery of tests and scans my colleagues in the land of the living performed. So our job this morning, Ash?'

'Is to determine what *caused* the heart attack.'

'Right, well, let's try and work it out.'

Kat enjoyed watching the interplay between the two mortuary staff. Jack was an excellent teacher, despite his occasional patronising lapses, and Ash clearly a willing and able student.

Beside Kat, Abby was keeping very still and breathing heavily. Kat thought she was either trying to control a vomit reflex or, as Kat had been in her time, she was intensely focused on what was happening on the stainless-steel table in front of her.

'Y-incision,' Abby muttered.

'I'm sorry?' Jack said, glancing up.

'Oh. I just said the Y-incision. It's what comes next. I was just preparing myself.'

'I'm sorry but you'll have to wait a little longer. First, I'm going to subject the body to a detailed external examination.'

'Sorry, Dr Beale.'

'First time, isn't it?'

'Yes.'

'Well then, don't be sorry. Everybody has to go through this. Isn't that right, Kat?'

'It is,' she agreed, momentarily nonplussed by Jack's compassion for the rookie.

Jack bent over the body and began scrutinising every square centimetre from the crown of the head down to the toes. As he worked, Kat peered closer, following Jack's progress as he stretched and palpated the skin, examined the hands, the torso, the genitals, all four limbs. With Ashleigh's practised help, he rolled the body over and repeated the process.

Although Jack was the expert when it came to corpses, Kat couldn't see a single sign of trauma. Just the accumulated signs of deterioration that accompanied the onset of middle age. Especially in men who treated their bodies not as temples but as man-caves. Rolls of fat, wrinkles and patches of eczema on the elbows, old scars, thread veins, even some cellulite on his buttocks.

Jack lifted the left calf and examined the foot, checking the sole then the instep. Finally he spread the toes. Kat was giving up hope he'd find anything when he put down the left foot and lifted the right. Then he leaned closer, maybe a few inches from the spread toes in his fingers.

'Hello. What do we have here?' he murmured.

'What is it, Jack?' Kat asked, leaning forward along with everybody else.

He beckoned her closer with his free hand. 'See for yourself. What does that look like to you?'

Kat peered at the spot between the big toe and its neighbour. The pinkish skin looked uniform at first, then she saw it. A small, inflamed puncture wound.

'Is that a needle mark?' Abby asked. 'Was he a heroin user, do you think? Could an overdose cause a heart attack?'

'Hold your horses, PC Greene,' Jack said. 'It's a puncture. That's all I can say at this point. It could have been caused by anything. A thorn in his sock, a wasp, or, yes, a needle. As to heroin, we'll need to wait for a toxicological screen before we can rule it in, or out. Ash, can you pass me a magnifier, please?'

Ashleigh handed him a rectangular cream plastic magnifier. He thumbed a black switch on the handle and a set of white LEDs around the frame illuminated the puncture mark.

'This doesn't look like a needle mark at all,' Jack said. 'For a start, it's turning necrotic, which means— Sorry, Ash, you explain.'

'Dead tissue.'

'Thank you. The diameter's all wrong, too. If anything, it looks like an insect bite.'

'Can I have a look, Jack, please?' Kat asked.

He handed her the magnifier and stood back, giving her room to hunch over the foot. She'd seen the same injury the previous year. On Van. He'd put his hand into a gardening glove a hornet was using as a summer house. The noise he'd made!

'My husband got stung by a hornet last year,' she said. 'It looked exactly like that.'

'Maybe Pete was stung, too,' Abby said. 'He could have been allergic.'

'Very good,' Jack said. 'Now, if only we had the creature that did it, we'd be able to close this one out.'

'Where are his clothes?' Kat asked, seeing a link to Van's unfortunate encounter.

'On the bench there,' Jack said. 'Did you miss Ash cutting them off him?'

'Not his hospital clothes. The ones he was wearing when he was brought in. If it happened the way it did to Van, the hornet or wasp or whatever could have crawled into his shoe.'

'Good point. Ash, do you know where they are?'

'They came down with the body. But in a separate bag. I'll fetch them.'

A few minutes passed during which everybody took a turn peering at the foot. Ashleigh returned and laid out the clothing on a workbench. Faded Arctic Monkeys T-shirt, Levi's 501s, white

M&S pants, and a pair of grey felt slippers with curled up pointy toes, embroidered with red and gold Arabic lettering.

Kat pointed at the slippers. 'Not exactly in keeping with the whole dad-rock look, are they?'

'Maybe he took a trip to Marrakech?' Jack said, before humming a snatch from an old tune.

He took the right slipper and very carefully upended it. Using the torch on his phone he peered inside. Kat held her breath.

'Bloody hell!' he said, dropping the slipper on to the bench. He took a quick step back. 'Ash, can you hand me some artery forceps, please?'

'What is it, Jack?' Kat asked, her belly fizzing with adrenaline. Whatever it was, it was clearly bigger than a domestic wasp. Maybe it was one of those newcomers. An Asian hornet.

Gingerly, Jack inserted the jaws of the forceps into the toe of the slipper, opened the handles and then closed them again. Very slowly, he withdrew the stainless-steel implement until its payload came into view.

There were a couple of sharply indrawn breaths. Abby swore and then apologised. And Kat stared. What the hell?

'Is that a scorpion?' she asked.

Jack opened the forceps and dropped the crushed and mangled creature into a white plastic tray.

'I think so, yes.'

Kat studied the multi-legged body, the two-legged one behind her forgotten for now. She pointed, from a safe distance, at the curled-up tail with the characteristic sting-tipped bulb at the end.

'I think we've just found our murder weapon.'

'Well, unless scorpions have suddenly become native to south-east England owing to climate change, I'd have to agree with you,' Jack said.

But as Kat stared at the creature, and tried not to think of the excruciating pain it must have caused Pete Vaughan, a more pertinent thought entered her brain.

Given that venomous scorpions weren't native to the country, how had the murderer acquired one, and then got it into Pete's slipper?

Chapter Twenty-Six

The scorpion went into a plastic debris pot with the lid screwed on extra tight, at Kat's insistence.

'I don't want anyone getting stung if there's any venom left.'

Jack and Ashleigh rolled the body back over so the chest was facing upwards.

'Right, now that little excursion into Scorpion World is over, let's get back to the internal exam,' Jack said.

His voice sounded shaky.

'You OK, Doc?' Kat said.

'Not a massive fan of scorpions, to be honest,' he said. 'I spent my gap year in Botswana. One morning, when I was getting dressed, I tipped up my boot – standard practice – and this bloody great black scorpion fell out. The guides said they could hear my screams from across the camp.'

Kat was impressed. First, he'd been nice to Abby, then he'd admitted to a little weakness. And there'd been that emotional outburst after he'd PMed the girl who'd died in the bombing. Was this a new side of Jack Beale? If it was, she approved.

'PM40, please, Ash,' he said.

Ashleigh handed him a large-bladed scalpel and without preamble he sliced deeply into the skin at the right shoulder.

Abby coughed, mumbled something, and rushed for the doors.

Jack looked up, just for a second, and made eye contact with Kat. She found she couldn't read him. But for her part, she was a little saddened that Abby had fled before the PM proper had got underway.

Being sick in a bucket was one thing. But to actually leave the room? It was a disappointing reaction from the peachy-keen PC, especially as she seemed to have her sights set on a career in plain clothes.

The post-mortem over, Kat went to find Abby.

She found her standing by the Golf, her head bent over her phone, smiling and scrolling. What the hell, was she checking her socials? Kat had expected more.

'Hey, Abs,' she said as she approached. 'How are you feeling?'

Abby looked round and hurriedly closed whatever app she'd been so interested in a minute before.

Her face crumpled. 'Oh, God, boss, it was awful. I don't know how you can stand it. That stink, and then when Dr Beale cut into that poor bloke's body with that massive blade. I thought I was going to throw up right there.'

'I told you that's what the bucket was for,' Kat said, trying to hold her irritation in check.

'Yeah, but I was, you know, embarrassed.'

'But you didn't come back, Abs.'

'I couldn't, could I? Everyone would look at me.'

Kat frowned. Had she misjudged Abby? Was she really more concerned about her self-image than gaining actual experience at the literal sharp end of homicide? Yes, uniforms might see more 'DBs' *in situ* than plain-clothes cops, but that meant nothing if you couldn't hack the actual work of investigating murders. Had

Abby fallen for the supposed glamour of homicide work without thinking about the grisly realities? She wouldn't be the first. Kat tried again.

'Look, it's tough, I get it. But if you're serious about the work, it's just one of those things you have to get used to. One way or another. Tom was the same. He chucked up in an empty sharps bin, but after that he was fine.'

'I'm sorry. It won't happen again.'

Kat sighed. Wondering whether she'd be comfortable giving Abby another opportunity. 'It's fine. But something in there made me think. Come on, we'll talk while I drive.'

In the car, Kat voiced the thought that had formed in her mind as she had walked back from the mortuary. Something Van had said in one of the endless discussions they'd had about his team's future.

'What's the name of the Al Jumairi sovereign wealth fund? The one that's buying the Eels?'

'Hold on, I'll check,' Abby said, unlocking her phone. 'It's Scorpio Investments.'

'That's what I thought. So, on a scale of one to ten, how likely is it that the murder by scorpion venom of a journalist is connected to a deal he was investigating involving a fund called Scorpio?'

Abby went silent for a few seconds. 'Eight?' she said, cautiously. 'I mean, I know it's obvious but there are other possibilities. Aren't there?'

Kat shook her head. 'It's a ten, Abs. A solid ten. It has to be. Coincidences like that don't just happen. I mean, yes, maybe if it happened in Botswana, where our revered Dr Beale took his *gup yah*,' she said, using a posh drawl for the final two words, 'I'd buy it. But Middlehampton? No. I mean, it's not as if scorpions are exactly wandering around town like the rats down by the canal, is it? The bloody thing must have been imported, surely?'

'I guess we'll never know.'

Kat flicked a glance at the young woman sitting next to her. Really? That was her response. 'Well, no, we *will* know, because we're going to find out. This is our first concrete piece of evidence, and we are going to run it into the ground.'

'Oh, yeah, right, of course. Sorry. I just meant, you know, it's a bit odd.'

'"Odd" would just about cover it, mate. No, the real question is not *if* they're connected but *how*. And why, given that the link is so obvious, did whoever did it choose that particular MO?'

'To point the finger at the Al Jumairis?'

Despite her misgivings a moment ago, Kat thought that Abby had at least reached the obvious conclusion. But what if it was too obvious? Maybe it was a double bluff. The Al Jumairis deliberately using the scorpion because no sensible copper would think they'd choose something so obviously linked to them.

As she drove, rolling this thought around in her head, Kat realised something else.

They had the time of death. But what they actually needed was the time of poisoning. It had to have been shortly before Pete's 999 call. So before 21.32 p.m. on Tuesday.

They needed a timeline.

Chapter Twenty-Seven

Kat stood in front of the team's murder wall – a long, deep whiteboard, that was now scrawled with a rudimentary timeline. She tapped each point with the pen she'd just used.

'At some point, presumably not long before half nine on Tuesday, Pete Vaughan pulls on a pair of Arabic-style slippers. As we now know, the right one contains a scorpion. It stings him between the toes and, in agony, he calls 999 at 21.32,' she said. 'At 9.51 p.m., which is a pretty decent response time given the bombing, the paramedics arrive, break down the door and find Pete on the floor, unconscious. He's taken to A&E, stabilised and then moved into the ITU. He regains consciousness on Wednesday at 11.06 a.m. But, sadly, he dies shortly after that, at 11.39 a.m. when the attending doctor pronounces recognition of life extinct.'

'ROLE,' Abby muttered. Just like Tom had done in his first week. Trying to impress the boss with their knowledge of the jargon.

'Now, normally in a murder investigation, time of death is critical because we can organise all our CCTV searches, door-to-doors and so on using that as a reference point,' Kat said. 'The murderer has to be on the scene to commit the crime. But here, they were long gone when the death actually occurred. So what do we need?'

'We need to know when Pete put the slippers on,' Abby said, looking around at the other three. 'He pushes his foot in, disturbs the scorpion, and then it stings him.'

Tom shook his head. 'That only gives us another variant on time of death. What we really need is the time when the killer put the scorpion into the slipper. That's as close as we're going to get to the time when the murder was committed.'

'Tom's right,' Kat said, noting that Fez and Leah were both nodding. 'So we need to check the house, and talk to Dalma, see if they'd had any break-ins in the days before he died. Leah, how's her alibi looking?'

'It's solid. She appears on the restaurant's CCTV through the evening. We picked her car up on council-operated cameras on the drive home as well.'

'Yeah, bab, but now we know the MO, that doesn't matter, does it? That's just an alibi for time of impending death,' Fez said. 'You know, when he was stung. We need alibis for time of—' He shrugged. 'What do we call it, Kat, time of placement?'

Kat nodded and wrote up a few new labels on the timeline. 'Let's call the three critical moments TOP, for time of placement, TOS for time of sting, and TOD for time of death,' she said. 'TOP is when the crime was committed.'

'How long can a scorpion lie dormant inside a slipper?' Leah asked.

'Good question,' Kat said.

'Unless they're hunting for food, scorpions love to just curl up and sleep. A bit like cats,' Fez said. 'Footwear is perfect. It's warm and dark and defendable.'

'The human Wikipedia has spoken,' Tom said with an ironic tip of his head.

'Encyclopaedia Britannica, please,' Fez said with an answering smile. 'My parents spent more than they could afford on it for their annoyingly precocious son.'

Thinking they'd need the services of a 'scorpionologist' or whatever the correct term was, Kat was about to start assigning tasks when a voice interrupted her.

'DS Ballantyne? Is that you? Acting SIO on the Peter Vaughan case? I was told I'd find you here.'

She looked past her team to see a pair of perfect cheekbones crossing MCU towards her corner.

The woman who'd won the genetic lottery spoke in a clipped upper-class voice that had Kat visualising horses, country houses and Swiss finishing schools. She sported the sharpest hairstyle Kat had ever seen outside the pages of a magazine. The textured pixie cut perfectly set off wide-set grey eyes that radiated confidence, breeding and – more than either of those other attributes – a fierce intelligence.

She stopped in front of Kat, a willowy figure in a navy V-necked jumper over a crisp pink-and-white striped shirt, tailored grey trousers and a pair of navy crocodile-patterned moccasins with gold snaffle bits Kat just knew would be handmade. Leah was checking her out unashamedly, and Fez and Tom weren't shy about looking this vision up and down.

'Victoria Palmer, MI6,' she said, shaking Kat's hand in a firm, bony grip. 'Don't repeat that or I'll have to kill you.' She smiled. 'Joke. Actually not a joke. I *will* kill you.'

Kat smiled, half in amusement, half in bewilderment. How old was this woman? *Late twenties, tops*, she decided. 'Not if I kill you first,' she replied.

Palmer threw back her head and laughed loudly, setting a few heads turning. 'I think we're going to get on famously,' she drawled.

'So, you're probably wondering what the hell a spook is doing poking her beaky little nose into your little murder investigation.'

'What – because I'm just some bumbling local plod, you mean?' Kat said, keeping her smile in place. 'Let me guess. You're here because someone in the Home Office got nervous about the proximity of a delegation from a Gulf state to a terrorist incident, and the murder of a journalist investigating the deal they're here to sign?'

Palmer clapped her hands delightedly. 'Oh, we are going to have *such* fun, Kat, I can just tell.' She beamed at Abby and the three DCs and dropped her voice through about five social registers. 'Your *guvnah* is a righ' old 'oot, ain't she?'

'She is, but she's also in the middle of a murder briefing,' Kat said, suddenly tiring of the pantomime. 'Was there something specific you wanted, Ms Palmer?'

She widened her eyes. 'Well, for a start, I want you to call me Vicky. Ms Palmer is so formal. You make me feel like I'm back at school. Zermatt was hell on earth, believe me. But more specifically, I want to know how you're getting on?'

'Can I ask why?'

Vicky tapped the side of her nose, which was, far from being beaky, perfectly proportioned and a little uptilted. On another woman, Kat would have suspected plastic surgery. This looked to be simply the product of generations of breeding.

'You *could*,' she said, drawing the word out and then winking. 'But then . . .'

'. . . you'd have to kill me. OK, I get it.'

Kat should have hated the young agent on sight. Or on hearing. They were so different. In education, in social class. In job, for God's sake! Even physically: a catwalk model versus an everyday mum-bod even netball couldn't prevent from softening with each passing year. And yet, something in Vicky's playful manner chimed with Kat. She sensed another of those bright, sparky personalities she always warmed to. Like Liv.

She filled Vicky in on what they knew about Pete Vaughan's murder, and the potential suspects and their motives. Vicky listened attentively without once interrupting. When Kat fell silent, she still said nothing.

Finally she nodded sharply. 'Thank you. Eminently concise. Here's what *I* can tell *you*. I don't know if it will help. Desert Sun have a history of committing terrorist outrages. Usually, though, in the Middle East. This is the first time they've mounted an operation in Europe.'

'I have it on good authority that they're *not* responsible,' Kat said.

Vicky arched one perfectly shaped eyebrow. 'Really. How fascinating. From whom?'

'I can't say.'

'Ohhh, right. A confidential human intelligence source, eh?' Vicky turned to the others and dropped into her mockney accent. 'Your *guvnah's* got 'erself a *chiz*, ain't she?' Then back to Kat and her own cut-glass tones. 'I'm willing to bet on my horse rather than whichever local hack you've been talking to, Kat. And mine says it *was* Desert Sun. It's sort of what I do, after all.'

Wondering, with a twinge of anxiety whether MI6 had monitored her meeting with Dawn in the pub, Kat tried another tack.

'What about my theory that Pete's murder is linked to the Al Jumairah sovereign wealth fund?'

'Well, obviously it's *linked*, but perhaps only linguistically. In my experience, state actors tend to go for lab-produced toxins. Our friends in Moscow, for example, or Pyongyang,' Vicky said. 'This MO – is that the right word? I love learning new bits of lingo – well, doesn't it strike you as just the tiniest bit baroque?'

'Like sending a swamp adder to climb down a dummy bell pull,' Fez said.

Victoria spun round to face him. 'Another Sherlock Holmes fan, I see, DC Mohammed. How delightful,' she said, beaming, before turning back to Kat. 'Tearing ourselves away from literature for a moment, Kat, I wonder whether the coincidence isn't just a little *too* convenient, if you take my meaning?'

'It had occurred to me. It could be an attempt to frame the Al Jumairis for a crime with a less *baroque* motive. Money, sex, drugs.'

'Sounds like a Saturday night at mine,' Vicky said, grinning wickedly. 'You were at the Powerhouse on Tuesday night.'

'My husband and son were there. I went to get them. Try to, anyway. They made their own way out.'

'Men can be so resourceful, can't they? How *are* Ivan and Riley? Not too shaken up?'

'They're fine,' Kat said, not wanting to share anything personal with Vicky, even if she was impressed by the twenty-something agent's research into her team and her own background. *Spies will be spies*, she thought.

'Tell me, what's your take on the bombing?' Vicky leaned closer and dropped her voice to a theatrical whisper all five officers could clearly hear. 'I know our friends from the Met are doing their best, but honestly? I've seen blue-arsed flies with more organisation.'

Kat smiled. The woman was clearly very intelligent, but all the matey play-acting was too pat to be anything other than an act. Whether it was just for her, or part of Vicky's regular shtick, she had no idea. But it was funny all the same and she got a great vibe off her. And it wasn't every day a regional DS got to share theories with an actual spy.

'I think the CTC team *want* it to be terrorists. They're the hammer that sees every problem as a nail. It's in their name, after all. But there are things that don't make sense.'

'Such as?'

'Why issue a warning? And why no shrapnel? From what we've learned, the bomb wasn't high-explosive. Why? The main effect was noise, smoke and fire damage to the property. Although two people were killed in the aftermath.'

Vicky pooched out her lower lip. 'Leaving aside that fact, I'm inclined to agree. And it would be counterproductive to say the least to massacre innocent Brits to make a point against a foreign regime. Although terrorists aren't always models of rational thinking.'

'I don't think it was terrorism at all. I think it was a distraction put in place by whoever murdered Pete Vaughan,' Kat said. 'It threw the whole town, and our police force, into panic mode. Us four are literally the only people not working on the bombing. Have you heard anything else? Something that points away from that?'

'I'm afraid there's not much I can say, Kat. MI6, MI5, CTC? We all live in our little silos, and by and large we stay in them. But despite all that, I'll tell you one thing we all agree on.' Vicky cleared her throat theatrically and stood straighter. '"Punishment, that's the justice for the unjust." Saint Augustine, dontcha know? Would have made a half-decent copper.'

Leaving the assembled cops open-mouthed at this final verbal flourish, she turned on one expensively shod heel and left the room. 'Lovely to meet you all. Leah, Fez, Abby, Tom. Keep me posted yes, Kat,' she called over her shoulder. 'I'm around.'

Kat caught Leah giving Fez a knowing smile. 'What?'

Leah turned back, the grin widening. 'You couldn't tell?'

'Tell what?'

'Kat, she was totally into you.'

'No she wasn't!'

'Must be my wonky gaydar then. It's like the crappy old Airwaves they give us.'

'Not everything's about being gay, you know? She was just being . . . I don't know, playful?'

Leah nodded. Frowned. '"Playful." Right. So the smile, the eye contact, the open posture, the way she ignored Fez and Tomski. All that, "I'll have to kill you, no I won't" stuff?'

Kat frowned. Really? Was the MI6 agent flirting? She shrugged. Maybe she was. It didn't mean anything. Her phone buzzed. A text from Darcy in Forensics.

It's stinger time!

'Regardless, although we now have a murder to solve, we do have the murder weapon. Leah, if you can switch off your gaydar for a minute, maybe you could find out all you can about the Eel Deal? My feeling is that's where we'll find our killer. Either a direct participant or someone with a vested interest in seeing it go through.'

'I'll get straight to it, yah,' Leah said, in a passable imitation of Vicky's upper-class drawl that had Abby frowning and Tom and Fez exchanging glances and trying hard not to giggle.

'You two overgrown schoolboys can help Leah, OK?'

Over laughter, Kat left them to it, taking Abby with her.

'Where are we going, boss?' Abby asked.

'Forensics.'

Chapter Twenty-Eight

Darcy and her small team were clustered at an examination table. The focus of their collective horrified gaze was the scorpion.

Lit by a halogen inspection lamp, the little creature crushed by Pete Vaughan's foot looked hardly big enough to have felled a child, let alone a grown man. Darcy greeted Kat then used two plastic rods to straighten the scorpion out.

'Can you measure it, Dougie? she said to a male CSI standing beside her.

He laid a clear plastic ruler alongside the mangled remains.

'It's 75 mm, end to end,' he said. 'Watch that stinger.'

'Don't worry, I am,' Darcy replied with a shudder. 'Horrible little thing.'

Kat leaned closer to get a better look. The scorpion's body was actually a rather lovely shade of pale lime green, with lemon-yellow legs. The stinger was curled over a little, just like every illustration she'd ever seen.

She stepped back from the table to give Abby more room and googled 'world's deadliest scorpion'. The same species topped every list she could find. Scientists in this field obviously had a sense of the dramatic. It was called the Deathstalker aka the Naqab Desert scorpion. And – this was interesting – it was native to the

Middle East and North Africa. Another link to the Al Jumairis and the bombing.

She read on, horrified by the toxic brew of neurotoxins in the venom and the havoc it would wreak on any poor soul unfortunate enough to be stung.

The article said that an adult human male could survive if he was healthy, but Pete had been a smoker and a drinker. This would have been, if not public knowledge, a decent bet given his physical condition.

Kat's little inner detective voice whispered to her, louder than ever. *Who would know his medical history better than anyone? His doctors. And his wife.*

'Do you think you can lift fingerprints off it?' Kat asked Darcy as she rejoined the little group.

Darcy wrinkled her nose. 'Maybe. We'll try fuming it. That's probably the best bet.'

'Any joy on the laptop?'

Darcy shook her head emphatically. 'As I suspected, we couldn't crack it. Mr Vaughan was nothing if not security conscious. We'll have to wait for Apple. I'm afraid that could take weeks.'

'Or months?'

'You said it, not me. But yes.'

After sending Abby back to MCU, Kat finally made the journey she hated most in Jubilee Place. The starting point varied but the destination was always the same. Carve-up's office. She was going to have to update him.

Preparing herself for another toxic dose of her line manager's animus towards her, she took the stairs back to the fourth floor.

Carve-up's office door was closed, as was increasingly the case. Kat felt sure that since she'd thwarted his attempt to get her and Tom killed by Tim Paxton, he'd been avoiding meeting her in the open if he could manage it.

She'd have given anything not to be doing this, but he was the only ranking MCU officer directly working with the CTC team. It was her town that had been under attack, and he needed to hear what she had found out.

She knocked and entered, not giving him time to utter his usual 'Come'.

He raised his head from the pile of paperwork in front of him and regarded her with a baleful stare.

'What?'

'Pete Vaughan was murdered. The weapon was a deadly scorpion. A Deathstalker. They're native to the Middle East.'

He shrugged. 'So far, so David Attenborough.'

She stared at him. Was Carve-up really this dim? Surely he had to have some kind of smarts to have been made a DI? Or had her father pulled strings to get his tame DC booted upwards through the ranks?

'Do you need me to join the dots for you, Stu? The Al Jumairis are in town for a week buying Middlehampton FC. Their money is held in a sovereign wealth fund called Scorpio,' she said, adopting a precise, scholarly tone she'd heard the old pathologist, Dr Feldman, employ with students. 'An investigative journalist trying to expose *corruption*' – she leaned hard on that word, but if Carve-up noticed he gave no sign – 'at the heart of the deal is murdered using a scorpion you can literally find in the Al Jumairah desert. On the same night as a bomb detonates in Middlehampton. Then we get a statement saying Desert Sun did it, a journalist telling me they didn't, and an actual spy, who I'm inclined to believe, saying they did.'

'Whatever. Thanks for the update, now run along and find out who wanted your hack dead. I've got a terrorism incident to solve.'

'Take it to Sharon.'

He looked up at her from the document he'd started reading. 'Pardon?'

'She needs to know.'

'No, she needs solid, reliable intel. Which she's not going to get from some over-ambitious DS with her eye on my office.'

'Fine. I'll tell her, then.'

He jumped to his feet and rounded his desk. 'Absolutely not. I'll do it. But forget about getting a pat on the back from Critchlow. You keep your distance, you hear me? I'll take this new intel to her myself.'

Kat left the office before Carver had a chance to get any closer. For his safety, rather than hers.

She needed to see a man about a scorpion.

Chapter Twenty-Nine

Seething from the encounter with Carve-up, Kat drove over to the university.

It turned out that the man she wanted to consult wasn't a 'scorpionologist' but an arachnologist. Dr Milo Smith was a specialist in all things eight-legged including spiders, ticks and the wonderfully named 'vinegaroons'. These last ones turned out to be scorpion-like creatures able to squirt acetic acid from their nether regions.

Kat presented herself at the biology department, where a briskly efficient secretary informed her that Dr Smith was on annual leave, and wouldn't be returning for three more days. Kat considered asking for a Zoom meeting, but evidentially she really needed Dr Smith to see the scorpion in the scaly, chitinous flesh. Thwarted, she booked an urgent meeting with him for 9.00 a.m. the following Monday.

She returned to Jubilee Place to ask Fez to try and hunt up another forensic arachnologist. Half an hour later he showed up at her desk with a long face.

'Sorry, Kat. There's only one other I could find and he's in Belize leading a field trip. Golden jumping spiders, if you're interested.'

Shaking her head, she called over to Tom. 'Any news on Pete's financials, Tomski?'

He scooted over on his swivel chair. 'Dalma's account of their finances checks out. No assets to speak of apart from the house, which is pretty heavily mortgaged. Nothing worth killing over.'

'Thanks. We'll rule that out as a motive then.'

'Which points the finger more firmly at his story on the Eel Deal.'

'Indeed it does.'

Wanting to brainstorm ideas to move the investigation forward, she called the team into a huddle. Abby sat directly in front of Kat like an over-eager child in a junior-school classroom.

'What do we think?' Kat asked, employing a neutral, open question to set the ball rolling.

She had her theory, and they all knew it, but it was dangerous to get tunnel vision on a case.

'It's obvious,' Abby piped up. Kat's heart sank. It was exactly the sort of phrase Carve-up would use, usually just before getting things monumentally arse-about-face. 'Someone who stands to gain financially from the takeover murdered Pete Vaughan to stop him publishing a story that could potentially derail the deal.'

'Yes, but this is early days. Maybe not the golden hour but close. My mentor had a saying. "If someone's stolen your ice cream, look for seagulls before polar bears".'

'Nice,' Fez said, with an appreciative nod.

'Thank you. In other words, if the wife's been murdered, look at the husband. If the husband's been killed, look at the wife.'

'But she's got an alibi,' Abby said.

'Which we know doesn't cover the critical point, Abby,' Tom snapped. 'Look at the timeline. Kat said we need alibis for TOP, yes? Time of placement. Not time of death. Or even time of stinging.'

Abby flushed and looked down at her notebook.

'I hear what you're saying, Kat, and I'm not saying we tool up for a polar bear hunt,' Fez said, perhaps to give Abby some time to recover her composure. 'But as a point of interest, our local multi-millionaire, John Morris, and his wife, stand to book a £331 million profit from the sale. Just saying, our kid.'

'Point taken. I'm saying we still need to cover the obvious bases before we get into conspiracy land,' Kat said, suddenly angry all over again with Carve-up's dismissive tone when she'd briefed him.

Leah opened her notebook. 'I've been looking into the key players. Aside from the Al Jumairis buying, and the Morrises selling, you've got the directors of Middlehampton Development Corporation. It's a limited company set up by the town council. Without their agreement, the whole deal goes nowhere. You've got Don Byatt, he's Middlehampton Council director of planning. Cory Whittaker, she's director of finance. And Kirsten Blake, the leader of the council. Reuben Starling MP sits on the MDC board as a non-executive director.'

'Is that all of them?'

Leah looked off to one side. She looked uncomfortable. Why? Kat soon found out. Wished she'd kept her big mouth shut.

'The other non-exec is Colin Morton, CEO of Morton Land. He's there because of all the property investment the Al Jumairis are talking about. They're an integral part of the deal. The council is issuing planning permissions for everything from a new retail park to social housing.'

Great. So her dad was involved. Of course he was! Where there was money, and construction, and the powerful elite who ran the town, you'd find Colin Morton. Kat's heart sank. He was there on the wall in her home office, a connection to the unexplained deaths of her half-sister's parents. He was there when Kat and Fez discussed Carve-up's corruption. He was bloody everywhere! Every time something dark happened in Middlehampton, her father was there, with his hand on the light switch. Could he be involved in Pete Vaughan's death, too?

Sending the team to their desks to start researching the list of people involved in the deal, Kat went back to thinking about the Deathstalker scorpion that had fatally poisoned Pete Vaughan.

Where had the murderer got it from? A pet shop? A zoo? A private collector? Or, as she'd surmised earlier, had they imported it? How easy would that even be? Surely for a creature so deadly it topped every list of the world's deadliest scorpions, there'd be all kinds of controls.

But her thoughts jumped the tracks. Not only did she need to find out the source of the scorpion, she also had to determine how the killer had managed to get it into Pete's slipper.

As she wondered how it had been done, her phone pinged. She picked it up, hoping it would be Van. She'd been messaging on and off all day but he'd been stuck at MGH waiting to be discharged.

hi honey im home

Smiling with relief, she called him.

'Hey, lovely. How are you? Are you OK?'

'I'm fine. Still got a sore throat, but they signed me off half an hour ago. I had to wait for ages while they found my paperwork.'

'Oh, darling, I'm so pleased. I can't wait to see you.'

'Me, too. I phoned your mum to let her know Riley and Smokey can come home. She actually sounded disappointed. I think she's been enjoying having them there.'

'I'll call her to thank her. Oh, God, Van, I'm so happy! Look, I'm in the middle of things, but I'll be home as soon as I can, OK? We'll open a bottle.'

At 4.00 p.m. that afternoon, Kat rang the doorbell at the Vaughans' house. Abby stood beside her, clutching her notebook like a talisman.

The door opened. The person standing there wasn't Dalma but her FLO.

'I was just leaving,' the FLO said. 'Dalma's in her study.'

'How does she seem to you?'

She put a finger to her lower lip. 'I think she's trying to avoid thinking about it by burying herself in work. She's just suppressing all her emotions. She's gone really cold. I've seen it before, Kat. It never ends well.'

Kat entered and led Abby through to Dalma's downstairs home office, which was located at the rear of the house overlooking a small unkempt garden.

They found Dalma studying a text on the screen of her laptop and then peering at the pages of a large book that appeared to be an Arabic-English dictionary.

'Hi, Dalma,' Kat said quietly, not wanting to startle her. 'It's Kat, and I've brought a colleague.'

Abby stepped forward. 'PC Abby Greene. I'm sorry for your loss, Mrs Vaughan.'

Kat was impressed. It was a professional yet sympathetic tone and she'd managed it without fluffing the line. Maybe there was hope for Abby yet.

Dalma offered a stiff nod. 'You'll have to wait a second, I need to just find a word that means tempestuous but without the sense of a sea storm. I've been struggling with it for ages.'

Abby shot Kat a puzzled look. Kat shook her head in return. Hoped Abby would understand. The FLO had been right on the money. Here was a woman suddenly widowed in the most awful way and unable to process it.

'Dalma, we really need to talk to you about Pete. I've got some news and some questions as well, I'm afraid.'

Tutting loudly, Dalma slammed the heavy book shut. She spun round in her chair. 'Fine. I wasn't getting anywhere with it anyway. Have you found out who murdered Pete?'

'Maybe we could talk in the kitchen, where there's a little more space. Abby could make you some tea.'

The process of decamping to the kitchen and getting tea sorted took five minutes. Once they were all seated round the table, Kat turned to Dalma.

'Pete was poisoned by a scorpion sting. A variety called a—' She stopped herself just in time from using the popular name. 'A Naqab Desert scorpion. We found it in his slipper and I'm wondering whether you noticed any signs of forced entry to your house in the couple of days or so before Pete died?'

'No, nothing like that.'

'You're sure?' Abby asked.

'We both work from home. I think we'd have noticed.'

Dalma had been frowning as they spoke. Why? Was it the unusual nature of her husband's death?

'I know it's a pretty strange sort of weapon, but there's no doubt,' Kat said.

'It's not that. Although I agree it is strange. I thought people just used knives or guns. No, what I mean is, it can't have been in his slipper. Pete didn't own any. He hated them. He always walked around barefoot in the house no matter how much I tried to get him to protect his feet,' she said. 'He was always stubbing his toes. I even bought him some for his birthday. They're still in the box.'

Kat's cop whiskers twitched. She pulled out her phone and showed Dalma a photo of the embroidered slippers with their distinctive upturned toes.

Dalma's frown deepened. 'The ones I bought him were regular sheepskin. Like soft boots. Those are *babouche*.'

'What did you say?' Kat asked, a memory pricking her brain.

Dalma pointed at the image on the phone's screen. 'Those! They're traditional Arabic slippers called *babouche*.'

Kat recalled Pete's dying words. He hadn't been stammering 'buh-buh-*bomb*' or 'buh-buh-*booze*' – he'd been trying to say '*babouche*'.

The murderer hadn't broken in and placed the sleeping scorpion in the slippers. He'd found a way to get the slippers into the house with the scorpion already in place. Although as fast as that conclusion arrived in her brain, a puzzle followed through the open door.

If Pete hated slippers, going so far as to refuse to wear a pair his wife had bought for his birthday, why on earth had he put on a pair that had been delivered to the house?

Chapter Thirty

After getting Dalma's permission to search Pete's home office, Kat and Abby went upstairs and into the small back bedroom. It stank of tobacco smoke.

'Chaos' would have been a poetic word for the mess of documents, books, files, folders, crumpled balls of paper, discarded sweaters, a toppled-over acoustic guitar and dozens of notebooks, pen pots and dishes full of cigarette butts that littered every surface.

'What are we looking for, boss?' Abby asked, pulling on a pair of purple nitrile gloves.

Kat put a hand to her forehead, dismayed by the mess in the cramped study. 'Something that gives us a clue as to the origin of those *babouche* slippers.'

'Where the hell do we start?' Abby hissed.

'You start by the window, I'll start by the door.'

They turned away from each other and Kat dropped to all fours to start rummaging among the stationery and reference materials scattered over the carpet.

From here, she had a view under the over-laden desk. And what she saw gave her hope that they wouldn't be spending the next three hours sifting through thousands of pieces of paper.

Lying against the wall was a cardboard carton roughly the size and shape of a shoebox. She leaned under the desk and retrieved it.

On the upper surface was a printed courier label. It was addressed to Pete and bore all the usual marks and insignia including a QR code. But no company logo. That was interesting. The bottom had been slit with a very sharp knife and the flaps pulled apart. Inside, there was a note printed on a small slip of paper.

> *To Pete, in gratitude for the work you are doing to expose the wrongdoing of the parasitic Al Jumairi royal family. Wear these and think of us. Your friends in Al Jumairah.*

She turned to Abby.

'I found it, Abs.'

'Oh, thank God for that. I thought we were going to be here all night. Not that that would have been a problem. I mean, I totally want to prove to you I can do the job.'

Kat smiled. She felt she could afford to, now that pieces of evidence were starting to stack up.

'It's fine, Abs. Sometimes you do have to pull an all-nighter, and sometimes a messy bloke just drops the evidence on the floor.'

Returning to the ground floor they found Dalma at the kitchen table, drinking mint tea, the smell invigorating after the stuffy, smoky interior of Pete's office.

'Dalma, do you have a doorbell cam?' Kat asked, holding the carton in her gloved left hand.

Dalma nodded. 'Pete insisted. He said it helped screen out door-to-door salesmen.'

◆ ◆ ◆

The footage had caught a courier calling at the house on the night of Pete's 999 call. Above a blue face mask that some people in Middlehampton still wore, his skin colour suggested someone of Arabic heritage. He was wearing a black jacket, the logo of a local firm – Middlehampton Express – on the right breast pocket, although there was no sign of a van in the background. The video was time-stamped 21.22 p.m. Ten minutes before Pete called the ambulance.

What must have happened beyond the view of the doorbell played out behind Kat's eyes like a secondary video feed.

Pete checked the video app on his phone. Saw it was a courier. Left what he was doing and went downstairs to sign for the parcel.

He thanked the courier, closed the front door and took the box back upstairs.

Was he worried about the contents of the package? He was an investigative journalist who was on the receiving end of frequent death threats, so he must have checked before opening the box. Kat realised they'd never know this part of the story, occurring as it did away from any cameras.

Maybe Pete hadn't taken the threats seriously. Thinking those who made them were just keyboard warriors. Either way, he'd opened the box from the bottom. A basic security precaution. Amid the detritus of his work, he'd reached in and lifted out a beautifully embroidered pair of *babouche*. He would have read the note and maybe smiled.

But if he hated slippers so much, why did he put them on?

She asked Dalma. At her answer, kicked herself for not figuring out the reason already.

'My husband worked from the purest of motives, DS Ballantyne. But he wasn't a saint, and his sin was vanity. He loved the thought of being a saviour. He probably felt flattered.'

Kat nodded. She found it easy to imagine Van being similarly tempted. Most men had a weak spot, usually sex-related, but sometimes ego – if they were different things – and a smart con-artist could always find a way to exploit it.

'In the days before he died, Dalma, did Pete mention meeting anyone?' she asked. 'A source, for example? Especially someone from Al Jumairah? Or had he received any threats specifically telling him to leave off his investigation into the Eel Deal?'

Dalma shook her head. 'No. Not that it would have made any difference. I said he wasn't a saint, but he truly believed in what he was doing. And now . . .' Her lower lip trembled and her chin pruned. 'And now, he's gone. My beautiful man is gone!'

Her face crumpled, her lips stretched over her teeth, and she emitted an unearthly wail of grief that made the hairs on Kat's arms erect. All Kat could do, all she could ever do in the face of overwhelming grief, was to offer Dalma a small, cellophane-wrapped packet of tissues. The latest in a series that would, she knew, have no end until she handed her badge back. And she was a long way from that day.

As she tried to comfort Dalma, Kat felt that here was an innocent woman. Evidentially, Kat knew her gut feeling counted for nothing. But as the lead investigator, she had to prioritise leads, and right now, Dalma Vaughan was falling to the very bottom of her list of potential suspects.

Which meant other people rose higher.

Chapter Thirty-One

Back at the station, Kat took the carton to Forensics, where she handed it to Darcy.

'I think this is how the murderer got the scorpion to Pete,' Kat said, handing over the note in the glassine bag she'd slid it into before leaving Dalma.

Darcy took the box from Kat and turned it over in her hands. 'The label looks genuine. Surely they didn't just send it like an Amazon delivery?'

'The courier was wearing a Middlehampton Express uniform. I couldn't see a van in the doorbell cam video, but for now I'm assuming he was genuine. The murderer could have bribed him to deliver the parcel.'

A chilling thought occurred to her. Had the killer murdered the courier for his uniform? There'd been no calls of an unclothed dead body being discovered in the last couple of weeks. No anxious enquiries from the firm's MD or HR manager. The courier had to be genuine. But she made a note to speak to the company anyway.

Darcy frowned. 'I suppose you want it analysing. Prints, DNA?'

'Ideally today.'

'Hmm. Ideally I'd have dinner with Tom Hardy tonight. I've got DI Critchlow on my case, literally, asking for help with artefacts from the bombing. I'll do my best Kat, but you're looking at days, possibly weeks.'

'Really, Darce? You can't VIP it? For me? Your favourite DS?' Kat sidled closer. 'I know, I'll be a stylish supermodel who wants to skip the boring queue, and you be a nightclub door-lady.'

Darcy grinned.

'Even for her. But I tell you what I can do. Come back in half an hour and I should have the results from the scorpion. That I *did* let past the velvet rope.'

◆ ◆ ◆

Kat huddled the team, explaining she really wanted to read Pete's article-in-progress, but with the laptop stalled in Digital Forensics, that could take months.

'Did he have any hard copies in his office?' Tom asked.

'Shit! I didn't even think to look.'

'Me and the boss were focusing on how the murderer got the scorpion into Pete's hands,' Abby said defensively. 'I didn't see anything except research notes. Although, that study. It looked like a bomb had hit it.'

The air thickened. A deafening silence descended over the small group.

Kat glanced at Abby, who was, once again, blushing furiously.

'Well, that killed the mood,' Tom said.

A second of quiet followed. Then Fez snorted, spraying coffee into the air. Kat shook her head as Tom leaned back, a sardonic grin on his face. If he'd caught the look Abby was aiming his way, he'd have been hastily strapping into an anti-stab vest.

Sometimes when you were dealing with the very worst things human beings could do to each other, gallows humour was the only safety valve you had. Firefighters and medics were the same. You just had to make sure you were out of sight of the public's smartphones. Nobody wanted to see a social media post captioned 'Murder cops laugh as town mourns'.

Kat patted the air for silence.

'OK. Easy, easy. Let's get back to the case.'

'What about the rest of the house?' Leah asked. 'Could we search?'

'What would be the point?' Abby asked. 'It's hardly likely, is it? If he was that secretive, changing his password regularly, all his precautions, he'd hardly leave it all lying about.' She turned to Kat. 'I'm right, aren't I, boss?'

Fez said, 'No, bab, *Leah's* right. Naz is co-writing a text book about paediatric cleft-palate surgery. She always prints out each draft because she's paranoid about losing it all.'

'Yeah, but I checked his desk,' Abby said. 'The filing cabinet. I didn't see anything.'

'Naz keeps *her* printouts in a drawer, but it's not top-secret stuff like Vaughan was working on,' Fez said. 'Maybe he hid it.'

Kat thought that could be worth looking into. 'I'll send a search team over in the morning. Tom, I want you to look at CCTV, ANPR, doorbell cams, dash cams, the usual. From the Vaughans' house out in all directions for a radius of five miles. I want all Middlehampton Express vans flagging, especially if the driver is non-white. And, Tomski, can you check with the firm? See if they've got a record of the package on their system. Between you and Leah we ought to be able to shake something loose.'

'What shall I do, boss?' Abby piped up.

Kat saw an opportunity. Abby had been pushing for 'proper' detective work all week, so here was her chance.

'I want you to track down and talk to the courier who delivered that parcel to Pete Vaughan.'

'I won't let you down,' Abby said as she grabbed her bag and car keys.

Shaking her head at her eager-beaver rookie's determination to prove herself, Kat ended the briefing and went back to Forensics, praying Darcy had recovered a print, even a partial, from the dead scorpion. Was the impatient nightclub patron about to get past the velvet rope?

She was not.

The scorpion bore no fingerprints at all.

Swallowing her disappointment, Kat started looking at the second part of her question. She knew how Pete's murderer had got the scorpion into Pete's hands. And he'd used psychological insights into Pete's character to get him to break a long-held preference and put on the *babouche*.

But where had he sourced the Deathstalker?

Back at her desk, Kat read the profile Leah had compiled on Gerald Hynde, the elderly man who'd begun sending Pete abusive messages after his wife had died.

As she read, she became surer that Hynde wasn't a genuine threat. His emails, beautifully spelled and punctuated and grammatically precise, if a little on the fussy side, were more the unhinged ravings of a grief-stricken husband.

However, one thing that did pique her curiosity was a sentence in the eleventh email Hynde had sent.

'Perhaps you find yourself able to laugh off my poison-pen letters. Beware! Peter Vaughan, Investigative Journalist *par infériorité*. I can do a lot worse.'

Had he decided to switch from the metaphorical to the literal? Gone out and bought a poisonous scorpion to add real menace to his poison-pen campaign?

She ran a quick search for exotic-pet retailers in Middlehampton, first, then Hertfordshire.

She had a list of five.

Kute Kritters, Middlehampton

Claws 'n' Jaws, Welwyn Garden City

Dancer Exotics, Abbots Langley

Exotix-R-Us, Hemel Hempstead

Scuttlies, Watford

They'd all need calling. Kat looked around for Abby then swore as she remembered she'd sent her off after the courier.

'I'll just have to ring them myself then, won't I?' she muttered.

Four minutes later, she put the phone down on the fifth virtually identical message informing callers the shop was closed until the following day. She tried the shops' websites next. They all had online stock lists. Two stocked scorpions – Claws 'n' Jaws and Dancer Exotics – although neither one appeared to have any Deathstalkers. But maybe they were updated in real time, in which case they might have had one and sold it to the murderer.

Kat decided to visit them in the morning. That left zoos. She called up the site for the local zoo at Whipsnade. They did have arachnids, but no Deathstalkers. The same went for London Zoo, and Battersea Park Zoo.

Kat shook her head. She couldn't see a zoo being lax enough to let a member of staff walk off with a deadly scorpion. Those things had to be locked down tight. And anyway, it felt like a stretch.

Tom arrived at her elbow a little while later.

'Bad news. I just got off the phone with Middlehampton Express. The package was a total fake. The QR code was for a children's soft-play area in Watford. They've got no idea how it got into their workflow. But it does look like the guy who delivered it was genuine. They've not got a record of sickness, annual leave or unexplained absence for the driver on that route.'

Kat paused, working through the chain of events in her mind.

'So, our guy puts the slippers inside a box, fakes up an official-looking label and then, in order to make sure it gets to Pete Vaughan's, finds a way to get it into the courier's van.'

'No. It would have to be into his hands. If it wasn't on the worksheet, it wouldn't get delivered,' Tom said. 'Maybe he bribes him. Or even threatens him. Or his family.'

'Good point, Tomski. So even if we can't trace the package back through the courier company's system, there's a moment where the murderer gets it into the hands of the driver. Which we might find on CCTV. Thanks, Tomski. This is good work.' She looked up at him, wanting to check in. 'You all right?'

'Yes, why? Shouldn't I be?'

'No, no. It's fine. If you're good, that's good.'

He frowned as he turned away. 'Whatever.'

Surer than ever her bagman was lying about his state of mind, she resolved to keep a closer eye on him from now on.

Abby arrived back an hour later. She hurried over to Kat's desk and in a breathless tone, delivered a report.

'I caught up with the driver who dropped off the package. I found him in South Lane. I asked him if anyone gave him a parcel or tried to get him to deliver something off the books. Honestly? His English wasn't great, but he didn't seem to be hiding anything. He showed me his work app. Everything looked kosher. I did push him, boss, but his daughter was caught up in the Powerhouse bomb, poor thing. He was distracted, to put it mildly.' She shrugged. 'I'm sorry it's not much.'

'OK, thanks, Abs. You did your best.'

Two hours later, fatigue making her eyes feel sandy and hot, she called it a day. On the drive back to Stocks Green, she smiled. Thinking of Tom's impression of a surly teenager reminded her that she had the genuine article at home.

Chapter Thirty-Two

Kat pushed through the front door, excited to see her boys again.

'Hi, I'm home!' she called out.

Smokey reached her first, barking delightedly, his claws skittering on the hall floor as he banged into her shin, stubby little tail wagging so hard she feared it might detach. She crouched to scratch him behind the ears. Then straightened and went into the kitchen.

Van was working at one end of the table, Riley at the other, his head almost touching an exercise book. Kat hugged Riley first, then Van, bestowing kisses on the tops of their heads.

'Oh, my God, I've missed you both. Are you OK? How was it staying with Granny and Grandpa, Riley?'

He shrugged. 'Good, I guess. Granny's like a dealer for chocolate cake. I might be addicted.'

'Did you call her?' Van asked.

'Damn, I forgot,' Kat said.

'I did. Thanked her from all of us.' He was smiling, but then his expression slipped. 'You all right, love? Not to be horrible but you look like shit.'

'I love you, too. Actually I feel like shit, too. Any wine open?'

Van rose to pour her a glass from an open bottle of Pinot in the fridge, then stopped as a coughing fit overtook him. Kat ushered him back to his chair.

'I'll do it.'

She poured herself a glass of wine then sat beside Riley.

'How was school today?'

Riley shrugged.

'He's been like that since he got home,' Van murmured.

Kat put an arm around her son's shoulders. He was filling out. She felt another of the tugs of emotion she'd been experiencing recently whenever she talked to him. He was growing up fast. Turning into a man. Even if it was a man with periodic outbursts of volcanic temper. But this was something else. Something darker. She thought she knew what.

'Is it the bomb, Riley? Or because Dad was in hospital? Is it troubling you, lovey?' she asked quietly. 'Because it's troubling me.'

Silently he nodded. Then his shoulders hitched and a sob escaped his lips.

'Oh, Riley!' Her heart filled with pain for him. Fourteen-year-olds shouldn't be dealing with the shock and terror of bomb attacks. It wasn't right. 'Hey, hey. It's OK.' She gathered him into her arms as he turned towards her.

'No! It isn't! Casey Hall was in my year at school. And those bastards killed her. And her dad. *Her* dad didn't go to hospital. He died!'

'I am so sorry, Riley. Was she a friend?'

'No, but it doesn't matter, does it, Mum? Those evil bastards murdered her. They should all be killed. You should catch them and then they should be killed for what they did.'

She looked over the top of his head at Van, who was standing by Riley's other side, a hand laid on his heaving back.

He opened his mouth and she knew he was going to say something about the death penalty. She shook her head quickly and mouthed, 'Not now.'

This wasn't the time for that kind of debate. And anyway, as she murmured soft, reassuring words into Riley's hair, she couldn't help feeling that a small part of her agreed with him.

Later, after Riley had gone up to bed, Kat and Van cuddled on the sofa. No TV, just one of her old nineties albums playing quietly on the stereo. Smokey padded in from the kitchen and stood in front of Kat, his little tail wagging. He whined softly.

She smiled. Patted the sofa cushion next to her. 'Come on, then.'

Smokey backed up, bunched his haunches and then leaped. His landing wouldn't have won any prizes and he had to pedal frantically with his back legs to make it to the sanctuary of the cushion. Kat grabbed him and hauled him on to her lap and began scratching him behind his ear. He grunted contentedly, wriggled his weight down on to her thighs and then gave himself up to the serious business of receiving attention from his mistress.

'How's the case going, love?' Van asked. 'Yours, I mean, not the other one.'

'I'm not sure there *are* two cases,' she said.

She told him what Dawn had shared about the nature of the device the bomber had used.

'What do the Met lot say?'

'Nothing. They just swan around the station acting like they own the place.' She twisted round to look at him. 'How are *you* doing? Are *you* all right?'

He frowned and sighed. 'Yeah. Yeah. I'm OK. Apart from this cough. The doctor said it might take a week or two to go away completely. It was pretty frightening at the time, but, you know, we got out, and you were there, which was unexpected. But then having to go to hospital. It's just . . .'

'I know. You don't think something like that is ever going to happen to you. Or your home town.'

'Exactly. But you're going to catch them, love, aren't you? The people who did this?'

'Well, technically, that would be Sharon the Terrible and her team of suited-and-booted counter-terror Robocops, but yeah, we are.'

They played some more music, then Kat let Smokey out for his final wee in the back garden, and settled him down for the night. Van came to find her and they went up to bed early. After a long cuddle, she fell into a troubled sleep.

◆ ◆ ◆

Kat woke with a start. She'd been dreaming of Jack Beale. He was performing an autopsy in a hotel bedroom and she was watching. In her underwear. Shaking her head to dispel the not entirely unpleasant mixture of guilt and desire, she checked the time – 5.15 a.m.

She dressed and showered, neither of which woke Van, then took Smokey out for a walk. They headed up to the Gallops, a big field bordering the village of Stocks Green. Nobody knew for sure how it had got its name, but the consensus was it had something to do with the broad grassy swathe along one edge.

She let Smokey off the lead and he dashed away, a blur of darkness in the pre-dawn light. Then he barked, and she smiled. He only yelped with that particular tone when he met his best friend.

She peered ahead and caught a flash of white – Lois, a black-and-white lurcher owned by Barrie Price, an ex-copper.

If Lois was here, then Barrie would be ahead somewhere.

She met him a few minutes later, standing and watching as the two dogs played in the field.

'Morning, skip,' he said as she came to stand beside him. He held out a white paper bag. 'Allsort?'

She selected a blue jelly covered in tiny bobbles and popped it into her mouth. The bobbles crunched between her teeth releasing an intense hit of aniseed.

'Thanks,' she said around the sweet. 'You're up early.'

'It's my age, skip. These days I count half six as a lie-in. What about you? I suppose you lot are all working flat out on the bombing.'

'Actually, that's a bunch of counter-terror cops from the Met. We're looking into the murder of a journalist. Pete Vaughan. Ever come across that name?'

Barrie nodded. 'Yes, but not in the line of duty. He was a reporter, wasn't he? Wrote those big exposé pieces the *Echo* runs now and again.'

'That's him. He was working on a piece about the Eel Deal when he died. I think it was murder *and* I think it was related to the bombing.'

Barrie popped another sweet – orange, black and white sandwich layers – between his lips. Chewed ruminatively. 'Someone didn't want him to finish his story.'

'It's a possibility. But there are two men who'd been sending death threats and making a lot of noise on social media about him. The article might have been convenient for them.'

'What's your gut telling you, skip?'

'Oh, Barrie, mate, I wish I knew.' She lifted her chin to the middle of the field where Smokey and Lois were running round in circles, yelping delightedly. 'Sometimes I worry I'm chasing my tail like those two over there.'

He shook his head. 'You've got a detective's instincts, skip. Whatever the specifics, your gut's telling you *something*. Go with that. And maybe let the boys, and girls, from the smoke worry about the bomb, eh?'

Maybe Barrie had a point. After all, Jack had confirmed her instincts. The scorpion in Pete's slipper proved he'd been murdered. At the thought of Jack, her dream came back to her. Cheeks flaming, she glanced guiltily at Barrie, glad the early hour meant he couldn't see her blush.

She took her leave and walked home. She planned to take Van breakfast in bed. And see if he was well enough for a bit more than just a cuddle. But when she arrived it was to a note propped against the kettle telling her Van had gone to get a prescription filled.

Work, then. And a visit to Dalma Vaughan.

Chapter Thirty-Three

At 9.00 a.m., Kat called Dalma.

'I'd like to send a couple of officers round to search your home. Pete might have recorded a threat without showing you that he'd received it.'

Dalma answered immediately. 'No.'

'Can I ask why not?' Kat asked.

'I'm staying with my sister and her family. Brighton. I won't be back until Monday.'

'Then could I send an officer down to you to collect your keys?'

'No. I'm sorry. My life is already in a mess without Pete. I don't want my home violating: it's all I have now.'

'I understand, Dalma,' Kat said. 'But without a full search of your house, we might miss a clue that will help us solve his murder.'

'I said no!'

Kat flinched and held the phone away from her ear. Did Dalma have something to hide? She'd wondered about her earlier, after all. If Pete had been murdered in a more straightforward fashion, Kat would have told Dalma she was empowered to search without a warrant. But that would be less than helpful right now.

'I'm sorry. I shouldn't have shouted,' Dalma said, her voice catching. 'I have to go. My niece and nephew want me.'

The line died. Kat sat back and pocketed her phone. She frowned. The woman was in the stranglehold of grief, but was there another reason she was being so unhelpful?

Kat checked her emails to find Jack's post-mortem report sitting in her inbox.

> *Cause of death:* *a) pulmonary oedema, cardiac arrest and multiple organ failure, caused by . . .*
>
> *b) scorpion venom*
>
> *Manner of death:* *homicide*
>
> *Time of death:* *11.39 a.m., 19/3/25*
>
> *Observations:*
>
> *Blood alcohol at time of death would have been around three times the legal limit. I also found traces of benzodiazepines in his system. The combination of tranquilliser and alcohol would have severely impaired his judgement and ability to assess risk.*

Kat paused. Whether he'd taken the tranquilliser recreationally, because of an addiction or genuine mental health condition, or even if it had been slipped into his drink, Kat saw a man who had already been disorientated by alcohol and prescription medication. Easier to kill by any method, let alone one as stealthy as that used by his murderer.

She continued reading.

> *P Vaughan was a heavy smoker, which would have contributed to risk factors. Lung damage, tar build-up.*

Beginnings of coronary heart disease (CHD). Also a drinker. Liver was damaged by alcoholic hepatitis. Build-up of fatty tissue around the internal organs. However, none of these health conditions, at the time of death, would have been fatal on their own, and all could have been reversed with the correct medical treatment. Mr Vaughan cannot be considered to have been a 'dead man walking'. In my opinion, he was murdered.

The scorpion venom clearly had a delayed effect. We can conclude that although the time of death was 11.39 a.m. on 19/3/25 (when his fatal heart attack happened at MGH in the presence of Mrs D Vaughan, DS Ballantyne and several medical staff), the time he was murdered was 21.32 on 18/3/25 (when he called 999 and told the operator, 'They killed me').

Kat closed the document. Jack was wrong. Pete Vaughan had been a dead man from the moment the murderer got his deadly package into the hands of the courier. She called her team together.

'Despite what the Middlehampton Express courier told Abby, I want everyone helping Tom look for the moment when that parcel found its way onto his van or into his hands. All I need is a single frame and we'll have the killer on camera, and, by the way, an accomplice. I also want to know how whoever did it got hold of that scorpion.'

'If it was the Al Jumairis, maybe one of them brought it in to the UK,' Fez said.

'I'm going to see them straight after this, but yes, good. Can you look into that, Fez? Talk to the security people at the airports. See how easy that would be.'

'What about me, boss?' Abby asked.

'We've got our local exotic-creature dealers, and I'll be talking to them later, but we need to eliminate the possibility the scorpion came from elsewhere in the UK. Call every exotics dealer, every zoo and any other sources anyone you speak to suggests. If you turn up a purchase of a Deathstalker, follow it up. When you've finished, help Tom with the CCTV.'

'But that's grunt work. It'll take ages!' Abby protested. 'I could be much more useful if you'd let me come with you to interview the Al Jumairis.'

Behind Abby, Tom raised his eyebrows at Leah. The body language was easy to read. *'Look at the new girl trying to impress the boss.'*

Kat could hear her own mentor, Molly Steadman, suggesting, kindly, that DC Ballantyne would be better off learning to walk before trying to run. Although at least DC Ballantyne hadn't abandoned a post mortem in order to check her socials.

'It's not grunt work, Abby. It's important. And if you do find the purchaser of a Deathstalker, that could well be our murderer.'

Abby brightened at that.

'Sorry, boss. Of course. I'm on it.'

When the briefing was finished, Kat called Dawn Jacobs for a favour. She told Kat the Al Jumairi delegation were staying at a new luxury hotel in old Middlehampton called The Garland.

Kat called the hotel and introduced herself. 'I'd like to speak to a member of the Crown Prince's . . .'

Yes, what *did* she call the people surrounding a visiting billionaire? His entourage? Retinue? Given the reason for the Crown Prince's visit, she settled on 'team'.

'Certainly, DS Ballantyne. Please hold.'

Classical music played.

And played.

Kat doodled an eel facing off against a scorpion.

And played.

She wasn't a fan of classical. Became even less enamoured as the piece started playing from the beginning again.

The phone clicked. She sat upright.

'This is Saleem Elwani, DS Ballantyne. I am the Crown Prince's head of security. Is this about the bombing? Do you have someone in custody?'

'I'd like to talk to the Crown Prince about the bombing, certainly. To see if he has any insights into Desert Sun.'

It wasn't true. But Kat thought the ruse would yield more results than suggesting she wanted to talk to Elwani's boss about Pete Vaughan's murder.

'His Royal Highness has already spoken to the Metropolitan Police about the bomb. He has nothing further to add.'

'I'm sure he has, and on behalf of my colleagues I'd like to thank His Royal Highness for his help. But there are other matters that fall within my jurisdiction. Please could you ask His Royal Highness whether he will agree to meet me?'

Elwani sighed deeply. It sounded put on to Kat. An attempt to show this interfering local detective that she was an amateur playing on a pitch designed for professionals. She was already chafing at the strangled diplomatic language she was using, and didn't appreciate being patronised by Elwani.

'I'm happy to wait,' she added.

The classical music returned. Kat sighed, genuinely.

After a few minutes, the line clicked and clonked.

A man's voice. The same deep timbre and accent as Elwani's, but laced this time with affability rather than suspicion. 'DS

Ballantyne? I believe you wish to speak to me. I am Sheikh Omar bin Hamad Al Rashid.'

After Elwani's tough-guy talk, the sheikh's friendliness left Kat struggling to find her way back into the conversation. 'I was hoping to talk to you about the bombing.'

'Of course. Anything to help the police. Come to my hotel for tea this afternoon. I am in meetings for most of the day but would 4.00 p.m. suit you?'

'Thank you. Yes. That would be perfect.'

'Until then, DS Ballantyne.'

Kat's hopes rose. Not least because under the legitimate cover of investigating Pete Vaughan's murder, she was also a step closer to the terrorism case, which had almost robbed her of her husband and son.

But before she could talk to the Sheikh, she had some creepy-crawlies to visit.

Chapter Thirty-Four

Glass tanks lined the walls of Claws 'n' Jaws.

Half-dreading, half-curious about what sort of beasts she might encounter, Kat peered into one. It appeared to be empty. Just a curling bark shelter and some leaves. She shaded her eyes and pressed her face closer.

A large, black, hairy spider hurled itself at her. The thump as it bounced back off the glass was audible.

Kat recoiled, heart pounding. 'Oh, Jesus!'

'You've met David, then?'

Kat turned to see a lady in her sixties standing watching her, a crooked grin on her face. Pulse still jittering along, Kat left the display and approached the counter.

'Are you the owner?' Kat asked, producing her warrant card.

'Eileen Forster. I take it you're not here to buy. I can let you have David for a very reasonable price. He's quite beautiful, isn't he? Goliath birdeater. Although that's a misnomer. He prefers cockroaches.'

Kat suppressed a shudder. 'I'll stick with my Cairn Terrier, thanks.'

'Each to her own. So, what can I do for you?'

'I'm interested in Deathstalker scorpions. Do you stock them?'

Eileen shook her head. 'People on the forum love talking about them but they're hard to sell. I might if it was a special order.'

'Forum?' Kat prompted.

'I'm the admin for an online forum called UglyBugs. Ironic really, because our members all find their pets beautiful. But the normies go all squeamish,' she said, giving Kat a searching look, as if spying an example of this lily-livered species. 'I've got the next best thing – a Black Spitting Thick-tailed scorpion. Want to see it?'

Not wanting to be saddled with the 'normie' label, Kat nodded. 'Sure. Why not?'

Eileen led her to the far side of the shop. In a large glass tank with a sandy floor and a few rocks and dead twigs, another bark shelter leaned against the back wall. No need to peer in to find this tank's occupant. The scorpion was motionless, dead centre on the sand. It resembled Kat's inner picture of what a scorpion would look like. Much bigger and shinier than the little Deathstalker in Darcy's specimen cabinet. And possessed of a big, bulbous, black stinger curved over its glossy back.

'How would you go about buying one of these?' Kat asked.

'You'd need a DWA off the council first. Then I'd want to satisfy myself you knew what you were doing. These need a lot of care. People rock up here thinking it'll be cool to own a scorpion, or a tarantula, but then they neglect them, the poor little things die and they come back here wanting a refund.'

'What's a DWA?'

'Dangerous Wild Animal licence. Yours from East Herts Council for £421.'

'Do you know a man called Gerald Hynde? Older gentleman. A widower. He might be a collector.'

Eileen shook her head. 'Doesn't ring a bell. I know all my customers by name. Well, the ones who come in in person. I do a lot online these days.'

'But you have a customer database, yes?'

Eileen's eyes narrowed. 'I do, yes.'

'Could I have a look? See if he's on it?'

'Well, now, there's rules about that sort of thing, aren't there? GDPR? Privacy?'

Kat had expected this response from the moment Eileen had squinted at her like she was planning to steal a spider. And she had a workaround that was often effective.

'There are,' Kat agreed. 'But you could look for a G Hynde and just tell me if he's on there, couldn't you? All you're sharing with me then is the fact of his existence, not his personal data.'

Eileen wrinkled her nose. She folded her arms too. Not promising. 'Rules are rules,' she said.

'How about a Nick Chater?' Kat asked, not really expecting anything more than another brush-off.

Eileen's eyes narrowed. 'What's he done?'

That was interesting. So she knew the Supporters' Trust founder.

'Nothing. Why do you ask?'

'Look, it's nothing, OK? Nick's a regular customer. A *good* customer. His mum and I were friends,' Eileen said. 'She's got dementia now. Early onset, poor love. Breaks my heart to see her like that. Anyway, Nick was a bit of a tearaway when he was younger.'

Wanting to know whether a teenage tearaway had evolved into an adult killer, Kat tried to find a way to get answers without losing a boot in the GDPR swamp. Maybe sharing a small piece of information would loosen Eileen's tongue.

'I'm investigating a murder. The victim was poisoned by a Deathstalker. I'm trying to find out whether anyone local bought one recently.'

'You mean Nick?' Eileen exclaimed, eyes widening. 'No! He'd never.'

'So he hasn't bought a Deathstalker from you?'

'No!'

'It would be really helpful, Eileen, if you'd let me have a copy of your stock lists and purchasing records. Just so I can eliminate Nick from our enquiries.'

Eileen placed her hands down on the glass countertop. Smiled. 'Of course I will.'

'Thank you.'

'When you bring a warrant.'

Thwarted, for now, Kat thanked her and left. Next stop: Dancer Exotics.

◆ ◆ ◆

Kat entered the shop, setting a bell jangling overhead. Where Claws 'n' Jaws had been spick and span, Dancer Exotics was a little more rundown. The posters on the walls were faded and the floor was scattered with sawdust. A man sat behind the counter, speaking in a low voice into his phone. *Fiftyish and shiftyish*, was Kat's first-glance assessment. He looked at her, smiled briefly and held up a couple of fingers. Mouthed 'Won't be long.'

She approached the counter and waited for him to finish the call. When it showed no sign of concluding, she held up her warrant card. His eyes widened.

'Gotta go, mate. There's a . . . customer here.'

He smiled at Kat. Properly this time. 'Sorry, Officer. Old friend. I'm Phil Dancer, owner of this fine exotic-creature emporium. What can I do for you?'

Kat went through the whole speech again, asking if Phil knew Gerald Hynde. Drew her second blank of the morning. Asked about online sales.

'Don't do it. I know I should. My son's always on about e-commerce, but I prefer seeing people in the flesh. Old school, I suppose.'

'Me, too.'

'Yeah, well, I suppose it comes in handy, your line of work. Spot the liars more easily.'

'And the truthful ones,' she said with a smile, revising her initial impression of him. He seemed happy to help.

'Fair play,' he said.

'How about a Nick Chater?' she asked, wondering whether she'd need to bring her real-world, lie-detecting skills into play. But there was no need.

'Yeah, I know Nick. Bit of an oddball. Obsessive, you might say.'

'About what?'

'Middlehampton FC and his pets.'

'What kind of pets?'

'You name it. Snakes, spiders, lizards, stick insects.'

'How about Deathstalker scorpions?'

Phil pulled his mouth down. 'I don't touch them. Literally. Vicious little things. Give me a nice tarantula any day. A Mexican Red-Knee or an Antilles Pink-Toe. They're really popular. Turn them over faster, make better margins.'

He willingly showed Kat his sale-and-stock records on his ageing desktop PC. No scorpions.

'Where would I get a Deathstalker if I wanted one?'

He drew in a long, noisy breath through his nose. 'Well, maybe Germany. There are sites there that'll ship to the UK. But I doubt you'll find a shop in the UK selling them,' he said. 'They're just too bloody dangerous.'

Another bust. She thanked him and left.

On her way to see Gerald Hynde, Kat called Abby and asked her to talk to the council and find out all she could about the DWAs they'd issued over the last five years. Specifically to either Gerald Hynde or Nick Chater.

Chapter Thirty-Five

Kat knocked on Gerald Hynde's door.

The house – a Victorian terrace – had seen better days. The paint on the window ledges was grey and flaking, and weeds grew through the gravel in the tiny front garden.

The man who answered was in his eighties. He looked wary, tired, with the haunted stare Kat had seen in the faces of burned-out cops who took medical retirement.

He invited her in for a cup of tea.

Sitting opposite him, in a sitting room that felt like a museum to a long marriage, she saw a rounded indent in the sofa cushion beside him. He rested a liver-spotted hand there.

'I am investigating the murder of Pete Vaughan, Mr Hynde,' she said. She glanced at a folded copy of the local paper on a side table. 'Did you see the story in the *Echo*?'

'Of course I saw it. And I can't honestly say that I'm sorry. Does that shock you, Detective Sergeant?'

'Nothing very much shocks me anymore,' she said, meaning it, 'although a bloody great spider just launched itself at me. That came as a bit of a surprise.'

'You've come about the letters, I suppose,' he said resignedly.

'I have. Can you tell me what happened to your wife? I hope it's not too painful.'

'It is painful. But I'll tell you all the same. Esther died from an acute asthma attack after inhaling epoxy resin fumes in an industrial accident at the Hunter Chemical Industries factory in Middlehampton. We'd been married for fifty-one years.'

It sounded like a recitation; something he'd said so many times to so many people, it had become an unvarying sentence he could probably deliver first thing on waking.

'Pete Vaughan contacted me about the accident because he was writing a piece on lax health and safety in Middlehampton factories. He led me to believe he could expose Hunter Chemical Industries and get a criminal investigation launched for corporate manslaughter, but nothing came of it.'

'You wrote death threats to Pete, care of the *Echo*.'

Fire ignited behind Hynde's watery blue eyes. 'I was grieving! I know it wasn't a particularly *elegant* response, but death isn't elegant, is it?'

'I totally understand. Grief really twists you around until you don't know which way is up,' Kat said. 'But you kept it up, Gerald. For years.'

'They meant nothing. I would never have followed through on them. What do the young call it? Venting? I was venting, that's all.'

'I need to ask you for your whereabouts for the last week.'

He stared at her as if she'd asked him to solve a cryptic crossword puzzle without looking at the clues.

'I'm an eighty-three-year-old widower. My children live hundreds of miles away. All my friends are dead. I shop at the Co-op on Bridge Street. I go to the doctor. I visit Esther's grave. The rest of the time I sit here and I watch television. Is that what you want to hear?' He held bony wrists out towards her, veins and tendons distending his crêpey skin. 'Are you taking me in?'

Kat shook her head and thanked him for the tea. 'I'll see myself out.'

The alibi – if you could glorify it with such a label – was patchy, even if bits did check out. But really? An eighty-something murderer? She didn't buy it. The motive was there, but it was weak compared to the others on her whiteboard. And she had no evidence he'd actually procured a Deathstalker. Still less evidence that he'd found a way to insert a bogus package into the courier company's distribution system.

The single point in the other column, the one labelled 'Gerald Hynde's Guilt', was the MO itself. At least poisoning someone with a scorpion didn't involve brute force, or require you even to be in the room with the victim.

On the list of people of interest she kept in her head, a 'Fantasy Football League' of murder suspects, she moved Gerald Hynde to the free transfer list. It wasn't him.

Maybe her next interviewee would be more of a star striker.

Chapter Thirty-Six

Ahead of her, Middlehampton FC's stadium loomed. The stands rose over the end of the terraced street like a cruise ship in a port town. Kat parked and headed for the main entrance.

Leah had sent her a brief profile. Nick was a groundsman there as well as the president of Middlehampton Supporters' Trust. He also had criminal convictions for being drunk and disorderly and low-level drug possession with intent to supply. Which meant that Eileen from Claws 'n' Jaws hadn't been entirely honest with her. A little more to Nick's past than being 'a bit of a tearaway'.

Inside the ground, she asked at the front office where she could find Nick. Learning he was 'on the mower', she made her way down a long flight of concrete steps. Roughly in the middle of the pitch a figure was driving a large, black machine. This had to be Nick Chater.

She walked towards him, struck by the distance from touchline to centre spot. She discovered a newfound respect for the players who ran from one end to the other every match day. The netball courts she and her Malbec Mafia teammates played on were roughly fifteen by thirty metres.

Chater wore orange ear defenders. He glared at her as she approached and signalled for him to cut the engine. He did so, snatching the defenders off his head and shouting at her.

'What the hell do you think you're doing? I have to get this ready for tomorrow.' He pointed at her boots. 'You'll ruin it.'

Could it really matter that much, given the fact twenty-two players would be tearing the grass up with their studs the very next day?

She held up her warrant card. 'DS Ballantyne, Hertfordshire Police. I need to ask you a few questions.'

'Can't it wait? I've got the other half to do yet.'

'Not really, Mr Chater, this is a murder investigation.'

Chater looked nervous. He glanced past her. She turned her head, expecting an irate head groundsman or whatever the senior grass man would be called, but there was nobody there. She turned back to Chater.

'It's about Vaughan, isn't it?' he asked.

'Why do you say that?'

'Oh, come on, let's not play games. This is about my social posts, isn't it?'

She ignored that. You never answered their questions. That wasn't how things went.

'I'd like you to come in to Jubilee Place police station to attend a voluntary interview under caution, Mr Chater. You'd be free to leave at any time, and you'd also be entitled to have a legal representative present.'

'What if I don't want to? Like I said, this pitch won't mow itself.'

'Then I will have no option but to place you under arrest on suspicion of murder.' She hit him with a low blow. 'Maybe with your record, you'd prefer to avoid that.'

Grudgingly, he agreed. 'But can I at least finish the pitch?'

'Get someone else to do it.'

◆ ◆ ◆

Nick Chater waived his right to have a lawyer present.

'I've got nothing to hide.'

Kat thought if he knew how many suspects who'd uttered the same threadbare line had subsequently gone to prison, he might have thought harder. His loss.

Feeling the need to throw Abby a bone in the shape of some interview experience, Kat had asked her to attend.

'To listen only. Leave the questions to me. But you do the caution, OK?'

'Of course, boss. And thanks. I won't let you down.'

Abby seemed to have given up on calling Kat by her first name. And Kat didn't have the energy to keep trying. 'Boss' it would be for the rest of Abby's rotation.

Abby leaned forward. 'Nick Chater, you are voluntarily attending this interview in connection with the murder of Pete Vaughan. You do not have to say anything but it may harm your defence if you do not mention when questioned something which you later rely on in court. Anything you do say can be used against you. Do you understand?'

Kat winced as Abby fluffed her lines. Chater had noticed, too. She saw it in his eyes.

He smirked. 'I understand you just bollocksed up the caution. Nobody says, "used against you" anymore. It's "given in evidence".' He turned to Kat. 'Is she even a real detective?'

It was a well-aimed barb, but cops were used to smart-alec nominals. You just rode it out.

Abby hadn't got the memo. 'I'm not the one being interviewed about a murder, am I?'

Kat felt the disappointment keenly. One mistake in an interview was forgivable. But two? No. Bickering with a suspect was a real lapse of judgement. Correction, another lapse. Kat had no option: she laid a hand on Abby's forearm. Turned to Chater. Delivered the caution, correctly this time.

Ignoring Abby's laboured breathing, and worrying she'd made a mistake asking her to take part in the interview, Kat eyeballed Chater. Time to wipe the smile off his face. And to wrong-foot him.

'The bomb at the Powerhouse exploded at 8.30 p.m. on Tuesday. Where were you at that time, Nick?'

His eyes popped wide. 'What? I thought this was about Vaughan? Why are you asking me about the bomb? I'm not a terrorist!'

'Answer the question, please.'

'I was in the pub with a few mates from work. We saw the whole thing on the news.'

'Which pub?'

'The Coach and Horses on the Bramalls.'

'We'll need names and contact details of your co-workers.'

'Fine. You can have them.'

'Tell me about your disagreement with Pete Vaughan.'

Perhaps relieved to be on safer ground, and not looking down the barrel of a terrorism charge, Chater started talking immediately, his attitude suddenly gone. 'I disagreed with Vaughan's take on the Eel Deal. It'll be brilliant for the club, and for the town. It'll mean thousands of jobs, new homes, retail, more inward investment, the works. It's a win-win.'

'Not for Pete Vaughan.' Kat spread out a few sheets of paper where Chater could see them. 'These are screen grabs of a few of your tweets about Pete. They go a bit deeper than "disagreement", don't they, Nick? Let me read you a couple.' She picked up a sheet. '"Pete Vaughan—" Actually you used his Twitter handle and called him @PV_investigates but that's a bit of a mouthful. So, you wrote, "Pete Vaughan ought to drop his pointless crusade against the Eel Deal before someone drops something on him." So far, so mild. But then two days later, you wrote, "Pete Vaughan is a toxic waste of space. Shut the" – I'm going to say "eff" here – "up and crawl back under your rock." This one's the really dark one, though. "Stop trying to kill the deal, Pete Vaughan. What goes around comes around. Maybe it's not the deal that'll be dead in the water." What did you mean by that?'

He shook his head. She'd rattled him, she could see that. 'It doesn't mean anything. Just trash-talk. Twitter's full of it.'

'Yes, I know. It's why I'm not on it,' Kat said. 'But it's hardly nothing, is it? The clear implication is that if Pete didn't stop digging into the deal, he'd end up dead. Did you want him dead, Nick? Did you kill him to preserve the deal and all those win-win benefits?'

'No!' he said in a panicky over-loud voice. 'Of course I didn't kill him! I just gave you my alibi, didn't I?'

'Which is worthless,' Abby interjected. 'He was poisoned on Tuesday night but technically the murder happened earlier.'

A guarded look entered Chater's eyes. Kat was furious. First Abby had bungled the caution, giving Chater an early advantage. Then she'd let him provoke her into an outburst. Now she'd blurted out a material fact about the timeline to a potential suspect. She needed to change the subject, get Chater relaxed again before pressing him.

'Tell me why you're such a fan of the deal, Nick,' she said firmly, holding him in her gaze and, beneath the table, pressing her boot down hard on Abby's foot.

'I'm a lifelong Eels fan, yes? I got my dream job at the ground. I run the Supporters' Trust. But I'm a realist. We're struggling. The stadium's hardly state-of-the-art. The big clubs, the ones with all the money, they're accelerating away. We need that kind of investment. In talent, management, coaching, facilities. Everything,' he said, spreading his hands. 'Vaughan was obsessed with "sportswashing".

He saw corruption and double-dealing everywhere. It was like this crusade with him. He kept turning over rocks looking for something bad to crawl out.'

Like a Deathstalker scorpion, Kat thought.

'Go on.'

He shrugged. 'In any case, even if the Al Jumairis are a bad regime at home, what does that have to do with MFC? This is a straight business deal. Everybody wins. I just couldn't stand by and watch him sabotage it for some high-flown idea about moral purity. I mean, get real. If you only took money from squeaky-clean investors, who does that leave?'

Kat had no intention of getting drawn into a philosophical discussion about international human rights. It was well above her pay grade and whatever opinions she did have, she wasn't going to get into them with a person of interest in a murder investigation.

Time to switch tack again. 'You're an Eels superfan, aren't you?'

He smiled. 'Man and boy.'

'Any other hobbies apart from football?'

He shrugged. 'Pub, like I said. Reading, the usual.'

'Yeah, but those are hobbies for "normies", aren't they?'

He tucked his chin in towards his chest, frowning. 'Sorry, I don't follow.'

'Do you like creepy-crawlies? Cute critters? Things with claws 'n' jaws?'

A scowl flickered across his face. But it vanished as quickly as it appeared. 'I have a few exotic pets, so what?'

'Which ones?' she asked innocently.

'Spiders, a couple of stick insects. A snake. Terrapins.'

'Any scorpions?'

His gaze flicked away from hers, to Abby, then back to Kat. 'No.'

'Do you have a current DWA?'

'Yes.'

Kat closed her folder. 'Thanks for coming in, Nick. Please don't leave Middlehampton until we advise you it's OK to do so.'

She had no legal power to keep him in the city, but saying something like that tended to put anyone with a guilty conscience on edge.

He got to his feet. 'I'm hardly likely to do that mid-season, am I? We're a man down at the ground so I'm working flat out.'

Kat stayed in her seat, asking Abby to escort Nick to the main entrance. When she returned, Kat met her at the door to MCU. 'Quick word in the ladies, Abs?'

Her eyes downcast, Abby preceded Kat down the corridor. Kat checked they had the loos to themselves before speaking. 'You can't let them wind you up, Abs,' she said, trying to keep her voice steady. 'We've all messed up a caution or some other bit of procedure. But you let him get under your skin. The moment that happens you let them take control of the interview. Make sure you don't let it happen again.'

'I won't, boss. I'm sorry. I just . . . He was being so sarky,' Abby said, on the verge of tears. 'I didn't mean to say "used against you", it just came out.'

'Little tip. Try cautioning yourself in the mirror. At home,' Kat added quickly. 'Do it ten times. Then ten more. Say it when you're loading the dishwasher or going for a run. Repeat until you're sick of it. It should be like muscle memory.'

Abby nodded. 'Thanks, boss. I will. That's great advice. So do you think he did it?'

'I don't know. If it means anything, I didn't get a vibe off him. But he collects creepy-crawlies, he clearly hated Pete's guts and I bet you his alibi will be as patchy as all the others.'

'So what now?'

'Go and give the others a hand. Make yourself useful.'

'What about you?'

Kat checked her watch. Isaac Handy's mum's funeral was at 2.45 p.m. She had half an hour and she really wanted to be there for him. Even if most other detectives at Jubilee Place thought he was 'a weaselly little scrote', Kat still had a soft spot for him. 'I have a personal matter to attend to.'

Kat led Abby back into MCU and called Leah over.

'Can you see if you can track the provenance of the slippers the scorpion came in?' Kat turned to Abby. 'I want you to check that Nick Chater has a current DWA. The holder has to list the animals they want to keep. If it says scorpion, we'll get him back in.'

'But what if the council cites GDPR?'

Kat sighed. 'Get creative. Tell them you're involved in an active murder investigation.'

Feeling once again that Abby's enthusiasm for plain-clothes work outstripped her appetite for actually getting on with it, Kat left for the funeral. At least she was already suitably attired.

Chapter Thirty-Seven

The early-afternoon traffic was heavy – a fact not helped by yet more roadworks in the centre of town. Sometimes Kat wondered whether the council had taken a five-year lease on the diggers and bulldozers and had to keep finding ways to use them.

She checked the time: 2.30 p.m. She could still make it, although when the car in front of her stalled at a temporary set of traffic lights she swore in frustration. Finally she reached Northbridge Crematorium and found a parking spot with five minutes to spare.

Mourners were clustered outside, chatting, waiting for the signal to go back in. Smoke issued from a tall chimney and as she watched it drift and dissipate in the breeze, she thought how insubstantial life was and yet people still tried to rob others of theirs.

Kat spotted Frank Strutt talking to a couple of old ladies. She nodded to him, receiving a brief answering tip of the head. Isaac was standing off to one side, wiping his eyes on a grubby handkerchief. Bony wrists protruded from the cuffs of his suit jacket.

She went straight up to him. 'Hello, Isaac. I'm so sorry about your mum.'

His eyes were red and a pearl of mucus hung from the end of his nose as he answered. 'Ah, thanks, Kat. It's good of you to be here. I know you've got a lot on your plate.'

She touched his shoulder. 'You OK? Is there someone here who's looking after you?'

He turned and indicated a matronly figured woman in a black trouser suit. 'My Aunt Tracey. Mum's older sister.'

'Good. I'll see you afterwards, Isaac, but I need to have a word with Frank Strutt.'

He sniffed. 'OK.'

Her heart went out to him. He'd loved his mother, of that she was sure. She wished her relationship with her own was as straightforward.

Frank spotted her coming and touched one of the old ladies on the elbow, making his excuses. He came to meet her in a small unoccupied patch of paving stones.

'Kat,' he said. 'Sad business.'

'Hello, Frank. I didn't realise you were a friend of the family.'

'I knew Donna quite well. We used to drink in the same pubs back in the day. I promised her I'd keep an eye on Isaac.'

'That's good of you, Frank. Tell me, have you heard anything about the bombing? Or Pete Vaughan's murder? I think they're connected.'

He jammed his hands deep into the pockets of his grey herringbone overcoat. Drilled her with a hard stare. 'I didn't appreciate being dragged out of bed yesterday by some goons from the Met thinking they're a SWAT team. Sue nearly had a bloody heart attack,' he said. 'I'm Middlehampton born and raised, just like you, Kat. Do you really think I'd blow up kids at a bloody pop concert?'

Telling Frank the truth was easy. 'Honestly, Frank? No, I don't, and I'm sorry. It's not the same as being rousted from your bed at whatever unearthly hour it was, but we're getting treated like a bunch of Hendon wannabes as well.'

'My heart bleeds.' He leaned closer. 'But, seeing as you do show me a modicum of respect, despite our obvious differences, I'll share something I found out with you. If you want to hear it?'

'Of course! What is it?'

'I had a couple of my lads ask around. See if anyone knew anything. You know, Kat. The kind of people wouldn't tell the police the time off an interview room clock. You remember Ray?' Kat nodded. Raymond Jeavons-Hume, Frank's fixer. 'Wednesday night, he had a chat with this bloke who handles bulk chemicals. Agricultural stuff mainly. Fertiliser, that kind of thing. Ray comes back to me and says this bloke sold a load of stuff last week to an Arab who said he wanted it for a – quote-unquote – fireworks display.'

Kat's pulse sped up. He was telling her Ray had spoken to a man who supplied bomb-making materials. Anger surged through her.

'Fireworks display? Jesus, Frank! And this bloke, he didn't think to tell us he'd helped a terrorist make a bomb that killed two people?'

He held his hands up, placatingly. 'No. That's not all of it. So the guy, the supplier, not the Arab, he says exactly that. And the Arab says, not to worry, it's all about noise and distraction, nobody's going to get hurt.'

'Did he get a name?'

Frank looked at Kat. Raised his eyebrows. 'That's a serious question, is it?'

'Fine. But this is a murder investigation, Frank. And a terrorist one, too. This guy Ray spoke to is involved in a bombing that killed two people.'

'I know. *He* knows. And believe me, he's cut up about it.'

'How about a description of the buyer?'

Frank shrugged. 'Arabic.'

'Seriously? No distinguishing features? Height, weight, clothing?'

'If I had something. A photo, maybe. You'd have to swear on your family's life not to share it with the Met.'

She was shocked. 'What the hell, Frank? It's my *duty* to tell them.'

'Is it? Or is it your duty to find who did it? I give you this, you can use it to find the guy. Arrest him, throw him in prison and chuck the key away. But *you* do it, Kat, not those Met arseholes who broke into my house and scared my wife half to death,' he said. 'And like I told you, the Arab said he didn't want to hurt anyone. So it's not terrorism, is it? Not really. It was all a distraction. Someone wanted you lot looking one way while they offed Pete Vaughan. That's what it looks like to me.'

It looked like that to Kat, too. But was she about to cross a line? Withholding evidence of a crime was already breaking the law. But to withhold it from the CTC team? No. That was a step too far. Except if she didn't she knew the photo would disappear. Frank would never talk to the Met. The identities of the man who'd sold the Arab the chemicals and the Arab himself would vanish like the smoke drifting in the cold damp air above the cemetery. And she *could* investigate the bombing herself.

'Show me,' she said.

He slid his hand inside his coat. It emerged holding an envelope, which he handed over. She slipped it into her own jacket pocket.

'You owe me, Kat,' he said.

'What?'

'I do you a favour now, you do me one in the future. It's how the world works.'

She eyeballed him. '*Is* it, Frank? Is *that* what you think? Why do I "owe" you for doing what any normal person would do as their civic duty?' She squared her shoulders. Frank Strutt towered over her and could probably lift her over his head from a standing start, but right then she didn't care. 'People died on Tuesday night, Frank.

People were murdered. Your right-hand man talked to someone who supplied bomb-making materials to a terrorist. This is so far beyond a quid pro quo.'

Her chest was heaving and sparks wormed round the edge of her vision. Anger surged through her at the casual way this gangster assumed they were simply trading favours.

Frank held up his hands placatingly. 'Look, maybe that was the wrong word to use, Kat. I'm sorry. Follow the lead. See where it takes you. If you get a result maybe just remember I helped you. We'll leave it at that. No harm, no foul, eh?'

'Fine,' she said.

Frank checked his watch and looked over Kat's shoulder. 'Time to go in. I hope you won't mind, but for form's sake I won't share a pew with you.' A beat. 'No offence.'

'None taken. It wouldn't do my promotion chances any good to be seen sharing a Bible with you either, Frank.'

They separated. Kat was still furious with Frank but she calmed down, eager to take a look at the photo that was burning her skin through the cotton of her shirt. She found a discreet corner, retrieved the envelope and slid out the photo. Black and white, grainy. From a security camera, obviously far from state-of-the-art. The man caught with a sheaf of banknotes in his hand had dark skin and hair, a beard and moustache. The angle made it hard to be sure but he seemed to be average height and weight. One of those desperately useless descriptions that members of the public, though eager to help, often supplied. She sighed, put it away and went in.

As the service progressed, and the celebrant talked about the importance of family, Kat's thoughts spiralled away down darker paths. For Frank, family was everything. His blood relations, and those who'd married into the Strutt family. He'd sooner go to prison than betray one of them. It was an old-fashioned standpoint, but as unshakeable as her conviction in the law.

And what of her own family? She pictured the whiteboard in her home office. She was convinced that Tasha and Connor Starling's deaths were linked to Tasha's business dealings with her father. She didn't care what the AAIB inspector's report said. Mechanical failures could be procured deliberately as well as accidentally.

The question was, by whom? And for what reason? She glanced at her watch. Not long before her appointment with the Crown Prince.

Her private investigation would have to wait.

Chapter Thirty-Eight

On a hunch, Kat took the *babouche* slippers to her meeting with the sheikh.

She arrived at the hotel at 3.55 p.m. and was escorted upstairs to the sheikh's suite. In an anteroom stood a tall, tough-looking man in a dark suit, white shirt buttoned at the neck, no tie. He nodded to her.

In his physique and bearing, he resembled the firearms officers at Jubilee Place. Had to be ex-military. And strongly built inside the clever tailoring.

'I am Saleem Elwani, head of security for His Royal Highness,' he said. 'I must search you.'

Kat hadn't been expecting this. She stepped back. 'I'm unarmed. This isn't America. We don't carry guns.'

He shrugged. 'I have my orders. If you wish to meet His Royal Highness, this is the procedure. He has many enemies. The Desert Sun terrorists are right here in Middlehampton, in case you hadn't noticed.'

She took a breath and raised her hands out from her sides. But at the first sign of anything dodgy, he would discover she remembered plenty from her unarmed defence tactics course.

The frisking was fast, thorough and professional. He donned a pair of black nitrile gloves, used the backs of his hands to brush down across her chest, and never once made her feel uncomfortable.

From a kneeling position, where he had just encircled both ankles with his hands, he stood and nodded to her. 'Just your bag and then you may go in.'

She handed the cotton tote bag to him and her own briefcase.

He opened them in turn, frowning at the sight of the *babouche* but saying nothing.

When he had finished, handing them back to her he said, 'I apologise. It is to protect the sheikh.'

'You're just doing your job. I get it.'

He held his right hand out to his side and nodded towards double doors. 'Please. Ladies first.'

She opened the doors and entered a room so large she gasped. A polished wooden dining table with ten chairs around it occupied one end. A sofa and three armchairs all in matching green leather clustered at the other end.

From the sofa rose a tall Arab man in traditional clothing. White floor-length robe in heavy cotton. A red-and-white headdress. And a doubled black rope binding to keep it in place. *Thobe*, *ghutra* and *egal*: Kat had looked them up before leaving Jubilee Place. He smiled, bright white teeth that had to be veneers splitting the dark mass of beard and moustache.

'DS Ballantyne,' he said. 'Welcome to my humble abode.' The smile widened. 'Actually it's not terribly humble, is it? My secretary makes all my travel arrangements. I think she worries I will suffer if the floor area doesn't exceed that of a football pitch. Please come and sit down. Are you thirsty? Hungry? I have tea and biscuits here. Very British, although maybe with a little twist.'

'That would be lovely, thank you.'

He poured tea from a tall silver pot into a glass encased in a silver metal cage. The aroma of mint filled the air. He passed it to her and held out a plate of tiny sugared biscuits, each studded with a blanched almond.

She took a bite of the biscuit. It tasted of marzipan.

He raised his eyebrows. 'Good?'

'Perfect.'

'And the tea?'

She sipped the steaming liquid. The taste of the steeped mint leaves was bold, not tannic – with no tea, it couldn't be – but more intense than the ancient mint teabags she occasionally resorted to at the station.

'If it's too much for you, try adding a sugar lump. I myself prefer it sweetened.'

She took the proffered silver bowl and tonged a brown sugar lump into her glass. Stirred it and tried again. 'It's good. I just wasn't expecting it to taste so strong.'

The sheikh smiled. 'That's because you are used to that dreadful packet stuff. Floor sweepings, my father calls it.'

She placed the glass on the low table between them. Time to begin. 'Thank you for making the time to see me, Your Royal Highness. I know you have a busy week here.'

'Of course,' he said. 'And please, drop the "Your Royal Highness" bit. Call me Zizou. My schoolfriends named me after Zinedine Zidane. I was a good football player. Not at his level, of course. But I like it.'

'Then I would like you to call me Kat. Would that be all right?'

'Of course. Zizou and Kat it is.' He laughed. 'Sounds like a pair of cartoon characters. Maybe we should have our own podcast.'

At the mention of the p-word, Kat's good humour dampened. Podcasts these days only made her think of Ethan Metcalfe and that was never a pleasant connection.

'Could I ask your opinion about something, Zizou?' she asked, reaching for her tote bag.

'Please.'

She withdrew the slippers in their plastic evidence bag and held them out. 'Could you tell me what you make of these?'

He took the bag from her and turned it in the light, examining them from every angle. 'They are very fine. The design is from my country. Have you had the Arabic translated?'

Kat cursed herself. She could picture the page in her policy book with her endless list of tasks to complete. The translation was on it, but with the worry over Van and Riley, and the spiralling connections between the murder of Pete Vaughan and the bombing, it had slipped through the net.

'Not yet.'

'May I?'

'Please.'

'It says, "He who would shake hands with a scorpion should wear gloves". It is an old Al Jumairi proverb. It is commonly taken to mean that you should protect yourself when doing business with shady characters.'

To Kat, the connection was plain. The proverb pointed to the Eel Deal. But why would Pete's murderer say it to *him*? Did it imply *he* was doing business with shady characters? Had he really been an investor while publicly criticising the deal? It would be a disappointment to his wife and presumably his editors.

But money was right up there with sex as a motive for murder. Perhaps someone had found out about his hypocrisy and killed him for it.

She filed this idea for now. It was just speculation and that was something she liked to ration herself.

'Have you come across an investigative journalist named Pete Vaughan?'

He inclined his head. 'I have seen one or two incautious social media posts. Mr Vaughan is not, shall we say, one of the deal's most fervent supporters.'

'He was preparing an article on the Eel Deal alleging corruption.'

'Was?'

'Mr Vaughan is dead. He was murdered the same night as the Powerhouse bombing.'

'I am sorry to hear that. He had family?'

'A wife.'

'Please send her my condolences.'

The sheikh's words were flat, rehearsed-sounding. Much like the standard, '*I'm sorry for your loss*' cops had to utter by rote. Why should they be otherwise if he didn't know Pete? Although Kat wondered whether someone as rich and powerful as the Crown Prince would really be ignorant of a vocal critic of his regime's attempts at sportswashing.

It was time to test the extent of Zizou's willingness to help the authorities.

'With the deal on the brink of being signed, any bad publicity would have been a problem for you. I can imagine you might have wanted him silenced. Perhaps permanently.'

Elwani stepped out from his corner, into her eyeline. 'That is an outrageous accusation! You dare to suggest His Royal Highness had anything to do with the journalist's murder?'

The sheikh smiled and waved his minder away. 'Relax, Saleem, Kat is only doing her job.' He turned back to Kat, still smiling, and shook his head. 'Wherever Scorpio Investments does business, there are those who want to stand in the way of progress. But there are swathes of sub-Saharan Africa, long considered unfarmable, where dams we have built now supply water. Minefields in South East Asia now cleared and free to have schools and hospitals built upon them. Even in the developed world, right here in England, our acquisition of Middlehampton FC will bring much needed jobs, social housing and prosperity.'

It was a nice speech. Kat imagined it wasn't the first time he had delivered it. But she wasn't finished yet.

'If Pete's report into the deal had exposed wrongdoing, the bad publicity would have stopped the deal from going ahead.'

He offered her a look mixing compassion with amusement. As if a child old enough to know better had suggested that Father Christmas was real. 'Listen, Kat. Mr Vaughan had every right to investigate and publish, free speech and all that? But preventing the deal from going ahead? No. Not even a leader in *The Times* could do that.'

He'd echoed Daniela Morris's words. Perhaps it was true.

'He was poisoned by a scorpion,' she said, watching him closely for a reaction. 'Pretty unusual way to kill someone for a British murderer.'

'Indeed. Although did I not read that you caught a serial killer who choked his victims with lavender-scented wheat grains? I am afraid when it comes to that gravest of moral transgressions, man's imagination knows no bounds.'

If he was hoping he'd wrong-footed her, he was mistaken. So, he'd looked into her background . . . Or more likely had someone do it for him. The big man standing in the corner, presumably. It didn't surprise her that he'd done this. A man with the sheikh's power would want to know everything he could about anyone poking her nose into his business.

She maintained a straight face. 'But it's interesting that the murder weapon matches the name of your own sovereign wealth fund, wouldn't you say?'

He smiled. 'What are you saying, Kat?'

'I'm just looking at an obvious connection. Nothing more, Zizou.'

He shrugged. 'If somebody wanted to cause me trouble by murdering a journalist opposed to the Eel Deal, then it would be a pretty smart, if obvious move,' he said. 'Perhaps a little *too* obvious, wouldn't you say? I mean, why not go all the way and leave one of our corporate brochures on the body?'

'You're right.' He wasn't. It could just as easily have been a double bluff. 'I wonder whether you could provide me with a list of everyone in your entourage?'

'To what end?'

'To eliminate them from our enquiries.'

'I can save you the trouble. They work in shifts, either in my presence or resting in their rooms. They are under orders not to leave the hotel except in my company. There. Eliminated.'

His phrasing made her think of one of Carve-up's favourite put-downs. *'There. Sorted. You're welcome.'* It didn't endear him to her.

'It would still be helpful.'

Instead of answering, he checked his watch and sighed. 'Sadly, we have run out of time. I must prepare for my next meeting.'

'May I ask who you're meeting with?'

'You may *ask*, of course. Regretfully, I must decline to answer. It is a private meeting.'

Kat got to her feet. She wasn't going to get anything out of him. And somehow she doubted the brass would give her any help if she went looking for a warrant.

'Thank you for your time, Zizou, and for the refreshments. What are those little biscuits called?'

'*Hadji bada*. I will have my personal chef send the recipe to you . . . if you'll let me have a card?'

She handed one of her cards over before leaving the sheikh in the company of his head of security. Outside the double doors another security man escorted her down to the lobby.

However sweetly Zizou had denied that Pete was a thorn in his side, she remained unconvinced. For her money, which might only be a minuscule fraction of the sheikh's immense wealth, the culprit was someone connected to the Al Jumairis. Perhaps even Saleem Elwani, his head of security, who looked like he could have snapped Pete Vaughan in two with his bare hands, let alone poisoned him remotely.

But without anything more to go on than gut feeling, how could she take the investigation forward? She needed a piece of hard evidence.

But where the hell was she going to find one?

Chapter Thirty-Nine

Abby rushed over to Kat as soon as she entered MCU.

'Boss! I got what you wanted,' she said breathlessly, waving a couple of stapled sheets of paper. 'It's Nick Chater's DWA licence. It's up to date and it lists "arachnids". That's spiders and scorpions. So basically anything with eight legs. He could have done it.'

'Any evidence he purchased a Deathstalker, Abs?'

Her face fell. 'Oh. Well, no. But me and Leah are looking into it.'

'Good work. Keep at it, yes? We need something concrete. Some actual evidence.'

Evidence. Kat had been struggling to find any, and yet she had a photograph of the bomber in her inside pocket. Frank had made her swear on Van and Riley's lives not to share it with the Met. But something the sheikh had said had resonated with her. The quote embroidered into the *babouche*. 'He who would shake hands with a scorpion should wear gloves.'

Frank had casually assumed that because he'd given her information about a terrorist, she 'owed' him. Her own reaction – *no, she didn't* – had been the truth. But the proverb encapsulated their relationship for her. Every time she visited Frank at the Hope and Anchor, or met him at some dimly lit haunt where they could talk unobserved, she was shaking hands with a scorpion. And eventually, she'd get stung. As the ending of another proverb went, 'I'm a scorpion. That's what we do.'

She took a picture of the CCTV image on her phone and went to find Sharon Critchlow.

The Met DI had taken over a whole corner of MCU and her team had rearranged the desks to create an enclave dubbed by one of the older Middlehampton detectives 'Fort Apache'. After some film, apparently. Van would probably know it.

Sharon looked up. Grey circles under her eyes and a worn expression. 'Please tell me you've got something, Kat.'

'I have.' Kat handed the printout over.

'Who's this?' Sharon said, peering at the photo.

'Last week, he bought a large quantity of raw ingredients for making an explosive device.'

Sharon's fist clenched and she punched the air. 'You bloody legend! Where did you get this? Where was it taken?'

Kat felt she owed the scorpion this, at least: 'Anonymous tip. It was left for me in a bin in town.'

Sharon locked a hard stare on to Kat, who waited her out. 'Anonymous?'

Kat nodded. 'If he's our guy I can see why one of my snouts wouldn't want to identify themselves as the one who fingered him. Probably end up dead from a scorpion sting, too.'

Sharon huffed a weary half-laugh. 'Fair play. We'll do what we can with this. And thanks, Kat. You really came through.'

'I was wondering whether you knew anything about the Crown Prince, or his head of security?'

'Not a lot to be honest. The person you need to speak to is Victoria Palmer. I'll get her over here later and we can have a drink.'

'Thanks, I'd like that. Value it, I mean.'

'Look, we got off on the wrong foot. I apologise for coming in here with my size tens.' She looked down. 'Not a joke, my feet are bloody huge.'

Kat wrinkled her nose as an all-too familiar smell enveloped her. Aramis. 'Value what, DS Ballantyne?'

She turned to face Carve-up. 'We were just talking about the case, Stu.'

'I thought I made myself perfectly clear. You're nothing to do with the case. You act in a strictly local role on the Pete Vaughan murder. Leave the serious stuff to those with the seniority to deal with it.'

'Are you joking?' Sharon asked, her hands on her hips. 'Kat's just brought me the first decent piece of evidence since we arrived. We've got an ID on the bomber.'

'Oh, great. Well, give it to me and I'll put a team on it.'

'No. I'll handle this, Stu,' she said, catching Kat's eye for an instant. 'Now, if you'll excuse us.'

She waited him out. Barely managing to suppress a scowl, he about-turned and stalked back to his office.

The two women shared a look. *Arsehole.* Which he was. But only Kat knew he was much, much worse than that.

Back at her own desk, she found a plain cream envelope sitting on top of her keyboard. The printed legend in the top-left corner read, 'The Garland, Country-house Luxury in the Heart of the City.' She slit it open with her thumbnail. Inside was a handwritten note on a sheet of the hotel's matching notepaper.

Dear Kat,

Good luck with your Hadji bada.

My chef says buy whole blanched almonds and grind them in a food processor. Shop-bought powdered almonds are no good.

My best,

Zizou

She smiled. Something to keep for the family scrapbook.

Tucked behind Zizou's note was a neatly handwritten recipe. She scanned it, decided it was probably within her capabilities, and pocketed the note.

◆ ◆ ◆

Vicky Palmer turned up at the station just before 8.00 p.m. Kat had just texted Van to tell him she'd be working late, again. His reply, a dismissive 'kk', left her feeling anxious. Was it passive-aggressive? Or was he just being a typical man?

Sharon drew Vicky and Kat – Met, MCU, MI6 – into a meeting room.

'I thought it would be helpful if we pooled our knowledge,' she said. 'I know we're all in our little silos, but seriously, we're not going to crack this unless we start cooperating.'

'I agree,' Vicky said with a bright smile. 'Although naturally there are areas of this case that touch on matters of national security where, sadly, I shall have to be circumspect.'

'Understood. Kat, you had a question, didn't you?'

Kat nodded. Turned to the MI6 agent. 'What can you tell me about Saleem Elwani?'

It was as though Vicky had been expecting the question. She didn't hesitate before replying. 'Studied engineering at Masrah

Arabic University. Joined the army straight after. Served for three years in the Al Jumairi Special Forces. Even trained with the SAS in Hereford for six months in 2017.'

'Could he have been behind the bombing do you think?'

'Why would he do that?' Sharon asked.

Kat thought she'd never get a better opportunity to air her own – and Frank's – theory about the bombing than now. 'What if it wasn't terrorism at all? What if it was just a massive distraction so we'd not focus on Pete Vaughan's murder? Everyone seems to agree it was an unconventional bomb for a terrorist to use. No nuts and bolts, no high-explosive. It was really just a glorified flash-bang.'

'Or maybe it was a false-flag operation,' Vicky said thoughtfully. 'After all, minimal casualties, and from what I hear it's solidified local support for the Eel Deal, as it's so charmingly called.'

'But local support is already sky high,' Kat said. 'The Supporters' Trust is backing it. Everyone you speak to in town says it'll be good for the club. The council are on board.'

'I don't know, Kat,' Sharon said. 'It seems like a lot of trouble to go to just to muddy the waters.'

'But perhaps someone was trying to, forgive me, kill two birds with one stone,' Vicky said with a quirk of her mouth. 'The bomber wanted to bolster support ahead of a potentially negative article coming out *and* remove the source of future negative publicity. Although I'd be *extraordinarily* surprised if the Crown Prince got anywhere near the sharp end.'

'I'd really like to talk to whoever trained Elwani at the SAS,' Kat said.

'Who dares, wins, eh?' Vicky said. 'I can arrange that. Leave it with me. I'll call you. So, ladies, it appears we are to work together. Anyone else feel like sealing the deal with a little drink? I don't know about you two, but I'm parched.'

They decamped to a nearby pub, took a corner table, well away from the other drinkers. Drinks bought by Vicky, they clinked glasses.

'So, what's Carver's deal?' Sharon asked. 'Is it some kind of shtick or is he really a seventies tribute act?'

Kat took a sip of her drink to buy a little time. How much should she share about Carve-up? That he'd tried to have her and Tom killed? That he was a bent cop in her father's pocket? In the end, she settled for part of the truth. 'I think it's fair to say he has a problem with women.'

'No shit,' Vicky said.

Over shared laughter, the three women, anti-terror cop, homicide investigator, intelligence agent, struck up a bond. And Kat found herself feeling something strange.

Optimism.

The following day was Saturday. Kat planned to spend it at home, maybe doing an hour's work, but trying to keep it free for some precious time with Van and Riley.

That 'kk' text was niggling at her. Van would deny it, but she knew a passive-aggressive text when she saw one.

She flashed on her dream of Jack once more. Did Van suspect something? How could he, when there was nothing there to suspect?

Chapter Forty

Kat slid from beneath the covers at 6.30 a.m. and went into the back bedroom – her personal incident room. She picked up the AAIB inspector's report again and started at the beginning, looking for something she might have missed from before.

She consulted the appendix – a densely printed set of pages covered in graphs, tables and reams of technical data. And there, sandwiched between a long technical spec sheet and a set of stress measurements, she found it.

The plane was less than a year old when it had crashed, killing Connor and Tasha instantly. Surely that was a bit soon for a fuel pump to develop a fault. Had it been sabotaged? That spoke to murder, confirming her suspicions.

Resisting the temptation to lose herself in the rest of her material, she slipped back into bed with Van, who grunted contentedly in his sleep. Wanting to reassure him, and herself, on some deep, not-quite-knowable level, that she still fancied him, she cuddled round him and dozed back off for a guilty hour.

On waking, she tiptoed from the room and returned twenty minutes later bearing a tray of cooked breakfast: eggs, bacon and tomatoes, toast and coffee. She set it carefully on the floor then bent over her sleeping husband. Kissed his bristly cheek.

'Hey, handsome, I brought you breakfast in bed.'

He rolled over, eyes still closed, and kissed her.

Ignoring his morning breath, and thinking of his last text, she kissed him back, harder.

He took her hand and guided it beneath the covers. She rolled her eyes when she found him hard under the duvet. She slithered on top of him, feeling that old familiar tug for him, low in her belly. Then her phone rang.

'Leave it,' he said breathily.

'I can't, love, it might be work.'

'That's why I want you to leave it.'

She was in two minds. Whatever it was, it could wait. But then she saw who was calling her. Vicky.

'I'm sorry, darling,' she said. 'I have to take this.'

She sat up, ran a hand through her hair and composed herself. Took Van's hand away from her breast as she answered the call, trying to block out his huff of disgust and the bounce as he threw himself on to his other side, presenting her with his back.

'Morning, Kat. I bring you news from the Marches. The guy who trained Elwani will meet you at 1.00 p.m. Off base, naturally. A pub in Hay-on-Wye called The Old Black Lion on Lion Street. He'll wait for five minutes then leave. But he won't reveal anything operational.'

'You're a star, thanks.'

Kat showered and dressed, while Van attacked his breakfast as if he were a serial killer, and the food his latest victim.

She bent to him, and he stopped eating for a moment, tilting his cheek just enough to accept her kiss. 'I'm sorry, love, but this could be important.'

'Fine. I suppose my needs will just have to come second. As always.'

'It's not "as always"! We do it lots.'

'It doesn't feel like it.'

'Well, I'm trying to solve a murder, and possibly a terrorism incident, so you'll just have to sort yourself out. I need to go. I'll see you later. I love you.'

She paused at the bedroom door, waiting for the reflexive response.

'Van?'

'Yes, I heard you. Go.' A beat. 'Don't keep your boyfriend waiting.'

She stopped in the doorway.

'Pardon?'

'What is it this time? Another post-mortem? Or do you just need to discuss something cheery like blood spatter?'

She shook her head. Had she been mentioning Jack more than usual recently? She couldn't remember, but it seemed unlikely.

'Van, love, I don't know what you're talking about.'

'The other night you had a dream. I don't know what it was about, but you said his name in your sleep. Sometimes it feels like you spend more time with Jack Beale than you do with me.'

She felt the blush creeping up from her neck to her cheeks. Turned away from Van so he wouldn't see it.

'You know that's not true. It was about the post-mortem, that's all. But in any case, I'm not seeing Jack. I'm meeting a contact in Wales, then I'm going to drop in on Liv. I'm sorry, love, I really need to get going.'

'Go, then, I'm not stopping you.'

Reluctantly, she left the room. Christ! What was happening? Her marriage was her rock. Now, all of a sudden, it felt like it was crumbling beneath her feet. And she hadn't done anything. What was it the nominals all said? *'I've got nothing to hide.'*

But I haven't! she wanted to shout. *I haven't!*

Trying not to obsess about Van's refusal to say 'I love you' back, and replaying every one of her recent conversations with him to see if she'd given him any cause to be jealous of Jack – *you mean, apart from moaning his name in your sleep*, her mischievous inner voice piped up unhelpfully – Kat hurtled westwards towards the border with Wales.

The traffic was light, what little there was shifting leftwards as she loomed behind it. Using her blues and twos when she needed them. M1. M40. M42. M5. Then A roads. Ending up in the pub car park three hours and fifteen mins later, bursting for a wee. According to the satnav, she was eighty-one metres inside the Welsh border.

She entered the dim interior of the pub, seeing immediately why her contact had chosen it. What little light entered through the tiny mullioned windows seemed to falter halfway across the room.

She looked around for a hulking man-mountain super-soldier. The type she could imagine rappelling down the sides of foreign embassies or stalking terrorists across rocky islands. She was disappointed. The bar contained a few elderly couples. Three young mums with babies in strollers. A grizzled old boozer with rheumy eyes, a dirty face and a half-drunk pint of Guinness. And two business types loudly discussing quarterly sales projections. She checked the time. She was five minutes early. He'd be on military precision timekeeping. She had time to visit the ladies and relieve her cramping bladder.

In the loo, she rehearsed her questions about Elwani. After washing her hands, she came back into the bar and ordered a Diet Coke and grilled halloumi, red onion and spicy mayo on focaccia.

While she waited to tap the card machine, she took another glance round the pub. He wasn't there yet. She glanced at the door. Then back at the room.

The crusty-looking geezer nodded to her. Surely this couldn't be him? He looked like he'd have trouble opening his own front door, let alone storming an embassy.

She walked over anyway.

He mumbled, 'Ballantyne?'

She nodded, sat. 'Yep, that's me. Call me Kat.'

He shook her hand. Warm, dry, no trace of the grimy, greasy grip she'd been expecting. 'You can call me Dave.'

Up close, she could see he was actually somewhere between his mid-thirties and early forties.

'Great disguise,' she said. 'I'd never have guessed.'

He shrugged, twitched, eyes flicking to the door, over her shoulder. Did he have PTSD? She'd seen it in cops. Hypervigilance.

'Wouldn't have been much good if you had.'

'Thanks for agreeing to meet me.'

'You want to talk about Stinger?'

'Huh?'

'Elwani. That's what we called him. Outside the wire he might be a Grand Panjandrum of Araby. In the regiment he was Trooper Elwani aka Stinger.'

'How did he get his nickname?' she asked, feeling sure she already knew.

'He brought a live scorpion back from the Gulf in a jam jar. Dared the other guys to let it crawl on their hands,' he said, holding out his own, palm uppermost. 'When they wouldn't, he did.'

'What kind was it, do you remember?' Kat asked.

'Yeah. Pretty little thing, really, with lime-green legs and stripes.'

Kat showed him one of the photos she'd taken on her phone. 'Is that it?'

'That's the little fellow. Looks so harmless. Believe me, it's not.'

'Oh, I believe you. It killed a man.'

Kat reckoned up the balance of her trip. She had witness testimony that Elwani had already once brought a Deathstalker into the UK. And clearly was unafraid of handling them.

A waitress arrived with their food. Kat's focaccia sandwich and falafel, hummus and Lebanese salad for Dave.

'I got the taste for it in Afghanistan,' he said, after Kat had thanked the waitress. 'So what's Stinger done, then? Must be bad if you came out all this way.'

'As far as I know, he hasn't done anything. I just wanted to eliminate him from our enquiries.'

He favoured her with a long, considering stare. Said, 'OK.'

Two short syllables. But they were as eloquent as a gabby nominal ready to spill their guts in return for a word in a prosecutor's ear. He knew it was more than she'd just said. She knew he knew that. And round and round it went.

'This is all confidential. It's an active murder investigation,' she said, suddenly worried that maybe there was some sort of SAS honour code and he'd be duty-bound to let 'Stinger' know of her visit.

'You had that terrorist bombing in Middlehampton, didn't you?' She nodded. 'I hate those mad bastards. Blowing up kids. So let's agree. This meeting never happened.'

That seemed like a good plan to Kat and she felt she could trust him implicitly. They finished their food in near-silence and she left ahead of him.

As she reached the door, she looked back. His posture had relapsed into the slouch she'd first taken for a drunken stupor.

Outside, she stood by her car for a moment, dragging fresh air deep into her lungs, trying to order her thoughts. Could the genial billionaire who'd asked her to call him Zizou and fed her *hadji bada* also have ordered his head of security to plant a bomb and murder a journalist?

But what if Elwani *had* brought a Deathstalker into the UK eight years earlier? It proved nothing beyond the fact that illegal importation was possible. Although it did suggest that even without the requisite paperwork, someone like Gerald Hynde or Nick Chater could have brought one in themselves.

It was 2.30 p.m. Liv's farm lay a few miles south-west of the pub. She put the Golf in gear and pulled away.

Confiding in her best friend about Pete Vaughan's murder the other morning had felt like walking a line. But that wasn't the case Kat wanted to talk to Liv about.

Chapter Forty-One

Sitting with Liv in the *Bryn Glas* farm kitchen, mugs of tea before them, Kat reached down to scratch Duffel the border collie behind the ear. Then she told Liv about the newness of the plane in which Tasha and Connor Starling had died.

'Am I reaching, do you think?' Kat asked.

'You have to draw out all the lines of the spider's web. If Tasha was having an affair with your dad, then he's right in there, near the middle. Who else? Obviously that arse, Carver.'

'Remember you told me before about your friend from Shirley House who went out with him when he was a PC?'

'Yeah. Silly cow.'

'I found out he was basically running an extortion racket with two mates on the force back then. Getting sex from prostitutes in exchange for not arresting them. But handy with his fists, too, if he didn't get what he wanted.'

Liv looked straight at her. 'Couzens, Carrick, Carver. Straight line.'

Kat remembered something else that had passed between her and Terrie Leonard, the escort who'd told her about Carve-up and the other two members of the 'Three Musketeers'.

She'd asked Terrie if she thought Carve-up could have been the serial killer she was hunting. Terrie had said given the right circumstances, any man could be a killer, but in all honesty she didn't get that vibe off Carve-up.

That thought sparked another. The Crown Prince was in thick with her dad. How long had that relationship been going? It was an interesting question. Because even if her dad had wanted Tasha Starling dead, no way would he have got anywhere near the actual deed. It would have gone through layers of deniability. Perhaps Colin Morton and the Crown Prince were following moves from the same playbook.

And then she saw a connection in the spider's web – a looping line of sticky thread lighting up between five points. Her dad. His dog-loyal PA Suzy, who'd already admitted to trying to fit Kat up on a bogus corruption charge. Stuart Carver. Tasha and Connor Starling. The only missing node in the electrifying theory was the person who'd actually tampered with the aircraft's fuel pump.

'Earth calling Thelma, earth calling Thelma!'

Kat refocused. Liv was staring at her over the rim of her mug, an amused look on her face. 'Sorry, I was just thinking about my dad.'

'Do you have to? I am a bride-to-be, you know.'

'Go on, tell me all about it. What about the dress?'

As Liv talked excitedly about her wedding plans, Kat fought to stay present for her best friend. She'd have to go soon if she was to be back in Middlehampton in time to patch things up with Van. No way did she want to let the sun go down on their quarrel.

The two friends hugged on the doorstep, and then Kat left, waving to Liv out the window as Duffel sat beside her, looking up at his mistress in the expectation of a walk.

That night, Van resisted Kat's efforts to engage him in conversation about his reference to her 'boyfriend'.

'I was half-asleep anyway,' he said, unconvincingly. 'Forget it. I have.'

She took Smokey for a walk, and formulated a plan to prove to Van he had nothing to worry about.

The following morning, Kat woke the second her phone started to vibrate on her nightstand. She turned it off then crept out of bed to silently close the bedroom door.

She slipped back beneath the duvet and took Van in her hand. Time to remind him she was more than a cop, a wife and a mother: she was a woman. And that there was only one man in her life.

Afterwards, as he lay beside her, panting heavily, she allowed herself a smile.

'Better?' she asked, triumphantly.

He could only nod. Although he, too, was smiling.

Later that morning they went to watch Riley play football. Kat's friend Jess Beckett was on the touchline, too, with her husband. Over teas and bacon rolls, they chatted, while the husbands compared notes on each team's players, before veering into a discussion of the Eel Deal.

'That bomb really frightened me, Kat,' Jess said. 'Alfie wasn't at the gig, but he knew the girl who was killed. He's been crying in his room. It's so unlike him. Was it terrorists? That's what they're saying on the news. But Mike says if it was they'd have used, you know, ball bearings, or nails or whatever. Horrible people.'

'Honestly, mate, I wish I knew what to tell you. But I'm really not allowed to talk about it. But I do think you shouldn't worry. This isn't breaking any rules, but my gut's telling me there's nothing to worry about.'

'Your gut? Or something you know?'

'Just try not to worry. Things will be fine.'

Cheers broke out on the pitch. Kat spun round in time to see Riley streaking away from the opposing goal, arms aloft, his face split by a huge grin.

At home, Van cooked roast beef. Kat noticed Riley watching closely as his dad poured a glass of red wine.

'Can I have some? Please?'

Kat and Van exchanged looks. Riley'd never asked before. A look of agreement passed between them.

'Sure. Grab a glass off the dresser, then,' Van said.

He poured out a small glass and added water from the jug on the table.

Riley looked at them both, then took a gulp. His face contorted and for a second Kat thought he was going to spit it back out. But he forced it down, his sharp Adam's apple bobbing in his throat.

He looked at them, big brown eyes full of reproach. As if they'd tricked him into drinking poison.

'How the hell do you drink that? It's rank. It tastes like petrol.'

'You asked for it,' Van said with a smile.

'Where did you get a taste for alcohol, then?' Kat asked, wanting suddenly to broach another subject she'd always dreaded. Ironically they'd had the sex talk before the alcohol talk.

'Me and Millie had some at hers after school.'

'Millie?' Kat repeated.

He shrugged. 'We're like going out?'

Kat was amazed, pleased and anxious all at once. Van seemed unbothered. All of a sudden Kat saw Riley growing not just upwards and outwards as his adolescent body filled out and his incipient beard grew darker with every passing day, but away from her. The tug felt like distant grief, but not in the past: in the future.

Kat woke early the next morning. Monday. A week had passed and she'd not made an arrest. The fact that Sharon's lot hadn't either – or not one that had stuck – was scant comfort.

Her best lead right now was Saleem Elwani. He had a motive of sorts. To protect his master's precious deal. No alibi, since she didn't count the Crown Prince's assurances. And access to the species of scorpion used to murder Pete Vaughan. As for the bombing, that would have to wait. It wasn't him in the photograph Frank Strutt had given her.

So, no arrest. But there was another option.

Chapter Forty-Two

At 6.45 a.m., Kat entered the lobby of The Garland.

Showing her warrant card, she instructed the receptionist to telephone the Crown Prince's suite and ask his head of security to come downstairs.

Elwani appeared five minutes later, stepping out of the lift looking fresh and well rested, not a hair out of place, as if he had been waiting for her all along.

'Good morning, DS Ballantyne. How can I help?'

'I'd like you to come to Jubilee Place police station with me to attend a voluntary interview under caution. You'd be entitled to legal representation and you'd be free to leave at any time.'

He stared at her for a few seconds. She assumed she was supposed to be intimidated. She stared back. Stares didn't matter. Only words. One in particular. Yes.

'No.'

'No?'

'I have diplomatic immunity. I'm not going anywhere with you. Was that all?'

She glared up at him. Visualising his strong-looking hands unscrewing a jam jar and tipping a deadly scorpion into his palm. 'For now.'

She spun on her heel and left him, just knowing he was smiling but not giving him the satisfaction of a backward glance to confirm it.

At that time of day, the drive from The Garland to Jubilee Place only took ten minutes. Frustrated and angry, she rang the Foreign Office. After the usual Civil Service run-around, she found herself talking to a very helpful young man – Young? He sounded barely older than Riley – who informed her that 'the gentleman is labouring under a misapprehension. Only accredited diplomats have immunity. We have no record of Mr Elwani on our database.'

She thanked him and put the phone down, seething that she'd been tricked so easily.

'Who were you talking to?'

She whirled round, startled.

Vicky Palmer was behind her, head cocked to one side. Her tone of voice was mild, but there was a sharpness to her gaze.

'I went to talk to Saleem Elwani. He refused to come in voluntarily. Said he had diplomatic immunity. I just got off the phone with the Foreign Office. He doesn't. So now I'm going to go back and give him a second chance.'

Vicky's perfectly uncreased brow, which Kat felt sure was the result of lucky genes and possibly an incredibly expensive skincare routine, and not Botox, did now furrow. Just a little. A single ripple in that flawless skin.

'I'm not one hundred per cent sure that's the best or wisest course of action, Kat.'

Kat nodded, suddenly angry not just with Elwani, but with his suave, hospitable boss, with Sharon, with Carve-up and with Vicky. They all seemed bent on preventing her from doing her job.

'Noted,' she said.

◆ ◆ ◆

Kat left the Golf in The Garland's car park. She found Elwani outside the hotel, supervising a couple of his men as they checked the road outside the hotel. Two blacked-out Range Rovers were idling on the hotel's drive.

Reassured by the weight of the cuffs she'd clipped to her belt underneath her jacket, and the bulky piece of equipment on the other side, she marched over to Elwani who straightened as she came into his eyeline.

'DS Ballantyne. You're back,' he said, the corners of his eyes crinkling.

'I checked with the Foreign Office. You don't have diplomatic immunity,' she said. 'So, I'm going to ask you once more, politely, to come with me voluntarily. If you decide not to, which is your right, I will arrest you and that will be that. Your choice, Mr Elwani.'

'You are making a big mistake, DS Ballantyne,' he said.

'No. I am following the law. My car's round the corner. Are you coming voluntarily or not?'

'His Royal Highness needs me.'

'I'm sure he can manage for a couple of hours.'

'May I call him?'

'Be my guest.'

He turned away and made a call. It was short. He said little, and what he did say was in Arabic. Finally, he turned back. 'It would be my pleasure to assist Middlehampton Police with their enquiries, although this is in no way an admission of guilt.'

Gratified that he was complying and she wouldn't have to call on the services of the two burly uniformed PCs she had on standby in a marked van, she led him to her car.

She held the rear door open for him. As he bent to climb in, his jacket fell away from his body. Clipped to his belt was a large black pistol.

Every nerve in Kat's body lit up. Her pulse started racing and she drew back instinctively as if stung. She stepped back and grabbed the Taser off her belt. 'Armed police! Hands in the air!'

He withdrew his head from the car and straightened slowly. Looked down at his right hip. Smiled.

As if in slow motion, she watched his hand move towards the butt of the gun.

'Leave it!' she shouted. 'Hands in the air!'

He turned fully to face her. He was still smiling. His right hand twitched. She tightened her finger on the trigger of the Taser. And then he raised both his hands high over his head.

Kat reached for the gun. Time snapped back into normal motion. Elwani stepped back quickly, out of range, dropping his arms.

'No!' he barked. 'Do not do that.'

Struggling to control her breathing, unable to do much about her pulse, which had skyrocketed, Kat stared at the gun. Behind Elwani two of his men had turned at the commotion and were looking at their boss. He waved them away. Kat did the same to the two uniforms clambering out of the van.

'Left hand, thumb and forefinger,' Kat said. 'Pick it up and drop it to the ground. Now!'

He inhaled through his nose. 'I am sorry. I can't do that.'

She hit the switch that sent a bright-blue electric arc crackling across the Taser's contact points. A visible and audible warning that had most nominals who faced the business end of the bright yellow weapon complying like Sunday school kids.

'Do it!'

'I have a permit. I am His Royal Highness's personal bodyguard. You will have to kill me to take it away.'

'What permit?' she gritted out. 'The same kind as your diplomatic immunity?'

Her arms were shaking but she kept the Taser levelled at his torso.

'There is a government arrangement between HMG and Al Jumairah. It was brokered by your MI6. Perhaps you should ask Victoria Palmer.' He lifted his chin a little to get a better look at the trembling Taser. 'That looks heavy. Put it down. I swear I will come with you without causing any trouble.'

He held up his right hand, moving away from the pistol. Slowly, he curled his little finger in until he could trap it beneath his incurved thumb. Some sort of Arabic gesture?

He raised the three straightened fingers to his forehead. 'Scout's honour.'

The gesture was so unexpected, Kat actually laughed. Shocked, she lowered the Taser.

'You're serious?'

'Eagle Scout.'

She sighed. Although her heart was still thumping, and the trembling in her hand had now travelled to her knees, she knew he wouldn't shoot. But that didn't mean she would abandon all her training.

She held out her left palm. 'Give me the magazine. You can have it back after I finish interviewing you.'

Smiling, he complied, moving with great care and slowness, and showing her the way he never let his finger stray towards the trigger. He depressed a catch and popped the slim black magazine out. Handed it over. 'Happy?'

'And the round in the chamber.'

He racked the slide and caught the round that jumped upwards with a metallic ping, its brass casing sparkling briefly as it caught the sun. That too went into Kat's pocket.

'Get in, please,' she said, heart still racing.

She drove him to Jubilee Place, ignoring every attempt he made to engage her in conversation, and led him downstairs to the custody suite.

After further argument, he agreed, with ill grace, to be fingerprinted. But he refused to say anything else bar request a lawyer. That would take most of the day and he refused to go into a cell.

Feeling she was already pushing her luck, given the sensitivities involved in the case, she left him to sweat in an interview room under the watchful eye and Taser of the largest uniformed officer she could find.

Chapter Forty-Three

Closing the door to the interview room, Kat checked the time. And then swore. She'd completely missed her meeting with Dr Milo Smith, the arachnologist.

She called his number as she headed down to the car park. 'Dr Smith, it's DS Ballantyne. I am so sorry for missing our meeting. Something urgent came up, but I could still have called you.'

'It's fine. I get it. But I'm about to head into a seminar so it'll be 11.00 a.m. before I'm free.'

'I'll wait. Wouldn't want to miss you a second time. You might not want to work with me again.'

He laughed. 'Believe me, if you call, I'll be there. Unlike blood spatter analysts or handwriting experts, us arachnologists don't get the call too often. This'll only be my second.'

Kat drove over to the university, reasoning she could find somewhere quiet to update her policy book and attend to the growing mountain of paperwork the case was generating.

She found a cafeteria near the biology department, where she sat hard at work on her laptop until she yawned widely, cracking her jaw. Rubbing the painful spot, she got up to stretch her legs. Would Abby really want a full-time job as a detective if she knew just how much time Kat spent filling in report templates, online forms and all the rest of it?

The campus looked inviting, with its stands of trees just coming into leaf and spring sunshine filtering down. As Kat strolled among the students she reflected on the fact that this might once have been her life. Except her two weeks at Nottingham University had been lost in a fog of tranquillisers and sleeping-pill hangovers – plus the real ones – until she'd bugged out, unable to cope with losing Liv.

Mixed emotions warred in her breast. Liv's actions had denied Kat the chance to finish, or even properly start, her studies. But Liv been running from what she believed to be a genuine threat to her life. And Kat had met Van during her time in Thailand, where she had gone after dropping out. Without Liv doing what she had done, Kat might never have met Van.

And now it was Liv's turn to get married. Kat smiled as she imagined the hen night. Something rowdy, knowing Liv, probably in Cardiff. Barry Island. Pink fur-trimmed cowboy hats. Far too much prosecco.

Still smiling as she wondered whether Liv would go the whole hog and hire a stripper, Kat turned a corner and stopped dead. What the hell? Her mouth dropped open. Surely it couldn't be him? Could it?

He was walking straight towards her, arm in arm with a woman in her late twenties or possibly early thirties. Smiling, and obviously hugely enjoying her company judging from his relaxed body language. Resisting the urge to turn around or hide, she checked, and double-checked. No mistake. It was Ethan.

As they drew closer, she saw he wasn't wearing those old-fashioned square, gold-rimmed glasses that she'd come to associate with him, as though they were a part of his body. They locked eyes and Kat was stunned into silence, as much by his radically changed appearance as the fact he had an apparently normal woman on his arm who clearly didn't find him repellent.

Smiling, and revealing straight, white, non-cruddy teeth, he stopped in front of her. 'Kat! This is weird, right? How are you?'

He turned to the woman on his arm who was regarding Kat shyly from beneath lowered lashes. Pretty, but a bit doe-eyed, was Kat's immediate summary. The sort of girl-next-door attractiveness she could imagine a creep like Ethan going for. Anyone more striking would probably terrify him.

'This is my girlfriend, Dr Ada Monk,' he said with obvious pride. 'She's an associate lecturer in the department of media studies. Ada, this is DS Kat Ballantyne, one of Middlehampton's finest. We work together occasionally.'

Reeling with shock, Kat mechanically shook hands with the young woman, whose small soft fingers seemed to melt inside hers. *'Work together?'* She wouldn't share a stale canteen cheese sandwich with him, much less a case.

'Pleased to meet you . . . Kat,' Ada said. Her voice was light, girlish and she seemed somewhat over-awed.

'How . . . How did you guys meet?' Kat asked, finding she was genuinely interested, given Ethan's personality.

Ada's face broke into a wide, toothy grin. 'Eeth contacted me about his podcast? *Home Counties Homicide*? He suggested doing a session for my students on podcasting. It was going to be a one-off, but they absolutely loved it. And him,' she added, turning to a beaming Ethan. 'He's a regular now. We've just come from a studio workshop, actually.'

Kat became aware her mouth was hanging slightly open, and shut it. She couldn't think of a single thing to say. How had her former stalker turned into some sort of media expert? Never mind that, how had he got himself a *girlfriend*?

Perhaps sensing her discomfort, Ethan disengaged his arm from Ada's and held both hands up.

'Kat, I've been waiting for the right moment, but I think now is as good as any. I want to apologise to you. Really. I am so sorry for my behaviour before. It was wrong. *I* was wrong. I've been doing a lot of work on myself. I even have a therapist. The missus recommended one here at the university,' he said, smiling at Ada. 'We've been exploring childhood trauma. I'm learning to understand the roots of my behaviour. My lack of self-care. You may have noticed I've lost some weight. I work out now. And I went for laser eye surgery. Even got the old gnashers fixed.'

Kat felt as though she'd just got off the waltzer at the Middlehampton Summer Fair. Disorientated. Completely wrong-footed by Ethan's dizzying change in appearance, outlook and character. She looked from Ethan to Ada. Should she say something about Ethan stalking her? Or would that be churlish given the apparently genuine apology he'd just made?

Ada smiled up at Ethan before turning her soppy gaze on Kat. 'I know about Eeth's previous focus on you, Kat. He told me everything on our first date. The poor lamb was in a really bad place but he's made such amazing progress. I'm so proud of you, baby,' she added, turning back to Ethan and booping him on the end of his nose.

Stunned, Kat could only manage, 'It was lovely to meet you, Ada. I'm on a case, though, and I have a meeting to get to.'

Ethan nodded earnestly, his face serious. 'Of course. The Pete Vaughan murder. I'm investigating, too, Kat. I'd be happy to share what I've learned. Anytime.'

Ada nodded and smiled at Kat. 'Isn't he adorable?' Then linked her arm through Ethan's, and stretched up to kiss him. The lovestruck couple turned as one and walked past her along the path.

Kat wanted to slap them both.

Instead, she swallowed her irrational anger, and made her way back to the biology department.

She found Dr Smith in his office. A cramped cubbyhole decorated with box-framed specimens from his field of study. Improbably large, brown, hairy-legged spiders and glossy black scorpions with curled tails tipped by stingers.

In contrast, Milo Smith was a rather unthreatening specimen. Sandy hair, a mild look in his eyes, soft-looking hands. They shook. His grip was weaker even than Ada's. Boneless, like his wall-mounted friends.

Kat apologised again but he brushed it aside. 'What do you need? And when do you need it?'

'I have a scorpion. It was used to kill a man. I believe it's a Deathstalker, but obviously I need a professional opinion.'

His eyes widened. 'Wow. That's a rare creature to find in the UK. Is it alive?'

'Dead.'

His face fell. 'Oh, that's a shame. Beautiful animals. Quite make you believe in a higher power. Now, you said?'

'Now would be ideal.'

He stood. 'I'm all yours. My next class isn't until this afternoon.'

They walked back to the car park, Kat keeping an eye out for Ethan and Ada, but the route was podcaster-free.

As they drove, she asked Dr Smith – 'Call me Milo, please' – about the Deathstalker.

'Is it legal to keep them in this country? Even if you have a DWA?'

'Absolutely. I have a couple myself.'

Kat's fingers tensed on the steering wheel. 'Where did you get yours?'

'I bred them. In the department. We're looking at pharmaceutical uses for their venom. Some very promising work with brain tumours. Early days, obviously.'

Kat swallowed. 'And you have all the paperwork.'

Milo laughed. 'Don't worry, it's all legal. I've got DWAs coming out of my ears. You don't need to worry that I'll be poisoning my academic rivals.' He paused. 'Although there are a couple of centipede guys I'd like to see with a Deathstalker in their slippers.' He laughed, over-loud in the cabin. 'Sorry. Arachnology humour. We all get on fine.'

Kat drove on in silence. Skin crawling.

Chapter Forty-Four

A small group were gathered around the table on which Darcy had displayed the Deathstalker.

Looking at it afresh, Kat was struck by the poor state of the creature compared to those displayed in Milo's office. Only natural, she supposed, given it had been crushed inside a slipper. And how, by the way, had Milo known that was where it had been glued? Or was it just a coincidence?

Wearing blue nitrile gloves, Milo expertly wielded a pair of artery forceps and a scalpel to tease apart the little arachnid. Even though it was dead, Kat could see the way he avoided the stinger. No sense getting close to the business end when it might still have venom to deliver.

He straightened. Nodded. 'It's a Deathstalker. Or, to give it its scientific name *Leiurus quinquestriatus*. Basically translates as five-striped smooth-tail.' He turned to Kat. 'Where's the rest of it?'

'Sorry, what do you mean? That's all of it.'

Using the scalpel, Milo pointed to a bent and twisted limb near the head. 'That's the front left pincer. Where's the right?'

Darcy frowned. 'That's how he arrived from the post-mortem.'

Milo sighed. 'In common with all other arachnids, scorpions have eight legs. They may have other appendages – palps, and so forth – that evolve until they *resemble* legs, but they're not,' he said fussily. 'Now, this little fellow here does have the requisite number of *legs*, i.e. eight. But he only has one of the two required *pincers*. So nine appendages in all, where there should be ten.'

'Do you have the slippers, Darce?' Kat asked.

Darcy signalled to a CSI who'd been watching over her shoulders. He hurried away and returned a couple of minutes later with an evidence bag containing the *babouche*.

'May I?' Darcy asked Milo, pointing at the scalpel.

After opening the evidence bag, she lifted the right babouche out and slit the toe, cutting a wide curve across the front. She widened the opening with the artery forceps, and there, stuck to the underside of the instep, was a shiny, yellowish-beige pincer.

'Can you hold it open for me?' she said to the CSI.

Darcy repositioned the forceps and cut the pincer free, bringing a tiny portion of the grey felt with it.

'It could have a fingerprint on it!' Kat said. 'Sorry, Darce. You knew that.'

Darcey smiled. 'I'm excited, too. Although I've never lifted a print off a scorpion pincer before.'

As everyone watched, she carried the pincer over to another work table on which rested a glass fish tank. She placed the pincer on a small Perspex block inside the tank and then put a few drops of super glue on to a little glass tray on a warming plate. She closed the lid of the tank and flicked a switch on a control panel.

Kat peered through the glass. As the heated pad warmed first the glass and then the glue dropped on to it, white fumes began to curl upwards, eventually filling the tank with a faint mist.

Darcy waited until a timer pinged. She flicked another switch and a small vacuum pump sucked the fumes out of the tank, leaving the pincer on its mount.

Kat peered inside. Her heart lifted with excitement. 'Is that a print?'

Darcy lifted the specimen out and then scrutinised it through a magnifier ringed with tiny LEDs that cast a fierce, blue-white light over the pincer.

'Partial. We're lucky to get that, given the available area, but it is hard forensic evidence and basically the best we've got so far.' She turned to Kat, smiling. 'You might call it a forensic breakthrough.'

Kat was delighted. Even though the partial would in all likelihood be too small for what Carve-up liked to call a slam-dunk, it might be enough to compare to samples on the IDENT1 national fingerprint database.

'Can you get it analysed pronto, Darce? We want a comparison with Nick Chater's from his criminal record on the PNC and also Saleem Elwani's.'

'Sure. Urgent?'

'Yes, please. Fast as they can. I'll sort the budget.' She turned to Milo. 'Thanks. You just earned your fee.'

He beamed delightedly. 'Fantastic! Not about the money. I mean just being able to help. You know, it's such a privilege to be at the centre of a murder investigation. I know it looks glamorous, but really my job can be so dull sometimes.'

And there it was again. There was something just a little off about him. First his odd remark in the car about poisoning his colleagues. And now this boyish excitement at being involved in the case. A little voice whispered into Kat's brain. *He has a couple of Deathstalkers. He's a bit weird. I wonder if he had anything against Pete Vaughan.*

She wasn't ready to start asking him for an alibi, though, so she filed the thought for now. But maybe there was a subtler way to get him talking.

'If we're done here, I'll drive you back to the university, Milo,' she said with a smile.

On the way, she asked, as lightly as she could manage, 'So the venom really is deadly, then?'

'Oh, God, yes. It's seriously dangerous. I mean, in chemical terms it's a work of art. You've got chlorotoxin, charybdotoxin, scyllatoxin, agitoxins types one, two *and* three, and Lq2. You couldn't design a better killing substance,' he said, growing animated. 'The combination of neurotoxins immobilises the prey and then, well, basically screws every system until they all shut down.'

'Charming.'

'Oh, but it is! And guess what? Deathstalker venom is literally the most expensive liquid on earth. Guess how much for a litre?'

Kat found she didn't care for the excitable scientist's enthusiasm for a creature that had been used to commit murder. But she supposed he was just doing his job, and he *had* been helpful.

'I don't know,' she picked the largest number she thought might be reasonable, 'a thousand pounds?'

'Eight.'

Kat was shocked. 'Eight thousand pounds a litre?'

Milo grinned. 'Million.'

'Bloody hell!'

'I know. I'd say based on the average load per sting, your victim probably died from about ten pounds' worth of venom. Quite good value for money, when you think about it.'

'And that's definitely what would have happened, you think? The venom itself killed him, not some underlying condition it just tipped over the edge.'

'Absolutely. They say children, the elderly and those with allergies are most at risk, but the literature is full of stories of fatalities among otherwise healthy adults. I, myself, published an article a couple of years back. Chap I was working with in Iraq was fatally stung. The progress of his deterioration was fascinatingly fast.

Doctors couldn't do a thing for him. Sad, obviously, for his family, but still. It's in *Papers in Arachnology.* I could let you have a copy?'

'I'm not much of a reader, to be honest,' Kat said, wondering how, precisely, Milo's colleague had got stung.

Kat signalled right for the university campus and after thanking Milo again, wished him a good rest of his day and let him out.

As he leaned back in to say goodbye, she said, 'You said you wouldn't mind seeing a colleague with a Deathstalker in their slippers.'

He grinned. 'I was joking. As I think I said.'

'Why did you say "slippers"?'

He shrugged. 'Scorpions love dark places. It's almost a cliché.'

He straightened and closed the door. She watched him all the way up the path to his department.

'But you could have said "shoes",' she murmured before pulling out her mobile and calling Tom. 'Can you run a background check on a Dr Milo Smith for me? He's an arachnologist at the uni.'

'Am I looking for anything in particular?'

'I want to know if he's had any interactions with Pete Vaughan over the last five years. Also, any criminal record, speeding tickets, cautions. And if there's any way you can find out what he was doing at the key points on our timeline, that, too.'

'Person of interest?'

'I'm not sure. Maybe just an interesting person. But he's got a couple of Deathstalkers and he's just weirdly into them.'

'Surely that goes with the territory. I mean, forensic ballistics experts tend to love their guns, don't they?'

'Yeah, maybe. But do it for me, will you?'

She started the car and drove back to the station. She'd almost reached Jubilee Place when her phone rang. It was Dalma.

'Hi, Dalma. Are you back in town?'

'Yes. I'm sorry for giving you the brush-off on Friday, but the stress is killing me. I had to get away.'

'It's fine, Dalma, I understand. Really, I do.'

'Thank you. Anyway, I am working from home today so if you wanted to come round and search, that would be fine. But please, just you, Kat. I don't want a horde of men tramping through my house.'

Kat swung a right. She had a fingerprint that almost certainly belonged to the murderer. Would she find evidence at Dalma's house that could put a name to the print?

Chapter Forty-Five

Kat sat amidst the clutter on the floor of Pete's office and picked up a sheet of paper. She looked at all the others and sighed.

An hour later, rubbing her stiff neck, she went downstairs to find Dalma.

'Anything?' Dalma asked, looking up from her laptop.

Kat shook her head.

'Did Pete have anywhere he kept hard copies of his work-in-progress? I know he was security conscious so I'm hoping he had paper backups.'

Dalma frowned, deepening the lines that grief had grooved into her forehead. 'I mean, not normally. I often suggested it, but Pete was a stubborn man,' she said, with a sad smile. 'But actually, maybe he did for this project. I kept hearing him stomping about in the loft. All hours of the night. Early mornings, you know? Maybe he was stashing copies up there.'

'Can I have a look?'

'Of course. I'll show you the way. The trapdoor's a little sticky. There's a knack.'

Kat followed Dalma out of the kitchen and upstairs. After some jiggling with a hooked metal pole, Dalma freed the trapdoor, which swung down so suddenly that both women jumped back.

'If anyone *had* tried to steal it, that would have knocked them out cold,' Kat said.

She climbed the ladder, reaching inside the open hatch to switch on the light – a bright, bare bulb dangling from a length of dirty white flex. Dalma came up behind her and Kat turned to offer her hand, helping Dalma into the roof space.

The space was a mess. Cardboard boxes from kitchen appliances. Half-used rolls of peach-coloured fibreglass insulation. A pedestal fan. Bits of junky-looking furniture. A disassembled flat-pack wardrobe.

'Did you get a sense of where Pete was working?' Kat asked, hoping she wouldn't have to spend hours up here.

Dalma nodded. 'It sounded like he was on top of my head.' She pointed to the far end. 'Maybe there? It's above our bedroom.'

Picking her way across the joists – anxious not to put a foot through the ceiling and add a repair bill to her spiralling case budget – Kat reached the far end of the loft. Here, a few click-fit chipboard panels had been laid together, forming a basic platform. Clearly this was where Pete had stored his old paperwork. Black-and-red plastic box files covered in a thick layer of dust sat cheek by jowl with an equally dusty desktop PC. Sainsbury's carrier bags full of what looked like old receipts lay in an untidy heap beside a towering stack of copies of the *Echo*. Sighing, she stepped over the PC and peered at the chaotic assemblage of the dead journalist's records.

She kneeled in front of the nearest box file and pulled it towards her, sliding an index finger under the lock to pop the latch. She stopped. Lying flat behind it was a burgundy leather briefcase. The old-fashioned kind with shiny gold combination latches. Unlike the box files and the PC, the briefcase was glossy and dust free. Frequently used, then.

Excitement flickering in her gut, Kat lifted the briefcase out of its hiding place and laid it on the board in front of her.

'I've never seen that case before,' Dalma said from right behind her, making Kat jump.

Kat thumbed the latches but they wouldn't move. 'I think this could be it,' she said. 'Let's get it downstairs and try to figure out the combination.'

Back in the kitchen, Kat laid the briefcase on the table, angling Dalma's work lamp on to the locks.

'How about Pete's birthday?' Dalma suggested. 'Sixth of July, 1985.'

Kat thumbed the wheels round.

060785

Nothing.

'How about *your* birthday?' Kat asked.

'Tenth of November, 1986.'

Kat entered the date.

101186

Nothing.

She ran through a few more memorable dates, the Vaughans' wedding day, date they met, date Middlehampton FC were promoted into the Premiership. Forward and backwards. Nothing worked. She ran out of patience.

'Have you got a sturdy knife, or a screwdriver?' she asked.

Dalma nodded, and after scrabbling through a narrow drawer handed Kat a scuffed, brown leather pouch. It contained a stainless-steel multi-tool. Kat prised out the bottle-opener and inserted its flat-head screwdriver tip under the left-hand catch. A sharp shove and twist. The lock gave with a nasty metallic crack. She repeated the process and laid the multi-tool to one side.

Hoping the case would reveal Pete's working documents for his exposé and not some deviant sexual kink, or a cache of love letters, she lifted the lid.

If it had been a film, she felt sure a blinding golden light would have wavered and shone from inside, accompanied by the harmonious chanting of a celestial choir. As it was she had to settle for her own muted gasp.

Lying on top of a thick wad of papers was a single sheet. It bore a two-word heading.

Eel Deal.

The briefcase was full of photographs printed out on glossy paper, stapled A4 sheets of what looked like bank statements, and thick wads of internet printouts. Further down were sheet after sheet of printed-out article drafts, each one meticulously hand-identified with a code across the top of the front page.

She turned the briefcase round to Dalma so she could see the contents. 'Can I take this?'

'Of course. If it will help catch Pete's killer. But take care of it. I hope I can still find a way to publish it when this is all over. As a testament to Pete's spirit.'

'I will. I promise,' Kat said, shutting the lid.

She thanked Dalma and left her at the front door, waving, as she settled behind the wheel of her car. Was this it? The moment the case broke? It felt like it. First the fingerprint on the scorpion pincer and now a treasure trove of documents. Would the name of Pete's murderer be typed out on one of the sheets of A4 sitting inside the case on the passenger seat?

Kat hadn't entirely ruled out Gerald Hynde or Nick Chater. But her instincts were telling her that the person who'd procured and then used the Deathstalker to commit murder was utterly ruthless. Neither man fitted the bill. The MO was simply too convoluted. Stolen courier uniforms? Faked-up shipping labels? The Deathstalker itself? It felt to Kat more like the sort of thing she could imagine Vicky Palmer orchestrating rather than a groundsman or a frail widower.

She'd continue with efforts to eliminate them both, but for now, her focus was on the Al Jumairis, and the man nicknamed 'Stinger' – Saleem Elwani.

She just needed his lawyer to turn up.

Chapter Forty-Six

The first thing Kat did when she returned to MCU was to check in on Saleem Elwani.

He was sitting stoically in the interview room. There was a cup of water on the table in front of him.

'No lawyer,' Leah said, when Kat asked. 'He's been sat in there like a statue.'

'He'll have to just stew for a bit longer, then.'

She found Tom at his desk and handed him the thick file of Pete's research. 'Can you do me a summary, Tomski, please? As soon as possible?'

An hour later, he came over to her desk. 'It's massive, Kat. According to this, half the council were involved in a corrupt property scheme allied to the Eel Deal. And Pete was just days from blowing the whistle on the whole lot. He's identified the people due a payout. They'd have got nothing and probably been investigated by Fraud. Talk about a motive.'

'Who are they, Tomski? Please tell me he used their real names, not codes?'

He went over to the murder wall and picked up a marker. 'He did. We've got Don Byatt, Cory Whittaker and Kirsten Blake,' he said, underlining their names. 'Director of planning, director of finance and council leader respectively.'

'Bloody hell, Tomski, this is awful.'

'Yeah, and it gets worse. Reuben Starling, MP. John and Daniela Morris. And uh— I mean, you have to understand, Kat, none of this is proven. They're just the names in his files.'

With a sinking feeling, Kat knew who the final name would be. 'It's OK, Tomski, you can say his name.'

Tom dropped his eyes for a second, then looked back at Kat. 'Colin Morton.'

She nodded. Finally, a piece of evidence pointing at her father that she could hand over to Fraud. She called the others over.

'Leah, Fez, I want you to start TIE-ing these seven.'

'Sorry, boss,' Abby said, 'tying?'

'Trace, interview, eliminate.'

'Sorry, I should have known. But there's just so much to take in.'

'It's fine, Abs.' She turned to address the others. 'This is standard procedure, but do I actually think one of that lot committed murder? If the weapon had been a blade, a bat or a brick, I could see it? But where the hell would one of those people get a Deathstalker from?'

'Not from a registered supplier in the UK,' Abby said. 'I finally finished checking them all. Nobody's sold one in the last five years. And none of those seven people have a DWA. I checked based on Leah's original list.'

Kat nodded. Abby had her faults, from ducking post-mortems to not knowing basic acronyms, but that was decent detective work.

'Nice work, Abs,' she said, earning a wide grin. 'Fez, can you look at flight details, passport records, the usual, see if any of them have been to the Middle East recently.'

She ended the meeting, more convinced than ever that they were looking in the right direction for Pete's killer, and maybe even the bomber.

Fez surprised Kat by returning to her desk just twenty minutes later. 'You're going to like this, our kid,' he said. 'Guess who out of our magnificent seven has been to the Gulf recently?'

She smiled. 'Go on.'

'All of them.'

That really *was* a surprise. 'Details?'

'They all flew out to Al Jumairah last month on a private jet.'

Kat nodded. 'So they're all out there, some sort of jolly. Nice bit of shopping. Beach time. Little bit of business before the fun starts.'

Fez nodded. 'Maybe some falconry in chauffeur-driven Bentley SUVs. You can get a Bentayga fitted out with special perches for the birds.'

Kat rolled her eyes. 'Do I want to know how you know that?'

He shrugged, grinned. 'What can I say? If I had a spare three hundred grand, I'd consider one.'

'So any one of them could have brought a Deathstalker back to the UK?'

'If they could get it through security, yes. Which would have been minimal, especially with the kind of money the Al Jumairis can throw around.'

'This is great work, Fez.' She called over to Leah. 'Any news on our magnificent seven? Anyone we can talk to this afternoon?'

Leah heeled her swivel chair over.

'If we're quick we can catch them all together. They're in a meeting right now at The Garland.'

'OK, great. Leah? With me. Let's go and see them now.'

The young man behind The Garland's reception desk listened to Kat's polite request for admittance to the conference suite, then offered an apologetic smile that didn't reach his eyes.

'I'm afraid our conference rooms are private. It's part of our client confidentiality package.'

'I see,' Kat said, glancing at his name badge. 'This is an active murder investigation, James. I have reason to believe one or more of the people in the meeting may be involved. So unless you'd like my colleague here to arrest you for obstruction, you'll tell me which room they're in and give me a card for the locks.'

He blinked, pale lashes fluttering. Fiddled with his tie. 'Oh. It's just . . . I'd have to check with my manager.'

Kat didn't want to get too heavy with him. But she needed to talk to the people just a few feet over her head. 'James, you're just doing your job, I get it. But so am I. And right now, I think catching a murderer beats preserving client confidentiality. So call your boss, but please make it very quick.'

He nodded. Picked up the desk phone and punched a number. While he waited, he shot her a nervous grin. Poor bloke. He'd probably been drilled on the need for client privacy at a training course.

Then he nodded. 'It's James, Mr Robard. I have two police detectives in reception. They need access to the conference suite . . . Yes, I told them, but they said they'll arrest me if I . . . OK, I'll tell them.' He replaced the receiver in the cradle. 'Mr Robard says you need a warrant.'

Kat sighed. Mr Robard was correct. But time was tight and she didn't have any to spare. But taking in James's youthful looks, another idea occurred to her.

'What do you do in your time off, James? Pub? Clubs? Ever go to any gigs?'

He looked puzzled. 'Yeah. I mean, it depends who's playing, obviously.'

'Were you at the Powerhouse last week?'

'Oh, God, no. But a couple of my mates were. They said it was terrifying.' He frowned. 'I thought you said you were investigating a murder.'

'We are, but it's linked to the Powerhouse bombing. You can help us catch the people who did that, James. But I'm going to need that access card and I don't have time to go back to my station and sort out a warrant.'

He looked at her, then Leah. Finally, he nodded. He pulled open a drawer, took out a blank white rectangle of plastic and fed it into a small black machine. He tapped a few keys on his PC and after a few seconds of electronic whirring, handed her the card.

'Stairs are probably quicker. They're in Pennyroyal.' Seeing Kat's frown, he added, 'Our conference rooms are named after wildflowers.'

She nodded her thanks and ran for the stairs, Leah right behind her.

They followed the signs to the end of a short hallway and Kat pushed through the door beside a neatly typeset sign bearing an illustration of a purple spiked flower.

The ten occupants turned as one. Nine were seated, one stood with his back to the floor-to-ceiling window. A security guard. She recognised the type. Muscular build. Watchful gaze. And was that artfully tailored suit jacket concealing a weapon? She decided to avoid that line of enquiry for now.

She recognised all but one of the people around the table. Sitting beside the Crown Prince was a balding man with a glance like a blade. She just knew he would be the Crown Prince's chief lawyer. The others were the men and women listed on her whiteboard. She caught her father's eye and felt the heat of his glare burning her. She stared back before turning to address the Crown Prince.

'Forgive the intrusion, Zizou,' she said, deliberately using his nickname to show the Middlehampton contingent she had a personal relationship with him. 'But it's vital to my investigation into Pete Vaughan's murder that I ask your guests a question.'

The others were all either frowning or staring at Kat and Leah with barely disguised anger.

'This is outrageous!' Don Byatt said. 'Who the hell are you, and how did you get up here?'

'DS Ballantyne,' she said, showing him her ID. 'And this is DC Hooper. It's come to our notice that everyone in this room was named in a document prepared by the murdered journalist Peter Vaughan. In the document, he alleged that illegal transactions were taking place in connection with the deal to acquire Middlehampton FC. I'm wondering how you all felt about that?'

She scanned the room. Waiting to see who'd break cover first. After all, the delay between the scorpion entering the courier system and the fatal sting meant asking them for alibis was of limited value. This was about getting a read on a potential suspect. If someone had a guilty conscience, it could prompt them to react differently to the others.

'This is ridiculous!' Daniela Morris said. 'Kat, you know me. You've sat in my lounge and talked about . . . family matters. How could you think any of us is involved in murder?'

'If Pete was right, and there were illegal payments being made, that would be a strong motive for murder for anyone frightened of exposure in the media.'

The Crown Prince's smooth voice broke in. 'Vaughan was an obsessive. He saw corruption everywhere. But in reality I'm afraid he was himself tainted. I know he liked to paint himself as a sort of saviour of the downtrodden and the powerless, but the truth is rather different,' he said. 'I tasked my head of security, whom I believe you are still holding, with doing some background research into Pete Vaughan. His findings make for interesting listening. If I may?'

'Please.'

'For years, my security services have been digging into the various dissident groups active in Al Jumairah. As soon as we shut one down, another springs up to take its place. They breed like jerboa. Desert Sun is merely the latest to appear. A more radical, violent offshoot of a group named Free Al Jumairah. Now, this may be no more than souk gossip, but we received word that Peter Vaughan was linked to Desert Sun *and* their bomb plot. Perhaps he changed his mind and they killed him to silence him.'

This was *not* information Kat had been expecting. 'Would you share anything else you learn about this alleged link with me, please?'

'Of course. We will be happy to help in any way we can. As soon as I learn something, you will learn it too.'

There was nothing else to be gained by staying. And the business with the keycard sat uneasily with Kat. She thanked the Crown Prince, and then glanced at her dad. His expression was unreadable.

Satisfied for now, but still suspicious, Kat left them to their deal-making.

Could the Crown Prince's story be the answer? Kat found she had no clear idea if he was telling the truth. Dalma had said her husband had fallen in love with the country. Could love have turned to hate for the regime? Enough for Pete to get involved in a plot to destabilise it?

If he had, and then got cold feet, it would have been a powerful motive for a violent group to murder him.

Chapter Forty-Seven

Kat had barely set foot in MCU before Sharon accosted her.

'Have you been investigating the bombing?'

'No. I've got enough on my plate with Pete Vaughan's murder. Why?'

'Because I'm hearing nasty little rumours that Middlehampton cops have been asking all kinds of people about terrorism links. I know you think it's linked to your murder but my experience tells me otherwise.' Sharon tried for a smile, but it came off as false to Kat. 'I thought we had an agreement, Kat. You'd stay out of my hair and report anything you found out about the bomb plot to me.'

'Which I will do. But as of now I have nothing concrete about the bombing at all.'

Sharon raised an eyebrow. 'What about anything non-concrete? Squidgy, maybe?'

Kat met her stare. Didn't blink. 'Nothing. Have you heard anything about Pete being involved with Desert Sun?'

'Why, have you?'

Unsure whether she believed the Crown Prince's claim about Pete, Kat opted for a half-truth. 'No.'

'Well, then. There we are. More evidence the two cases aren't linked.'

With that, Sharon walked off back to the office she'd commandeered. Kat looked after her, baffled by the way Sharon's mind seemed to run on rails.

'Boss!' It was Abby. 'Elwani's lawyer's here.'

'At last. Any idea who it is?'

Abby shook her head. 'A woman.'

Kat had a feeling she knew which woman she'd find sitting beside Saleem Elwani in interview room 2. 'Come on, then. Let's go and talk to Mr Elwani and his lawyer.'

Abby's eyes widened. 'You mean me?'

'Unless there's another detective-in-waiting standing behind you . . . Yes, Abs, you!'

'Cool!'

Out of Abby's eyeline, Kat shook her head, sighing. It really wasn't 'cool'. It was actually Abby's last chance to prove she had what it took to be a detective. Kat had reluctantly concluded that – barring a miracle – she didn't. Kat should have seen it earlier. But she blamed herself for being swayed by Abby's relentless fangirling.

As Kat had suspected, sitting beside Elwani was the holy terror of Middlehampton's criminal defence bar, Beth Sharpe. Kat and the fearsomely intelligent solicitor saw each other so often, Kat wondered whether they should have a 'ship' name, as in 'relationship', like Fez and his wife's FezNaz.

Katabeth? Bethryn?

Catching Beth's curious stare, Kat nodded to Abby who inhaled and then, word perfect, delivered the official caution.

Relieved Abby had got it right this time, Kat began. 'You're the Crown Prince's head of security, Saleem, is that right?'

'It is.'

'Can you tell us briefly what your job entails?'

He bowed his head. 'I am charged with preserving His Royal Highness's personal safety at all times. Predicting, removing or eliminating any and all threats.'

'I see. Thank you. Was Pete Vaughan a threat?'

He smiled. 'Pete Vaughan was a typical Westerner. Dabbling in matters of which he had no understanding. You have heard of the phrase "white saviour"? He thought it was his job to *save*' – air quotes – 'the people of Al Jumairah. The fact they had not asked him for his help seems not to have bothered him.'

'Was he linked to any dissident groups in Al Jumairah?'

'Dissident?' Elwani scoffed. 'Desert Sun is a *terrorist* organisation. As designated by the UN, the EU and your own government. But in any case, who knows? It is possible.'

That was interesting. He was less definite than his boss had been.

'Can you tell me where you were last Tuesday night between 6.00 p.m. and midnight, Saleem?'

'I was alone.'

'Yes, but where?'

'His Royal Highness gave me the evening off. I went for a walk.'

Kat frowned. She'd formed the impression the two men lived in each other's pockets. 'Was that normal? To dispense with your services?'

'I have men under my command. His Royal Highness was safe at all times. Anyone trying to harm him would have found they were running into the lion's mouth.'

'So he gave you the night off?'

'His Royal Highness was concerned I had been working too hard. He said I should relax for a few hours.'

'You were walking all that time?'

'I like to walk. At home, I walk many miles in the desert.'

'Where did you go, on this walk of yours?'

He shrugged. 'Nowhere in particular. I just walked. The park with the river in it. Around the town. The market.'

'The Powerhouse?'

For the first time since Kat had begun the interview, Beth stirred. She leaned towards Elwani and whispered behind her hand. He looked at Kat as he listened, nodding.

'On the advice of my legal counsel I decline to answer that question.'

Kat didn't even bother trying to get round Beth's advice. Any further questions about the bombing would, she knew, earn a repeat of the standard formulation Beth would have coached him to deliver.

'You see, Saleem, I'm just trying to establish your alibi for the night Pete Vaughan was murdered,' Kat said. 'And it would really help me if you could, for example, give me the name of someone you spent time with. Or a place you went. They usually have CCTV these days. Then I could eliminate you from our enquiries.'

She couldn't. She *wouldn't*. The key time to be alibied was when the scorpion-loaded *babouche* were introduced into the courier company's system, not when Pete was stung. But Elwani, apparently, didn't know this.

He dipped his head respectfully once again. 'I understand.'

'And?'

'I cannot help you. I am sorry.'

'That's OK. Have you ever gone by another name, Saleem?'

He frowned, dark brows drawing together over those deep-brown eyes. And then he smiled. 'When I was a little boy, my older brothers called me Mouse. I was small for my age. It is now merely' – he spread his muscular arms wide – 'ironic.'

Was he taunting her? Time to ratchet the questioning up a notch. 'I see. So, no others. From your army days, perhaps? I know soldiers in this country often get nicknames. Bit like the police. You know, Timesheet, Batman . . . Stinger.'

His features flashed over with anger. She saw it as clearly as if he'd held up a hand-lettered sign. A man used to being in control finding he'd been outmanoeuvred. Did the fact Kat was female have anything to do with it?

He clenched his fists on the table. His suit jacket tightened across those massive shoulders.

'You don't know what you are dealing with here.' Beth leaned towards him a second time, but this time he shrugged her off. 'Quiet, woman!' He glared at Kat. 'No. I have never gone by that name.'

'How would you react, Saleem,' Kat continued in a soft, friendly and oh-so-reasonable tone, 'if I were to tell you that I have evidence you *did* go by that nickname, during a training period with the SAS?'

He was breathing heavily. She'd scored a point. In his anger he forgot the legal protocols he'd agreed with Beth.

'That's confidential! How did you know about that?'

'Have you ever brought a Deathstalker scorpion into the UK? In a jam jar, for example?'

'No. But it seems like a stupid thing to do.'

'So you didn't show it to your comrades in the SAS and dare them to let it crawl on their hands?'

'No.'

'Are you aware that Pete Vaughan was murdered using a scorpion just like the one you brought to Hereford?'

Elwani's eyes were ablaze. Kat truly believed that at this moment, he would have killed her if their meeting was taking place in his country, not hers.

'My client has denied doing such a thing,' said Beth. 'Please move on.'

'Have you ever killed anyone, Saleem?'

The look he bestowed on Kat mixed contempt with anger. 'It is dishonourable to speak of such things.'

Kat believed she heard an unspoken 'with a woman' but let it go. She wasn't there to fight culture wars. She just wanted to solve Pete Vaughan's murder.

Apart from Elwani's lie about his military service, he'd been open and more or less courteous in answering the rest of her questions. His answer to the question of his whereabouts on the night of Pete's murder seemed genuine, too. Unlike most half-witted suspects, he'd made no attempt to cook up an easily disprovable alibi where none existed.

So was he innocent of everything except a silly stunt involving a Deathstalker in 2017? Or was his casual refusal to establish an alibi a double bluff, and he was guilty? There was no point holding him any longer. She had nothing. With a minute nod to Beth, she informed him he was free to go.

He left, taking her hopes of an early resolution to the case with him.

Chapter Forty-Eight

The afternoon turned into evening.

Nearly a week had elapsed since the bombing. Kat was no nearer to solving Pete's murder. That Sharon Critchlow and her team were drawing blanks identifying the Powerhouse bomber was no consolation. Kat thought Sharon's resistance to the idea that their two cases were linked was going to hamper her chances.

What sharpened her sense of frustration was the looming deadline for the Eel Deal. It would be signed the following day and then the Al Jumairis would board their jet and be gone, to a country with which the UK had no extradition treaty.

She really liked Saleem Elwani for the murder. He was surely capable of killing: he'd all but admitted as much in the interview that afternoon. And, despite his denials, he'd imported a Deathstalker into the UK in 2017, fooling around with it to impress his new friends in the SAS.

But what she lacked was hard evidence connecting him to the murder itself. Her best hope right now was that his fingerprints would yield a match to the partial Darcy had lifted from the Deathstalker's pincer.

She called the team together. Out of the four younger officers, only Abby appeared to have any energy. The other three looked tired and fed up. It wasn't uncommon. When a case refused to break, frustration, fatigue and the pressure of other cases, plus the never-ending paperwork, would sap the spirit from even the most dedicated detective.

'Look, I know we're chasing our tails here, but we're going to keep pushing on, OK? And we need to work fast. Once the Al Jumairis fly out of the UK we lose them. If it's one of them, they'll escape justice. We'll never get them back here.'

'What do you want us to do, boss?' Abby asked, practically standing to attention.

Kat puffed out her cheeks before she could stop herself. The DCs weren't the only ones feeling the strain.

'Let's get on with TIE-ing the people Pete named as recipients of Al Jumairi money. Leah and Abby, you take Don Byatt and Cory Whittaker. Tomski, Reuben Starling. Fez, you talk to the Morrises. And I'll talk to Kirsten Blake.'

'Er, Kat?' Leah said.

'What?'

'You forgot your dad.'

Kat flushed with guilt. Her subconscious was playing games. 'Of course. Tomski? Can you handle that? You've played golf with him, after all.'

Tom nodded. 'With pleasure.'

Pleasure looked to be the last thing on his mind. Tom had told her on their first case together that after seeing how her father operated, he'd decided he'd rather make his way honestly.

It turned out council leaders kept the same long hours as homicide detectives. Kat found Kirsten Blake in her office at the Town Hall and was waved in by an assistant.

Kirsten cracked a smile as Kat took a seat, but there was no offer of coffee or tea. Or even water. Fine by Kat. Dispensing with the social niceties sped things up.

'We meet again, DS Ballantyne. What is it this time?'

'Did you have any dealings with Pete Vaughan?'

'No. Why would I?'

'If he was investigating the Eel Deal, and your involvement in it, he might have asked you for an interview.'

Kirsten's lips pinched. 'Oh, he asked, all right. And I told him to go to hell. That man is a bloody liability. He attends every council meeting and wastes everybody's time with his never-ending questions. Do you have any idea of the budget this council has, DS Ballantyne? No? Well, I'll tell you. Seven hundred and thirty-eight million pounds. *Million*,' she repeated as if Kat might have been hard of hearing, or possibly listening. 'And Pete-bloody-Vaughan thinks we spend all our time embezzling it. But we don't! We spend it trying to keep this town supplied with services, the roads fixed, social care, libraries . . . It's never-ending.'

Interesting that Kirsten had referred to Pete in the present tense. Spouses often did the same, unable to face the fact their soulmate had been murdered. A way of refusing to confront the dreadful reality of murder. In Kat's experience, murderers tended to use the past tense. Obvious, really, since they knew for a fact the victim was dead.

'Do you even know why he was killed?' Kirsten asked.

'We're pursuing a number of lines of enquiry.'

'And you think it had something to do with the Eel Deal and his stupid campaign to stop it.'

'It's one of our working theories.'

'Well, here's another one for you,' Kirsten said slyly. 'Pete wasn't quite as saintly as he liked to paint himself. And I don't mean that line about him being in league with Desert Sun, either.'

'What *do* you mean?'

'A little bird told me that Pete Vaughan was, to use a phrase, playing away from home.'

Kat maintained an impassive expression. 'Any idea who he was playing *with*?' she asked.

'Not by name. Some protégée of his wife's, though, is what I heard.'

◆ ◆ ◆

Sitting in Dalma's kitchen twenty minutes later, Kat asked her a hopefully innocent-sounding question. No sense insinuating her husband was having an affair if it was just vicious gossip. Or even a murderer's clumsy attempt to throw Kat off the scent.

'Do you have anyone you're training? Or an intern?'

Dalma laughed. 'I'm a freelancer. How could I afford an assistant?'

Kat nodded. She didn't give Dalma's denial much weight. If she knew Pete had been having an affair with her own assistant, she might well lie about it.

'I suppose your work gives you opportunities to travel back home,' Kat said, wondering in that moment if it was Dalma who'd imported the Deathstalker.

'I haven't been back to Al Jumairah for years. Pete always wanted to go, but things have changed so much since we met.' A tear broke free of her lid and trickled down her cheek. 'Now we'll never go back.'

Kat thanked her and left. On the way back to Jubilee Place she called Tom and asked him to check on Dalma's movements over the last year.

Then she went back to wondering about the gossip. *What* protégée? Dalma's denials had seemed genuine enough, but maybe she wasn't entirely sure of the meaning of the word.

It could wait. What Kat needed now was a team with enough morale to keep going. And there was a tried-and-tested method of raising it. She arrived in MCU with a loud 'Right, pub.' She gathered her flock up like a mother duck and whisked them out to a local bar that did decent beer and cheap but drinkable Pinot Grigio.

By 8.00 p.m., spirits had lifted, and Abby had shown a superb ability as a mimic, reducing everyone to tears of laughter as she took off first Kat, then Linda and then, drawing the loudest shrieks, Carve-up.

Only Tom seemed distracted. He'd been downing pints like a man on a mission to rehydrate his soul with beer. He got to his feet unsteadily and wove off towards the toilets.

Kat got to her feet too and waited for him outside. When he reappeared, she touched him lightly on the shoulder.

'You all right, Tomski?'

'Me? Why wouldn't I be? My career's in the shitter thanks to that bastard Paxton and now so's my love life.'

'Oh, Tomski. What happened?'

'Eleanor dumped me last night. Said I've got "unpredictable mood swings". I tried to explain it's a side-effect of being in a coma but she said it didn't matter. She couldn't cope with it anymore.'

He looked at her with reddened eyes already glistening with tears. Instinctively she drew him into a hug. 'Hey, hey,' she crooned, as he sobbed in her arms. 'It's OK. Let it out.'

He did, drawing the odd inquisitive look from drinkers passing them on their way to the loo. Finally he pulled away, dragged a paper tissue from his pocket and scrubbed at his eyes.

He cleared his throat. 'God, sorry, Kat.'

'Don't be. It stinks, getting dumped. I'm really sorry.'

'Thanks for not telling me there are plenty of fish in the sea.'

'You really liked her, didn't you?'

'I did. She was the first girl since Janis I actually had proper feelings for.'

Janis. Tom's university girlfriend had also left him, after a fight in a pub that had ended in the death of a biker. Not Tom's fault, but Janis had returned to the US soon after.

'Listen, if you ever need to talk, I'm here. And, Tomski,' she said as he turned to go. 'It's OK not to be OK. Yes?'

He nodded. Managed a half-smile. 'Yes, boss.'

Kat left a short while later, texting Van to say she was on her way home.

His reply pushed the boundaries of conciseness into a whole new dimension.

k

Not even two k's this time.

He was probably just busy. But she drove home hurriedly all the same.

Van seemed fine when she arrived. They had dinner with Riley, watched TV, chatted and went to bed. But Kat couldn't shake the idea that he was playing a part. That somewhere he was keeping his true feelings from her.

In bed, lying next to him in the dark, she voiced the thought.

'Is everything OK?' she whispered.

'Yes. Why?' he whispered back.

'Your text was so short. I was worried you were still cross about the other morning.'

'What do you mean?'

'That thing about Jack being my boyfriend. He really isn't, you know.'

'I know.' He rolled over, pressed his face close to hers so the tips of their noses touched and she could feel his breath on her cheek. 'It's just . . .'

'What, Van. Tell me!'

'Even when you're here and you've left the case at work, you're sneaking off to the back bedroom to stare at that bloody murder wall or whatever it is. It's like I'm still only getting half of you when you're at home, if that.'

'I'm sorry, darling,' she whispered. 'I know I'm preoccupied, but I have to know what turned Jo into a monster. I have to! You understand, don't you?'

The silence between them stretched out. Finally Van pulled his head back.

'I do, yes. Of course I do. Now go to sleep.'

Kat tried. But it took a long time.

Despite it vibrating on her nightstand at 6.00 a.m., Kat's phone alarm didn't wake her. She'd been on mental high alert for at least an hour, lying silently beside a snoring Van, worrying at the case like Smokey when a treat got lodged under a radiator.

But it did tell her it was time to get out of bed.

Van made a grab for her but she wriggled from his grasp before turning to kiss him.

'Can't. Got to walk the dog then get into work. I'll bring you some tea before I leave.'

He grunted something that might have been a 'thank you' or equally a complaint, rolled over and went back to sleep.

She ate standing up – toast and Marmite, and coffee, black – clipped Smokey's lead on and headed out. Reaching the Gallops, she let Smokey off and he raced away, yelping delightedly, already zipping into the crops looking for pheasants.

She looked down the straight swathe of grass, searching for a long-legged, black-and-white flash heading for Smokey, but they had the field to themselves. Maybe Barrie was having a lie-in. He was retired after all.

Kat tried to imagine what that would feel like. Putting her thirty in and giving up the chase. Found she couldn't. Her work gave her life meaning. Her marriage did, too, of course, and she'd never once regretted having a baby young. But deep down, in the place she kept all to herself, she knew that without cop work, she'd struggle.

Was it because of Liv? That desperate deception when they were teenagers had scarred Kat mentally, but it had also given her the impetus to find her purpose. She smiled at the thought of her best friend getting married. It didn't matter what case was going on at the time, Kat would be there for Liv at the dress fitting, the hen, the rehearsal and the big day itself. Nothing, and nobody, would get between them again.

While Smokey tore around the young wheat, she pictured the murder wall at Jubilee Place. Her investigation into Pete Vaughan's murder was as fast moving and twisty as Smokey's progress through the crops. One minute, a widower's grief and a groundsman's fury were likely motives. Then international power politics and municipal corruption. And now, thanks to Kirsten Blake's revelation, sex? Was it really going to come down to the oldest motive for murder in the book? One the writers of the Bible would have recognised. It had to be a strong possibility.

And if it was, then one person had the clearest motive to murder him.

Had Kat been chasing polar bears all along, when she should have been looking for a seagull?

A seagull named Dalma Vaughan?

Chapter Forty-Nine

Ten past eight. Her team were assembled in front of the whiteboard. *Good*, she thought, *everybody still keen*. Maybe the trip to the pub the previous night had been just what they needed.

'According to Kirsten Blake, the council leader, Pete was having an affair,' Kat said, scrawling up a stick woman beside his photo and a question mark, plus the word 'affair'.

'Can we take her word for it, though, boss?' Abby asked. 'She could be trying to throw shade because she's already in the frame herself.'

Kat caught Tom offering Fez an eye roll. *Let it pass*. Abby was doing her best.

'No. But we can follow it up. So now we have three strong lines of enquiry. If there really *was* an affair, then I'd expect it to be Dalma or the girlfriend,' Kat said, tapping the marker against the stick woman. 'If Kirsten was lying, then we're back to looking at the Al Jumairis, Nick Chater or Gerald Hynde.'

Abby's mouth was already working. Kat could see she was desperate to come in again.

'Abs?'

'It's just, I thought you were convinced it *was* the Al Jumairis? Elwani specifically?'

'That's what my gut's telling me, yes. But we can't afford to get tunnel vision. So here's what we do today. Tom, I want you and Abby to keep on at the CCTV. We need to find that courier van and the person who dropped off the *babouche* at Pete's. It looked like a man and either he did the whole thing himself or he was working for someone else. Either way, we find him, we find our killer. Leah, can you keep digging into Chater and Hynde? We need to eliminate them one way or another. Fez, you and I are going to look at Dalma. And I have an idea where to start.'

Middlehampton had five mosques. The closest to the Vaughans' house in Northbridge was Makkah Mosque.

It occupied the corner between Merryvale Road and Dunston Road a few hundred yards from 31 Viking Way. Kat thought it was stunning, and admired the way it was built from alternating courses of rust-red and pale-gold bricks. Tall, arched windows outlined in deep blue, a huge central dome of blue-green patinated copper, and at each corner an octagonal tower surmounted by a smaller copper dome. The tower on its south-eastern corner was half as tall again as the others and built to narrower, more graceful proportions.

'The minaret,' Fez supplied. 'Where the call to prayer comes from.'

'And you're sure it's OK for me to go in? Not being a believer, I mean. And a woman?'

He smiled. 'It's fine, our kid, I told you. Women *are* allowed in mosques. Actually they're encouraged. It's just not compulsory. And the black suit is definitely "modest attire" so you're golden.'

She tried to push down her nerves. She'd never been a churchgoer, so entering any kind of religious building put her on edge. As if she'd unintentionally cross some invisible line of protocol and have an outraged cleric hustling her off the premises.

'OK, but can you lead?'

He shook his head, grinning. 'Stick with me, bab, you'll be all right.'

After removing their shoes in the vestibule, they went in. Kat gasped. Where the exterior had been impressive, the interior was downright beautiful. With no interior pillars, the central hall was as big as the sports hall at the leisure centre where Kat played with the Malbec Mafia. But instead of polished pine floorboards with their overlapping netball court outlines in coloured tape, the mosque floor was covered in a carpet of royal blue with golden designs woven into it. Above their heads, the underside of the central dome was tiled in intricate turquoise, purple and blue patterns comprising geometric figures and Arabic script, reminding Kat of their purpose in being there.

Fez had called ahead, and the imam was waiting for them. A slightly built man in his forties with prematurely greying hair, black-framed glasses and a look of kindly curiosity on his face.

They met in the centre of the carpet, directly under the dome.

'*As-salamu alaykum*, Imam Hamza,' Fez said.

'*Wa alaikum as-salaam*, DC Mohammed,' he replied, shaking Fez's hand.

Fez gestured to Kat. 'This is my boss, DS Kat Ballantyne.'

'*As-salamu alaykum*, Imam Hamza,' she said nervously, echoing Fez's greeting, which she'd been mentally rehearsing on the drive over.

'*Wa alaikum as-salaam*, DS Ballantyne. Welcome to Makkah Mosque and thank you for your greeting. Most police officers don't bother with such niceties.'

'You've had dealings with the police before?'

He shrugged. 'Graffiti, from time to time. Assaults on worshippers leaving the mosque. It is rare, but sadly, it happens.'

'I'm sorry to hear that. I hope my colleagues were helpful.'

'They were, don't worry. Would you like to come to my office? We can have tea.'

'Thank you, that would be lovely.'

The imam led them to an office which contrasted with the ornate decoration elsewhere in the building. It could have been the office of a DI back at Jubilee Place. A functional space with bookshelves and filing cabinets, a desk, two visitor chairs.

Once tea was made and poured, he clasped his hands on his desk. 'How can I help you?'

'This is a sensitive matter, Imam,' Fez said. 'It concerns the murder of Pete Vaughan. You read about it?'

The imam bowed his head. 'I did. Terrible business.'

'Is Dalma Vaughan a worshipper here at Makkah Mosque?'

The imam nodded at once.

'Yes. She comes regularly. With no children to raise, the traditional exemptions for women do not trouble Dalma.'

'Imam, we have been told that Pete was having an affair. Did Dalma ever mention anything like that to you?'

'No. Never. As far as I knew, Dalma's marriage was a happy one.'

Kat leaned forward. 'Imam, I was told that the woman in question was a protégée of Dalma's. Do you know of anyone who might fit that description?'

He shook his head. 'I'm afraid not. But Dalma volunteers at a local charity for refugees and asylum seekers. Perhaps they could help you? It's on Merryvale Road here in Northbridge. The Salam Project. Like our greeting. It means "peace" in Arabic.'

'Thank you, Imam, that's really helpful,' Kat said.

They finished their tea and after thanking the imam again for his time, made their way back through a sparse group of worshippers and out to the car.

Time to locate Dalma's protégée and possible love rival. Would one of the two women turn out to be the murderer?

Chapter Fifty

The Salam Project's office couldn't have presented a greater contrast to the Makkah Mosque.

The tiny charity occupied shopfront premises along a stretch of Merryvale Road characterised by vape shops, fast-food places and phone repair places, usually spelling their stock-in-trade 'fone'.

Inside was a small reception area with a couple of battered armchairs and a desk and chair, currently unattended. Somewhere towards the back, children's voices were raised in laughter and songs, like in any infant school or nursery in Middlehampton.

A woman in her thirties appeared, smiling a little, but anxiety showed behind her eyes. 'Can I help you? I am Yasmina Koussa, the director here.'

Kat and Fez produced their IDs.

The worry lines in Yasmina's forehead deepened. 'All our paperwork is in order. We are doing nothing wrong.'

'I'm sure it is,' Kat said, injecting as much reassurance into her voice as she could manage. 'We just need to ask you a few questions.'

'I'm afraid there isn't anywhere very private to talk. We are very short of space.'

She led Kat and Fez to some under-sized plastic chairs, and they grouped them into a triangle in one corner of the large room that served as a play centre.

'Do you know Dalma Vaughan?' Kat asked.

The woman's face fell. 'Poor Dalma. Her husband being murdered like that. She volunteers here, interpreting for our service users and helping with form-filling. That kind of thing.'

'Does she have a protégée?'

Yasmina frowned. 'I am sorry, I do not know that word.'

'Sorry. Someone she is training or working closely with? Another volunteer, perhaps? A young lady?'

Yasmina smiled. 'Oh, of course, yes! That would be Illy. Well, she is Iliana Nassar but everybody calls her Illy. She is Jordanian. She studies at the university, but she also volunteers here.'

'Is she in today?'

'Yes. She is in the office. It's why we are speaking here. Shall I fetch her?'

'Please.'

Two minutes later, Yasmina reappeared. Beside her was the most beautiful young woman Kat had ever seen. Tall, svelte, with large dark eyes, lustrous long auburn hair and a wide smile revealing perfect teeth framed by plum-coloured lipstick.

Beside her, Fez's jaw had all but unhinged. She nudged him and he closed his mouth with an audible *clop*.

'Detectives, this is Illy. I will leave you to talk,' Yasmina said.

The young woman folded herself into the chair, knees together and swung to one side as if she'd studied deportment.

Kat introduced herself and Fez, since he seemed to have temporarily lost the power of speech.

'Is everything all right?' Illy asked.

Kat smiled back. 'I think he's just having a boy-moment. I'm sorry.'

'Don't be. I'm studying for a Masters in computing now at Middlehampton University. Even my professor forgets I have a brain sometimes.'

Kat warmed to the young woman sitting before her. Beauty, brains *and* a self-aware sense of humour. A powerful combination as long as she could ride out the male gaze.

'Can I ask you, Illy, do you work with Dalma Vaughan?'

Illy's lower lip trembled. She nodded. 'She mentors me.'

'And how about Pete Vaughan? Did you know him at all?'

Illy gasped. Her face crumpled. Tears broke over those immaculately mascaraed lower lids and coursed down her cheeks. Kat offered a tissue, sure now that Kirsten Blake wasn't simply spreading vicious gossip. Or trying to dig herself out of a hole.

'Tell me about Pete,' Kat prompted softly. 'Were you two involved?'

'He was so lovely. Kind. He told me he was in love with me. I knew it was wrong. He was so much older than me. But I was alone here in Middlehampton. He was so interested in me. I fell for him.'

To Kat's cynical ear, Illy's tearful words sounded like something from a romance novel. 'You were having an affair?'

Illy shook her head. 'Nothing, you know' – she swallowed – 'physical happened. But I believe we had a connection. But then he broke it off just a week before he died. He broke my heart,' she sobbed.

Kat nodded. Offered the rest of the packet of tissues. But as Illy pulled herself together, she found herself wondering whether she was sitting knee to knee with a murderer. Despite her intellect, or perhaps because of it, Illy was clearly an innocent in the ways of male-female relationships. A woman as beautiful as her would be catnip to a middle-aged bloke like Pete Vaughan. Or, for that matter, any straight guy over fourteen. She could imagine Riley's reaction to Illy. It would make Fez look like a model of restraint.

'Illy, can I ask you, where were you last Tuesday night, between 6.00 p.m. and 10.00 p.m.?'

Illy dabbed delicately at her eyes, blotting rather than wiping her tears away. 'I was here, working with a group of women. Teaching them IT skills. Why?'

'Just a routine question. And Yasmina would be able to confirm that?'

'No. I have my own key. I run the classes on my own. But the women I was teaching could, if it's important? We have a list of their names in the office. Shall I fetch it?'

'That would be great, thank you.'

Illy unfolded herself from her chair and left Kat with Fez.

'You managed to get your eyes back in their rightful place, then, our kid,' Kat said, grinning. 'Wait. Is that a blush under that goatee, DC Mohammed?'

He smiled back. 'OK, OK. Guilty as charged. But you have to admit, boss, she's a bostin' wench.'

Kat raised her eyebrows. 'I'm going to assume that's a Brummie term of admiration for a beautiful woman and not a sexist insult?'

'Absolutely. Here she comes, look, with her alibi.'

Kat and Fez got to their feet to meet her. She handed Kat the list. It contained names but no contact details.'

'If you want to speak to them, you need to go through Yasmina. These women have escaped persecution. They are very frightened of the authorities.'

'Of course,' Kat said. 'We will do, and I promise we'll be respectful and discreet.'

Leaving Illy, she and Fez went back to the car.

'You like her for it?' Fez asked, once they were both seated and Kat had pulled away from the kerb.

'I don't *not* like her for it. If Pete broke it off, whatever *it* was, that could give her motive. But whether he did or not, it also gives

Dalma motive. Which would mean I've been wrong about her almost from the beginning.'

'And no brute force required, which would fit with what we know of female killers.'

'On the whole,' Kat agreed. 'And Illy comes from Jordan. Can you look up if they have Deathstalkers there?'

'Hold on. Just checking Wikipedia. Yep. It says they're found right across the Middle East.'

◆ ◆ ◆

Kat and Fez arrived back to MCU at 11.00 a.m. She hadn't even got her bag under the desk before Sharon Critchlow stormed over, her face a mask of fury.

'What the hell are you doing, Kat?'

Kat bridled at once, fed up with being treated like a criminal in her own house. 'I'm investigating a murder. Why, Sharon? What's up?'

'Your team, that's what. PC Wannabe has been sneaking off with our files, thinking she's going to solve the bombing *and* the murder. A regular twofer. You need to shorten her leash or I'll do it for you.'

Kat's heart sank. What had Abby done now? But whatever the ambitious young woman had been up to, no way was Kat going to let an incomer, especially one as snotty as Sharon, lay the law down or refer to her team as dogs, even by implication.

'Nobody's shortening anybody's leash,' she shot back. 'That's not how I run my team. If PC Greene's trod on your toes then—'

'*Trod on my toes?* Did you not just hear what I said? She's been making illegal copies of confidential Met files for her own purposes. You need to get her in line, pronto. This isn't bring your daughter to work day, it's a terrorist investigation!'

Kat's heart was banging uncontrollably against her ribs and her breath was coming in short gasps. She was dimly aware of faces turned in their direction as the argument heated up.

'Yeah? I'm not so sure. And from what I can see, either way, you and *your* team aren't making any headway. The only bit of real intel you have was the one *I* provided.'

They were mere inches away from each other. Close enough for Kat to see the lines above Sharon's mouth where her lippy had tracked out of its boundaries.

'Ladies. Ladies, stand down!' Kat spun to see Vicky Palmer walking towards them, the MI6 agent patting the air and sending the watching cops back to their work with a commanding, 'Nothing to see here. Back to it, everyone.'

'You have no standing here,' Sharon said, breathing heavily. 'This is a police matter.'

'*Au contraire*, Sharon,' Vicky said, offering a wintry smile. 'If, as you say, this *is* a terrorist incident, and one perpetrated by *foreign* actors, then MI6 absolutely *does* have standing. And by the way, you ought to learn some manners. We're all guests in Middlehampton, and Kat and her team are doing a frankly marvellous job under trying circumstances.'

Kat wondered whether she was about to witness Sharon having a heart attack. Her face had turned puce and she was actually clenching her right hand around her left bicep. Then, abruptly, she turned and marched off, bellowing to her sergeant, 'With me, Michael. Now!'

Kat turned to Vicky. 'Thanks for that.'

'Don't mensh. Though I'm rather glad I arrived when I did. Blood is so hard to get out of a white shirt, no?' she added, brushing the backs of her fingers over Kat's shoulders.

How could Vicky be so calm when Kat felt wrung out, sweaty and decidedly uncool? Must be the training, she supposed.

'What are you doing here, Vicky?'

'Apart from breaking up catfights, you mean?' She poked Kat playfully in the shoulder. 'Or should that be *Kat* fights? Just keeping an eye on things for HMG. Believe me, this famous Eel Deal is being talked about in all kinds of unexpected quarters.'

'Like where?' Kat couldn't resist asking.

'One couldn't possibly say. But I hear that Oliver Baka is Middlehampton's top goal-scorer this season. Which shirt does he wear again?' Vicky leaned closer and murmured in Kat's ear. 'Oh, yes. Number Ten. Anyway, must dash. Keep your chin up.'

She left Kat standing, open-mouthed, in a cloud of expensive-smelling perfume and with the vague sense of having been flirted with. Again.

Kat tugged on her left earlobe. *Number Ten? Really?*

She didn't have time to consider the implications of Vicky's barely disguised hint. Leah came up to her, her face split with a smile.

'You're not going to believe this, Kat. I've been digging into Dalma's background. Guess what her maiden name was?'

'Leah, please, I've just nearly come to blows with a Met DI. I'm not in the mood for games.'

'Sorry, sorry. OK, well, get ready for this. It's Elwani. She could be related to Saleem Elwani.'

'OK, that is officially a massive clue and a proper pat on the back for you. Are they related? Is it a common surname?'

'Not sure yet. I've started looking.'

Fez and Tom came over.

'What's going on?' Fez asked.

'Leah just found out Dalma's maiden name was Elwani.'

Tom nodded. 'If they *are* related, that would give Saleem Elwani a personal motive over and above anything to do with the deal.'

'How do you figure that, our kid?' Fez asked.

'Well, Dalma's an observant Muslim, we know that. And she married a non-believer, right? So maybe Saleem murders Pete as an honour killing. Which, before you correct me, I know is part of a spectrum of crimes under the honour-based abuse heading. We did it in my criminology degree.'

Fez had started shaking his head before Tom was even finished. 'Gonna have to pick you up on a couple of points, bab. One, it would be pretty unusual for a Muslim, even if he was committing an HBA murder, to kill the man. Sadly it's the woman who's normally murdered,' Fez said in a patient tone. 'Second, the fact he's a Muslim is secondary. The Qur'an expressly forbids *any* kind of murder. The reality is, HBA happens because of ancient tribal traditions, not prophetic teachings or Islamic law.'

Tom shrugged. 'I stand corrected. But my main point holds. It could point the finger at Saleem Elwani.'

'How are we going to find out if they're related?' Fez asked.

'Simple,' Kat said. 'I'm going to ask Dalma.' She looked around. 'By the way, has anyone seen Abby?'

Tom groaned. 'No. You know you told her to help me with the CCTV? Well, she did for about twenty minutes then she disappeared.' He glanced in the direction of Sharon Critchlow's office. 'Now we know why.'

Kat nodded. Pulled out her phone and called Abby. Maybe she didn't want to shorten Abby's leash, but she still needed to rein her in.

Chapter Fifty-One

It was the part of the job Kat hated most. Even more than paperwork. Even more than death-knocks.

Management.

And specifically, *people* management.

What she enjoyed as a team leader was working with self-starters who needed a push in the right direction and then got on with it.

She didn't care if they were fast-trackers like Tomski, or up-the-hard-way streetwise cops like Fez and Leah. But what she couldn't deal with were the ones who needed both hand-holding *and* disciplining.

Like Abby Greene.

With the Met contingent occupying every spare meeting room, and the ladies loos seemingly host to a women's policing convention, Kat asked Abby to meet her on the roof.

Clearly Abby knew what the meeting was all about. She wouldn't meet Kat's eye, staring at her feet and toeing the scatter of cigarette butts into the pale grey grit.

'Do you want to tell me what's going on, Abs? I just had Sharon Critchlow shouting in my face and I didn't enjoy the experience.'

Now Abby did look up and Kat saw defiance mixed in with the shame.

'It was just some background on the bombing. I got friendly with one of the CTC guys,' she said. 'I thought if I could find a way to prove it was connected to our investigation, like you were saying the other day, they'd have to leave and we could work both cases together.'

Wow. It was the worst case of naivety mixed with over-confidence Kat had ever encountered. She needed to let Abby down gently. But she also found herself in agreement with the substance of Sharon's complaint, even if not her approach. Abby was out of her depth and unwilling to listen. Kat knew with depressing certainty that she'd be writing a negative evaluation at the end of Abby's time in MCU.

'Abs, you can't just start copying Met files. Especially not CTC. You've seen what they're like. They see terrorists lurking round every corner. They could even haul *you* in.'

'Don't be daft, Kat. They'd never do that.'

Abby grinned. In the moment, she looked girlish. Dismissive.

Kat lost it. 'Really, Abs? Really? That's your judgement, is it? Based on, what, a week in MCU? Compared to the Terrorism Act, PACE is like an etiquette guide. They could totally arrest you!' She paused for breath. 'You know, I was really pleased when your rotation came through. I thought I could help another female officer make the grade. But this isn't some sort of game. Three people are dead! Whether I think the bombing wasn't terrorism is neither here nor there. Sharon Critchlow thinks it was, and that's all that counts. She's got the rank, the rationale and the resources to steam through this town looking for whoever did it like a weapons-grade enema. I don't want you anywhere near their investigation again, you hear?'

Abby nodded. Her eyes glistened and she looked so forlorn Kat had to pull her into a hug. Then she held her out, at arms' length.

'We're good?'

'Yep,' Abby said quietly. 'It's just, I wanted to impress you, boss.'

'The best way you can impress me is by helping me catch Pete Vaughan's killer, yes?'

'OK.'

'Good. No more honey-trapping some butch counter-terror DC into sharing his files with you.'

Abby smiled tearfully. 'He is pretty handsome, though, boss.'

Kat rolled her eyes. 'Get inside. It's bloody cold up here.'

With Abby gone, and hopefully behaving herself at last, Kat called Dalma and invited her to meet at Hatî, the Kurdish cafe on North Street, in half an hour.

Chapter Fifty-Two

Dalma was drinking mint tea. Kat ordered her usual Americano and, as she'd skipped lunch, a smoked salmon and cream cheese bagel.

'Dalma, I need to ask you something about your family,' Kat began cautiously. 'Are you related to a Saleem Elwani? I know that was your maiden name.'

Dalma crinkled her nose. 'No. Who is he?'

'His name came up in our investigation, that's all. He's about your age. I wondered whether he might be a cousin, or someone closer. A brother perhaps?'

Dalma smiled easily. 'I wish I did have a brother. But I am an only child. My parents wanted more children, but it was not to be. They are both dead now.'

'I'm sorry.' Kat sipped her coffee and took a bite of bagel. She took her time chewing. Her next question was even more personal. And potentially devastating for Dalma. 'We went to see Illy Nassar today. She took my bagman's breath away.'

Dalma smiled. 'Poor Illy. Her looks are a blessing and a curse. Men find it so hard to talk to her without staring.'

'Did Pete have that problem?'

Dalma frowned. 'What do you mean?'

Kat observed the other woman's face. Either Dalma knew nothing of her husband's infidelity or she was a shoo-in for a best-actress Oscar. Earlier, she'd denied he was unfaithful. But there could be many reasons for that.

'Dalma, I'm sorry to have to ask you this, but did you know that Pete and Illy were having an affair?'

Dalma sighed. Cupped her tea glass and rotated it on the table. She didn't speak for a long time. 'Pete was a good husband. Faithful, in the ways that truly counted. But he was having one of his periodic midlife crises. He was infatuated with Illy. You've met her: you can understand how that might have happened,' she said. 'The poor girl went all starry-eyed that this mature, educated, Western man should have fallen for her. I know he wasn't much to look at, but Pete was an excellent listener, especially to women. He could be very charming.'

'You said he was faithful in the ways that mattered.'

'There was nothing physical. Just some silly teenage trysts. It meant nothing. I knew it would blow over. And it did. He told me he'd ended it just before . . .' Her voice cracked and she swiped at the tears gathering in her eyes. 'Before.'

'Is that why you told me he was faithful when I asked you?'

Dalma nodded. 'I didn't want his private indiscretion diverting attention from his investigation into the Eel Deal. It would have been a travesty if that's how he was remembered.'

Dalma's answers were convincing. But Kat had met murderers before who could have convinced a Geordie to buy coal. On the face of it, though, sexual jealousy as a motive for murder was looking less and less likely.

So the meeting was a bust. Almost. Kat nibbled her bagel, sipped her coffee and continued to make small talk until, eventually, Dalma finished her tea and stood.

'I hope you don't mind but I have to get back to work. I have a deadline.'

Kat stood. 'Of course not. Sorry, my mum always says I'm a slow eater. I'll keep you informed if we discover anything new.'

She watched Dalma leave, cross North Street and turn up a narrow side street leading to a car park.

A waiter appeared at her elbow and reached for the empty glass.

Kat gently placed her hand on his arm. 'Leave that, please,' she said, showing him her warrant card.

He backed away with a nervous smile and she lifted the glass by the handle of its metal cage with a spoon and dropped it into an evidence bag.

Darcy would be getting a new sample to send off to IDENT1.

Chapter Fifty-Three

After dropping the bagged tea glass off with Darcy, Kat made her way up to MCU. Tom and Abby were at their desks, reviewing CCTV footage. Fez was out.

'Hi, guys. Where's Leah?' Kat asked.

'She just arrested Nick Chater. They're in interview room one,' Tom said. 'He waived his right to a lawyer.' He stopped for a moment and seemed to think about something. 'Oh, and talking of potential suspects, I finished my background checks on Milo Smith, our scorpionologist. He's a proper Boy Scout. No criminal record. No speeding tickets. Easy for him as he doesn't drive. No links to Pete Vaughan. I phoned him with a few follow-up questions about Deathstalkers and got him chatting. He's got an alibi for Tuesday night. He was delivering a lecture in London. Hundred and thirty in the audience.'

'Thanks, Tom. Good work.'

Kat hurried out, entering the observation room neighbouring IR1. She switched on the monitor. Leah sat facing Nick Chater.

Leah turned over a page in the folder in front of her. 'When DS Ballantyne asked you whether you had a Deathstalker scorpion you denied it, Nick. Can I ask you why?'

He folded his arms. 'Because I don't.'

'How would you react, Nick, if I were to tell you that I have here a record of a purchase you made three months ago on a German website called, and forgive my lousy pronunciation, tödlichekreaturen.de? The English translation is "deadly creatures". For the recording, I am showing Mr Chater a copy of a sales receipt, exhibit number PV/MI/DCLH/17.'

Kat nodded her appreciation of Leah's trademark calm, unthreatening interviewing style. They all tried to use it, but Leah was the best at maintaining her cool, however uncooperative, hostile or just downright evil the person sitting across the table from her.

He glanced away from Leah. Then tried to meet her gaze. Failed. Looked away again. Started biting a fingernail.

'I thought she meant what I actually had at home. Last time I checked, it wasn't even in the UK. It's a really complicated process. You can check with HMRC. You'll see what I mean. If you check my phone you'll find all the paperwork on it. I'm telling the truth.'

'I see. So this is the truth, and what you told DS Ballantyne before? What was that?'

He shrugged. 'A misunderstanding?'

'Right. I'm just going to remind you, Nick, that you are being interviewed under caution. It doesn't mean you *have* to tell the truth, although obviously that would be a good idea. But if you tell me lies now, in this interview, and remember we're recording this, well, it would look bad if you were in court and I showed the judge you'd lied, wouldn't it?'

'I suppose so.'

'You know so. What I'm wondering, Nick, is whether the scorpion you ordered from the Deadly Creatures website is a replacement for the one you sold or gave to the person who then used it to murder Pete Vaughan. We know you sent threats to him. Very serious threats. Are you part of the group that conspired to murder him, Nick?'

'No! No way. Look, I admit it, OK? I sent him threats and abusive messages. That was wrong. I shouldn't have done it. But he was trying to bollocks up the Eel Deal and we need it. The *town* needs it.'

'Just to clarify, you admit to sending threats to the deceased. You admit to lying to my DS about owning a Deathstalker. And you admit to having ordered one three months ago?'

'I didn't kill him.'

Leah got to her feet. 'Interview suspended at 1.37 p.m. DC Hooper leaving the room.'

Kat left the room next door a moment later, and met Leah in the corridor. 'You're the queen of interviewing, mate.'

'Thanks, Kat, but I need to check what he told me about this bloody deadly creature he ordered. If it's already cleared customs he might look good for it. How have you been doing?'

'I've got Dalma's fingerprints on a glass. Maybe they'll match the print off the scorpion pincer.'

'This is good, right. We're getting evidence.'

'Yeah, but we need a proper breakthrough. So far it's all bits and pieces. Nothing definitive. Come on. Let's get back to MCU. You can check on Chater's little friend and I'll see where the others have got to on the CCTV.'

Arriving in MCU, Leah went to her desk to call HMRC.

Tom and Fez were chatting animatedly at Tom's desk. Kat joined them, hoping for the best. 'What's up?' she asked.

'I found the delivery guy,' Tom said with a tired smile. 'Well, the guy in the Middlehampton Express uniform anyway. Do you want to see?'

'Of course,' Kat said, feeling that familiar buzz of excitement in her chest. The sensation of the tumblers clicking into place on a complicated lock just before it sprang open.

They gathered round Tom as he loaded the video player and pressed play.

'I stitched the clips together to make it easier to watch,' he said. 'I'll run it forward from when we pick him up to when he leaves the Vaughans' house.'

Kat peered at the footage as a man of Middle Eastern appearance carrying a shoebox-sized package handed over cash and then swapped jackets with a Middlehampton courier driver, also dark-skinned, just beneath a railway bridge. The Middle Eastern man climbed into the cab and drove away, leaving the real driver – who'd lied to Abby – counting his cash. This was the pay-off. They'd found, if not identified, the guy she'd seen on Dalma's doorbell cam footage.

Just to be sure, Kat called Abby over and pointed at the guy holding the cash.

'Is that the Middlehampton Express driver you interviewed in South Lane, Abs?'

Abby peered at the screen. 'That's him.'

'You're sure?'

'Positive. It's him.'

'Great. Thank you.'

'I've tasked a couple of uniforms with bringing the Middlehampton Express courier in for questioning,' Tom said, 'but obviously the other bloke is our priority.'

They watched as the video skipped ahead in a handful of jump-cuts, always showing the same van and the same man driving. He parked a few doors up from the Vaughans' place and climbed out, holding the cardboard box. He disappeared out of the frame, then reappeared a few minutes later, empty-handed.

In another series of short clips, they watched as the van drove through Middlehampton before parking on a side street. A blacked-out Range Rover drew up alongside and the bogus courier climbed into the back. Finally, the Range Rover drove into the car park of The Garland hotel.

'That's where it ends,' Tom said. 'I've contacted the hotel about their CCTV but they're being difficult. I'll keep on it. Also, the Rangie is rented. I contacted the hire company. The contract was signed by one Saleem Elwani.'

'This is fantastic work, Tomski,' Kat said. 'I mean that. I don't think you need to worry about your career prospects if this is what you're pulling out of the hat.'

'Thanks, Kat.'

Abby drew in a sharp breath, then winced and rubbed her stomach.

'You all right, Abs,' Kat asked.

'Not sure. My tummy feels a bit weird.'

'Kat?' It was Leah, coming to join them. 'I just got off the phone with HMRC. Would you believe there's a quarantine rule for scorpions? Well, deadly creatures generally? Chater's Deathstalker is locked up in a fish tank in the HMRC facility at Dover. It won't be released until all sorts of conditions have been met and investigations concluded. It could be weeks more.'

'What do you want to do with Chater?'

'Release him under investigation?'

'Do it.'

'Boss?'

Kat turned to find Abby standing in front of her, clutching her stomach and looking as though she might throw up.

'Abs? You look a bit green. Are you sure you're OK?'

'No. I feel awful. I think I ate something that disagreed with me at lunch. I had the canteen lasagne. It didn't taste right but I was so hungry I finished it and now I wish I hadn't.'

'Right. Go and see the doc. Or take the rest of the day off. Just get yourself sorted and come back when you can, all right?'

'Thanks, Kat.'

Abby made a brisk exit, heading for the door closest to the ladies.

'She said she wasn't feeling well earlier,' Leah said. 'Hasn't been sleeping well, either, apparently. Poor girl's been overdoing it. She's too keen to impress you, Kat.'

'I know. I wish she wasn't. I wonder if the stress of the case is getting to her,' Kat said, feeling a pang of guilt. 'Plus I had to give her a bit of a bollocking over the business with the CTC files. I meant to stay calm but it got a bit heated. Well, I did, anyway.'

'She was out of line. You did what you had to do.'

Kat nodded ruefully, remembering her own peachy-keen efforts as a wet-behind-the-ears DC to impress Molly Steadman. But her sympathy for Abby had to take a back seat. She needed to figure out what to do about the guy Tom had found on the CCTV. He'd got into a Range Rover rented by Saleem Elwani and returned in it to the hotel where the Al Jumairi delegation were staying. Despite the evidence that pointed away from Elwani, she was convinced he was involved. Possibly at the top of the chain.

Could she go over to The Garland and demand to see every man in the sheikh's team? She could just imagine how that would go down. A warrant wouldn't fly, either. Without a confirmed ID she couldn't apply for an arrest warrant. And without a warrant she wouldn't be able to match a face to the CCTV footage.

She tried again. Squeezing her eyes shut she tugged on her earlobes as she fought through the thicket of distractions, trying to home in on the essence of the problem.

The courier was just the help. Someone had told him where to deliver the scorpion and he had followed his orders. So who'd given the kill order? It seemed obvious to her. But she wanted a second opinion.

And the person whose opinion she valued most right now was somewhere inside the station.

Chapter Fifty-Four

It took Kat half an hour to track Vicky down.

She found her in the general CID office, sitting at a desk in a quiet corner enclosed by an L-shaped barrier of filing cabinets.

Vicky looked up. She casually closed her laptop as Kat came over.

'Kat! Just when I thought I'd found somewhere quiet to play solitaire.'

'I need to ask your opinion about something,' Kat said, not for a moment believing her.

'Ask away. If I can help, I will.'

'We've traced the man who delivered the scorpion to Pete Vaughan. It looks like he's part of the Al Jumairi delegation. Probably one of the security team,' Kat said.

'And you're sure of this? Because, and forgive me, Kat, but "looks like" and "probably" don't sound massively convincing.'

'That why I need to ID him. But that would mean comparing all the Al Jumairi men with the CCTV footage we recovered. Do you think there's *any* chance the Al Jumairis would cooperate?'

Vicky put the tip of her index finger to the point of her chin. Furrowed her brow. 'I mean, you could *ask*,' she said finally, sounding sceptical.

'But they'd say no.'

'They're here to close a strategically important deal for the Kingdom. Why would they let one of their goon squad go off and murder a frankly insignificant journalist on the eve of the contracts being signed?'

'I know! But the thing is, I don't think he acted alone. It makes no sense. He must be working for Elwani.'

Vicky nodded slowly. 'I see. So you want to go in, batons twirling, Tasers flashing, and arrest the top security guy. I really don't think that's such a good idea, Kat. Do you have any proof he was involved?'

'It's possible he's related to the victim's widow. There might be an honour-based component to the murder.'

Vicky smiled. 'There y'all go again, girl,' she drawled in a comedy hillbilly accent, 'leapin' to one a them gosh-darned conclusions what y'all ain't got no evidence fer.' She flipped back to her natural, cut-glass tones. 'It's "possible"? There "might" be? Kat, I may only be a lowly spook, and not a highly experienced murder detective, but even *I* know that doesn't really pass the threshold for an arrest on a murder charge. Is there a fingerprint on the murder weapon?'

'We're still waiting.'

'DNA at the crime scene?'

'No.'

'A purchase order for a, what are they called again? Deathdealer?'

'—*stalker*. No. But he could have brought one in. He's done it before.'

'How do you know?'

'That SAS guy I met told me.'

'And you have that in writing?'

'No.'

'Recorded?'

'No, but . . .'

Kat saw it, then. She had no idea of the real identity of her witness. And presumably marching up to the front gate of a Special Forces training base and demanding to see 'Dave' would not go well. Penetrating the levels of security that would surround the men who belonged to the SAS could take months. Years, maybe. By which time the Eel Deal would be a matter of historical record and the Al Jumairis long gone.

Vicky pursed her lips into a sorrowful *moue*. 'Look, I didn't mean to be a wet blanket. At school, the other girls used to call me Pollyanna for my' – she waggled her head from side to side and bared her teeth in a madcap grin – '*relentless optimism*. Leave it with me. I have access you don't. I'll get it sorted. Give me an hour.'

'You can really fix this?'

Vicky took Kat's left hand in her right and gave it a quick squeeze. 'I promise. Now, get yourself back to MCU and prepare for victory. I have a call to make.' She winked. 'And a solitaire game to finish.'

Kat left the flirtatious MI6 agent to her laptop, on which she knew beyond a shadow of a doubt no card game was being played, and rejoined her team in MCU. She felt, perhaps not relentlessly optimistic, but positive, all the same.

She'd soon have Elwani in custody and this time there'd be no guns, unloaded or otherwise.

Chapter Fifty-Five

Exactly fifty-nine minutes after Vicky made her promise to Kat, her desk phone rang. Surely it wasn't going to be this simple.

'MCU, DS Ballantyne,' she said, her stomach fizzing with excitement.

'Kat, it's Polly.' The receptionist sounded puzzled. Kat's pulse started racing. 'I have a young man here, calling himself Ibrahim Al Hammadi. He says he wants to speak to you about Pete Vaughan's murder.'

Vicky had come through. Kat could hardly believe it. 'OK,' she said. 'I'll be right down. Make sure he doesn't leave, Polly. Get a couple of uniforms to watch him.'

'I don't think there's any need for that, Kat. He's just sitting there on a chair with his hands in his lap.'

A horrifying thought ran through Kat's brain, like a drenching of iced water, as she thought of the Powerhouse blown apart, flames and smoke boiling from its collapsed roof.

'Polly, is he carrying anything? A rucksack, briefcase, even a Tesco bag. Is he wearing a coat? Anything bulky?'

'No. He's just, you know, normal.'

Kat grabbed a pair of cuffs and ran out of MCU, hurtling down the stairs two and three at a time. She burst out into the bustle of the reception area, looking over at the big plant she knew Polly talked to when she thought nobody was looking.

Sitting beside it was a young, dark-skinned man with a beard and moustache. He was dressed simply, narrow-legged trousers, a collarless shirt in beige linen and a white crocheted skull cap. She scanned the area around him but saw no bags or boxes of any kind. No bulk beneath the thin fabric of his shirt. She relaxed, just a little. No suicide belt. No bomb.

She stood in front of him, keeping a half-metre gap between them.

'Are you Ibrahim Al Hammadi?'

He raised his head and looked her in the eye. His were wide and a beautiful shade of brown with long curling lashes.

'I am.'

'I am DS Kathryn Ballantyne. Did you have something you wanted to say to me?'

'I wish to confess to the murder of Pete Vaughan. Also to planting the bomb at the Powerhouse.'

Chapter Fifty-Six

Kat handcuffed Al Hammadi.

Striving to keep her voice level, even as she flashed on Van's and Riley's smoke-blackened faces as they emerged from the gloom at the Powerhouse, she recited the official arrest script.

'Ibrahim Al Hammadi, I am arresting you on suspicion of the murder of Pete Vaughan, and of the murders, by planting a bomb, of Casey and Jonathan Hall. You do not have to say anything—'

'—but I *want* to say things. I confess freely.'

'Let me finish, please.' She rattled through the rest of the caution. 'Do you understand?'

'Yes.'

'Good. Right, let's get you booked in and then we can begin.'

As she marched him downstairs to the custody suite, more images of that terrible scene at the Powerhouse flashed through her mind. Her blind terror as she drove crazily through the night, terrified she'd lost Van and Riley. The carnage. The dead girl and her father. And then Pete Vaughan's final moments, gasping for breath, his face a rictus of agony as the Deathstalker's venom wreaked havoc on his internal organs.

Julia Myles was the officer on duty. Kat was relieved. She was the most efficient custody sergeant at Jubilee Place and a consummate professional. No matter the crimes which the detainee in front of her stood accused of, she never, ever lost her cool.

'Afternoon, Kat. Who do we have here?' she asked, her unvarying formula.

'The suspect's name is Ibrahim Al Hammadi.' She turned to the young man beside her. 'Double M?'

He nodded.

Julia's fingers flashed across the keyboard. 'Offence?'

'Murder.' A beat. 'And terrorism.'

Julia raised her eyes from her keyboard to regard Al Hammadi. 'You planted the bomb at the Powerhouse?'

'Yes.'

'I see.'

More tapping. Then: 'Well, Mr Hammadi. It is my job to inform you of your rights. You are entitled to legal representation. You are entitled to reading matter connected to your detention, and writing materials.'

Al Hammadi nodded as Julia recited the standard script. When she'd finished he looked her in the eye.

'I do not wish for a lawyer. I do not wish for reading matter or writing materials. I would like to make my confession to Detective Sergeant Ballantyne now, please.'

Kat stared at him. She'd arrested numerous murder suspects, from tearfully repentant husbands who'd murdered their wives and then called 999 themselves to impassive psychopaths with the cold, dead eyes of sharks. But none had ever struck her so forcibly as the strangely passive killer standing beside her now.

What the hell had Vicky done? Had she told the Al Jumairis the jig was up, and it was better to submit to British justice quietly rather than cause a scene from which they would emerge the loser? In truth he did look like the figure on the CCTV. But would he really have acted alone? She began to suspect she'd arrested not a lone wolf but a sacrificial lamb. But right now, her theorising would have to wait.

'Ibrahim, you have been arrested on suspicion of committing heinous crimes. These are very serious charges. You really ought to have a lawyer present.'

She wasn't trying to persuade him because she cared about him. If he really had murdered Pete Vaughan, and planted a bomb at a gig attended by hundreds of Middlehampton kids and their parents, including Riley and Van, he could rot in prison for all she cared. But she knew a defence barrister would pounce on anything that even hinted at a lack of correct legal procedure being followed by the police.

He turned to her slowly. No trace of threat or aggression. Just this weirdly still presence as if he wanted to go down. Was it a martyrdom thing?

'I understand my rights. Your colleague explained them very clearly. I do not want to have a lawyer present. I wish to . . . I am sorry, I do not know the correct word. Is it "renounce" my right?'

'Do you mean "waive"?' Kat asked.

He smiled. He looked so boyish. How could someone who looked so innocent be guilty of such barbarity? She chided herself. Easily! It happened every day. Then why was she having this reaction? *Because you're being played*, the quiet, insistent voice that stood in for her cop intuition whispered.

'Yes. I waive my right to legal representation.'

She nodded. She'd done her best. And she'd be sure to get him on tape repeating his refusal to have legal counsel.

'Right. Come with me. We'll get you processed. That means taking your photograph, your fingerprints and a DNA sample, and then, yes, I will interview you.'

Leaving him to be processed, Kat headed upstairs to find a free interview room. Sharon met her as she entered MCU.

'I heard someone just walked in and confessed to the bombing.'

'That's right. I'm about to interview him.'

'I'll do it. My offence takes priority.'

Kat eyeballed her. 'We'll *both* do it. I'll ask him about Pete Vaughan. When I'm done, you can ask him about the bombing.'

Sharon regarded Kat for a few seconds.

'I can work with that.'

◆ ◆ ◆

Kat switched on the recorder.

When it finished its teeth-grating, seven-second introductory whine, she spoke.

'Interview with suspect Ibrahim Al Hammadi.'

She added the date and time and her own name and rank. Sharon followed suit. If Ibrahim was bothered about being interviewed by two female officers, he didn't show it.

Kat repeated the official caution, closing with, 'Ibrahim, do you understand your rights as I have explained them to you?'

'I do.'

'And would you like to have a lawyer present?'

'I would not. I waive my right to legal representation,' he said, speaking in a calm, clear voice as if competing at a school spelling bee.

'Thank you for confirming that. Are you a resident of Middlehampton?'

'No.'

'Where do you live?'

'Masrah, in Al Jumairah.'

'And why are you in Middlehampton?'

'I am part of His Royal Highness's security team.'

Kat nodded. So at the very least he reported in to Saleem Elwani.

'Did you murder the freelance investigative journalist, Pete Vaughan?'

'Yes, I did.'

'Can you tell me how you killed him?'

'I put a Deathstalker scorpion inside a pair of *babouche*. They are traditional slippers from my country. I delivered them to his home dressed as a courier.'

'Why did you murder him, Ibrahim?'

His black brows pulled together. Perhaps he thought he'd just confess and then that would be that. But she intended to dig a lot deeper. 'Why?' he asked.

'Yes, why? Did you know him before you came to Britain with His Royal Highness?'

'No.'

'Had he done you harm in some way?'

'No.'

'Did he owe you money?'

'No.'

'Did he attack you?'

'No.'

'So why did you kill him?'

'I thought it would please His Royal Highness.'

'Did His Royal Highness *ask* you to kill Pete Vaughan?'

'No.'

'Did anyone else ask you, or order you, to kill Pete Vaughan?'

'No.'

This was so frustrating. Instead of going 'No comment' he was answering every question readily, quickly and politely. And yet she had the exact same feeling. That he was hiding something.

'Where did you get the Deathstalker?'

'The desert. There are many.'

'How did you get it into the UK?'

'I hid it in my cabin luggage. In a cigarette carton.'

'How did you make sure it didn't escape from the *babouche* before it stung Pete Vaughan?'

'I used super glue.'

'And you did it because you wanted to please His Royal Highness?'

'Yes.'

Kat shook her head. She had what she needed. Tied up neatly with a bow on the top. A confession, given voluntarily and willingly. A motive, of sorts. He knew details of the MO that had not been released to the public. She ought to take the win. That's what Carve-up would say. But deep down, she knew Ibrahim Al Hammadi wasn't the ultimate villain. Someone was pulling his strings. Someone with a jokey SAS nickname that pretty much nailed his guilt.

She had one last try.

'When we compare your fingerprints to those we found on the scorpion, will we find a match, Ibrahim?'

'No.'

'Why is that, please?'

'I wore gloves. The ones doctors wear. I did not want to get my fingers stuck together, or to the scorpion.'

She sighed. Leaned back. The signal for Sharon to take over.

Sharon leaned forward. She didn't bother with any theatrics, opening files, saying nothing for an age to see if the suspect would crack. She just looked him calmly in the eye.

'Ibrahim, did you plant the bomb at the Powerhouse that killed two people, injured many more and caused extensive property damage?'

'Yes, I did.'

'What can you tell me about the explosive used?'

'I made it myself. I bought fertiliser, sugar and bleach from a man here in Middlehampton. I made the detonator from a mobile phone. I set it off remotely with my own phone. You have this in your evidence locker.'

'I see. There's something that's been bothering me about the bomb you claim you planted, Ibrahim. Maybe you can help me out?'

He nodded. Smiled. 'I will try.'

'Why did you use ball bearings as shrapnel, and not nails and screws? That's the more usual way of causing damage to people, isn't it?'

Kat kept her face neutral. It was a smart question. Sharon might be a shouty, aggressive woman who treated other cops like a joyrider treated traffic cones, but she was damned good at her job. If Ibrahim explained his choice of shrapnel, rather than denying he'd used any, he'd be admitting he didn't make the bomb.

Ibrahim frowned. 'I did not use ball bearings, or any of those other things. I only used the explosive. No shrapnel.'

'And why was that?'

'I only intended to frighten people. That is why I phoned in my warning. The call will also be recorded on my phone.'

'So you planted a bomb in a place where you knew hundreds of children would be present, only there to have a good time, and you're telling me you didn't want to hurt anyone?'

'Yes. I am deeply sorry that the girl and her father were killed. That will be on my conscience always.'

'Why did you plant the bomb, then, if not to kill people?'

'I thought it would help His Royal Highness. If people believed terrorists were trying to stop the deal going ahead, they would feel sympathy for him.'

Really? Kat wanted to shout. *That's what you're going with? How stupid do you think we are?* If Sharon found his explanation equally unconvincing, she gave no sign of it.

'And it wasn't to divert police resources away from the murder you committed?' Sharon asked.

'No.'

'Who told you to plant the bomb?'

'Nobody.'

'Who sold you the raw materials?'

'I do not know his name.'

Sharon finally betrayed a hint of irritation, her lips tightening fractionally.

'Ibrahim, come on. Look at me, I'm not some twenty-something rookie straight out of university. I'm a middle-aged counter-terrorism detective inspector and I've seen, and heard, it all before. I work for the Metropolitan Police Service and I spend every working day hunting down, listening to and interviewing terrorists. I have *experience* in these matters. From the sounds of it, more than you.' She scrubbed her fingertips through her hair. 'Are you seriously asking me to believe that you planned, resourced, built, placed and detonated a bomb – committed a terrorist attack, in other words – entirely on your own? With no intention to actually hurt people. Because you wanted to please your *boss*?'

He frowned at her. 'His Royal Highness is not my boss.' Then his eyes shuttered for a second and he bit his lip.

Kat kept her breathing steady but inside she was dancing. Sharon had tricked him into giving something away. 'Then who is your boss?'

'I am tired. I wish to go to my cell now.'

'Sorry, Ibrahim. Not going to happen. Not yet, anyway. My colleague DS Ballantyne has arrested you on charges of murder and terrorism. Now, under the regular law in this country, the Police and Criminal Evidence Act 1984, she can hold you for twenty-four hours without charge. But you see, I work within the confines of the Terrorism Act 2000. And that gives me all kinds of additional powers. I can keep you here for a lot longer than DS Ballantyne can. So, I'm going to ask you again. Who is your boss?'

'No comment.'

'Really? No comment? I'd have thought it was a bit late for that, mate. You've just confessed to murder and a terrorism offence. Who is your boss? Is it Saleem Elwani?'

'No comment.'

'Well, he must be, mustn't he? You told DS Ballantyne that you are a member of Omar's security team. Saleem's the head honcho so that makes him your boss, right? Or did I miss something?'

Kat watched Ibrahim closely. She knew what Sharon was doing. Using first names for the Crown Prince and his head of security was an unforgivable lapse in protocol, if not basic cultural norms.

Ibrahim's lip curled. 'You do not refer to His Royal Highness so insultingly, woman. He is the Lion of the Desert. Who are you, *kuffar*? A nobody.'

'Sticks and stones, Ibrahim. Well, we know Saleem Elwani is your boss. So my guess is, he put you up to it. Maybe we'll pay him a visit once we've tucked you up for the night. Arrest him, too. Tell him you confessed and told us it was all his idea.'

Ibrahim's eyes popped wide open. He looked genuinely terrified. 'No! It was me. I acted alone. That is the whole story.'

'But it isn't, is it, Ibrahim?' Sharon's voice had switched from mocking to motherly in a heartbeat. 'I'm worried for you. You see, what if we do charge, try and convict you? You'll go to prison, yes. But I'm sure the sheikh has long arms. Long enough to reach you in prison. And then what? We do everything in our power to keep prisoners safe, but the prison service in this country is stretched to breaking point. Accidents happen. Deaths in custody are thankfully rare, but they're not unheard of. He might even break you out and have you brought back to Al Jumairah. Then what?'

Kat turned her head fractionally towards Sharon. She wasn't crossing a line, but she was approaching it pretty boldly.

Suddenly her rage at the man who'd caused all that mayhem, destruction, death and grief evaporated. She didn't want him spouting half-truths or lies, or even the actual truth, because Sharon Critchlow was issuing thinly veiled death threats. That could come back to bite them at trial.

'Ibrahim,' she said, trying to ignore Sharon's sharp intake of breath beside her. 'We are both grateful for your cooperation. But something else has been puzzling me, apart from who told you to plant the bomb and murder Pete Vaughan . . .'

'I already told you,' he said, a note of desperation evident in his voice.

'I know. And we may come back to that. But for now, answer me this. Why did you decide to come here and confess to murder? Your plane is leaving tonight. You could have waited it out at the hotel and then left the country. We have no extradition treaty with Al Jumairah. You would have got away with it.'

She thought she knew the answer. The heat on his boss, Saleem Elwani, was intensifying. They were worried he wouldn't be allowed to fly out of the UK.

'It is as I said, my conscience was troubling me. The Prophet, peace be upon him, told us not to murder.'

'I'm not a religious scholar, Ibrahim, of your faith or any other,' Kat said, 'but as a detective, what puzzles me is that you only started thinking about the Prophet's teachings this afternoon. If he forbade murder, why did you commit it in the first place?'

'My loyalty to His Royal Highness blinded me to my faith. I am sorry. I must take my punishment.' That sounded like so much post-rationalised bullshit to Kat. Thinking suddenly of Abby and her need to impress Kat, she readied her next question, and then stopped as he added something else.

'That is the justice for the unjust.'

Gooseflesh prickled along Kat's forearms. Vicky had used the same phrase the first time they'd met. '*Punishment, that's the justice for the unjust. Saint Augustine, dontcha know?*'

How had the young man in front of her come to use it? He hadn't known the word 'waive' yet here he was uttering the same obscure quote. And by a Christian saint at that. Had he heard Vicky saying it? Had she told him to come in? Or had a word in his boss's ear? Wondering whether she'd been too trusting of Vicky, Kat swallowed. Changed tack.

'I understand the concept of loyalty, Ibrahim. There are people we look up to, people we'd do anything for,' she said. 'But did anyone come to you today and encourage you to make this confession? If not His Royal Highness or Mr Elwani, someone else perhaps. A police officer?' Her inner voice butted in. *A posh British spy with a cute nose and cheekbones to die for?*

He'd been shaking his head as she spoke. Now he straightened in his chair.

'No. I confess my crimes of my own free will. I am a murderer. I am a terrorist. I murdered Mr Vaughan. I planted the bomb. Nobody told me to. Nobody helped me. I acted alone. I accept my guilt and expect my punishment.' He folded his arms. 'That is all I have to say.'

Kat knew finality when she heard it. Sharon tried for a few more minutes. But after the fifteenth 'No comment,' she, too, gave up.

Ibrahim Al Hammadi was removed to his cell. His days of freedom were over.

Kat and Sharon returned to MCU. And to cheers from their fellow detectives.

Chapter Fifty-Seven

Carve-up emerged from the centre of the crowd of cheering officers.

His suit, a shimmering teal, looked as though he'd just bought it. Not a crease to be seen. It presented a stark contrast to the rumpled look of the thirty or so other detectives all crowding round Kat and Sharon.

He shouldered his way to the front and approached Sharon. 'Well done, Sharon. I always knew we'd do it.'

She eyeballed him. '"We" didn't do anything, Stuart. This was all Kat.'

'It wasn't,' Kat said. 'I just kept shaking the tree. I have a great team,' she added, making eye contact in turn with Tom, Leah and Fez. Wishing Abby could be here to share the triumph.

Carve-up turned to her now. 'I suppose congratulations are in order then, DS Ballantyne,' he said, sounding about as pleased as a dental patient informed they'd need a root canal. 'And you're right, an individual copper can't achieve anything without a strong team. I'm just glad that's one more Muslim terrorist behind bars. Allah isn't so great now, is he?'

Kat noticed Fez wince at Carve-up's racist slur. She was about to jump in but Sharon beat her to it.

'As a senior officer involved in this operation, you ought to know the difference between Islam and Islamism, DI Carver,' she said crisply. 'But then, I don't suppose the Parks police spent much time giving you counter-terror training.'

Carve-up scowled before sliding an obsequious smile on to his face. '*Touché*, Sharon,' he said, holding his wrists out so his gold-linked shirt cuffs slid out of his jacket sleeves. 'Send me to the workers' re-education camp before the PC police come for me.'

The silence congealed like day-old blood. The crowd dispersed, back to desks and the mountains of paperwork that would now need to be processed, completed, bundled, labelled and sent to the CPS.

Sharon drew Kat to one side. 'That man is a liability. How do you stand it?'

Kat sighed resignedly. 'I just try to ignore him. Failing that, I keep our conversations to the bare minimum.'

'And that works, does it?'

'What do you think?'

'I think we need to have a drink at some point. Minus Carve-up.'

Kat inhaled, gave voice to her inner doubts that had surfaced as Ibrahim had echoed Vicky's quotation. 'Do you think we've got the right guy?'

'You mean, it all seemed a bit too easy?'

'Exactly. Your questions were so on point. And that guff about his conscience pricking? I didn't buy that for a second.'

Sharon frowned. 'What are you saying?'

'I'm saying it stinks like knock-off perfume. No way was he acting alone when he planted the bomb *or* murdered Pete.'

'So who gave him his orders? Elwani?'

'It has to be. He's Al Hammadi's boss, we know that. And *his* boss is the Crown Prince.' Kat counted off the points on her fingers. 'Elwani told me his job is basically to anticipate and eliminate threats to the Crown Prince. Pete was a threat. Elwani eliminated him.'

'Using the bombing as cover.'

'Yes. Hence the lack of shrapnel. They didn't want the heat a massacre would have drawn. I'm not saying your team weren't a big enough threat . . .'

Sharon shook her head. 'It's fine, I know what you mean. If we'd had another Manchester Arena there'd have been hundreds of us. The town would have been in lockdown until we caught him. No way would the Al Jumairis be allowed to leave, either. So what do you want to do?'

'Can we put Elwani and the sheikh and his entourage under covert surveillance?'

Sharon offered a small smile. 'We put cameras and mics inside the hotel this morning. You want to know if they're all there?'

'Yes. I do.'

Sharon pulled out her phone and made a call. Asked a couple of questions. Nodded. Ended it.

'They're all there. The Middlehampton lot, too. Apparently they're having a press call then they're going into the conference room to sign the deal.'

'We need to get over there.'

Sharon nodded. 'Come with me.'

They turned to go only to meet Leah running towards them, a sheet of paper in her hand.

'Kat, wait!'

'What is it?'

'This just came in from IDENT1. The fingerprint on the scorpion. We got eleven points of comparison for Saleem Elwani. None for Nick Chater yet. His prints only went off today. Or Dalma. But that puts Elwani in the frame, right?'

'Yes. You're a bloody star, Leah. Right. Can you formally de-arrest Nick. Tell him he's not wanted anymore.'

'Where are you going?'

'Sharon and I are going to see Mr Elwani. I need to stop him leaving town.'

'Boss! Boss!'

Kat turned. It was as if her entire team were conspiring to stop her leaving MCU. 'What, Tomski? We really need to go.'

'I know, but you should see this.'

Kat and Sharon hurried over to Tom's desk. A CCTV feed from outside The Garland was freeze-framed on his PC screen.

'Watch,' Tom said, then pressed play. 'This is from last Tuesday.'

Standing face to face with Saleem Elwani was Ibrahim Al Hammadi. No mistake. The hotel's CCTV quality was full-colour HD.

No sound, but Tom zoomed in on Elwani's face. His lips moved.

'What's he saying?' Sharon asked.

'I think it's Arabic,' Tom said. 'Keep watching. There!'

Elwani's lips came together, parted, touched again, then pouted outwards.

'I'm not a lip-reader, especially not of Arabic,' Tom said, 'but doesn't that look to you like he's saying "*babouche*"?'

'Play it again,' Kat said.

He rewound, slowed it down to ninety per cent and played it again. Seventy per cent. Again. Fifty. Again. The sounds around them faded as Kat focused on Elwani's lips.

'I don't know, Tomski. It could be. It could be all sorts of things. But I have an idea.'

Kat called Dalma.

'I need a favour. Can you lip-read Arabic?'

'I can probably manage a little. It depends how close I am to the speaker.'

It was good enough. Kat told Dalma to stay put and sent a car to pick her up.

Kat spent the next twenty minutes in a fever of anxiety. Powerless to do anything but wait. If Dalma could confirm that Elwani was asking Al Hammadi about the slippers, it would be strong enough to arrest him.

But would Dalma come through?

She arrived in MCU escorted by a young uniformed officer who spotted Kat, nodded then pointed her out to Dalma.

Kat rushed over to greet her. 'Dalma, thank you so much. Come with me. I want you to watch a video.'

At Tom's desk, Kat asked him to play the video for Dalma from the beginning of the sequence. Ibrahim Al Hammadi arrived at The Garland. As Saleem Elwani appeared on-screen, Dalma froze. Her hand flew to her mouth, then dropped away as she spoke in a shaky voice.

'Is . . . Is that the man who ordered Pete's death?'

'I think so, yes. You may be able to help. Just watch him speaking and tell me what he's saying.'

Kat held her breath as Dalma, tears streaming down her cheeks, studied the few seconds of video. While Dalma watched the screen, Kat watched Dalma. She'd told Kat she had no brothers or sisters. But there was no mistaking the look of horror that had crossed her face as Saleem Elwani had appeared on screen. Dalma knew him.

'Can you play it again, please, slower?' Dalma asked Tom, her white-knuckled fingers entwined at her chest.

He spun it back and reduced the playback speed.

'Slower?'

He played it at half-speed.

'Now, back to normal.'

After the fourth play through, Dalma uttered two words under her breath. 'Oh, Saleem.' But Kat still heard them. She'd been waiting, after all.

Dalma stepped back and turned to Kat. She looked stricken.

'He is saying, "Did you give him the *babouche*?"'

Kat nodded. She had the evidence she needed, and something else, too. She turned to Sharon. 'We need to get a team together. An armed team.'

As Sharon left to make arrangements for Elwani's arrest, Kat drew Dalma aside. 'Before you go, Dalma, I need to ask you something. When we had coffee together in Hatî, you told me you were an only child. But I watched you just now when Saleem Elwani ordered Pete's murder. You looked shell-shocked. I know your maiden name was Elwani. Is Saleem your brother?'

Dalma nodded tearfully. 'I am sorry I lied to you, Kat. When I married Pete, an older Western man, my father was furious. My father wanted Saleem to kill us both.' She inhaled sharply. 'It is terrible there for everyone. We have a saying. "Face the wall, but say nothing. For the walls have ears." But for women and girls it is worse still. I was one of the lucky ones: I escaped. I have not spoken to my father or my brother since. I tell everyone I am an only child. That my parents are dead. It is easier for me than to admit the truth. I thought Saleem was still in the army. I had no idea he worked for the Crown Prince. I had no idea he was *here*.'

Kat felt unbearable sympathy for the woman in front of her. First, widowed, then asked to lip-read as her own brother revealed his role in her husband's murder.

'I'm sorry, Dalma,' she said laying a gentle hand on Dalma's shoulder. 'Truly, I am.'

But it was almost over. And then, at least, Kat could bring about some form of justice for Pete's killing and some form of closure for Dalma.

Kat prepared for her final confrontation with Saleem Elwani. And this time, nothing was going to get in her way.

Chapter Fifty-Eight

She checked her weapon again.

She felt oddly calm. No jitters, no urgent need to go to the loo. She felt purposeful. Powerful.

From her observation point across the street from the hotel's main entrance, she watched as Elwani ordered his men around. The press were still arriving, so the deal hadn't been signed yet.

She'd bought the suit specially. Charcoal grey, sharp cut. Jacket and trousers. She was glad the hotel didn't require its female staff to wear skirts. Sage-green shirt and a grey tie. Heels. Hair in a chignon. Just like the other employees. She didn't have a name badge but she reckoned she could wing it.

She checked both ways, although the traffic on this side street was light. Crossed towards the target, blinking as the wind flicked a stray strand of hair into her eye. She tucked it back in place.

When she was within a few feet of him, she called out. 'Mr Elwani!'

He turned. 'What? I am very busy.'

She recited her prepared line.

'Mr Robard sent me. The manager? One of your men has been taken ill. He's collapsed in the road behind the hotel. Please come with me.'

She held her right hand out wide. Shouting a couple of instructions, he turned and followed her as she led him to the mews street she'd selected. If the side street where she'd been watching was quiet, the mews was silent.

She almost stumbled as her left heel caught on a loose cobble.

Behind her, Elwani stopped. Looked around. 'Where is he?'

She produced her warrant card. 'I want to talk to you about the Powerhouse bombing and the murder of Pete Vaughan. I have reason to believe you were involved in both crimes.'

She edged her right hand behind her back until she found the stubby grip protruding from her waistband. Trying to be subtle about it. If he lost it, she needed to be ready.

But he didn't look angry. In fact he looked amused.

'You are making a big mistake.'

'No. I'm not. But you are.'

A gust of wind whipped down the mews, swirling up dust and a few dead leaves from the gutter. His jacket flapped open and she saw the big black pistol holstered on his belt.

Panic overwhelmed her. She stumbled backwards, bringing her right arm round and levelling it.

'Armed police! Drop your weapon!' she screamed, her voice bouncing back off the nearby houses.

He went for his gun.

Abby squeezed the trigger on her own weapon.

Chapter Fifty-Nine

The last time Kat had tried to arrest a murder suspect without firearms support, Tom had ended up in a coma. She wouldn't make that mistake again.

She fought against her instinct to race straight over to The Garland and arrest Elwani, instead waiting until the firearms team was ready to roll. But, oh, God, it was an agonising wait.

She couldn't sit at her desk any longer. She got up and went to check in with Leah, Fez and Tom.

Then MCU was filled with an ear-splitting screech as the emergency alarm on everybody's Airwave went off.

Someone yelled, 'Red button!'

Kat checked the blaring red text on her Airwave. Abby! A location near the Al Jumairis' hotel. Everybody moved at once. The room was a mass of running cops as everyone raced down to the car park to grab a vehicle.

Kat was pulling away moments later, blue lights flashing, siren squealing. *Oh, Abby, what have you done?*

Maybe it was her local knowledge, or pure luck, but Kat arrived in West Lodge Mews first. Abby was on her back in the middle of the road, blood spreading outwards from her chest in a huge pool. A bright yellow Taser lay six inches from her out-flung right hand.

Kat skidded to a stop and jumped out, racing over to Abby and kneeling beside her.

Abby's eyes fluttered open. She coughed a fine spray of blood into Kat's face.

Kat bent closer.

'Abby! Abs! Can you hear me? It's Kat. Stay with me. Ambo's on its way. Stay with me OK, lovely? You're going to be all right.'

Sirens filled the air. The street strobed with electric-blue light as cop cars screeched to a halt behind her. As Kat lifted Abby's jacket to one side, uniforms started erecting a cordon around them both. Then a tent.

The front of Abby's shirt was soaked in blood. High on the left side, a dark, ragged hole. Kat stripped off her jacket and wadded it up before clamping it over the wound. She tried to stay calm. To follow her first-aid training. Oh, Jesus, there was so much blood.

'Who did this, Abs?'

Abby opened her eyes, but they were unfocused. 'I wanted . . . him to confess. I wanted to . . .' She coughed again, and a gout of blood issued from between her lips. 'He had . . . a gun.'

Kat was crying. She lay beside Abby and cradled her head, keeping one hand pushed down over the blood-soaked jacket.

'Who, Abby? Who did this?'

'It was . . . Saleem Elwani, boss. He shot me. I just wanted . . . make you proud. I'm sorry . . . let you down.'

Abby's head seemed to double in weight as the muscles supporting it relaxed. Her eyes closed and a long, guttural breath escaped her lips.

'Abby? Abs! Stay with me.'

Someone loomed over her. Green uniform trousers. A paramedic. Then another.

Ryan and Rosemah. Kat knew them. Counted them as friends. Just like Abby.

The petite Malaysian squatted beside Kat. She slid her hand between Kat's arm and Abby's hair. 'Let's just lay her head down, my dear,' she said. 'Can you move away for me? Ryan and I need to check on her.'

Kat stood. Staggered away from them and into Leah's arms. Sobbing, she looked back over her shoulder.

She didn't need the paramedics to tell her. She didn't need Jack Beale to confirm it.

Abby Greene was dead.

And she'd done one last, invaluable duty as a police officer. She'd given a dying declaration, naming Saleem Elwani as her murderer, knowing it would stand up in court. At the very end, Abby Greene had proved her dedication as a copper.

Kat pushed herself free of Leah's arms. She was going to see to it that justice was served.

Numbed by shock, wracked by guilt for not having realised just how desperate Abby had become to impress her, Kat backed away from the scene. Behind her, Ryan and Rosemah were loading Abby's body into the back of the ambulance.

A cold clarity descended on her as the reality of Abby's death – *murder!* her inner voice screamed – sank in.

This was different from when she'd thought Liv was gone, taken by the Origami Killer. Then at least Kat had been drugged up to the eyeballs, stumbling around the city in a haze of tranquillisers and sleeping pills.

Now, her vision felt pin sharp. Her ears were alive to the tiniest sound, from the rustle of a CSI's booties to the plink as they tweezed a brass shell casing from between two cobbles.

And her thoughts were travelling down arrow-straight rails that led directly to Saleem Elwani.

She called Sharon. 'Where is he?'

'Inside the hotel. They've abandoned the deal. It's chaos here. The Al Jumairis are checking out.'

'You can't let them leave!'

'Don't worry, we won't.'

Kat jumped into her car and tore off back towards the hotel, her squealing tyres throwing up acrid clouds of blue rubber smoke.

She arrived just in time to see the Al Jumairi delegation exit the building, wheeling suitcases and signalling frantically to the blacked-out Range Rovers parked haphazardly on the semicircular drive.

Elwani climbed into the front-most vehicle. Firearms officers were piling out of a black van, filling the air with their yells of 'Armed police!'

As the Range Rover containing Elwani peeled away from the kerb and shots rang out, Kat stuck the gear lever into first and lurched forward, straight into the Range Rover's path.

The driver tried to swerve round her. She locked her elbows, swung the wheel and rammed it, striking the huge squared-off bumper. AFOs were rushing over but Kat beat them to it. She leaped from the car and ran to the front of the Range Rover.

With a yell, she wrenched the door open and grabbed Elwani by the arm. Using strength she didn't know she had, she dragged him bodily from his seat, out of the car and on to the ground. She kneeled on his chest and screamed into his face.

'You're under arrest for murder, you bastard!'

Chapter Sixty

Kat grabbed her file and strode out of MCU.

Elwani was waiting for her in interview room 3 with his lawyer. She didn't care who he had representing him. With Abby's dying declaration and the ballistics evidence, he'd be going down for murder.

But as she reached the door, a familiar voice called out to her. 'A word, Kat?'

She turned.

Vicky was striding down the corridor towards her.

Kat greeted her with a grim expression. No smiles for Vicky now. None in return, either.

'What is it? I'm about to interview Saleem Elwani. He murdered one of ours.'

'Yes, I know. And I am so terribly sorry for your loss, Kat, you have to believe me.'

'Thanks. Was there anything else?'

'Yes. I need you to release him.'

Kat reared back. 'What?'

'I want you to de-arrest Saleem Elwani.'

'No! Why? Did you not hear me? He shot and killed a cop. Her name was Abby Greene. She was a friend of mine. What the hell are you talking about?'

Vicky took Kat's arm just above the elbow, but Kat shook her off angrily. 'I'm afraid I'm going to have to insist, Kat.' Vicky looked past Kat's shoulder. 'Ah, just in the nick of time. Linda, could you explain the situation to Kat, please?'

Was it a trick? Kat whirled round, pulse racing, a sick feeling spreading out from her stomach. No trick. Linda was striding towards her. She looked as though she was about to puke. Cheeks pale, lips compressed. She was shaking, visibly. Enraged. Kat knew the look.

'Let him go, Kat.'

'But, Ma-Linda! Why? He's a cop-killer. I can't. I won't!'

Linda heaved in a breath. 'That's an order, DS Ballantyne.'

'It's an unlawful order. I'd be breaking my oath as a constable if I obeyed.'

'No, you wouldn't. Oh, God, Kat, please don't make this any harder than it already is. I want you to go in there and de-arrest him.'

Kat stuck her fists on her hips, fighting back tears of frustration, rage and bone-crushing sorrow. 'And if I refuse?'

'Then you will be placed under arrest,' Vicky said quietly from behind her. 'And it will happen anyway.'

Kat stared at Linda, her eyes pricking. 'Ma'am, please.'

'I'm sorry, Kat. This has come down from on high. Beyond the brass in Welwyn. Way on high.'

'As high as that football shirt I mentioned,' Vicky breathed into Kat's ear.

'Do it yourself,' Kat cried out before marching away from them both, blinded by tears.

She took the stairs to the ground floor and slammed out through the double doors on to the terraced area in front of the station. Chest heaving, she felt she was suffocating, however hard she tried to drag oxygen into her lungs.

She leaned back against the metal railing, clutching the cold steel for support, her knuckles cracking as she squeezed the rail tighter and tighter. Not feeling the pain, just the crushing sense of being ground between the gears of a machine whose purpose she knew nothing about.

Minutes later, the doors opened again, more slowly this time.

Elwani sauntered out, accompanied by a tall, suited man carrying a bulky briefcase. Elwani caught her eye. Nodded. And then walked over to a black Range Rover and climbed in.

Kat wanted to run after him, rugby-tackle him to the ground. But her hands were welded to the railing behind her and she could only watch, impotently, as the Range Rover pulled away.

Then her sense of justice came roaring back.

Saleem Elwani would not escape her.

She headed to the car park.

Chapter Sixty-One

From behind the plate-glass doors, Vicky Palmer and Linda Ockenden watched as Kat stalked off, heading away from the front doors and round the side of the station towards the car park.

'Can she be trusted?' Vicky asked.

'Kat is a fine detective,' Linda gritted out. 'She is very keen on seeing justice done. Especially when it comes to murderers.'

Vicky nodded. She'd seen that for herself.

Chapter Sixty-Two

Kat looked up at the departures board.

She'd headed straight to Heathrow from Jubilee Place, hoping to beat the Al Jumairis.

It was 7.00 p.m. The flight to Masrah was on time. She had three hours left.

She scanned the vast space of the departures hall, searching for Elwani and the rest of the Crown Prince's entourage.

She had no idea if he'd still be armed. Whatever arrangement the Al Jumairis had struck with MI6 surely didn't extend to carrying firearms on a scheduled flight. In any case, she was sure he wouldn't use it. Not with airport cops wandering around strapped with machine guns.

Then she saw them: a tight group of figures, mostly dressed in black suits but a couple, including the Crown Prince himself, in *thobe*, *ghutra* and *egal*. The red-and-white headdresses certainly made them easier to spot in the crowd.

Clutching her handcuffs in one hand and a Taser in the other, Kat strode through the crowd, muttering 'excuse me' every few steps and pushing through if the passenger proved too slow in making room for her.

Ignoring the protests about her behaviour, she planted herself right in front of Elwani. He looked surprised. But he kept his hands in view.

'Saleem Elwani, I am arresting you, again, for the murder of Abby Greene. We have evidence linking you to the crime. You do not have to say anything—'

He looked over her shoulder and said, 'Oh, hello, Miss Palmer, you're just in time.'

Kat ignored the cheap trick. She stayed locked on to his eyes, the Taser out in front of her, her finger on the trigger.

Agony exploded along the nerves of her right arm. Then it lost all feeling and dropped uselessly to her side. The Taser clattered to the floor, where it was immediately trapped beneath a navy crocodile-patterned moccasin with a gold snaffle bit.

A hand was clamped above her elbow, the fingers digging in so hard they dented the fabric of her jacket. She twisted round, wincing at the pain it caused. Vicky was standing so close they might have been lovers enjoying their last moments together.

Something hard jabbed against Kat's ribs. She looked down. Vicky was pushing the muzzle of a squat, black, silenced pistol against her side.

'No arrest today, Kat,' she murmured. 'There are bigger issues at play here. We'll see all the victims' families are compensated. But it is *extremely* important to HMG that Elwani gets on that flight.'

Kat simply stared at Elwani. He came closer until he, Vicky Palmer and Kat made an oddly intimate trio amid the bustling crowd, and the onlooking group of Al Jumairi security staff.

'You are a smart detective, DS Ballantyne,' Elwani said. 'Maybe you worked this out for yourself, but Dalma *is* my sister. Our father did not approve of her marrying that man. Nor did I. I tried to talk her out of it, but she wouldn't listen to me. When he started making a nuisance of himself over the deal, I saw an opportunity to kill two birds with one stone, or maybe one bird with one scorpion. It was poetic, no? And his towering ego made my job so much easier.' Elwani leaned closer still. She smelled his aftershave. Fought down nausea. 'My father wanted me to kill them both, to preserve the family's honour. I had to disappoint him. He will say I rebelled against my faith, but I love my big sister too much. But now, enough. I must go or I'll miss my flight.'

Stunned into disbelieving, outraged silence, Kat stared after Elwani, as he strolled off. Just before he turned the corner into passport control, he turned, smiled, and offered an ironic salute.

Vicky remained though, her hand still gripping Kat's arm, though less painfully.

Choking with anger, Kat turned to the MI6 agent.

'What was it? Oil? Defence contracts? "My enemy's enemy is my friend?" That sort of thing?' she hissed. 'And take that gun out of my ribs right now unless you want me to smack you one.'

Vicky eyed Kat with a calculated air – a snake regarding a small desert rodent, perhaps. Or a deadly scorpion. Slowly, and discreetly, she slid the gun beneath her jacket and released her pincer-like grip on Kat's arm.

'Oh, Kat, I wish I could tell you all the details. But then I'd have to . . . well, you know.' She sighed. 'We're not that different, you and me. Successful women in fields still largely arranged to suit the boys. In a different life, I could imagine us being colleagues. Friends, even. But you serve justice on a very' – she bit her lip – 'I'm sorry, but a very *parochial* level. I, on the other hand, need to see the bigger picture. Which, in this case, touches on all three of the topics you just mentioned, and involves sums that make the Eel Deal look like the takings from a wet Wednesday night friendly.'

Kat fought back the rage that threatened to overwhelm her. She was angry with Vicky for betraying her trust, and with herself for having sold it so cheaply. Vicky had bedazzled Kat with her spook talk and one-of-the-girls matiness, when all along it had been Sharon, the experienced copper, who Kat should have listened to.

'So that's it, is it? Three people dead, murdered,' she choked out. 'You serve up a fall guy, pay out some comp to the victims' families, the real villains walk, and it's all swept under the carpet? Is that how you work?'

Vicky nodded. 'Pretty much, yup. It's a dirty job, et cetera.'

'What about your quote? "Punishment, that's the justice for the unjust".'

Vicky tapped the side of her nose once again. 'Ah, Kat. But who's to say who is just and who is unjust? The Crown Prince is front and centre in the war on terror. He is a friend to the United Kingdom. His steadfast support has saved countless lives not just in his own part of the world but ours, too. Is he unjust?'

'His head of security shot my friend dead. Why can't you see how wrong that is? Why are you helping a murderer escape justice?'

Vicky smiled sadly. Or was it just another of her masks? She turned to go.

'I hate to use such a honking great cliché, Kat, but that is rather a long way above your pay grade.'

Kat stood, unable to move, as if shackled to an iron ring in the floor, watching the slender, impeccably dressed, amoral spook drift away through the swirling crowd before disappearing altogether.

Her jaw clenched so hard she felt the joints crack.

Elwani had escaped justice. But it was Vicky who'd taken something from Kat: her unshakeable belief in the legal system she had sworn to uphold. There was no black, no white, just shades of grey. Where nebulous concepts like 'the greater good' trumped basic moral certainties like 'murder is wrong'.

Then, from deep in her soul – where lay her best intentions, and the fierce girl who had joined the police to catch murderers like the one she thought had killed her best friend – Kat fought back against this nihilistic vision.

No. *No!*

If Kat could salvage anything from the murders of Casey and Jonathan Hall, Pete Vaughan and Abby Greene, and the close brush with death suffered by her own family, it was this.

Vicky Palmer was wrong. Who was just and who was unjust wasn't a philosophical question. And it wasn't subject to considerations of money, power or politics.

The way Kat saw it, there were good people and there were bad people. There were selfless acts, like Abby's sacrifice. And there were evil ones. Like Ibrahim Al Hammadi committing murder on Saleem Elwani's orders. All while their ultimate boss looked on, using his unimaginably vast wealth to distract the world from his acts against his own citizens, in a country where women and girls could be imprisoned and tortured simply for wanting an education, or murdered for choosing their own husbands.

If Vicky's world – where justice was a commodity to be bought and sold – was above Kat's pay grade, then she was determined never to reach it.

She turned and headed for the exit.

As she drove home, a plane on an ascending flight path flew over the motorway, right above her. She looked up, wondering if Zizou and his team were on board, sipping Coca-Cola, nibbling those almond-flavoured *hadji bada* cookies and laughing. Kat gritted her teeth and drove on. This wasn't over.

But it was.

For now.

ACKNOWLEDGEMENTS

I want to thank you for buying this book. I hope you enjoyed it.

As an author is only part of the team of people who make a book the best it can be, this is my chance to thank the people on my team.

For their patience, professionalism and support, the fabulous publishing team at Thomas & Mercer, led by Eoin Purcell and Sammia Hamer. I want to thank Sammia specifically for her help in developing Fez Mohammed as a three-dimensional character (and for coming up with his nickname). Also, my wonderful editor, Victoria Pepe, who, as well as having a sure literary touch and the sort of commercial vision that turns books into bestsellers, I count as a friend. My developmental editor, Russel McLean, is a fiction eagle, able to see an entire plot from his vantage point, but with the visual acuity to spot a clunky phrase from half a mile up. And lastly (but not leastly), my copyeditor, Sadie Mayne, and proofreader, Jill Sawyer, without whom I am sure many of my authorial glitches would have escaped on to the finished page.

Plus the wonderful marketing team including Rebecca Hills, Jessica Sharples, Hatty Stiles and Nicole Wagner. And Dominic Forbes, who, once again, really smashed the brief with another awesome cover design.

For sharing their knowledge and experience of The Job, former and current police officers Andy Booth, Ross Coombs, Jen Gibbons, Neil Lancaster, Sean Memory, Trevor Morgan, Olly Royston, Chris Saunby, Ty Tapper, Sarah Warner and Sam Yeo.

I volunteer on Laverstock Ward at Salisbury District Hospital. The wonderful staff there have got used to my occasional (and sometimes worrying) questions about aspects of clinical practice. For her help sorting out the precise nature of Van's treatment, I want to thank Danni Parker.

The members of my Facebook Group, The Wolfe Pack, are an incredibly supportive and also helpful bunch of people. Thank you to them, also.

And for being an inspiration and source of love and laughter, and making it all worthwhile, my family: Jo, Rory and Jacob.

Andy Maslen

Salisbury, 2025

ABOUT THE AUTHOR

Photo © 2021, Kin Ho

Andy Maslen was born in Nottingham, England. After leaving university with a degree in psychology, he worked in business for thirty years as a copywriter, while also continuing to write poetry and short fiction. In his spare time, he plays blues guitar. He lives in Wiltshire.

Follow the Author on Amazon

If you enjoyed this book, follow Andy Maslen on Amazon to be notified when the author releases a new book!
To do this, please follow these instructions:

Desktop:

1) Search for the author's name on Amazon or in the Amazon App.
2) Click on the author's name to arrive on their Amazon page.
3) Click the 'Follow' button.

Mobile and Tablet:

1) Search for the author's name on Amazon or in the Amazon App.
2) Click on one of the author's books.
3) Click on the author's name to arrive on their Amazon page.
4) Click the 'Follow' button.

Kindle eReader and Kindle App:

If you enjoyed this book on a Kindle eReader or in the Kindle App, you will find the author 'Follow' button after the last page.